FRANKLY FEMINIST

Frankly Feminist

SHORT STORIES BY JEWISH WOMEN

FROM *Lilith* MAGAZINE

Edited by Susan Weidman Schneider & Yona Zeldis McDonough

Brandeis University Press / Waltham, Massachusetts

Susan Weidman Schneider

Brandeis University Press
Compilation © 2022 *Lilith* Magazine
"The Woman Who Lost Her Names," story by Nessa Rapoport,
© 1979, 2021 Nessa Rapoport
Manufactured in the United States of America
Designed and composed in Garamond Premier Pro, Weiss BT,
    and Mr Eaves Sans by Mindy Basinger Hill

For permission to reproduce any of the material in this book,
contact Brandeis University Press, 415 South Street, Waltham MA 02453,
or visit brandeisuniversitypress.com

Library of Congress Cataloging-in-Publication Data

Names Schneider, Susan Weidman, editor. | McDonough, Yona Zeldis, editor.

Title Frankly feminist : short stories by Jewish women from Lilith magazine /
    edited by Susan Weidman Schneider & Yona Zeldis McDonough.

Other titles Lilith (New York, N.Y.)

Description Waltham, Massachusetts : Brandeis University Press, [2022] | Series:
    HBI series on Jewish women | Summary: "An anthology of the best of feminist
    Jewish short stories published in Lilith Magazine by well-known and less-well
    known authors from all over the world"—Provided by publisher.

Identifiers LCCN 2022018488 | ISBN 9781684581269 (paperback) |
    ISBN 9781684581276 (ebook)

Subjects LCSH: Short stories, Jewish. | Short stories, American. | American
    fiction—Jewish authors. | American fiction—Women authors. | Jewish
    women—Fiction. | Feminism—Fiction. | BISAC: FICTION / Women |
    FICTION / Jewish | LCGFT: Short stories.

Classification LCC PN6120.95.J6 F73 2022 | DDC 808.83/1088924—dc23/
    eng/20220607

LC record available at https://lccn.loc.gov/2022018488

5 4 3 2 1

Contents

ANITA DIAMANT

Foreword

Frankly Feminist: Short Stories by Jewish Women from Lilith *Magazine* is a welcome celebration of women's voices. I have my favorites and you will have yours, but I doubt they'd overlap. I imagine us having a lively discussion—maybe even a worthy argument "for the sake of heaven"—about the merits of this one or that. The strength of this collection is its multidimensional breadth in style, subject matter, mood, voice, and message. Not that this should come as a surprise.

In college, I was assigned collections of Black poetry, Latin American stories, Native American writings, and Asian literature. The prefaces to those books tended to be breathless—as if Black, Latin American, Asian, and Native cultures weren't worlds unto themselves with long, illustrious histories full of genius. The official canon of Western literature had dismissed, overlooked, or simply ignored the existence of genius outside the narrow rubric of Western Civilization: male, white, and European. Those collections—even if worthy or well intentioned—implied the writers in these categories were "other," were "niche."

Frankly Feminist is not an introduction or discovery. We are way past that. Jewish women have produced stories, plays, poems, novels, essays, and reportage for centuries, though sadly, most of that work is known mostly through citations in the Jewish Women's Archive and the *Encyclopedia Judaica*. But for the past fifty-plus years, obscurity gave way to the limelight. Jewish women have won prestigious literary prizes (Pulitzer, Man Booker, Pen Faulkner), published countless bestsellers, received six-figure book advances, gotten front-page attention from the *New York Times Book Review*, attracted legions of loyal readers. And that visibility has inspired more of us to turn on our laptops and get busy.

The forty-four stories in this volume were selected from the two hundred

Lilith has published over the past forty-five years; and those two hundred were culled from more than six thousand submissions.

Frankly Feminist is distinctive in its focus on our experience of Jewishness, with kaleidoscopic results. There are some unforgettable stories from the worlds destroyed by the Nazis and a few remarkable narratives about life in Israel. *Lilith* is an American magazine so these are mostly American tales. Brooklyn and neighboring boroughs are well represented, but so are California, the Midwest, and the South, generation after generation from sea to shining sea. We meet immigrant grandmothers and great-grandmothers—some adored, some feared—then watch their grandchildren and great-grandchildren's adventures: summer camp, sexual awakenings straight and gay, testing the boundaries of tradition, brave, afraid, smart, foolish.

There are many more stories to come in the next forty-five years. More stories by and about Jews of color, Ladino and Mizrachi Jews, and LGBTQ rabbis and cantors: about Jewish life online and about the diverse constellations of our households—religiously and racially mixed, adoptive, informal, polyamorous. Also witty, clever, sharp, and naughty stories about the *mishegas/locura* of our lives.

I'm always telling people that there has never been a better time to be a Jewish woman. I have many proofs, including *Lilith*, which has given public voice to our concerns and our anger, celebrating our achievements, plumbing our sorrows, and creating a platform/living room for our conversations. And now *Frankly Feminist*.

Thank you to the contributors, editors, funders, volunteers, and interns who bring *Lilith* to life. Thanks to the subscribers. Thank you all.

SUSAN WEIDMAN SCHNEIDER

AND YONA ZELDIS MCDONOUGH

Introduction

S hort story collections focusing on Jewish writers have—no surprise—
typically given women authors short shrift, as have most general fiction
anthologies. Even those ubiquitous "Best of" volumes, for example, typically present only a moiety of their stories contributed by female authors,
often the same ones at that. Of the few previous, estimable collections of
short stories written by Jewish women, none has the geographic scope of
this volume; none were published in this century; and none used a particular Jewish feminist lens to scout out their selections.

This collection, though, has not been created to right past wrongs. It is a
unique sampling of the range of stories published in *Lilith* magazine since
1976. As the editors of the collection, we've been struck again and again
by the variegated cultures and contexts and points of view these stories
offer: Persian Jews; a Biblical matriarch; an Ethiopian mother in modern
Israel; suburban American teens; Eastern European academics; a sexual
questioner; a Jew by choice; a new immigrant escaping her Lower East Side
sweatshop; a Black Jewish marcher for justice in the streets of Washington,
DC; in Vichy France, a toddler's mother hiding out; and more.

Every person holds multitudes, and each of us brings more than one
identity to our encounters with one another. We identify ourselves—as
do the characters here—by religion or race or ethnicity, by our choices of
pastimes, friends, partners; by our causes, by our passions, by our worries
and joys; by what we say and what we signal. It's not simple, and these stories
reflect the complexities of history and geography, gender and sexuality,
blessings and their opposite.

These are subtle stories that explore complex relationships. There is the
attraction-repulsion energy and tension of both endogamy and exogamy,
and as readers, we too understand that the poles of "like" and "unlike" can

attract as well as repel. Characters' interactions here are not simply "girl meets boy, or girl," but include encounters comfortably familiar and dangerously illicit. No tidy stories here, wrapped up neatly; their conclusions are never foregone. They invite the reader in, often to experience an emotional world with the narrator, or to witness a fraught moment.

Moreover, these are distinctly modern short stories, sometimes open-ended and ambiguous. They tease, provoke, beguile, and challenge. We have gathered a few dozen, each uniquely of its moment and also distinctive in its feminist, Jewish perspective.

Like *Lilith* magazine, the matrix in which these stories appeared, the voices here turn a feminist lens on Jewish religious practice, Jewish history, and Jewish popular culture, spotlighting inherent inequities in gender roles and expectations while working to correct or subvert these constraints. At the same time—again like the magazine—their authors speak with a Jewish voice in the larger world of women's and gender issues. These stories face both inward and outward.

Since its launch in 1976, *Lilith* magazine has been committed to attracting and publishing short fiction that elucidates what we editors perceived as important truths or particularly revealing experiences in the lives of Jewish girls and women—both in the Old World and the New. Submissions have come from an annual short story contest and from an invitation on the magazine's own platforms: in print and also, from the 1990s onward, online at Lilith.org and face to face in more than a hundred *Lilith* "salons" where readers meet to discuss each new issue of the magazine.

Hundreds of published stories later, it's clear that some themes are forever with us. Family relations provide endless fodder: stories about our mothers, and mothers about their children. Persistent memories of the Holocaust—and the reverberations from this and other traumas of antisemitism and gender injustice through generations—surface, again and again. And familiar biblical narratives become a springboard for examining their modern-day parallels.

Small moments that connect one character memorably to another are at the core of many stories here, whether the touch points are tenderness, jealousy, or other hurts. Woven through this collection are dynamic relationships of women to one another, with bonds that provide emotional scaffolding for a pivotal interaction. Regardless of a story's theme, we have sought out good writing that offers intelligence and empathy, often seasoned with anger and humor. And it has not been easy to choose!

In *Lilith*'s early years, we considered some of the submissions a kind of necessary ancestor worship, homage to women of previous generations, grandmothers with various accents, avatars of traditional cooking, demanding while fiercely loving. But the excavations went deeper. Though fiction stands apart from the literal truth, many of the same experiences probed in memoir are present in this fiction: misogyny, tight control of women's options (and hence our lives), undercurrents of violence, and the joys of unexpected self-awareness, or of being seen and understood by another. And as with any stories that engage us, this collection brings us into imagined worlds similar to—and perhaps very dissimilar from—our own.

And there are pieces missing. You'll see that notably scant in this collection is the leverage that the workplace exerts on contemporary Jewish women's lives. Here, jobs and even professions are barely a means to an end, not in themselves provocations for this feminist fiction. Because the stories here came to *Lilith* starting in 1976, some subjects that appear in the magazine's nonfiction features seem not yet to have worked their way into our short story submissions: living with disability, for example, or undertaking gender transitions.

The stories have sorted themselves into categories, but the book reads comfortably as a thumb-through experience as well, useful as much for a gift to a friend as for a survey of women's issues in Jewish life. The first section, "Transitions," cycles through female lives, birth to burial, paving the way for the widening lens of the section "Intimacies." The stories that follow, in "Transgressions," imagine Procrustean pulls on women stretched between loyalties—to oneself, to another, to tribe, or family, or to a more abstract notion of how one ought to behave in the world. The category "War" should need no explanation. "Body and Soul," the next theme, is especially germane because so much of Jewish religious ritual is indeed embodied: what we're supposed to eat, the kinds of fabrics we're supposed to wear, sexual relationships we're supposed to honor or eschew. Regardless of where a woman might locate herself on the grid of Jewish identification or observance, the concluding category, "To Belong," is open to all. Except, of course, that belonging—whether to one's own kind or to the cohort one aspires to join—is a fraught subject.

In dividing this collection by theme, we have foregrounded content, but our hope is that in reading you'll appreciate the liveliness of the burgeoning self-awareness brought to life in each tale, and the occasional funny, call-your-friend-and-tell-her-about-it moment. Skip around, encounter an author whose other writing you may know, be enticed by a title, or an opening line. We hope you'll find both pleasure and enlightenment—and perhaps even revelation—within these pages.

TRANSITIONS

There was a time in some families, and not so long ago, when the arrival of a newborn daughter was not a joyous event. It was just another fact of life marking time until a son (or another son) was born. That's the cold reality of the world the narrator of "The New World" was born into, and the early life of the story's author bore out this unattractive truth.

But thanks to somewhat more enlightened attitudes toward gender (we said *somewhat*, remember) things have improved over the generations. Now, ceremonies and blessings welcoming a newborn baby daughter into a Jewish family are in many communities as common as the ceremonial welcoming of a son. Changes like these do not come about because of some general benevolence, or a sudden recognition of past injustices, but because strong women were brave enough to state, even to themselves, at least a little of what they wanted from life.

The stories in this opening section of the collection do not offer a linear progression from birth to old age, nor a collective portrait. Instead, each story frames a few episodes in the lives of their imagined protagonists, girls and women each sharp-eyed in her own way, trying to make sense of the world around her. Despite historical constraints on the options for females, the lead actor in each of these stories looks for ways to manage her own destiny.

The undervaluing of daughters is not unique to Jews, but in a religion where practices are determined so strongly by gender—who lights the Sabbath candles, who has the right to say aloud the Kaddish prayer in memory of a deceased relative, who is permitted to chant from the Torah—discrimination often seeped into secular conditions as well. The author of the opening story was sister to the celebrated writers Isaac Bashevis Singer and Israel Joshua Singer; their mother destroyed all of Esther's early writing, claiming it would render her unmarriageable. Messages like this weren't lost on generations of Jewish girls and women who were warned by concerned parents to be "smart, but not too smart."

Differentiation between the sexes provides a framework for understanding social strictures, including strife between women made to feel that they're competing for scarce resources—the attention of other girls, or a parent; later for the attention of males, if they're following the prescribed path into heterosexual marriage and childbearing. Which brings us to fertility, and the pressures on women to become mothers. As much as shame has been heaped upon unmarried females who were pregnant, there was equal shame (though perhaps easier to conceal or deny) for women unable to conceive.

In Jewish life there has never been an honored place for the celibate. Jewish texts—including the liturgy—elevate study, good deeds, and "chuppah"—the marriage canopy. The particular pressure on LGBTQ Jews has been profound (and is still so today, in some spaces). Sexuality isn't dismissed or frowned upon in Jewish life, but the formal expectation is that it will take place within a sanctioned marriage. Even in proudly secular or assimilated families, these social norms were maintained, despite the sexualization of girls and young women in twentieth-century Western culture at large. And then there's the ever-present threat of gender-based danger: harassment, discrimination, outright assault.

The fiction in this section references many of these matters, even if just by suggestion. Whether the characters are living in a contemporary Ashkenazi-American community or in the Sephardic Middle East in another era, the tensions between expectations and reality make for rich narratives.

ESTHER SINGER KREITMAN

translated from the Yiddish by Barbara Harshav

The New World

From the start, I didn't like lying in my mother's belly. Enough! When it got warm, I twisted around, curled up and lay still . . .

But, five months later, when I felt alive, I was really very unhappy, fed up with the whole thing! It was especially tiresome lying in the dark all the time and I protested. But who heard me? I didn't know how to shout. One day, I wondered if perhaps that wasn't how to do it and I started looking for a way out.

I just wanted to get out.

After pondering a long time, it occurred to me that the best idea would be to start fighting with my Mama. I began throwing myself around, turning cartwheels, often jabbing her in the side; I didn't let up but it didn't do any good. I simply gave myself a bad name so that when, for instance, I'd grow tired of lying on one side and try turning over, just to make myself a little more comfortable, she'd start complaining. In short, why should I lie here cooking up something, it didn't do any good—I had to lie there the whole nine months—understand?—the whole period.

Well (not having any other choice), I consoled myself: I'll simply start later! Just as soon as they let me out into God's world, I'll know what I have to do. Of course, I'll be an honored guest, I have a lot of reasons to think so. First of all, because of what I often heard my Mama tell some woman who (as I later found out) was my Grandma:

Grandma comes in and smiles at Mama. She looks happy—probably because her daughter has come through it all right. She doesn't even look at me.

"Mazal tov, dear daughter!"

"Mazal tov, may we enjoy good fortune!"

Mama smiles too but not at me.

"Of course, I would have been happier if it were a boy," says Mama. Grandmother winks roguishly with a half-closed eye and consoles her:

"No problem, boys will also come..."

I listen to all that and it is very sad for me to be alive. How come I was born if all the joy wasn't because of me! I'm already bored to death. Oh, how I want to go back to the other world.

All of a sudden, I feel a strange cold over my body. I am jolted out of my thoughts; I feel myself clamped in two big, plump hands, which pick me up. I shake all over. Could it be—a dreadful idea occurs to me—is she going to stuff me back in for another nine months? Brrrr! I shudder at the very thought.

But my head spins, everything is whirling before my eyes, I feel completely wet, tiny as I am! Am I in a stream? But a stream is cool, pleasant, even nice. But this doesn't interest me as much as the idea of what the two big, clumsy hands want to do with me. I am completely at their mercy.

"It does hurt a little but I almost don't feel it," Mama would say. "I'm glad! I was so scared I was barren. A trifle? It's already two years since the wedding and you don't see or hear anything... Minka the barren woman also said she would yet have children. And why should I be surer of it?"

"Well, praised be the one who survives. With God's help, it will come out all right; and God forbid, with no evil eye," Grandma would always answer. From such conversations, I assumed I would be a welcome guest.

I knew that, here in the other world, where I lived ever since I became a soul, when an important person came, he was supposed to be greeted with great fanfare. First of all, a bright light was to be spread over the whole sky. Angels (waiting for him) were to fly around; merry, beautiful cherubs who spread such holy joy that the person only regretted he hadn't... died sooner. It was quite a novelty that I, an honored, long-awaited guest, expected to be born into a big, light home with open windows, where the sun would illuminate everything with a bright light...

Every morning, I waited for birds who were supposed to come greet me, sing me a song. And I was to be born on the first of Adar—a month of joy. "When Adar begins, people are merry."

But right here "it" comes—the first disappointment.

Mama lay in a tiny room, an "alcove!" The bed was hung with dark draperies, which completely screened out the light. The windows were shut tight so no tiny bit of air could get in, God forbid; you shouldn't catch cold. The birds obviously don't like screened-out light and closed windows; they looked for a better, freer place to sing. Meanwhile, no happiness appears either; because I was a girl, everybody in the house, even Mama, was disappointed.

In short, it isn't very happy! I am barely a half hour old but, except for a slap by some woman as I came into the world, nobody looks at me. It is so dreary!

Thank God, I am soon taken out of the wet. I am brought back to the alcove, already violated, sad. I am carried around the alcove: everybody looks at me, says something. At last, I am put back to bed. Mama does put a sweet, liquid thing in my mouth: I am really hungry for what is in the world.

Mama looks at me with her nice, soft eyes, and my heart warms. A sweet fatigue puts me to sleep and I am blessed with good dreams . . .

But my happiness didn't last long, a dreadful shout wakes me with a start. I look around. Where did it come from? It's Mama!

People gather round.

"What happened? Where did that shout come from?"

Mama gestures, tries to point, her lips tremble, want to say something and can't. She falls back onto the pillow, almost in a faint.

Seeing they won't get anything out of Mama, they start looking for the reason in the closet, under the bed, in the bed.

All of a sudden, a shout is heard from the nurse, who keeps repeating in a strange voice:

"Cats, oh dear God, cats!"

The people look up, can't understand what she's saying. But, except for the word "cats," they can't get anything out of her—so upset is she.

Grandma is also very upset. But she takes heart, makes a thorough search in the bed and, laughing to hide her fear, she calls out:

"Mazal tov, the cat had kittens. A good sign!"

But apparently, this isn't a good sign. The people are upset:

"On the same day, in the same bed as a cat?"

"Hmmmm, a person and a cat are born the same way," says one brave soul.

They calm Mama. But again, nobody looks at me. Mama falls asleep. And with that, my first day comes to an end. I am, thank God, a whole day old and I have survived quite a bit.

The third day after my birth was the Sabbath. This time, a big, red Gentile woman puts me in the bath. I wasn't so scared anymore, already familiar with the way it smells.

Once again, I lie in bed with Mama. Mama looks at me more affectionately than yesterday. I open my eyes, I would like to look around a bit at the new world. I am already used to the darkness. All of a sudden—it grows even darker for me than before.

A gang of women burst into the alcove. I look at them. They're talking, gesturing, picking me up, passing me from one to another, like a precious object. They look at me, they look at Mama, they smile.

Meanwhile, Grandma comes with a tray of treats.

The women make her plead with them, pretend they don't want to try any of the cookies, whiskey, preserves, cherry brandy, berry juice, or wine; but, Grandma doesn't give up, so they open their beaks, and finally consent to do her a favor.

Males also stuck their heads into the female alcove. They talked with strange grimaces, gestured, shook their beards, went into a fit of coughing.

With them, Papa succeeded, not Grandma. And I am named Sara Rivka, after some relative of his.

Now they need a wet nurse. Mama is weak, pale, with such transparent, narrow hands without sinews, she can hardly pick me up. A middle-class woman, she cannot breastfeed me. I am the opposite: a healthy, hearty gal, greedy. I restrain myself from shouting, "all I want is to eat."

"Not to a goyish wet nurse," says Grandma. Not for all the tea in China. And she can't find a Jewish one. The pharmacist says I should get used to formula, which is better than mother's milk. But I say I don't want to get used to it and I throw up all the time.

This is bitter! Grandma is upset. Mama even more. But Papa consoles them, saying the Holy-One-Blessed-Be-He will help. And He does.

Our neighbor remembers a wet nurse named Reyzl. She has the voice of a sergeant major and two red eyes that scare me. She can't come to our home. She has six children of her own but there is no choice.

All the details are worked out, she is given an advance and may everything work out all right.

Reyzl picks me up out of the cradle, takes out a big, white breast, which looks like a piece of puffed-up dough, and gives it to me to suck, as a test. Well, what should I say? I didn't drown. Even my eyes fill with the taste of a good wet nurse.

Reyzl looks happily from one to the other:

"Well, what do you say?"

Mama and Grandma glance at each other furtively and are silent . . .

I have the good fortune to be a tenant at Reyzl's! Not that she needs another tenant 'cause she lives in a flat not much bigger than a large carton. When Reyzl brings me home, her husband comes to greet me carrying their smallest one in his arms and the other five heirs swarming around him. He seems to be pleased with my arrival.

"Well, what do you say about this, eh? Ten gulden a week, my word of honor! Along with old clothes and shoes. Along with the fact that, from now on, they'll give all the repairs only to you! You hear, Berish?"

Berish is silent. He turns around so his breadwinner won't see his joy.

"You're more of a man than me, I swear. You can earn a gulden faster . . ." he thinks to himself. But right away he becomes serious. "Where will we put the cradle?" They ponder a long time.

But Reyzl's husband, who is an artist at arranging things in his tiny flat, smacks his low, wrinkled forehead with his hard hand and calls out joyously:

"Reyzl, I've got it! Under the table!"

So in a tiny cradle, I am shoved under the table.

With open, astonished eyes, I look at the filthy wood of the table, covered with a host of spiderwebs, and think sadly:

"This is the new world I have come into? And this is its heaven?"

And I weep bitter tears.

In Every Girl's Heart

They stand in a circle wearing horrible shirts with the sun shining down. They are red-faced children with shirts the color of traffic cones and sharpened stones for eyes. It is already 90 degrees and it is Horse Day for Bluebirds (Age group 10–12, space is limited so register your daughter to-day!). Their counselors lead them in song. "Let me hear your camp spirit!" Cora, a red-haired counselor, has so many freckles it looks like a disease. "Marsha, I can't hear you."

Marsha is making the right shapes with her lips but no noise is coming out. The group with the most spirit gets ice cream after lunch.

"Sing," hisses a Bluebird between verses. Marsha sings.

The horses (Remember to include the riding fee with your application if you want your daughter to participate in this extra-special activity!) are kept in a stable at the edge of the camp. The counselors pick the Sunflower Girls (Age group 8–9, please indicate if you wish for your daughter to participate in the end-of-summer sleep-over!) as the spirit winners. It is the fourth time in a row the Bluebirds will not get ice cream.

"Bluebirds, line up." Cora is their leader. Every lunch, she sneaks to the boat house (Only campers with a white or red swim band allowed!) to meet her boyfriend. Her freckles don't stop at her neck.

"The Sunflower Girls keep getting the best of us." Cora's smile is widest when she is annoyed. "I'm going to start feeding you worms if you Bluebirds can't chirp loud enough." Her mouth is a hive of small, uneven teeth. "Let's sing the Worm Song on our way to the horsies."

They walk in groups of three and four, swinging their arms to stir the still air. "It's Marsha's song," one Bluebird whose name is Heather whispers to another, whose name is Jennifer. They trail Marsha, clipping the backs of

Marsha's shoes as she walks. They sing a special version of the Worm Song just loud enough for Marsha to hear.

"Nobody likes you, everybody hates you, you're just an ugly worm."

Marsha's heels smack against her flattened sneakers as she walks, flip-flop flip-flop, the sound of Granny's slippers. Marsha is pretty sure Granny stopped recognizing her. "Who is this darling child? I'd like to give her a big kiss," every time Marsha was made to visit. The toothless mouth opening and closing.

On the first day of camp (Don't forget to dress your daughter in a camp T-shirt!) everyone was told to decorate their name tag according to the name of their group. Marsha drew musical notes around hers (HELLO!! My name is Marsha!), turning the s's into treble clefs.

"What're those supposed to be?" Heather had asked, poking her finger into Marsha's chest. Heather has impossibly small lips the color of cherry chewing gum. Her barrettes and socks always match her shorts.

"It's birdsong. Since we're Bluebirds."

Cora had called Marsha "creative" in front of the whole group. After the first week of camp, Heather passed out invitations to a pool party in her backyard. One Bluebird was not invited.

There is a changing room next to the stable (Do not enter unless you're dressed to ride!) where the Bluebirds change together. Marsha tries to hide the sweat that has turned her T-shirt a darker orange under her arms.

Marsha doesn't wear a training bra like the others. Her mother thinks it inappropriate for a girl her age. Before Granny was sent away, she would feed Marsha milkshakes with raw egg and, later, whole sticks of butter. "You're a twig. Better drink this if you want boobies." Marsha's mother assures her that she will one day be thankful for the high metabolism that keeps her so thin.

"Worm." The word echoes through the room, the heat melting its source.

Marsha has a raised mole the size of a corn kernel just below her clavicle. She keeps her back to the other birds. Heather's training bra has a pink flower in the middle. She likes to walk around in it when she holds butt inspection. Her belly button is a perfect innie.

"Get ready, Bluebirds! It's tush time!"

Heather demands the full participation (Our wide array of camp activities build fitness and social skills!) of her fellow campers. From under the Bluebirds' shorts emerges a flock of cotton panties the colors of the pastel rainbow. Jennifer spreads her legs and pushes her butt out like a model for designer jeans. Despite the small fan in the corner (All facilities are climate-controlled for camper-comfort!) the room stinks of yesterday's sweat.

"Remember girls, stick out your ass to go to the head of the class! Even a little one can go a long way," Heather sings, passing each bird from behind.

"Oh, I forgot, worms don't have butts, do they?"

All the Bluebirds, even the shy ones, twitter. Marsha focuses on the tree outside the window, tries to think herself to a branch higher than Heather can reach. Through the window of Granny's room there was only a creek with thick, brown water.

"What's wrong? Don't you know how to talk?"

Marsha's head moves up and down.

Heather puts her mouth close to Marsha's ear. She whispers loud enough for everyone to hear her. "Do worms have butts? Yes or no?" Heather's breath smells like peanut butter.

"No," Marsha whispers.

"Then how'd you get chocolate stains on your underwear?"

Sound bounces off the concrete walls and floor until it is the whole world. Marsha smells the metallic stink of shame from her armpits. When Cora comes in, her birds are dressed and ready.

In the stable (Horses hold a special place in every girl's heart!), the flies have grown too fat to fly. The heat makes Marsha's clothes (Jeans and a long-sleeved shirt are absolutely necessary!) feel heavier. Marsha's horse that day is white with brown spots.

"My undies are clean," she says to no one in particular. The horse's name is Lightning. Its mane and tail are yellow-white like Granny's hair. When it breathes, the air rushes too loudly through its nose. Marsha doesn't like leading the horse into the sun, doesn't like being near its large yellow teeth.

Outside the stable, the dark spots on the horse's coat seem to spread like creeping stains. Marsha is afraid to touch them in case they are contagious like warts. When the horse moves, its bones make lumps ripple beneath its skin. Granny had a bump on the side of her neck that no one talked about. She would stroke it with her fingers until Marsha's mom would pull

Granny's hand away. Marsha is short for her age. To get onto the horse, she needs extra help.

Most of the Bluebirds came to camp knowing how to canter. Marsha slows the riding class (All experience levels welcome!) down. She has a difficult time remembering that kicking with the left heel means turn right and that the right heel means turn left.

Heat jellies the air Marsha breathes. In it, she can see specks of dust and hairs loosened from the horse's neck. She can see fly eggs and horse spittle. Heat melts the difference between the horse and Marsha's leg. Underneath her jeans, she feels rough hairs sprouting. By the time Marsha returns to the changing room, she will be white with chocolate stains. The thought closes around her like a scab.

"Marsha!" The voice of Graham (Our professional riding instructor knows children as well as he knows horses!) cuts through her thickening skin. "Why aren't you moving? Get your butt in gear. I know Lightning's ready for a ride."

"I have to get down. I can't ride today. Please let me get down."

Graham turns his horse around. Heather and the other Bluebirds stare. Heat blurs the lines of their faces. Heather's mouth shimmers small and red.

"Why do you even come here?" Graham leads Marsha from the ring. He wrenches Marsha's arm lifting her off the horse, then tethers Lightning to a post beside the stable.

Marsha watches the Bluebirds ride (Good horsemanship is something a girl can take pride in!) as if their bodies have been made for it. Beside her, Lightning snorts. The smell of fresh horse droppings amplifies the buzzing of the flies.

Inside the changing room, the air feels cool on Marsha's skin. Marsha looks for Heather's cubby. Today Heather's barrettes and socks are lemon yellow. Marsha finds a hard candy in the pocket of Heather's shorts and eats it even though it is unwrapped. She leaves with the shorts stuffed under her shirt.

Marsha stands beside Lightning (Be a careful Bluebird: never approach a horse from behind!), patting its side before reaching behind its legs. As Marsha rubs the shorts in the dung, she tells herself it is like twisting the top off an Oreo, the same feeling of give and slide as the cookie comes free from its creamy center.

"Horse patties," Marsha whispers, and giggles. Lightning shifts. Its hoof comes down on Marsha's shoe. The horse's hooves are thick and yellow like Granny's fingernails. The initial burst of pain becomes a dull throb.

"Let go," Marsha says. Marsha pictures the ground softening in the day's heat, the weight of the horse forcing her into the earth. Granny always worried she'd be buried before she died.

Heather's shorts are heavy in Marsha's hand. "Letgoletgoletgo." Lightning's tail swats slow flies. The Bluebirds (We try to make our youngest campers feel especially welcome!) are rounding the turn that leads back to the stable. Marsha shoves the horse with her free hand. She pounds it with her fist. Its pelt feels like little needles. She pounds between its spots.

Heather is at the front of the group. Marsha slams her shoulder into the horse, turning to avoid seeing herself touch its brown fur. Granny is behind Marsha's eyelids. "Little girl," Granny wheezes, "let me touch your face." Whenever it was time to leave. Granny would squeeze Marsha's hand and not let go.

The Bluebirds draw nearer, clip-clop clip-clop. Marsha begins to plead. "Let me go. Please. I'll kiss you this time." Marsha presses her mouth to the horse. Its hairs prick her lips.

Flies settle on the shorts in Marsha's hand. The Bluebirds see brown and lemon yellow. Their horses are breathing fast from being ridden in such heat. Their sides rise and fall, rise and fall.

Heather's face turns the color of cherry chewing gum. Her lips stretch and stretch. Graham begins to yell, but Marsha doesn't hear him. Heather's eyes are sharpened flint.

Rising temperatures are setting records up and down the eastern seaboard. Summer has just begun.

In Vegas That Year

A fter the Flamingo lost $300,000 in its first two weeks, Meyer Lansky forced Ben to close and retool. Mr. Lansky sent some of his men from the El Cortez to poke through everything in the hotel before he himself flew out in March to review the account books, to check the cameras in the counting room, to re-rig the tables and rewire the slot machines. Out front there were to be no more thieving Greek dealers. No more tuxedoes. This wasn't Paris or Havana. We needed to be friendly looking, not intimidating. The new dealers would wear regular suits, just like the patrons. There would be bingo and giveaways, and just the idea of either one of those made Benny, his manager, wince. I knew Lansky wasn't happy about Ben's recent divorce. There was nothing at all, really, that Lansky was happy about on this visit.

He and one of his men even made a point to watch the dress rehearsal of our new floor show. I'd been promoted from cigarette girl to dancing girl during the closure. When I'd told my father I wasn't going back to school after Christmas, he hadn't objected. Neither he nor my mother had finished high school, and the Flamingo was just too exciting.

And, anyway, who needed math and history lessons to be a dancer? I'd had more dance schooling than the rest, a bunch of local girls, pretty, but a little clunky. None of them could dance, not that we had much choreography to perform. Strutting, some waving of feather fans, a kick here and there, some tap. Our little numbers were scheduled between the real acts, a sip of water to cleanse the palate, the announcer introducing us with, "And now, from the Fabulous Flamingo Hotel, here's our lovely line of dancers!"

I don't think we lovely line of dancers were that important to the overall show, but still, I was nervous about making a good impression. We could be dumped just like the Greek dealers—and then what would I do? Sell cigarettes. Check hats. Or be sent back to school. So I was watching closely as Lansky, Benny, and a man I didn't know sat on chairs in the empty night-club, the three of them our only audience, their table the only one with a cloth over it, smoking and tipping their ashes into our flamingo-adorned ashtrays. The three kings.

It was the wrong time of day, of course, to see a nightclub floorshow. You needed night. The sun was bearing in on us despite the draperies, rendering the room vacant and dead, like any theater during the day. And having the men sitting there at the center front table with a tablecloth laid deferentially just for them made the rehearsal feel like an audition. None of the girls were wearing curlers like they usually did for four o'clock rehearsal. No one was wearing practice clothes. We wore our pink-feath-ered costumes, our rubberized mesh tights pulled up high and rolled at the waist, our red high-heeled shoes. What if the men didn't like what they saw? Would the costumes be taken from us? Would the opening be postponed still further?

Eventually, I would come to understand that our show, or any show here, had just one purpose, a purpose of paramount importance to Lansky and company, which is why they bothered spending any attention whatsoever on it and us, and that purpose was to send the exhilarated, titillated audi-ence out into the casino eager to part with its money. Because the casino was the heart of Las Vegas, the whole point of the whole city. The baying patrons, flinging their money down, always amazed me. Didn't they know the house always won, and the house would always win?

Benny, sitting there between Lansky and his friend, looked chastened, his normally ruddy, enthusiastic face a little empty, a little sandpapered, and he looked small, even though he was actually bigger than Lansky, who lacked Benny's sartorial flair. Mr. Lansky wore a shirt without a tie and a herringbone sports coat, his hair combed straight back. He was not handsome, but ordinary looking, middle a little thick. He could have been a shopkeeper in Boyle Heights. Or a rabbi. The other man, whose name was Nate Shapiro—though I didn't know this yet—wore a two-toned golf shirt and slacks. He was tall with a broad back and his hair was a black shock of a pompadour before there even was an Elvis Presley to sport one. Lansky might look to me like the rabbi at my grandfather's synagogue, but the way he held himself, the way both those men held themselves, the way they smoked, the way they looked around the club said they were not obedient servants of the Breed Street shul, but men who considered themselves as powerful as the God to whom its worshippers prayed.

My father wore a bouncy enthusiasm, always looking for the next opportunity to grab, sure it was coming around the corner. Lansky and Shapiro had already grabbed hold of opportunity and had twisted it into something miraculous. They were more powerful, I realized, than Benny Siegel, but I hadn't yet met anyone more powerful than Ben. I thought bigger than life meant powerful. But Lansky, and this Shapiro, lived smaller, they lived quietly, and there was nothing small or quiet about Ben, and for the first time, I realized that might be a liability. Quiet like my grandfather might be better, power hidden up the sleeve, not sprayed all over everybody in sight. I'd only ever seen grandstanding—in Ben, in my father, even in Louis B. Mayer with his big white semicircular desk up on a pedestal in his blindingly white office.

Under Lansky's disapproving gaze, everything around me seemed wrong. Our costumes looked cheap. In this glare, my short pink dress had a tacky sheen to it and my red shoes were silly and the pink feathers ridiculous. I wasn't sure the men would even understand that we were supposed to be flamingos, picking our way across the stage after the Andrews Sisters exited and before the Xavier Cugat band played again. Yes, I was finally going to have a chance to put my expensive dance lessons to some use, and I should have been thrilled, but our dour audience snuffed out any excitement. For me, anyway. The other girls, scooped up from dry goods store counters and restaurant cash registers in a pinch to fill the stage, seemed oblivious to anything but the fun of this. We're flamingos! At the Flamingo! Ha, ha, ha.

I watched the Andrews Sisters sing "Near You," watched the way they tapped their way toward the proscenium and back, swinging their arms in unison, doing a few step ball changes, singing their little songs, and I thought, This is boring. Even their costumes were boring, their hairstyles dated. Wartime entertainment. Patrons could get the Andrews Sisters back in Los Angeles or watch them in the movie houses. And they weren't even that pretty, one of them with a big nose. Any extra on the MGM lot was prettier than the prettiest of the Andrews Sisters. This wasn't what people would drive to postwar Las Vegas to see. The stark desert and the luxury hotels would need more riveting entertainment, more beauty. Not this.

And not a handful of chorines like me doing some kicks and tap dancing between the real numbers.

Of course, this was 1947, pre-Las Vegas showgirl, before the Copa girls and the Lido girls, before the sky-high headdresses and the sequins and beads. But I could see it all before it arrived—because I had already seen it in my mother's Busby Berkeley films. That was what Las Vegas needed. Goddesses. Long rows of girls descending staircases, curving staircases like the one my mother stood on playing the violin in "Gold Diggers," girls flying on trapezes, girls turning on spinning pedestals like the ballerinas in music boxes. I didn't know that girls like that were already performing in Parisian nightclubs or in some of the clubs Meyer Lansky was opening in Havana, girls ornamented in every way with the exception of clothing. But I could sense that what we were doing was not going to fly here for long.

I looked to Benny. His face was blank, obedient. Whatever Meyer wanted to see on that stage was what Ben was going to put on that stage, no matter how he felt privately. He would watch the cheerful Andrew Sisters retreads. He would cut the paychecks for the twelve of us girls dancing chastely in pink. If Meyer wanted the clean American West, friendly, welcoming, bring us your money, we would present cheerful Americana as we scooped up the tokens and chips. I wrinkled up my face as I watched those Andrews Sisters dancing and singing.

There's just one place for me, near you
It's like heaven to be near you
Times when we're apart
I can't face my heart

They swayed their arms as if they had no idea their days were numbered and that pretty soon they'd be a nostalgia act.

I had cut my teeth on Hollywood, and on the Sunset Strip. Not on a desert backwater. So over to the side of the floor where we girls were corralled waiting for our turn to flip and flap, I quietly defied Mr. Lansky. To "Near You," I stretched, threw my leg up, arched my back. I did a slow swirl that started in a crouch and then spiraled upward and ended with a head circle. I did the mincing steps of the high-heeled striptease artist, my arms thrown up to the heavens, hands wagging. By the window drapes where nobody could see me, I had my own private ball. And then, slowly, I became aware someone was watching me.

It wasn't the crestfallen Benny, or Lansky, the man who'd deflated him. It was the man beside Lansky. Nate Shapiro. He wasn't looking at the Andrews Sisters any more at all, just at me, only at me, and there was no censure in his face. Quite the opposite. He was smoking and watching me. I looked back at him for a moment and once I figured out that what I saw in his face was not disapproval, I continued dancing. I pretended I didn't know he was watching, but I knew that he was. I felt myself tugging on a long fluid string to make his hands and legs and lips move and if I wanted to, I knew I could pull him toward me, though I was too naïve, of course, to have any idea what to do with him once I'd gotten him there.

When the Andrews Sisters finished their number, I stopped, my back to the club floor, and I listened to the men clap. When I turned my head for a peek, I saw Benny and Lansky were applauding the Andrews Sisters, but not the third man. He was looking right at me, all approbation, and when I inclined my head in a small bow to acknowledge his pleasure in me, he smiled, eyes crinkling, all the former severity in his face banished and, suddenly, I liked him. All the men I knew on occasion used what I thought of as the bad face, the tough, unflinching stare meant to intimidate. The man had been wearing that face not ten minutes ago, but now his bad face was gone and he was looking at me as if he were delighted with me, this little girl he didn't even know. And he was the one who tugged at that string between us, not me, tugged me to him with that smile. And then he leaned over to Benny, and I knew he had asked Ben who I was. And Benny brought him over.

Maybe it was because I was wearing this costume. Or maybe it was be-cause I was finally grown up, which I'd been trying to do as fast as I could since we'd arrived in Vegas because there was nothing here for little girls and so many opportunities for young women. I didn't know yet how these men were protective of little girls but predatory when it came to women. But you couldn't stop growing up. The transition from girlhood to wom-anhood turned on a pivot. One day you were a child and then, all at once, you weren't. Well, that day was my pivot.

The man had a pinkie ring on his left hand and a cigarette in his right, and he transferred the one to the other as he approached, and that's how I knew he was going to touch me. I could see better now his Roman nose that counterbalanced all that hair. He was handsome, though not in a pretty-boy way like Benny. Still, he looked something like Ben, something like my father, some version of them. Without the intemperate rage. Without the failure. He moved with a tall, silky grace that actually reminded me of my old Hollywood dance teacher, Daddy Mack, who might have been short and fat, but when he moved all that weight on his two short legs, he wore his blubber like a mink coat. And that's how this man moved, as if he were wearing a mink coat.

"E," Benny said to me, not entirely happily. "This is Nate Shapiro."

Nate offered his hand. I took it. It was large.

"I'm Esme Wells," I told him, giving him my stage name, which was half my name and half my mother's stage name.

Nate laughed.

He knew exactly who I was, Esme Silver, fifteen years old, practically unschooled, a nobody, but he understood my affectation, even approved of it. All those men approved of ambition. Of reinvention. Naturally.

And we stood there, my hand in his while Benny frowned, probably because Nate was married, and not for the first time, not that marriage had ever inhibited Benny himself in any way in his various adventures, but because I was Benny's Baby E and Nate was staring at me in this certain way and Ben could see what lay ahead, just as my father did, and he didn't like it. He cleared his throat. He would have liked to clear the club, or rather, clear Nate from the club. But in the current pecking order, Ben didn't have the power to do this. So the rest of the girls clumped back to the dressing room, where they would smoke cigarettes and drink Cokes, while I stood here. I can only imagine how I looked to Mr. Shapiro, a piece of candy in a candy-colored costume, my face orange with Pan Cake and my lashes an elongated black, my hair long as a child's. The desert sun had turned my hair so blonde it was almost white and the sun had darkened my skin. Was I too dark? Did Nate think I was a Negro?

I didn't want to let go of Nate's hand and he seemed not to want to let go of mine, either. What was happening was perfectly proper, an introduction, a handshake, but somehow it didn't feel proper at all. And Benny, irritated, looked away.

My costume, though actually quite modest, suddenly seemed to feel riskily low cut and short, exposing too much of me. I flushed and Nate smiled at my transparency. Embarrassed as I was by my near nakedness, I nonetheless found myself in the grip of an absurd impulse to undress further, and all the while Nate Shapiro smiled at me. He's an old man, I told myself. But the fact that he was older was exactly what I liked about him. He wasn't striving to be something, he was already something. I had a feeling about him, the kind of feeling my father had when he knew his horse was going to come in win, place, or show.

But because I was underage, and because Nate was a careful man, more like Lansky the accountant than the id-driven Benny—who needn't have worried about me, at least not yet, and by the time he should have been worried he was dead—it was therefore too early to know what would become of us.

And so all Nate said to me that day was, "Lovely to meet you, Miss Esme Wells." His voice was a purr, with the slightest tinge of something foreign-sounding in it, which turned out to be just his flat Midwestern accent, though I was too ignorant to know it.

He was fifty, and I wasn't quite a third of that.

A Wedding in Persia

News of Solomon the Man's engagement to Peacock, the daughter of Joseph the Winemaker, spread faster and incited more animosity in Esfahan and Juyy Bar than any other incident in recent memory. In the ghetto, mothers of eligible young women dug their nails into their cheeks and mourned. Matchmakers ran to each other in a fury as they tried to discover which one of them had made the deal. Young men despaired at the thought of having Solomon removed from the circle of womanizing and debauchery that had become the object of all their fantasies.

Ever since Joseph the Winemaker had announced her engagement, Peacock had cried and begged and sworn she would not marry. It was preposterous—that Peacock should refuse the man everyone wanted.

Solomon sent to Kashan for his mother to come and take charge of the festivities. She arrived a week later, a big woman with light skin and nothing of the good looks that had blessed her son. She sat in the carriage she had hired with Solomon's money, complaining of the heat and the dust of the desert. She arrived at the city's gates and was forced to disembark, for no Jew could ride through town. She had come with her daughters, all eleven of them, and with another, darker than the rest and even uglier, whom she claimed was an orphan she had raised from childhood.

Ghadereh Khanum—the Able One—stayed in Solomon's house for a week and held court. She sat with her daughters around the receiving room. In Kashan they had been rug weavers. They had lived in a hovel and worked from the age of three, sitting cross-legged in front of wooden frames onto which they tied minuscule knots of wool and silk. And they would have worked till their eyes were blind and their lungs rotted from inhaling wool, except Solomon the Man had made them rich. Now they sat in his house and snubbed the visitors who came to offer their welcome.

At the end of the week of greeting, the Able One and her daughters paid a surprise visit to Peacock's house. As was customary, they arrived early in the morning, before Peacock could have a chance to comb her hair or hide her faults in deceiving clothes.

The Able One and her daughters stayed all morning. They inspected Peacock, commented on the thickness of her skin and the darkness of her gums, remarked that her hips were so narrow no child could ever come through them alive. They made Peacock walk from one side of the court-yard to the other so they could see her stride, examined her knees and complained that she was too thin—not fed well by her parents.

To the people of Juyy Bar, Peacock's wedding to Solomon the Man marked the end of the Great Famine of 1871. For although the earth did not yield a healthy crop for another decade, and although their poverty would become worse in the years to come, the three days and nights of celebration at Solomon's home managed to create in the minds of even the harshest of skeptics a lasting illusion of comfort, and a collective memory of never-ending wealth.

It began at dawn on a Monday, and did not end until after midnight on Wednesday. In between, the men gathered in Solomon's house and ate and drank and danced to the music of seven groups of entertainers he had imported from as far as Tehran and Rasht. They ate eggs and honey and sweetbread and halva for breakfast, drank cool essence of cherries and snacked on apples stewed in rosewater until noon, then feasted on roasted lamb, bread, rice, and golden cookies for lunch. In the afternoon, bands of musicians played, acrobats danced in the courtyard, and old storytellers recited verses from the Book of Kings while poets repeated the verses of Omar Khayyam. Before sunset, Joseph the Winemaker walked from room to room and poured Persian wine and Russian Vodka into everyone's cup. By the time Homa the Ricemaker served dinner, the men were all drunk.

On the women's side, the celebrations were more solemn but just as extravagant. As tradition dictated, they gathered at the house of Joseph the Winemaker, where Solomon the Man had paid all expenses. The Able One and her eleven daughters hosted the affair. On the first of the three days of celebration, they took Peacock for a marriage bath.

They left in the dark, equipped with food, nuts, and candy, jugs of cool drinks, and, most important, chunks of henna. In the bath, the Able One took Peacock into the well and watched as she performed the rites of purity. Then everyone came inside, around the pool, and undressed. A band of female musicians, courtesy of Solomon the Man, performed in the nude. Pari the Henna came forward, clicking her tongue to sound a cheer that echoed through the bath until it became deafening. She gave Peacock a dimpled smile and a reassuring pat, admired her beauty and remarked on her youth, then set about "turning her into a woman."

She tied the ends of two long threads around her thumb and forefinger, put the threads to Peacock's eyebrows, catching each hair and plucking them, until she had created two arched lines. Then she plucked Peacock's legs and thighs, the hair on her vulva and armpits. Finally she prepared a mold of henna, which she placed on the bride's fingernails and toenails, and on her hair. The other women, cheering, began to dye their own hair.

On Tuesday the women gathered at the winemaker's house to bless the bride. They brought Peacock into the courtyard and put her in a translucent chador made of gold thread. Grudgingly, while her daughters shed tears of envy, the Able One extended to Peacock the gifts Solomon had sent for her: a dozen gold chains, a sapphire necklace, turquoise earrings, and a diamond bracelet. Everyone gasped in awe. The Able One took out a bag of gold coins and placed a crystal bowl into Peacock's lap. One by one she pressed the coins against Peacock's forehead, letting each one stick momentarily—for luck, so that from now on the bride's forehead would be marked with joy and prosperity. Then Peacock bent her head and dropped the coin into the bowl as coal stoves burned wild rue seeds and smoke filled the air.

On the third day a delegation of women visited Solomon's house to arrange the bridal room. They spread the bed toward Jerusalem—ensuring that a son would be conceived of the first intercourse. Inside the sheets they sprayed rosewater, spread jasmine and rose petals. Above the pillows they put a white handkerchief that Solomon the Man would have to rub in Peacock's blood and present after the intercourse.

In the afternoon, Raab Yahya called at Solomon's house to perform the first half of the ceremony. Solomon the Man was bathed and shaved, dressed in a Western suit and hat. He repeated the vows and then raised his cup in celebration.

"Bring her to me," he toasted.

Then Pari the Henna left Solomon the Man's house to carry the bridal gown to the bride.

But in the house of Joseph the Winemaker, Peacock's mother Leyla was running from room to room, flushed and frantic, the other women were searching every corner, and rumors had begun to circulate that the bride was missing; she had disappeared sometime before noon, and no one could imagine where to look for her.

Joseph the Winemaker paced every inch of the ghetto and at last found his daughter in Mullah Mirza's basement which had been empty and abandoned since Muhammad the Jew's Massacre. Peacock sat there terrified by her own defiance, terrified also by the walls that reeked of poison and the smell of Mullah Mirza's dismay. Still, when Joseph grabbed her, she held his hand and begged that he call off the marriage.

"Solomon the Man," she cried, "will leave me."

Joseph the Winemaker took his daughter home and dressed her in a pearl-embroidered gown and a veil—a gift from Zil-el-Sultan's harem—made entirely of silver and gold threads. He saw her wear the jewels Solomon had given her, and fought back his own tears of joy.

"Believe in luck," he whispered to Peacock as he took her before Raab Yahya.

When the wedding ceremony was over, a caravan of women walked from the winemaker's house to that of Solomon the Man. Peacock rode in front, mounted on Solomon's black horse. At the top of the alley leading to the house, she stopped and waited for messengers to announce her arrival to the groom.

"What if they know she ran away?" Leyla asked Joseph, who trembled at the possibility.

But in Solomon's house the sound of music and laughter had never ceased, and the matter of the bride's disappearance was quickly forgotten. When they heard that the bride was about to arrive, the men cheered and all seven bands of musicians played at once as women burned espand seeds and threw sugar-laced almonds on the bride's path. Peacock was led into the house and straight to the bridal room, where she would wait for the end of the reception. Leyla took her inside and kissed her goodbye, and then, suddenly, Peacock was alone.

She stood erect, looking ahead, and tried to gather the courage she had lost along the way. She told herself she was not going to stay, that no one could force her to stay. She reminded herself of the dream she had had; an old woman, alone and brokenhearted, walking the streets of an unfamiliar town and crying Solomon's name. In the dream, Peacock knew that she was the old woman.

She looked around the room. The walls were plastered white, the ceiling decorated with hand-painted moldings. There was a window in this room. Peacock remembered the house of Muhammad the Jew.

"But I won't stay," she reminded herself.

She could smell food from outside.

"When he comes in, I will tell him he has to send me back. 'You keep whores,' I will say. 'I don't want a man who keeps whores.'"

She waited, but hours passed and her legs became numb from standing, and still the sound of laughter had not ceased in the house. She sat on the floor, her chador around her, and found herself admiring the softness of her dress, the shine of her jewels, the beauty of her veil. She put her head on a cushion away from the bed and fell asleep.

She dreamt that the door opened and a man came into the room. He was tall, with long arms, and the smell of rain on his clothes. He brought with him a piece of the moonlit sky.

She dreamt that he stood above her, looking, then bent down and lifted her from the ground to place her on the bed. She thought he was about to unveil her, that she should stop him, but he touched her and she was not afraid anymore. He took off her veil.

He stared at her—his eyes submerged in the blue light of dawn—and then he reached to the bottom of the bed and pulled a white sheet, as cool as the wind that came before every rain, over her body. He left. Without him the room was vast and empty.

Peacock sat up, jolted by the sound of the morning namaz, and looked about. She was still burned from last night's anger. She remembered her dream. She saw the white sheet that covered her. Solomon the Man, she realized, had seen her.

She stood up on the mattress and searched her clothes for blood. She looked on the sheets. There was no stain. She breathed with relief; he had not touched her. Then she realized why: he had seen her face, and decided she was too ugly to touch. She picked up her chador and walked out.

"Good morning," a voice greeted her on the porch. Solomon's eyes were full of sleep. His face was unshaved. He sat on the steps, smoking his water pipe and watching the sunrise.

"You wake up early," he said.

Peacock froze. She was disarmed by his casual manner, his smile. She thought his eyes played with her.

"I sent everyone home last night," he said. "I told them, 'My wife is asleep and I will wait for her.' Your father insisted I do the job. He's afraid I will change my mind about the marriage."

Peacock took a step back.

"No need for that," she answered. "I will go myself."

He raised an eyebrow and smiled.

"Where to?"

"Anywhere." But she had already lost her conviction. "Somewhere. I can't stay here. You keep whores."

Solomon the Man laughed and reached for her. She thought she would pull away, but she could not.

"You have married me." He picked her up off her ground. "You can't just leave someone you married."

He opened the door and walked in. She wanted to fight him, but he put her down and slowly opened the braids of her hair, undoing the string of pearls and letting each one fall into the bed of withering roses and dying jasmine, and then he took off her shoes and her gown, and lay her naked on the sheets and made love to her as if she were indeed a woman—as if he had chosen her knowingly, as if she were pretty, and desired, and worthy of his touch. Afterward he lay next to her and watched her cry—from the shock of encounter, perhaps, or the relief of being accepted, and then he kissed her and pulled the sheets back over her and told her to sleep.

"You are beautiful."

She heard his voice and wondered if he had lied and prayed she would never know. She saw him leave and missed his smell and his touch and the sound of his laughter. She fell asleep and dreamt of his eyes and loved him all her life.

News to Turn the World

T he summer I was fifteen, 1917, it was our first summer in Cleveland, my mother and I were up to our elbows in hot water, canning. This day must've been late August or September, because we were putting up tomatoes. Bessie and Evelyn, the littlest ones, my sister Mollie had taken to the park to keep out of our way, but Rita and Naomi, they were probably ten and twelve then, they kept coming in with their clothes sopping, soaked like they were fish. I guess one of the neighbors had set out buckets and a hose so they could cool off. Between the canning and all the water the girls brought in, the kitchen was a mess.

It was a big kitchen, bigger than we'd had in New York. We'd had to leave New York because Pa's work had gotten so sporadic. His brother Irving—my uncle—said in Cleveland a tailor could work year-round. Pa didn't like it, leaving his union, but he had to feed the lot of us. So, we packed up and took the train. Evelyn wasn't six months old when we made the trip. She hollered the whole ride.

I wiped a puddle of water from the floor, to keep us from slipping at least. "Maybe this kitchen will never be clean again," I said to Ma.

"*Ya*," she said. And then she turned her round body to my tall one. "*Estelle, ikh hob nayes vos ken iberkern di velt*," she said. [I have news to turn the world upside down.] "*Ikh hob nokh a mol farshvengert.*" [Again I've conceived.]

I turned my face toward her. I had an urge like a rocket running through me to take the tomato I'd just peeled, make like I was a baseball pitcher and smash it on the wall in front of me. Ma'd just scrubbed that wall the week before.

Well, I didn't do it. I don't even know where that tomato went, but my hands, all red they were, went to my hips. I kept my face toward hers, I put my lips together and locked them. And I suppose you'd call the eye I gave her a mean one. I felt an invisible kind of shawl come around my whole body, a wrapper that put me in my own world, sealed off from the rest.

This moment has stuck on me my whole life. Because here's where the world turned for me—from a hard place to an impossible one. By impossible I mean there was no way out for me. I adored my mother, just from chores she could make me feel good. "Oh Estelle," she'd say, "why don't you cut the salad? When you do it, it tastes the best." Or "Why don't you dust, *sheyn meydl*? Just give it a swish swash."

But right then, because she was pregnant, I had to leave the kitchen. I had to get out of the house! Because I couldn't stand to be near her.

I don't have to tell you, do I, what it meant for me that Ma had another pregnancy, a new baby due in March, just before we'd all be getting out of school? Evelyn was four by then, the youngest, just out of night diapers. We also had Abie and Sol, my Uncle Isaac's boys. Ma had taken them in just when we got to Cleveland—their mother had died from tuberculosis. The boys were eight and ten, pretty sweet, sure. But with them we made ten people altogether, and we had only three bedrooms for the lot of us. Well, a new baby meant whatever dreams I had of going on picnics with my friend Pearl Adler I could forget. Also there was a bookkeeping class I wanted to take special. I wanted that so I could get a good job after high school. I wanted to help my parents, and I wanted a little money of my own. My dreams weren't so wild. Oh, I had a crazy one of becoming a doctor or a scientist who'd invent a foolproof method of birth control. Or maybe I could go off with Margaret Sanger and teach women the methods she knew about. Mainly, I guess, I wanted a taste of the world outside of housekeeping—though I didn't have the foggiest notion of what that might be. Bookkeeping, of course, was a lot more practical; and then as now, I was practical.

Well. Two weeks passed from that afternoon where Ma told me she was pregnant again. The whole time, I didn't talk to her. It wasn't a plan or anything, I was just steaming mad, and afraid if I opened my lips to her I'd hear things that'd make the situation worse. So, like always, I got the groceries on my way home from school; I made a dozen chopped liver sandwiches every day and packed them into lunch bags, or maybe a hard-boiled-egg salad. I took each rug in the house to the backyard and whipped out the dust. If Ma was nearby, I'd feel that extra layer wrapped around me, fresh. If Pa was near, I lowered my eyes a little. I was mad at him, too, I suppose. I knew what it took to make a baby; I knew what it took not to make one. I didn't see why they couldn't stop doing it. I knew she and Pa had a love marriage. That wasn't hard to see. But couldn't they find other ways to love each other than make babies? These were my useless thoughts.

After I washed the dinner dishes—sometimes I got my sister Mollie to do them without me—I'd walk out the house and around the block, to cool off. Sometimes I'd stop by Pearl's, for company. She knew the gist of what was going on, and even though she probably would've preferred talking, she let us walk in silence. She was a good friend, Pearl.

I still took my moonlight baths, too. That's what I called them. I'd go in the washroom after I was sure everyone else was asleep. Ma used to call it my private *mikve*, which of course you don't take until marriage—to encourage your seeds to sprout, after your monthly. Ma used to joke I took so many I'd end up with more children than she'd had; or that once I did marry, I wouldn't have to bother going to the *mikve*, I did enough as a young maid.

That was not my intention.

I turned the light off when I took my baths. I soaked in the quiet as much as the warm water. I soaked in the dark, too, I suppose. I could often see the moon above us from the windows—it was a tiny bathroom, but it had a big window—good for watching the night. They say at Rosh Hodesh, the new moon, the moon draws inside herself, into that dark moment, you can't see it. It's alone. That's how it starts each cycle, bringing itself to a full circle then back to emptiness again.

I don't remember when I started taking these baths. I know we were still in New York; but as soon as I started, I knew I needed them. Going to my own quiet place, so dark it's like nothing, no effort, no name, only peace. I could feel quiet and stillness even with a world war getting started, and I could use that quiet to carry me through the next day.

Anyway, two weeks passed and I didn't say a word to Ma. Then one night after my bath, I'd just drained the water and pulled my gown on, someone tapped on the door. I knew it was her. I glanced at the moon, nearly full. I felt my lips tighten. When I opened the door, Ma squeezed in. We just stood there a moment, in the dark. Then she spoke. "I need help, Estelle, tomorrow. So, I ask you. But if you don't want with what I ask you, then please, I want you should say it. Okay?"

I nodded. I had my arms crossed over my chest. I felt like a horrible person, and quite frankly, I didn't care enough about that to make myself different. No: I didn't have an ounce of desire to take my arms down. I didn't want to see, either, that Ma looked like a ghost. Like a leech had sucked all her blood away.

Her eyes had caught onto the moon. So, we had another moment of quiet. I didn't mind. After a while she turned her eyes back to me. "I wonder would you stay home from school tomorrow, watch Bessie and Evelyn, and also make Shabbes. Mrs. Kaminsky told me, down on Woodland, she knows a man what can make me an abortion. Today I made my mind up, I'll go. Pa, he knows I'm pregnant, but I'll wait 'til my body is healed again to tell him this. Mrs. Kaminsky says she can finish her Shabbes making by two o'clock, she'll come meet me. So I'll have someone to walk me home."

Everything was already pretty closed in for me, and that washroom was tiny for one person, let alone two. I felt sick, whirly. I sat on the toilet, more like I melted onto it. I felt like I was the one pregnant. I couldn't tell who's who. I felt like I was the one who'd decided on an abortion. I started to cry. I worried I'd wake the others, but I couldn't control myself. "*Dos moyl ken nisht zogn vos iz oyfn harts, Ma*," I said finally, after my long cry. "The heart can't tell the mouth what it feels. But I feel bad, no matter what happens with this baby."

Ma put a hand to my head, which brought more tears. So then I sobbed in her belly, with that baby growing in it. "*Es iz tsu sliver tsu zayn afroy*," she said. "It's too difficult to be a woman sometimes."

Ma's face and her eyes were so kind on me, especially with all the moonlight there. I noticed, too, how much sad she had in her. I stopped my crying. I said I'd stay home for her the next day.

Just before Pa got back from the factory, and my sisters and my two cousins were all playing outside or, thank God, taking a nap, Ma walked in. I had a big hot pan of kugel in my hands when she leaned on the door and opened it. When I saw her I didn't dare take my eyes away, even if it meant burning my hands. She looked nearly dead. Maybe, I thought, if I keep my eyes to her, she won't slip away. You know, die on me. She moved heavy like an elephant, maybe I should say the ghost of an elephant.

We got her into bed and decided we could tell the others she'd taken sick with flu. Whatever that so-called doctor did to her, he said the baby wouldn't come out 'til the next day. If we said she had a bad flu, we figured she could have a few days in bed without the others disturbing her.

This time, it was me who said to her, "*Es iz tsu shver tsu zayn a froy.*"

"Ya," she said. She gave me a little smile, moved one arm behind herself, then the other, so I could pull her dress off. She'd gotten so doughy, Ma had, big. When she was pregnant with Bessie, no one had known; and all of us kids were tall, like Pa, though not so lanky. "Estelle," she said, as if to comfort me, "Ruchel's here."

Ruchel—that's the girl Ma miscarried before me, the one she talks to more than anybody. "The whole day," she went on, "Ruchel has talked. '*Vos du vilst,*' she tells me. 'Whatever you choose,' she says, 'I'll keep talking.' She said she knew, either way for me would not be easy. She says this soul I carry can manage, either way.

"My big scare was that if I put away this baby, Ruchel would stop her talking. And if she stops her talking, I will turn completely meshuge. But even when I was up on that man's table, she talked. '*A brokhe oyf dayn hop,*' she says to me, 'a blessing on your head.' And 'this too shall pass'; and 'breathe gently, the world can hold this too.'"

After this Ma fell to sleep. I told the others we'd have *Shabbes* without her. So—I lit the candles that night. I felt like Ruchel was nearby, Ma's angel in heaven. You know I wasn't jealous of her. But sometimes I felt jealous of Ma, that she had someone like that to talk to. Maybe, I thought, this one she killed today, maybe I should talk to that one. Maybe it has words for me. I even wondered should I give it a name, this baby I had wanted to stay in the Other World. I had these thoughts and then the next thing I had was to make sure Pa could have a little Shabbes even with his worry about Ma, also to see Bessie got her chicken cut up small enough, and that Abie not take too much kugel or else he'd get sick. He didn't take so good to potatoes.

I never named that baby. But even to this day I think of it, and I think of it as mine, too.

Sylvia's Spoon

I steal a sterling silver baby spoon from my great Aunt Sylvia, while her body, barely cold, rests under a blanket of disheveled earth at the Beth Shalom cemetery. I do it in the kitchen, on impulse, while I'm looking for a teaspoon to stir my chamomile, just before my family begins reciting the mourner's kaddish in my aunt's living room. *Yisgadal ve'yiskadash shemay rabah . . .*

My mother, loud and tone-deaf, can't even finish the prayer she's so weepy. We all are. She enters the kitchen to empty a fistful of dirty Kleenex into the trash, and I slide the spoon further into my pocket. I run my fingers around the tiny bowl and up along the skinny handle to the tip which is inscribed with the Hebrew letter *hey*. My name, Hannah, begins with a *hey*. This piece of flatware is my destiny. Besides, finders keepers.

I imagine that this spoon has survived pogroms and a long passage to Ellis Island, and I want to siphon its fortitude for my baby. I'm thirteen weeks pregnant, my new record for not miscarrying. Every morning I pray from *The Jewish Women's Guide to Fertility*, a book I would have snickered at two years ago. I suffer the indignity of progesterone suppositories—the added hormones make me throw up in my office trashcan—and I avoid foods I ate and clothes I wore while unsuccessfully carrying babies number one and two. I take pregnancy yoga classes to manage the stress from keeping it all straight.

My husband Danny can't win. If he's enthusiastic about the baby, I tell him not to jinx anything. If he's cautious, I interrogate him—a man of reason, not instinct—about his "true gut" on this pregnancy. My parents are no help; my mother worries so much that I end up comforting her, and my father changes the subject but then e-mails me the cell phone numbers of his old med school buddies who specialize in fertility. Most of my friends are reveling in their fecundity. I cling to this spoon and the hope that my dead aunt is taking care of my baby, somewhere out there in the ether.

On the flight home from the funeral, I watch Milwaukee disappear into a puff of clouds and sip lukewarm orange juice out of a plastic cup. I like the way my aunt's spoon burrows into my thigh. Aunt Sylvia used to laugh at my knock-knock jokes and hang my art projects on her fridge and look the other way when I pinched pieces of meringue from the top of her icebox cake. I feel more hopeful than I have in weeks.

I kiss Danny's cheek, breathing in the familiar scent of Dial soap. "Let's name our baby Sylvia." As soon as these words leave my lips, I want them back.

Danny gives me the wan smile that he's cultivated. "Let's just see what happens." He strokes my arm.

"Oh God, Danny. Don't tell me that you're too superstitious to name the baby," I snort, when in fact I cling to superstition like Velcro. I lean my head back and close my eyes, signaling that the conversation is over. My hand rests on my mildly distended belly while I daydream about my little Sylvia. It will be a warm spring day, and she'll sit on my lap licking vanilla icing off of a cupcake, wiping her sticky fingers on my knees. She'll smell like baby sweat and sugar. I'll pull her tangle of ringlets—auburn like Danny's—from her eyes. I can practically hear her giggle. Fear forms in the back of my throat and swells into my esophagus like a hive, as it always does when I allow myself to hope that this baby will survive.

Later that night, shortly after eleven, I feel like someone is yanking my abdomen shut with a drawstring. Fuck. Shit. Fuck. Cramps turn into nausea, and I beg my baby to stay put. Danny pages the obstetrician while I stumble to the bathroom, clutching the spoon for dear life, not mine. Talisman in hand, I negotiate with God. No deal. Before the sun rises, I deliver my baby.

I rest my head against the side of the toilet and gaze at the emptied contents of my womb. The acrid odor of my waste mingles with the smell of urine and Tilex, nearly making me gag. I try to capture the cluster of blood and tissue with my aunt's spoon, but my efforts only loosen the clump into a spray of red and greenish gray that dissolves into the bowl. I let my fingers linger in the cold, red water, before I close the lid. Aunt Sylvia appears to me: the slightly bulging gray eyes and the sad smile pasted on soft pink lips and the sound of her lisp.

Danny mops my forehead with a washcloth. I stand up slowly and rinse off the spoon, turning the faucet on full blast in a futile attempt to drown out the sound of the flushing toilet. My knees buckle.

One week later, Danny lounges on our bed—as he has done for each of the past six nights—staring slack-jawed at ESPN. Who gives a damn about the Cardinals?

I forage around our pantry for Tylenol. We're out of cereal. A jar of my friend Maggie's homemade raspberry jam (her annual holiday gift) sits next to a bottle of capers; the contrast of the green and the red reminds me that I did get to see my actual baby, instead of just a black sonogram screen, devoid of the pulsing light the size of a thumbtack. We disposed of those babies during tidy office visits followed by written instructions to call if there was too much blood. There's always too much blood.

I dump four tablespoons of jam and eight capers together in a bowl and then retrieve the spoon from my purse; I use it to mix and then ladle the concoction into a small zip lock baggie. Sylvia.

By the time I return to Danny, he's sprawled out on our bed, his face bathed in the blue TV light, his mile-long eyelashes—blond at the tips—fanning the tender skin beneath his eyes. He looks like he's eleven years old. A fresh soul. The phone calls and foot rubs aren't working, but at least he's trying. I can't muster up the energy to comfort him. I don't want to. Before the miscarriages, I would have cheered him up by taking him bowling or seducing him or renting a Monty Python movie; we'd sit in front of the television drinking cheap beer and eating potato chips, laughing—Danny at John Cleese's ridiculousness, me at Danny—until we could barely breathe.

It's hot for June, and the breeze from the air conditioning vent chills my toes. I pull my T-shirt over my head and crawl into bed beside him, cradling his smooth back against my breasts. He mumbles something and reaches over to grab my hip. I move slightly, and he rolls over and runs his hands through my dirty hair. We don't make love—too raw, too soon. Sleep finds me clutching the baggie of raspberry jam and capers and Aunt Sylvia's spoon.

The next morning, I cancel my 9 a.m. staff meeting. I was scheduled to fly to Boston the day after I miscarried, so now the whole office knows what happened, and I'm no longer the den mother of our "little nonprofit that could," my old hiding place from this relentless pregnancy angst. My coworkers now treat me like I've got a raging case of pink eye, except for Valerie, the stripper turned receptionist who has a six-year-old son. The morning I came back to work, she greeted me with a homemade loaf of banana bread. I almost cried.

I pull on an old pair of shorts from my college days—University of Michigan—and walk two blocks up M Street to a coffee house that doesn't sell anything ending with the letters "ccino." Danny wants to move to Bethesda, but the thought of living in the suburbs without children thoroughly depresses me.

A cell-phone-blabbing mother spills her latte on me; the hot liquid burns my thigh. "Watch where you're going," her brusque words crack me open like a walnut. Instead of crying, I find a table and rub my iced tea against my leg.

A man with kind eyes and a thumb ring sits down next to me and asks to borrow a pen. I reach into my backpack and the baggie falls to the table. We both examine what looks as though a sandwich has orphaned a glob of jelly and perhaps a few pumpkins seeds.

"Must have been a hell of a sandwich." He points at the plastic bag and laughs nervously.

"Keep it." I slide a pen at him with more force than I mean and then snatch the baggie from the table. These days, I go nowhere without my spoon and baggie; they make me feel close to my Sylvias. Totally weird, I know, but they comfort me when nobody else can. One miscarriage and you get "75 percent of women miscarry during their first pregnancy." With the second, it's "my sister/cousin/electrologist had two, you'll be fine." And three begets "I know of a fertility clinic out in Gaithersburg."

The day folds into itself; at five, I'm smothering a chicken breast in olive oil when Danny calls. "I have to show a house tonight, sweetie. Can I pick up some Ben and Jerry's on the way home?" He sounds both anxious and relieved to take a night off from our grief. I call my mom. Just because.

"Whatcha doin?" I try to sound like that plucky girl who beat the entire sixth-grade class in an arm-wrestling tournament, who trotted off to Mali to run an AIDS program, and not the hormonal casualty that I am.

"Thinking about you, honey."

"No need." I muster up some of my old bravado.

"We spent today at Aunt Sylvia's house, cleaning her things."

My cheeks turn warm and I feel like I did when I was sixteen years old and my father almost found a fifth of Southern Comfort I stashed in an old suitcase. "Am I in trouble?"

"Why?"

"I swiped Aunt Sylvia's baby spoon," I blurt out in a moment of lapsed impulse control.

"Not the one from your great-grandma Hannah from Minsk?" My mother sounds both amused and alarmed; she's a fourth-generation German Jew and often disparages her mother-in-law's Eastern European ways. "Your Grandma Goldie went on and on about that spoon when her dementia got bad."

My heart quickens as my mother tells me about some feud between my grandmother and my aunt over this spoon. She's fuzzy about the details but my grandmother was mad as hell that barren Sylvia kept their mother's baby spoon for herself instead of letting her sister use it for her babies.

I sleep fitfully. I dream that a pregnant Aunt Sylvia eats Neapolitan ice cream with the baby spoon, while Grandma Goldie sits on her favorite chair and watches a toddler with braids stand alone in a grassy knoll playing "Captain, May I?" Raspberries stain the girl's white overalls and her eyes bulge slightly. These images smash into each other like an MTV music video.

The next morning, I'm shampooing my hair when I retrieve a memory of the spoon. I was five when my parents let my brother Eric and me stay with Aunt Sylvia while they went to the Cayman Islands. She ran us bubble baths and wrapped us in towels that she had warmed in the dryer. Cocooned in our bathrobes, we curled up on the sofa bed and ate Jiffy Pop. She packed Hostess Ding Dongs in our lunchboxes, and I watched her polish silver until it sparkled. Only after she finished the candlesticks and kiddush cups, did she shine the baby spoon.

On the last day of our stay, I asked her if I could feed my doll Wendy with the spoon, which even as a child, I knew she didn't want me to touch.

I also knew that she couldn't say no to me. She nodded toward the spoon, and I grabbed it greedily.

"Here, here, my little Wendy." I placed the spoon gingerly against her plastic mouth. "My little baby, my baby." I rocked the doll back and forth. I could feel my aunt watching me, so I hammed it up. "Mommy loves you. Mommy loves you." On some level, I knew I was making my aunt feel like I did when my brother waved his extended bedtime or gum-chewing privileges in my face. My aunt never polished her silver in front of me again.

In an effort to rinse this memory out of my hair, I stand under the shower until the water turns cold. I e-mail my boss to tell him that I'm taking a few more days off and spend the morning Googling old lovers. I only want to know if they've had children.

I pop my old wedding video into the deck. Danny breaks the glass, and then we kiss as we practiced: affectionate but not too much tongue. I fast forward to Aunt Sylvia, who is fingering a stray rose petal when the camera zooms in on her. She fumbles with the microphone and holds it up to her lips, recently touched up with a fresh coat of lipstick. Pink Velvet. Revlon. Funny the things you remember. Her large eyes dart around the room, and she clears her throat several times, "Like someone pulled them off the top of a cake, this bride and groom," she giggles nervously and continues, "my wish for my Hannah is that she know every kind of *nachas* life has to offer." Her laughter fades.

I replay the clip over and over. My aunt is smiling, but her eyes are slightly watery. How could I have missed this? Maybe she suspected that I wasn't going to be able to have children. Maybe she is mourning Uncle Irving. No, he was an asshole; this has to be about me. What possessed me to swipe a fertility totem from a barren woman? How could I have stolen my aunt's birthright?

Tears are forming somewhere in my skull. To stave off another tidal wave of grief, I drive around the Beltway thinking about my aunt.

"Call me Aunt Sylvia, all the kids do," she told Danny seven years ago, when I presented him to her as a dry run for the later round of family introductions. She motioned to a wall of framed photos of my grandmother's progeny, while I poked around her fridge for a Pepsi. She loved to brag about me, "her bat mitzvah" . . . "voice like an angel" . . . "captain of the volleyball team."

I joined my aunt and Danny in the dining room, where they were laughing at one of his puns. And when I recited the blessings over the candles later that night, I surprised myself with my prayer that my walls would never be filled with photos of other people's children.

I pack toiletries, two shirts and a peasant skirt—my jeans don't fit because ten days post-miscarriage, I'm still sporting a sanitary napkin the size of a diaper between my thighs—into a duffel bag and drive to the airport. I fly Midwest Express to Milwaukee because the seats are roomy and they serve meals with real linen napkins.

A blonde woman in her sixties offers me two chocolate chip cookies. "I'm Lois. You got family in Milwaukee?"

"I'm visiting a relative."

"You got kids?" She adjusts her Coke-bottle glasses. "Those career women forget to have kids until it's too late and then that's that."

"I have a baby girl." I entertain a confrontation fantasy with Lois on my way to the bathroom: Lois. I've lost a baby. I named her Sylvia and I'm carrying a replica of the fetus made out of raspberry jam and capers in my backpack. Would you like to see? The tiny lavatory smells like asparagus pee and diesel.

I rent a Ford Taurus, whose air conditioning dries out my contact lenses, and drive to my Aunt Sylvia's empty, colonial house with a "For Sale" sign planted on the front lawn. I sneak into the backyard and sit cross-legged on her overgrown grass. A ladybug crawls up my big toe. Four raspberries cling to an anemic-looking bush, so I pick them. I open my baggie—the plastic forms a crease in the aging jelly concoction, which smells vinegary and sweet—and drop in the fruit.

The grass cools my feet as I walk back to the car. I'll call Danny after I make my next stop. I excavate a piece of licorice from the bottom of my purse and run it back and forth between my teeth until it turns into a skinny thread, while I concentrate on finding my way to the cemetery.

Seven white tulips mark Aunt Sylvia's grave. Sylvia Savitz Seigel. What a dreadful name for a woman with a lisp. The thought makes me smile.

I remove my sandals, and let my soles sink into the velvety soil. The dirt next to my aunt's grave yields easily, while I dig a hole with my fingers. I retrieve the baggie from my purse and place it into the crevice. I scoop small chunks of dirt over the plastic with my aunt's spoon, and then I raise its warm handle to my lips and kiss the Hebrew letter *hey*. I drop the heirloom into the earth. A warm breeze tickles me, and I hear a whisper, my whisper. *Yisgadal veyiskadash sh'may rabah. Amen.*

JUDITH ZIMMER

Max's Mom Goes to Camp

"*Tsimtsum*—contraction—ushers in the cosmic drama . . .
for it is God's withdrawal that first creates space."
GERSHOM G. SCHOLEM | *On the Kabbalah and its Symbolism*

Every mile of the drive from West 22nd Street to Hancock had felt right. How good it was to say the words to anyone who crossed her path that morning, "I'm going to visit my son." In her mind, she and Max were one big family, even though now it was just the two of them. Hers was a life wiped out by divorce. It was a miracle really that she'd even had Max in the first place, let alone gotten any other children out of his father. One loss is not another, her therapist said.

The wooden signs nailed to trees said, "Blind Curve, Honk Your Horn," and "Children on Bikes." It was the Saturday morning of Parents' Weekend—and the parking lot was full. She saw couples and dogs getting out of cars, strolling toward the main campgrounds. She felt a little out of place since she wasn't officially here for Parents' Weekend, even though it was when they told the parents of counselors to visit.

Out of the car, she took a long breath, inhaling the cool and fragrant Vermont air, so different from home. She reached the end of the path and the camp lay before her. Rustic red log cabins. A big stone building with a wraparound porch. Open fields leading to a lake.

The lawn might have been a jumble of ages and activities, but everyone looked like they knew where they were going and what they were doing. Children careened across the grass on bikes. They gathered in bunches on the lawn or walked in pairs and threesomes toward the main building, some holding hands without giving it a thought. Across the lawn, from the swings to the hammocks to the tetherball poles, she caught glimpses of movement and color, a Georges Seurat come to life.

You could see that it wasn't one of those glossy-brochure-type camps. It was, as Max had described it, low-key and not competitive, an "everyone's a winner" kind of place. No homesickness apparent here, she thought. Strange, really, that she'd never sent Max away to sleep-away camp when he was young. Had he missed out?

A few parents milled around on the path in front of her—and they looked content too, greeting their children, getting ready to join an activity, weighing the prospects of crafts or tennis or rowing. There must be some camp schedule that they all just knew. She seemed to be the only newcomer, the only one who didn't know the ropes.

Could she also be the only parent who had come alone? She counted heads. She did this wherever she went. She was always on the lookout for other single moms at restaurants, on the street, in the park. Seeing other single parents made her feel that she wasn't the only one raising a child this way.

As she approached the first log cabin, a young woman leaned out of the doorway. "Can I help?"

"I'm looking for Max Durbin. I'm his mother."

"Oh, hi Mrs. Durbin. I just saw Max."

She hadn't been called Mrs. Durbin in a while—and there was that moment where it felt wrong to even claim it as her name. There was another Mrs. Durbin now. This was one of those things you couldn't possibly plan for when you married and kept your maiden name. That one day another woman would have the same last name as your son, but you wouldn't.

"Mrs. Durbin? You can wait here. I'll have someone get him for you."

A few minutes later, someone shouted, "There's M-a-a-x." And there he was, all six-three of him, swooping down on a bicycle, toothbrush and razor in a net bag hanging from the handlebars, wearing flannel pajama bottoms and looking sleepy. His brown hair stood up straight as though it just woke up too.

At five-eleven she wasn't short. But Max hung over her like a giant sunflower. She gazed up, squinting to see his face. He bent down so she could kiss the top of his head, the woodsy, country smell of his hair.

"You're early," he said. "I was just getting ready."

"No problem. I'll wait."

"Give me five." And he took off on the bike, leaving her on the path.

She watched him go. Why the flannel pajamas? Not a good sign. They reminded her of his senior year in high school when Max wore pajama bottoms all the time and talked like an anarchist about how grades didn't matter. Then freshman year in college—Max had been recruited to play baseball, but never showed up at practice. "What's the point of it, anyway?" She'd had to answer the coach's concerned calls, the patient ones, the indignant one.

She didn't really know why he'd dropped baseball after all those years, except that he'd started reading philosophy. But she did know that it was a Division Three school and he hadn't signed a contract. He had simply walked away from a game he loved and, as people were always saying, his incredible talent. "He just doesn't need baseball anymore," one of her friends said.

But he'd ended his freshman year on every probation form they had. Too much partying. Missed classes. Bad grades. He had to see a counselor. Now, he was considering not going back, which made her crazy with anxiety. What would he do with himself? He'd get off track. She'd get off track. His father would see it as a failure. So would her parents. She'd get blamed. "He's dropping out. He's a drop-out." Where she came from, school was the most important thing. It was a bad idea to deviate from the four-year plan. If you did, you got lost. You were a loser, and so was your mother.

A bell rang, and now there were even more kids walking between buildings, mingling on the lawn, shouting to one another. She wanted to take in as much of the place as she could, the better to understand what Max was doing here.

And then there he was again, back on the bike. This time wearing shorts and a T-shirt, and it looked like he'd washed his face. He had only two periods free this morning and they had arranged to go out for breakfast in town.

At the café, they settled at a table outside, overlooking the main street. She was eager to hear from him. She was overly aware of the time, that they didn't have much. How was it all going? Did he like it? What was his actual job, duties? What was the schedule? How was Emily, the girl who had gotten him the job here?

"Whoa, Mom. Slow down," he said. "You're asking too many questions. It's like you're a mosquito, buzzing around me." And he made a shooing motion with his hand.

She sat back in her chair, looked out at the street, willed herself not to tear up. She knew she buzzed. She could feel herself buzzing. She buzzed because there was just Max.

She would never have spoken to her own parents that way. She wouldn't have dared. Even now with her parents, it was a one-way street. They spoke, she nodded. She had never been able to say what she meant. Half the time she had to settle for the surface, the buried words too hard to retrieve. She was untrained. But not Max. She'd given her child that, at least.

She took an intentionally long sip of iced coffee, hoping that the silence wouldn't go unnoticed. They were both quiet. She hated quiet. She looked out, past him, to the town's main drag, a hardware store and Laundromat across the street. What would it be like to live here?

"Sorry, Mom. But it's true."

"I know," she smiled. "But I haven't seen you in so long. I need to know how you're doing."

The food came. Max was hungry and dug into his omelet and home fries.

"That looks good."

"I order this every time we come here." The food lightened him up. Each bite was a huge forkful. "So, I've got this bunk of thirteen-year-olds," he said. "I got them because I'm taller than all the other counselors and it's the only cabin I fit into."

And she thought, really, they put you in charge of teenagers? Who would have thought that an anarchist could take charge of a group of thirteen-year-olds?

"The thing is," he continued. "I've got to come up with ways to get them to do what I want."

"Is it a little like me trying to get you to do something?"

"Sort of. Although with so many of them it's much harder. Some of the kids are easy to get along with and listen. But the others, not so much. At staff meetings, they give us ideas about how to handle the bunk."

It seemed safe now to venture another question. "What kind of ideas help?"

"One of the things we tell kids is—'Deeds not words.' We actually say it at camp all the time. Words are fine, but deeds are better. Anyone can talk, but actions speak louder."

"I like that. I'll have to remember it," she said.

After breakfast, they drove back to camp. Max had one more hour before he had to get back to work. He suggested swimming. "I'll show you my favorite spot."

They changed into bathing suits and headed down a narrow path through tall reeds to the lake. Groups of children dotted the shore on the other side. The noise drifted across. On their side, all was quiet. They had it all to themselves. "I come here sometimes to cool off," he said. "It's a good spot."

They walked to the end of the narrow wooden dock. Max jumped right in, but she went slowly down the ladder. The water was brisk, with the occasional warm spot. She paused for a little while in one of those pockets. She hadn't been swimming outside in a long time, and the view was brand new from this perspective, water stretching away at eye level, the big sky arching above. "Let's go to the float," Max said, paddling past.

She marveled at his stroke. As a child, it had taken him forever to learn to swim. Every sport that she loved, including swimming, had taken him ages to master. And now here he was, swimming right past her. Maybe not lifeguard material, but definitely holding his own.

Max was on the float when she got there, lying on his back soaking up the warmth. She stretched out next to him, feeling the float bobble along in the water.

"That was wonderful. I love swimming outside."

"I knew you'd like it."

"This just might be my favorite hour of the whole summer," she confided, closing her eyes.

They were quiet for a few minutes and then Max said, "Mom, you should know. I'm not going back. In the fall."

And just like that, it was no longer her favorite hour. She could feel little pinpricks of anxiety firing up inside. For a minute, she didn't know if she was angrier with Max for wrecking the moment or for ruining his life.

She heard his voice from across the float. "Look, I know it costs a lot of money and I don't want to wake up after four years and find I've wasted it. I'm going to get a job. Emily and I are going to get an apartment."

Before she could say anything, he added, as though he could read her mind, "You don't have to worry that I'm dropping out. Because I'm not. I'm taking a year off. There's a difference."

How could she argue with him when everything he said made so much sense? And for a second it seemed like he had the quiet wisdom of years and she was the wayward child caught playing with matches.

"Are you really sure it's what you want?" she asked. He sat up, and reached over to give her a little punch on her arm. "Deeds, not words, Mom. Remember?"

She lay there for a second longer. It wasn't what she'd wanted for him, but it did make sense. The light was bright and she closed her eyes, and the brightness stayed behind her eyes. Her wet skin warmed up in the sun. For a minute, she saw the little square wooden float in the lake from above. It was a patchwork square, dancing in the water. And from that high place she also could see her parents sitting in their house in New Jersey, the house she'd grown up in, her father so frail and dangerously thin, and her mother, fretting and worrying about how imperfect everything was, that nothing was ever right. And for those few moments she understood that few things ever were right, but that you could manage anyway.

"Wow. To be able to do this every day," she said in a low voice.

"Yeah, isn't it great?" Max said. "I love Vermont."

"Me too."

They swam back across the lake, and dried off on the dock.

"I've got to get back," Max said. "Third period starts in fifteen minutes." And she watched him take a well-worn lanyard with a whistle and several keys out of his backpack and put it around his neck.

As they walked up the path toward camp, they could see a group of campers and parents coming toward them. "That's one of my boys," Max said, as the group approached. "Jason, are you showing your parents a good time?"

The parents surrounded Max. They were glad to meet him. Jason was having a great summer in his cabin. Max put his hand on Jason's shoulder. "Did you tell them you learned to play tennis?"

She took a small step back, a painful one, but a necessary one. How strange. Then another step back. Heard the conversation, smiled. A third step.

She remembered the instruction. "At the end of the Kaddish, take three small steps back . . ."

That withdrawal from the path was her *tsimtsum*. In Hebrew, it meant contraction. But in the Kabbalah, she recalled, it was the word for the deity contracting to make room for the creation of the world. From her place just off the path, she felt the world shift. Something had changed yet again, whether she liked it or not.

My Daughter's Boyfriends

JACK

Jack is Naomi's first boyfriend. They meet the first day in nursery school and are inseparable. He is a red-headed boy with freckles and mischievous green eyes. Jack also likes to wear Naomi's dresses. A lot. Every time I arrive home from work, the babysitter says, "Jacqueline is wearing Naomi's ballet tutu again." Jacqueline is how Jack likes to be referred to during his play dates. His favorite outfit is a pink leotard and a pink tutu Naomi won't wear since she hates ballet class. He also favors Naomi's Cinderella costume that her grandmother brought her from Disneyland. Luckily Jack has not discovered my makeup cabinet. Since Jack just lives down the block, I usually drop him off at his apartment near Morningside Park. I am terrified that his father, a sergeant high up in the police force, could arrive at our apartment and discover him.

I am home from a too-long meeting with a magazine editor and my sitter is pale. "I didn't know what to do," she stammers. Jack's father is standing at the doorway of my daughter's bedroom. I slowly walk toward him and peek into the bedroom. Today Jack has chosen Naomi's best party dress, which is a shocking pink velvet, with several beaded necklaces. If he wore a black bob, he would resemble a flapper from the 1920s. Jack's father towers over me. He is still in his police sergeant's uniform. I hold my breath as Jack's father watches his son and Naomi jump up and down on the bed.

"Hello," I say nervously, but I am surprised. Jack's father is laughing. Laughing so loudly that for a moment I think he is crying.

"Holy Mother of God," Jack's father exclaims. "Just look at him! Jack, you're gorgeous. Absolutely gorgeous!"

And Jack's father is right. His son is gorgeous.

PEDRO

Pedro is from Buenos Aires and has already enchanted the entire second grade. According to Naomi, she, Elisa Schwartz, and Rosie Marks all want to marry him. Pedro is such a sensation that the second-grade teacher, Mrs. Levy, has called an emergency parents' meeting to discuss the discord that Pedro has brought into the classroom. It seems that the girls have been fighting over Pedro in the cafeteria, the gym, and on the playground.

One would expect Pedro to be a mini-Antonio Banderas, but he is just a soft-spoken little boy with long lashes and shiny brown hair, who is obsessed with turtles and doesn't have the remotest interest in girls. Sobbing, Naomi is convinced that Pedro will marry Sylvia Cohen, who brings food for Pedro's turtle. But her worries are for naught as Pedro's family is suddenly being transferred to London. There isn't even a going-away party, but he does leave his pet turtle behind. The turtle is duly taken care of by every single girl in the class until the school custodian turns the heat off one night and the turtle, named Nueva York for Pedro's brief home, dies from the cold.

HARLAN

Harlan is named after the famous science fiction writer Harlan Ellison; his father tells me this at our synagogue parents' night. Harlan likes to read comic books and does not like to cut his hair, so it's as long as the girls in Naomi's Hebrew class. Harlan is madly in love with Naomi and brings her scary comics with violent covers of exploding things, which Naomi tolerates. She doesn't really love Harlan, she tells me, but she will let him visit her and draw fantastic creatures in her notebooks. It helps that Harlan tells Naomi that she is beautiful about twenty times an hour. "Every girl needs to be told she is beautiful twenty times an hour," I tell my husband, who as usual is not listening to me, but reading his most recent legal brief. One afternoon Harlan is too preoccupied to notice that he is crossing against a red light and is hit by a delivery bicycle. Thankfully, Harlan only suffers a broken leg, but his parents keep him home for his recuperation. Naomi doesn't have time to visit him since she is currently obsessed with horses and spends hours in Central Park watching the riders gallop along the bridle path.

When Harlan finally recovers, he has fallen out of love with Naomi and in love with Jill Kleiner, the rabbi's daughter. Naomi is miserable for two nights and then decides that Harlan was a nerd and develops a crush on Kevin Bacon while watching *Footloose* at her older cousin Rachel's house.

ROGER

Roger is Naomi's first boyfriend who does not live in New York City. They meet during an eighth-grade dance at Naomi's sleepaway camp in the Berkshires. Roger lives in Portland, Maine. "I didn't know there are Jewish boys in Maine," Naomi told me. They have long phone conversations in Naomi's bedroom which has a large PRIVATE sign taped on the door. She is lucky she has no interfering siblings. I suspect that for the first time in his life my husband is jealous of a boy who is beginning to resemble a man. Roger has been left back a year in school and so technically should be going to high school. A photograph I discover hidden in Naomi's desk shows a giant who actually needs a shave.

One night, Naomi discovers through her friend Sharon whose cousin who by some incredible coincidence attends the same Portland, Maine, school as Roger that he is dating not one but three girls at the same time including a high school junior. The night that Naomi breaks up with him is also the night she has her first period. From then on, whenever she has menstrual cramps, she refers to them as "Roger's Revenge."

JOSH

Josh is the killer. He is Naomi's ninth-grade crush that lasts through the end of twelfth grade. Josh is devastatingly and dangerously handsome—a private-school version of Jim Morrison who plays guitar in a band that does terrible covers of the rock songs that I listened to in the 1970s. No one cares about his lack of guitar skills or that he forgets the lyrics. If I were fourteen, I would be mad about Josh too. He is famous for being thrown out of every Hebrew school, and insisting on wearing a leather jacket during his bar mitzvah. Naomi's love is the unrequited kind, the worst. I know that there are mornings she lingers on the street outside his apartment building. I hear her speaking about this to her friends on the phone and also about how she has made close friends with all of Josh's doormen. Has Josh ever acknowledged her? I know from my own experiences with boys like Josh that he is too cool to notice anyone except himself. Eventually Josh's parents will divorce and he will move with his mother to Asheville, North Carolina, which is too far for Naomi to follow. Yet he hovers still about her high school years like the weather—it is always there even though it changes.

Several years later, when Naomi is in college, I will find a torn napkin hidden deep in her desk with a scrawled phone number and Josh's signature. Did he give this to Naomi or did Naomi find this and keep it to herself as a wish or a souvenir? All I can hope is that Josh at some moment in time was kind to her.

ARTHUR

In eleventh grade, Arthur can almost make Naomi forget Josh. He is the child of two Deadheads who are now doctors, and with his ponytail, vintage tie-dyed T-shirts, and John Lennon glasses could be from a different decade. Naomi, who has recently been a punk rock fan with a fake leather jacket and blue bangs, has become a brunette again and favors hemp necklaces and clove cigarettes. She has confided in me about the marijuana plants that grow on the roof of Arthur's parents' townhouse and claims she doesn't smoke pot because it makes her contacts dry out. Her father, who is now my ex-husband, is not so sure. We had a good divorce—if you can have a good divorce. Naomi spends most of her time anyway in Arthur's huge Greenwich Village townhouse, so it is as if she had divorced us too. One night, Naomi arrives home with flushed cheeks and announces she is no longer a virgin.

"But I thought you would have done it already," I stupidly say. Naomi's mouth pops wide open.

"Do you think I'm a slut, Mom?" she shouts.

She slams the door before I can discuss birth control.

HARRY

Harry is Naomi's college boyfriend for all four years. They meet during freshman orientation and stay together even the last semester of senior year. They are a wonder to their friends and their parents. Harry irritates my ex-husband by his constant grins and guffaws. He is the ultimate frat boy who cannot walk down the street without at least eight people giving him a high five. I do not understand how Naomi, after Arthur, can stand him. But Naomi has turned into a sorority girl with cute pink terrycloth skirts and white tennis sneakers and blonde streaks in her hair.

Even in winter, Harry wears flip-flops, T-shirts, and shorts. He is from Aspen and has the sharp, chiseled features of his mother, a famous Swedish model, with blue eyes and high cheekbones. Harry is almost too pretty at times and he seems to compensate for this by always looking as grungy as possible.

"Hasn't he heard of deodorant?" my annoyed ex mumbles to me during Parents Visiting Day. When Harry is accepted into business school in California, my ex and I share a bottle of champagne. Surely this is the end of a too-long romance.

But we don't have a real reason to worry. I receive a phone call from Naomi the night before her college graduation.

"Harry's come out," Naomi announces.

"Excuse me," I ask, not sure about what I heard.

"Harry's gay, Mom. I'm glad for him. I guess I kind of knew."

I don't ask any more questions. At graduation, Naomi poses with Harry and they embrace in front of the camera as if they are still a loving couple.

Two years later, I will see Harry in a film and then another film and another. But he has never admitted he is gay, although Naomi knows all about his string of lovers. Every time I see him in *People* magazine with a "new" fiancée I have to laugh. I never thought Harry was bright, but I never took him for a coward.

OWEN

Owen is married. He is married with two beautiful kids and a beautiful wife. Naomi met Owen at the art gallery where she now works and he asked her to the Metropolitan Museum for advice since he knew nothing about art. There, in front of a Rembrandt, Naomi fell madly in love with him. Owen is twenty-five years older than Naomi and married to Jessica Carmel, a well-known opera singer who travels all over the world. So, there isn't much to hide from Owen's wife since she is so rarely in New York. But still. Owen is married, and I am the mother wolf.

I follow Owen from work one day (he also works in publishing and I know where his office is) and confront him directly outside Radio Music City Hall.

"I am Naomi's mother," I tell him. "Please leave her alone." Owen stares at me for a moment, switches off his mobile phone and sighs. He is a very handsome man with neat gray hair and very blue eyes.

"I know it's not fair," he answers. "It's wrong but I don't know what to do. She's threatened to kill herself if I leave her."

I immediately take the train to Brooklyn and ring Naomi's buzzer. When she opens the door, she is eating a yogurt and wearing sweats. She does not look like a suicidal young woman.

"Is it true?" I ask her. "Would you really kill yourself if Owen left you?"

She nods solemnly. I fight the urge to call the police, her father, my husband. The stricken look on her face is the same I saw in eleventh grade when she waited hours to see Josh and his band and he walked by her without giving her a glance.

But I needn't have worried. Six months later Naomi meets Rajiv.

RAJIV

Naomi has quit her job and, with an inheritance from my aunt, has bought discount around-the-world tickets. She begins in Australia and makes her way through distant continents. In Mumbai, she meets a young man from India named Rajiv, an engineer who lives in Jersey City. When she introduces us to Rajiv, they are so in love that they gaze into each other's eyes even when talking to other people. He is tall and funny and loves to cook and sing country and western songs. Naomi moves in with Rajiv to his small Jersey City apartment and finds a job teaching art history at a charter school. Naomi's father, my second husband, and I are relieved. She has finally found her true love. One afternoon, Naomi arrives at my apartment with a bouquet of roses.

"Thank you," I tell her.

"They aren't for you, Mom. They're for Rose. That's why I brought roses."

"Who is Rose?" I ask. Then I see the blush rise in her face and I understand. She is three months pregnant and instinctively knows that the baby will be a girl. I place the bouquet in my favorite crystal vase and we toast with ginger ale. Finally, happiness. She and Rajiv fly to London to visit his parents. She will be gone for a week and during that time I obsessively shop in every baby store in Manhattan and buy the most beautiful baby dresses ever made.

She is due home the Friday before July 4th. We all plan to watch the fireworks from their Jersey City apartment rooftop. When Rajiv telephones me, I think we have a bad connection because his voice sounds like he's underwater. I hand the phone over to my husband who listens, nods, and then starts to sob.

"My God, what happened?" I scream, I know. I know. My Naomi is gone. A brain aneurysm on the return flight from London. No one could do anything. These things happen. A famous actor's daughter had suffered the same fate a month ago and the story was in all the papers. I have lost not only my daughter but my granddaughter as well. Rajiv arrives at our apartment, but I cannot see him. I hear his and my husband's voices outside my bedroom door. I do not leave my bed for three days. Darkness is what I crave. Utter darkness. I lie on my bed, still and silent, like Naomi, like my daughter. Dead yet not dead, which is worse.

THE BOYFRIENDS

Somehow with the aid of drugs and my husband's and ex-husband's support, I make it to the funeral. The rabbi speaks to me, but I can't see him in my blur of tears. In one corner of the room, I see a group of men. Some converse with each other while others are quiet. There are no women or children with them. All of the men wear beautiful suits. And then I understand. These men are Naomi's past boyfriends. They approach me and one by one embrace me briefly and say a few words. Jack has grown up to look exactly like his father and is an emergency doctor in Maine with twin girls. He's six foot two with a bushy beard and it's so hard to imagine him twirling about in Naomi's shimmery Tinker Bell costume. Pedro, who lives in LA and was contacted by a mutual friend about Naomi, is tall and handsome and has long lost his Spanish accent. Arthur, Naomi's long-haired hippie, is now bald and a corporate lawyer in Washington. Harry wears sunglasses to hide his celebrity as well as his tears. Owen is here, too. He seems to have aged at least twenty years and blows his nose in a monogrammed handkerchief. He tells me he is heartbroken for any pain he caused my daughter. Another man, a good-looking man with dark glistening hair and deep-set eyes, approaches me and takes my hand.

"I am so sorry for your loss," he says softly.

"Who are you?" I ask.

"Josh. I knew Naomi in high school."

I stare and stare. The long-lost love of her life.

"You're too late," I say.

"We are all too late," he tells me, rubbing his eyes.

Finally, when the funeral is over, I take the pills the doctor prescribed and tell my husband I need to be alone in our room. But sleep or any sort of relief does not come easily. The only memories that bring me any sort of relief are the faces of Naomi's boyfriends—all of them traveling hundreds of miles to be at her side today. They're not boys anymore—they are men.

I drink a glass of water and walk unsteadily to my computer and begin to write about Naomi. Somehow my girl, my lost girl, has escaped me. Then I wonder if I really did see all the boyfriends or was I just hallucinating? No matter. I am comforted by the vision, real or otherwise, that I witnessed today. I can't bring Naomi back but I am compelled to write the names of her boyfriends.

Jack

Pedro

Harlan

Roger

Josh

Arthur

Harry

Owen

Rajiv

As I write this list, Naomi appears before me, laughing and shaking her head as she tells me of her latest romantic obsession.

Unveiling

"My dear beloved," Iris began the letter to her husband, who would tomorrow be a year deceased. "Today in *shul* I sat between my parents. I lay the blame at your feet. The feet I would entangle with my smaller, colder ones, when you were considerate enough to be yet living. I sat between them, the widow, pitiful and angry for all to see. My parents, Jerome and Rose, sat taller in their seats, relieved to think that perhaps I would be noticed, and with that their hearts unburdened.

"Imagine their disappointment, that their daughter, not so pretty but pretty enough, pretty enough to have distracted you, made you flat out stupid on what became our first date, a trip to the twenty-four-hour store in Cambridge for henna, no, cigarettes, the henna was an afterthought. But that's what we had told the children, the angels, don't get me started, so that they would not find it romantic to smoke. Imagine the disappointment of my parents that their daughter was theirs to carry once again and not just her, but also her children, who daily show their love in the form of anger. The boy, not yet ten, telling the grandfather to leave him the fuck alone and kicking him hard in the shins."

Iris Tellerman pulled her car into a space just feet from the five-dollar valet, not because she was miserly like the rumor of the Jew, but because in the year since her husband died she could barely organize getting her kids to school in the morning, let alone a job. And though her husband had been smart about money and had had insurance from the union, Iris knew now that you just don't know, and she had to be careful. The house was paid for, but there was college and now it was all on her. "I am getting my hair colored today. I know you think it is beautiful and smoldering with a touch of grey, very Anne Bancroft, but it's not about you anymore. It's about taking my photos for JDate, because Melora says that I have to. 'It's been nearly a year,' she tells me, and tomorrow is the unveiling and I could meet someone, kidding. Or not—Melora might bring a guy from work."

Stepping in the salon where Melora had made the appointment, Iris immediately felt steeped in a pleasant cynicism. She was none of the things that she needed to be to come here: not tall, not blonde, not vapid, not an actress. The man behind the desk had had his eyebrows waxed in a high arch that made him appear preternaturally interested. Iris gave him her name and continued her letter to her deceased husband.

"The receptionist informed me while I waited, that for my first visit, I was being gifted with a 20 percent discount on a Brazilian wax. This is a gift. To have the most personal hedge of all shaped into topiary. Can you imagine it? Do you? The soft triangle that was easily covered by your hand, shaped to a valentine or a landing strip or removed completely to have the nectarine-smooth surface of a porn star. Is this how I should make myself over for the lawyer who was cornered by my parents in a zone defense in the lobby of the sanctuary? Would he, in our breathless removal of each other's clothing, expect to slip his hand into the front of my jeans and find, nothing? Would the down you once petted offend? So be it. If that is what is called for, I will pour hot wax on myself and wrest it away at the root. Or better, not leave my house, nay my room, but to drive the children to school or to buy their food at Trader Joe's."

In the changing room, Iris removed her T-shirt. Her breasts, she knew, were small but lovely, her body not so different than when she had gone to Camp Ramah as a teenager and been felt up by the very delicious Abram Scheinfeld, whom she thought she heard was a rabbi now in Boulder. She unconsciously cupped her breasts beneath a bra she suspected it was time to replace and was posed that way when the perpetually surprised receptionist poked his head in and told her that Namaste was ready for her, the curtain drawn around his face like he was preparing to wash that man right out of his hair.

"Namaste, formerly Susan, suggested that I do a two-step process to add lowlights for warmth and to help brighten up my face, which she informed me was washed out by the unfortunate brown I was born with. This long-overdue transformation will cost, with blow-dry and tip, two hundred and sixty dollars, paid for by Melora who staged the intervention, because 'I can't spend the rest of my life in the house with the kids.' That's what she thinks."

In the chair, Iris endured the smell of the peroxide and paged through the vacation album of Namaste and her dog Johnny Depp. He was one of the dogs now popular that were children-light and could be smuggled onto airplanes and into movie theaters like guns and popcorn, respectively. The album featured Namaste and Johnny Depp at various dog-friendly destinations: in the snow in matching down jackets, at the beach under a color-wheel umbrella. They were well traveled and had plans for a visit to Nepal in the spring. Namaste and her assistant, Yzenia, guided Iris to the dryer as if she were both blind and clueless, each taking a hand. A third person, who was dressed in thigh-high striped stockings and platform Mary Janes like a saucer-eyed girl from a comic book, brought Iris a cup of rooibos tea.

For a moment, Iris thought she might leave her body and view the scene from above like her husband would if you ascribe to the floating-above-things version of death. She was relieved when they left her and, under the weight of the heavy *Instyle* magazines they had piled on her lap, Iris closed her eyes and resumed contact with her beloved.

"The children are well," she began. "We are like a small specialized unit—skilled at moving the groceries from the car to the house. Evan carries the heaviest things, like the man that he isn't, and Vered, with skill and precision, orders the couscous and macaroni boxes by height in the cabinet she makes tidy as a library. When she is done, Vered and I fold the bags and place them in a neat pile under the sink. I never have to tell them anything twice. They know it is just me, just us. We work together. I buy one special thing each for them when I shop. For Evan, it is Thai peanuts, and for Vered, fresh papaya with lime. After shopping, we snack on our treats and do homework.

"They both do their work at the dining room table and tuck the completed papers into their backpacks. They are uncomplaining and never whine. They do not dawdle or tarry like normal children. It is heartbreaking. Evan has a teacher this year who is a bastard. It is too much to tell you. He is punitive and mean and I would like to kill him with my hands. When I pleaded with him that Evan had recently lost his father, he countered that it had already been a year. I thanked him for pointing that out. I had lost track of it completely. I am teaching Evan how to deal with difficult people. The bad teacher is keeping Evan from the class trip to Space Camp because we have been late more than three times. Because there are some mornings when I open my eyes that it is too much and I have to shut them again and pull the blankets around me for a few more seconds to find my strength. Most mornings, all mornings, both children are in bed with me. It feels like we are riding a flimsy raft, but at least we are together." Namaste put her hand on Iris's shoulder and pushed the dryer back. Iris startled; it is that rare that someone touches her. "Do you want me to do those eyebrows?" Iris raised her hand protectively. No, she thought, I'll muddle through. "No thank you," she said. Yzenia guided her to the sink and rinsed the color from her hair.

"Do you remember before you were dead?" Iris continued, "Before you were sick even, when the children were small and we drove up to the redwoods? We were in the van and both kids were asleep in their car seats and the rain was coming down so hard that they kept closing the roads behind us. And we had that Van Morrison CD on that we would play when Evan was colicky? That's all. Just that day. I go back to it all the time. When we got back to LA, you got a pain in your shoulder you thought from playing basketball, and then it all happened like in a playbook. The diagnosis—the chemo. You know. You must have been sick already, but we didn't know. It was just our family then. It was all we ever wanted and the noise of the rain so loud outside and we couldn't see ten feet in front of us. And when we finally got there, after driving all that way, Evan and Vered refused to get out of the car to see the redwoods. They thought we were crazy and I guess we were. That is my perfect day. When I close my eyes on the mornings that are impossible, that is what I see. I can't believe you left me. I have to go. They are wrapping my head in a towel and wondering why I have tears running down my cheeks. Time for the big blow-dry."

Iris used the corner of the towel to dry her eyes and Namaste removed it like unwrapping a gift. Iris could see already that the color was beautiful and didn't know what to make of it. She looked like she had just come out of the lake at camp, her hair falling in long ringlets. Over the sound of the dryer Namaste stage whispered, "Is this a special occasion?" Iris resisted telling her the truth: that she was preparing to go to the cemetery and reveal the headstone of her year-dead husband. That after this she had to go to Neiman's and pick up the tasteful and appropriate dress that Melora had selected for the occasion, and panty hose and shoes that wouldn't sink into the damp earth at Forest Lawn. That she would pick up her sister-in-law and her husband and kids at the airport and that the housekeeper was due to vacuum the house and put the kids' toys out of sight for the thirty or so people that would come back to her house tomorrow after the unveiling. She could see her mother already fluttering from kitchen to table, table to kitchen, interrupting her flight plan only to tuck in Evan's shirt or adjust the hem of Vered's dress. If her husband were alive they would lie in bed afterward with the lights off and dish about Rose and Jerome, and his gentle laughter would make her like them better, relieved to be together in their quiet bedroom. He would bring her hand to his mouth and kiss it, and with the ease of a yawn pull her toward him, his arm hooked around her waist like a lifeguard. Iris let the warm air and the hum of the hairdryer lull her. She closed her eyes and remembered him in such detail that she caught her breath; her face flushed when she opened her eyes and saw herself in the mirror. Namaste stood back, pleased, and gave Iris a moment to take herself in. Her heart was still pounding from the dream of her husband, but it didn't alter or slow when she saw herself. A smile dawned on Namaste's face. "You see," drawing in her breath, ". . . beautiful." Iris brought her hand to the now cooling skin at her neck. In the mirror she saw the ring on her hand that belied that she was married to no one. Her hands moved to the sable smooth hair that cascaded down her shoulders. The room and the sounds around her receded and she felt a still quiet, like floating underwater, her heart beating hard. "How dare you," she heard herself say under the rush of sound that broke over her. Iris reached down to the floor for her purse and quickly arranged a tip for Namaste, tucking the folded twenty into a tiny white envelope and dropping it into a box that Namaste had brought back from her trip to India where it was used for donations for orphans.

Iris walked back to her car and fumbled with the keys as if she were being followed. When she finally managed the key in the lock, the alarm blared. From a high window of the Yeshiva near where she had parked, a group of students with *payes* gazed down at her from above like a human menorah. She pressed the button again, again, again until the alarm at last silenced and the minyan receded. Iris dropped into the driver's seat and locked the door behind her. She caught her breath as if she'd made a narrow escape and laid her head back on her seat, the air escaping her lungs in a stutter. She felt her hand clench in a fist and instructed herself to release it. Her husband was dead. She had known this before. She had, after all, attended his funeral. Had sat in the room at Cedars, had pressed her dry lips to his forehead, had released him. But for him to be dead still was too much. For a moment, Iris rocked herself to the sound of her own keening. Her head dropped against the wheel and two fat tears dropped onto her lap, and with that she righted herself. She sniffed and brought the back of her hand to the corner of her eyes. She knew well that her grief was useless. Her husband, day after day, remained dead. His children were proof of this. They were already taller, the shape of their very faces had changed. They ran, and on days when they might be distracted, they laughed. He was not in this world. He had left her, left them, and Iris, as widow, was a reluctant expert. What she needed most to endure this loss was to rest briefly on the wide plane of her husband's chest. She was without him and her mastery had left her only weary, only empty, only angry.

Iris felt an impatient congregation urging her on. The celebrity of her husband's death now waning, novel only to her, when, before she opened her eyes each day, it jolted her limbs. They were eager for her to shed her grief like a viscose robe trailing off her fingertips. She was meant to step into a future she did not choose and did not plan for, a future that she could barely contrive. Iris steadied herself, her hands holding the steering wheel of the parked car. "I miss you," she said, the sound of her voice soft and small. "What if tomorrow I don't unclutch the stone and lay it on your grave?" she asked, expecting no answer, "What if I refuse?" But Iris knew that tomorrow she would go and march as directed to mark the year anniversary of her husband's passing. Then, with the sun catching the warm highlights in her hair, she would take the hands of her children, first one, and then the other, walk back across the soft lawn to the waiting cars, and after washing the dust of death from her hands, head back to the house for a nosh.

Iris gathered her hair in a ponytail holder that she found in the glove box and, pulling on Evan's baseball cap, she tucked her hair away. She started the car and put it in reverse. Then, pulling forward and easing her car out of the space, she drove north on Alta Vista, halfway down shearing off completely the rear-view mirror of a parked Prius. She pulled over, gathered the broken pieces from the street, and placed them in the well of the passenger seat of her car. On the back of a lunch menu from Vered's school, she wrote in handwriting that was neat and easy to read, "Iris Tellerman," with her phone number and her promise to replace the broken mirror, which she knew from the last time would be about five hundred dollars.

INTIMACIES

Intimacy represents a risk a woman is willing to take. For the characters in these stories, a powerful relationship is a counterweight to any danger it might signal. That's where the excitement lies.

Each woman is living out a radioactive moment in which she knows she's locking into a connection with another—even if the connection is doomed to come apart. That's the problem with being conscious, as these women are; their stories are not fairy tales of lives lived happily ever after. There's a palpable and gendered maturity in these experiences of intimacy, no matter their circumstances.

Some topics are universal, aspects of life that affect everyone—like money, food, or even hair—that can bring people together or drive them apart as their differences surface. Getting a haircut, the occasion for the first story here, involves powerful physical intimacies, though they can't be mutual. One is client and the other laborer, yet the person holding the scissors wields power over the body of the woman she is touching. Status, safety, vulnerability, self-presentation—they're all in the mix, and though this story ostensibly centers on a haircut, just under its surface are tensions of race, sexuality, and loyalty.

Intimacies can bridge some differences, but intimate moments can also be reminders of social barriers that make the bridges inaccessible. Social convention declares a 1950s lesbian passion "impossible." The same for a liaison between an Orthodox single woman and the non-Jewish man she's drawn to. Love can—and does—turn sour and sometimes sweeten again. Refracted through particular Jewish experiences (prejudice, inherited disease, an uncertain Promised Land, the lure of exogamy), intimate relationships in these small dramas are perilous and pleasurable all at the same time.

1919: At the Connecticut Shore

Again, it is as if something between them happened before, but neither woman can remember it. There is something between them now, and they both know it, but neither one speaks of it. With all that going on—all the unsettling feelings moving around them, as if the air itself is saturated with something heavy, but without the shapes or colors that one of them might easily comprehend, or the words that might ease the other one in her mind—the two women stand for a moment, watching each other silently. Then they talk about hair.

"It's thick—you can see. Not as thick as yours. And not kinky—is that the word? Not really curly. But wild, and I'd like it evened out. Can you do that?"

Belle sits on a chair on wheels, an old lawyer's chair Samuel picked up at a junkyard and refinished for her so she could rest her feet from walking around the house. On this wonderful contraption, she can wheel around from fireplace to table and table to shelf when she needs something. On a lower chair, a soft green pillow at her back and a clean sheet around her to catch the falling hair, Hannah faces the fire. Behind her, Belle moves her chair to the left and right, holding the thick, wiry hair that hangs down past the white woman's shoulders.

"It is thick," she says, feeling it and spreading it out. She removes small, sharp scissors from the pocket of the long sweater she wears over her dress.

"Just an inch or two," Hannah says. "My husband likes it long, but the ends need trimming."

Belle lifts layers of the hair and pins them to the top of Hannah's head. Then she snips a slightly curved line around the under layer left hanging loose. Slowly, layer by layer, ten times in all, she evens the edges and cuts the split ends of Hannah's hair.

Meanwhile, Hannah has been looking at as much of the room as she can see without moving her head. She sees the wood, chopped and piled neatly to the side of the black iron chimney tools. She sees a dark shelf to the side of the fireplace and on it some pottery dishes in lovely blue and green flowered patterns, a series of tan mixing bowls, an earthenware jug filled with wooden spoons. When she lifts her eyes she can see a shelf above the fireplace, and on it a black Bible and an old brown ledger.

Belle's eyes follow Hannah's. "Keep your head still," she says, a bit harshly, pushing it so that Hannah's eyes face the floor again.

A handwoven, woolen rug of dark red and brown covers a small portion of the wide wooden planks of the floor. A closed door leads to what must be another room, the bedroom. It's only a closed door, normal for daytime when a visitor is in the house, but Hannah feels it is closed against her in particular, that Samuel's wife Belle doesn't want her to see in.

When Belle finishes the back, she asks, "You want the front a bit shorter?" They both feel the absence of the "Ma'am." It goes with the un-spoken thing between them, the one they know about, and somehow refers as well to the thing they don't know about but feel.

"Just a tiny bit," Hannah tells her. "I don't want anything fancy, or no-ticeable. Maybe just so the front and sides curl a bit more when I pull the whole thing up in a bun or a braid."

Belle gets up from the chair and walks in front of Hannah, lifts her chin up in one of her hands, tilting her head in the right position. "Keep still," she says, and combs a thin layer of Hannah's hair down in front of her face. Through the veil of dark brown, Hannah can see the curves of the other woman's breasts stretching the black woolen sweater she wears over a heavy blue cotton dress. Under her breasts, her stomach has begun to protrude, a small round mountain beneath two smaller hills. Hannah wants to touch the mountain affectionately, as she might have touched May if she'd ever had a child, but she folds her hands in her lap. She sees Belle's slender, brown neck, and when her chin is lifted slightly higher by the firm hand that parts the veil and pushes each side behind an ear, she sees tiny silver earrings in the soft ear lobes, and she sees the other woman's hair. She's never seen a colored person's hair up close, but heard many stories about how ugly and coarse it is, how it's greasy, and it smells. The desire to touch it is nearly overpowering. Curls as tiny and tight as the tightest woolen shawl layer thickly, pulled back into two fat braids wound around each other at the nape of Belle's neck. Perhaps some kind of grease, or oil, has been used, because separated by a narrow part, the hair on top of Belle's head lies flat and thick and glistening until it meets the braid. The braid and the strands escaping from it look soft and pliant—the opposite of ugly or coarse. Hannah keeps her hands folded so they won't move of their own accord and reach out to touch that wonderful-looking hair. Hair Samuel touches, she thinks, and shuts her eyes quickly, banishing the thought.

Belle has cut a neat line of hair from ear to ear at the level of Hannah's nose. Then she brushes it back in long, firm movements that bring Hannah's mother momentarily to mind, how each night Rena brushed her own hair, then May's, then Hannah's, tugging it into a braid that fell nearly to her waist. Finally, Belle twists all the hair into a bun and makes a sound of completion, a humming sigh. As she pins the large roll high at the back of Hannah's head, the shortened front layers wave out of the pins slightly, and a few strands curl entirely free down the sides of Hannah's face. Belle holds a hand mirror up to show Hannah, who utters a cry of pleasure. She loves the soft look framing her face, and as she touches the perfectly shaped bun, she knows she will not forget the feeling of Belle's fingers on her scalp, moving gently around her neck as she brushed and gathered the hair, combing the thick layers with her fingers as she pinned, brushing her cheeks, forehead and shoulders with a handkerchief she'd taken from her pocket when she was done.

Belle smiles at her, or at her handiwork, a broad, satisfied smile.

"The colors in this room," Hannah says, groping for words, wanting a connection she feels deprived of, despite the efficient, gentle hands, the careful brushing, the perfect cut. "I love the dark reds and browns next to the copper kettle. I love colors." She stands and reaches for her purse, one she's made herself, knitted in thick green and blue wool and lined with black cotton. "I made this." She holds the purse out to be seen. "I love shapes and colors so much I sometimes make up scenes in my mind that look better than the real world around me. My husband mocks me for it—I'm always changing our furniture around."

Belle is sweeping up the hair with a straw broom while the white woman talks. She tries to offer an mmm, hmm once or twice for the sake of politeness, but she wonders why white people always think you've got nothing to do but listen to their stories. And the time she hasn't got for white people is reduced even smaller in the case of this particular white person who is not only playing with the only human being in the world Belle loves but putting him in danger as well. Yet, her thoughts are interrupted by the memory of Samuel's words the night before, the knowledge that this particular white woman holds some interest for him, and despite herself, she understands how and why. She would never confess her own passionate relationship to stories, her stories made up of words not colors and designs, but she stops sweeping and looks straight into the other woman's eyes. "I understand about shapes and colors and stories and scenes," she says. "That purse you made is real nice. It's a nice shape. The detail is fine," she adds, pointing to the tiny stitches at the edge.

Hannah opens the purse, shows Belle the black lining. It's a secret she would share only with someone who understands the importance of detail in things you make, even when it doesn't show. "It took me days to get the lining to fit just right," she says, and pulls out several coins which she gives Belle, who says, "Mmm, hmm, thank you," and puts the money into her pocket where the scissors have returned.

"We—our people I mean—we don't believe in tempting the evil eye by wishing luck for things that haven't happened yet—." Hannah looks at the curve of Belle's stomach pushing at the cloth. "But when it happens, I'll send over some of my fish stew as a sign of best wishes. We say mazal tov."

Hannah looks eagerly into the face she feels she knows from someplace else. Or, perhaps it is not another time or place the face evokes, but a quality of sympathy Hannah has not known for years, has almost forgotten because the desire is so painful when it goes so long unfilled. Or maybe the desire is born into you, whether you ever knew it or not. Perhaps Belle has a face that communicates the special sympathy, or would if its color, several shades darker than Hannah's own, did not preclude its articulation. She can't get rid of the uncanny feeling that there is something between them, something besides the thing they both know is between them and would never speak about out loud. She stares at Belle, whose opaque eyes enable Hannah to overcome her own fear of looking too long. She wishes she could penetrate the hardness of those eyes, find a way to make that mouth open in uninhibited laughter.

Belle meets her stare, but there is no smile when she says, "Well, thank you. We will appreciate the fish stew." Then, as if to compromise with her own harshness with this woman who is so appealing today yet was so offensive the last time they met, as if to remind her of her rudeness and thank for her generosity in one perfect phrase, "No shellfish though," she says.

Hannah blushes, reminded and chastened, respectful of Belle's courage and precision with words. She tries to answer with equal precision, perhaps some courage too. "Shellfish are forbidden," she says, looking straight into the other woman's eyes.

All the things she wants to say to Belle flood her mind. That she understands how prejudice can frighten and harden you. That being a woman is a blessing and a curse too. That creating scenes and arranging rooms, fixing clothes and purses and hair, making the world more shapely and comforting is the strongest happiness there is, that it somehow heals the sore parts, even if only temporarily, even if you don't know how it works. She wants to say something about the shaping, because she is coming to recognize Belle now and she feels Belle would understand. She wants to say that she understands being part of a people who have been in slavery so long they have to keep close guard of their carefully honed rituals, public and private, that remind them how hard and important it is to be free. She wants to say she understands how it feels to be hated for nothing, just for being who you are. But she senses vaguely, yet clearly enough to ensure her own reticence, that she is deeply ignorant of the extremities this other woman knows, that the tiny piece of their history she's learned from Samuel is only the slender beginning of the story of brutality and unimaginable cruelty, cutting people to bits while they're still alive, slicing off body parts in public that should be too private and sacred to name except in the safest, most intimate places, selling children away from their mothers for profit, and all of it done in memory recent enough to be heard from their own parents' mouths. These are things Hannah had never imagined, still has trouble believing. And then there is the worse feeling. Hatred of Jews has always been a huge mystery to her; something undeniable and preposterous, because Jews are not only as good as others, they are better in many ways. She has always been told this. But the way white people feel about the colored has always seemed different to her. It is not exactly hatred, except for people like the Klan and those others who support them. It is more like Aaron said, thinking about Negroes as not really ordinary people like white people are—not only less beautiful and less smart, but with different feelings, not ordinary feelings like white people have. She looks at Belle hard as she removes her apron covered with Hannah's hair, straightens the chairs in the room. She tries to see her as a *schvartza*, the way she has been trained to see, not a person with a certain skin color but a creature who is her skin color, whose skin color determines what she thinks, or cannot think, how she feels, or does not feel, a creature very different from Hannah, or other Jews, or anyone white.

Facing Belle in her red and brown room, surrounded by kettles and pottery and a closed bedroom door, sitting in a wooden chair with a green pillow just where your back might hurt if it wasn't there, seeing the woman's hair and her ears and her breasts up close, and knowing a baby is inside her body that Samuel put there, Hannah is rocked again by the shifting feelings she's been subject to in the past few months of knowing these two. They seem less and less different from her in the way she assumed before. And more and more different from what she's always supposed. Belle has told her she understands stories and scenes, and the way she said shape and detail, as if she were holding up a mirror that reflected them both, told Hannah who she was.

"You let us know when the time comes," Hannah says as she covers her newly cut hair with her shawl. "And thank you. Working with the hair in layers is a wonderful idea."

Belle opens the door for her and stands on the wooden step. "Be careful," she says, pointing to a crack in the wood but hearing the echo of the words she had said to her husband, this time in a different tone, cold and distant to keep her heart from breaking. "Be careful, Mrs. Sokolov," she says, pronouncing the name just right, and Hannah hears all the layers of meaning in the words. She nods, then turns and walks away. After a few steps she turns back, perhaps to wave, perhaps only to look at Belle again, but the colored woman is already moving into the interior of her tiny house. Hannah glimpses the shelf over the fireplace with its dark ledger and Bible just before Belle shuts the door to number 20, and she proceeds down Knight Street toward home.

The Curiosa Section

J. Rothenburg Used and Rare Books on Fourth Street displayed a yellowing dictionary on a stand in its window alongside some antique maps that looked as if they'd been placed there when Columbus set sail. Charlotte Silver squinted into the shop, one flight down from street level and worlds away from the sunny day outside. She screwed up enough courage to ask the man hunched at the desk—J. Rothenburg, she figured—for books by Havelock Ellis, the scientific sex researcher. The eyebrows on his hangdog face lifted. "You're not from the Vice Squad, are you?"

"No, I'm a nursing student," said Charlotte. She removed her white gloves so he could see her wedding ring and know he wasn't contributing to the corruption of a minor. As an unseen clock ticked in the airless room, she held her breath and reassessed her white straw hat. Was it too plain— something a police decoy might wear—or just plain enough to be owned by a poor student? But Charlotte's disguise wasn't her hat or her gloves, it was the attitude she'd been cultivating in the streetcar all the way to Manhattan from Williamsburg, Brooklyn, after having proved too shy to ask for this book from the same librarian who had been stamping her selections since she began to read. At the library she had been hoping for nothing less than to understand what had transpired between her and Martha this summer, and had left because she was afraid the librarian would ask her what business she had in requesting such explicit material. Now she did her best to affect the persona of a nurse, efficient and aloof, a woman on a scientific mission. She willed herself to remember one certain thing—she would never see J. Rothenburg again.

"You're really a nurse, right?"

"A nursing student."

"Does your husband know you're here?"

"My husband is at home with our little boy," she said. At least that much was true. In the three months since she'd met Martha she'd been living with Perry as if she were Charlotte Silver's accomplished understudy, and Perry seemed to suspect nothing. All he knew was that he had accepted a job as director of Camp Idlewild to get his family away from the city during the time of the year when polio was the most contagious, and they had all come back healthy and strong.

"If anyone asks, I'm going to say you said you're a nurse. Where do you go to school?"

Charlotte had already thought of an answer to that question. "Beth Israel," she said, because all the Jewish nurses studied there.

"You're not Catholic?"

"No, I'm Jewish."

"Because the cops are Catholic. They say they're enforcing the Comstock Laws, that would be bad enough, but last time I looked we are in the year of their Lord, nineteen forty-four and the Pope is still deciding what they read. And don't let them tell you any different."

"I'm not Catholic. I'm Jewish."

"You know why I believe you? Because it's Saturday, and none of those barbarians work on the weekend, unless they're busting into bordellos or fairy bars. Then they get zealous. But books . . . they don't understand books. They aren't going to bother on a Saturday." He lifted himself out of his chair. "I'm not saying I have it," he said, as he indicated that she should follow him along the narrow path between the rows of books stacked in front of packed shelves. Once again, she had lied and someone had believed her, just as Perry believed her when she had said she was just going to spend this afternoon with a friend who was ill, and all through the summer, when she had said Martha, the swimming instructor, was just teaching her how to swim.

Charlotte could pinpoint the moment deceit had become second nature. It was the afternoon of the swimming lesson. She and Martha were waist deep in Lake Idlewild surrounded only by the red-winged blackbirds displaying their colors and flitting between the reeds. Charlotte had been trying to place her face in the water. Time after time, her lungs became stiff with air she couldn't seem to release.

"You're just scared," Martha said as she offered her outstretched arms. "Lie down. I promise I won't let go." How light Charlotte felt, buoyed by those strong hands. When she looked up, there was only encouragement in Martha's face as she began to move Charlotte's body in a slow circle. When her arms slid away from Charlotte's belly, it was as if scaffolding fell, and Charlotte could feel the plane of reality shift from vertical to horizontal. She was floating. This was how fish must feel—fish, and birds, and trapeze artists. "Well done!" Martha said when Charlotte managed to blow bubbles. In a maternal gesture, she removed a strand of hair from Charlotte's mouth. "We really need to get you a cap."

Charlotte allowed Martha to take her hands and tow her, kicking, around the dock. When they stood, Martha slipped her fingers under the strap of Charlotte's bathing suit, and pulled her near. Charlotte had a vivid experience of Martha's body then. It came like an eddy pooling around her. Martha's lips brushed Charlotte's mouth and returned again, this time the tip of her tongue rousing Charlotte from her stunned disbelief. She jerked her head back. "What are you doing?"

"I'm sorry. Did I misunderstand?"

"Misunderstand?"

Martha stepped back. "It's just the way you kept looking at me."

"I don't know what you mean."

"Look, I didn't mean to spook you. I thought . . ."

Charlotte could feel her heart pound against her back. "I have to get back." She sloshed toward the beach. Mud and dry leaves accumulated on her feet. The earth radiated heat. But Martha wasn't finished, calling something Charlotte couldn't make out. Charlotte had the odd thought that English was not Martha's first language and that this confusion was simply something of the clumsiness that came with translation. She almost turned to wave goodbye, but afraid of unintended communications, thought better of it.

"Wait," Martha shouted, rushing to catch up. "Charlotte, can I talk to you?"

Martha was standing so close it felt to Charlotte as if she was about to single-handedly gang up on her. "I won't tell—if that's what you want," Charlotte said.

"No, not that," said Martha, staring intently into her face. "Can I give you some advice? Take a look in the mirror sometime. You were truly giving me looks."

Charlotte moved quickly to pick up her towel and her beach bag. She knew Martha was watching her and she felt completely exposed. The skirt of her bathing suit clung to her behind. Water dripped down the length of her legs, and wetness turned cold in the air. *Take a look in the mirror?* That Martha saw something she couldn't made Charlotte panicky, for what was that thing?

She was still searching for it now as she followed J. Rothenburg. He walked like a horse pulling a millstone, past a grand piano not visible from the front door. It was piled high with travel journals and materials on the occult arts. Its lid was open and the ivory keys were stained. Charlotte had underestimated the depth of the store and the rooms leading to more rooms. Alert to the fact she could be foolishly following a stranger into his lair, she studied J. Rothenburg more closely. His back was curved. His belt was cinched around his ribs. His big, lumpy hands hung at his sides. If there were danger here, it would not come from him. A half-open door revealed a bathroom yellow with neglect, toilet seat up, looking like it belonged in a subway station, and pricking her with the feeling she was here to research filth.

J. Rothenburg stopped in front of a locked cabinet. Screwing up one eye and turning to look at Charlotte as if still debating her bona fides, he finally pulled a heavy keyring out of his pocket and opened the door. "This is the curiosa section."

The cabinet was filled with forbidden volumes—*Lady Chatterley's Lover*, Henry Miller, *The Kama Sutra*, Marquis de Sade, other French titles she didn't recognize, and boxes of postcards Charlotte was sure she didn't want to see. He ran his hand along the red-and-gold bindings of *Studies in the Psychology of Sex*. There were seven volumes. "That's what I'm looking for," said Charlotte.

"A beautiful edition," said J. Rothenburg.

"How much are they?" She had about three dollars in her pocket. Surely that was not enough.

"Seventeen," he said.

"Seventeen dollars?"

The look he gave her seemed to say no refunds, no returns, and most definitely no bargains.

"Could I buy just one?"

"It's a set in fine condition, not a spot on it. Plus I have to make it worth my while. I could get locked out of my store, the whole business down the drain. Someone's going to come in one day, a rich doctor, maybe, and buy the whole set. Who's going to want six volumes?"

A rich doctor? Taking another look around this faded, melancholy place, Charlotte thought this a gross case of wishful thinking, but J. Rothenburg wouldn't reconsider. He became decidedly less friendly, or at least less talkative, and looked at Charlotte like he smelled bad faith. He closed the door and turned the key. The metallic clack of the lock was so absolute and final, Charlotte felt as if she were being cast into the street. She made her way toward the door, trying not to feel defeated. She hadn't imagined the book would be the size of the *Encyclopedia Britannica*. Where would she hide such a thing in the cramped one-bedroom apartment she and Perry and their four-year-old son, Julian, shared with her mother? But the thought of emerging into the hot air and shimmer of asphalt as ignorant as she'd been when she came was unbearable. She walked back. "Do you think I could just read it for a while?"

"Here? This isn't a library, miss," he said.

"I'll wear my gloves," she promised.

Perhaps it was her sincerity, or her persistence, or the fact that she had nothing but wearing gloves to offer, but J. Rothenburg softened. He unlocked the door of the curiosa section again. Charlotte pointed to Volume II of the Studies, the volume titled *Inversion*. She sat where she was told to sit, at the piano. J. Rothenburg closed the lid, placed the book there, and left her alone. The only sound was the ticking of the clock and the creak of the tin ceiling as someone crossed the floor above.

Intending to take notes, Charlotte removed a pad and pencil from her purse. If the doctor were to reveal a path to a cure, she would want to remember it. She ran her bare hand over the pebbled binding and shivered. She put on her white gloves, grateful for the barrier between her skin and *Studies in the Psychology of Sex*. The cover, scarcely touched, creaked when she opened it. In the preface, the doctor seemed to be making the case for more scientific study and more tolerance of inversion: "Sexual instinct turned by inborn constitutional abnormality toward persons of the same sex." Inversion.

Through the keyhole of her imagination, the women in the case studies took on life. They all had a tendency to eccentricity or nervous diseases. She read with intense interest about Miss A., aged 38, with her good general health and coolness to men, who came from a family of "marked neuropathic element." Ellis described her "exemplary" self-control in using her impulses as a "stepping stone to high mental and spiritual attainments." What did that mean? And how could she, Charlotte Silver, muster similar self-control while haunted by memories of the slightly knock-kneed gait that made Martha's wide hips sway in a movement entirely necessary and provocative at the same time? Martha's hips, like her smile, had said I know a lot more than you do. Martha's little acorn earrings, souvenirs from a European adventure, and her stories of drinking and dancing in low-lit establishments in Greenwich Village, hinted of life lived large and was seductive beyond all measure.

Charlotte read on, scouring the section titled "Offspring" for some insight into how she might protect her son from the consequences of her actions. The new nightmares, the tears of fury—would this have happened anyway? Was there a way to ease his mind? Dr. Ellis seemed to indicate Julian's predicament would have been much worse if she were a degenerate, or had an early experience that turned her into a habitual fetishist or masochist, and she was not that. He wrote, "Unstable marriages were not beneficial for children." It was no news to her that children knew things their parents didn't tell them, and that their hearts could be broken.

She put her pen and pad aside. She couldn't write Ellis's words. His tone was clinical and benevolent, but the pages became hostile things, as the words "aberration," "abnormality," and "neurosis" proliferated. He wrote about women with abnormally large genitalia who had a preference for oral stimulation, as extreme, unashamed Sapphists. Charlotte turned the page to see a pen-and-ink illustration of what Ellis called cunnilictus. Her body ached. She was unable to look away as she remembered the very specific hum on her skin when Martha was near. But oh, the nights on the lakeshore, running her hands over Martha's body, feeling the curve of her spine, the tender muscle, the soft declivities and dark spaces that even now made her mouth dry with desire. Charlotte felt pressure in parts of her body only Havelock Ellis would name. She was "aroused," a word spread generously throughout Volume II like breadcrumbs leading her to the forest primeval, and she couldn't help herself. She rocked back and forth on the bench, something Miss M., aged thirty, might do, until her mind filled with an intense memory of the pressure of Martha's little acorn earring against her cheek, and she had an orgasm, a little private one, with her eyes squeezed shut and her chin tucked to her chest. And why not? This summer something free-floating inside her had surfaced and broken apart. It didn't seem there was much she could do to revert back to the normal girl she used to be. Havelock Ellis, she realized, had done nothing to make her feel less lonely.

Charlotte closed the book. She smoothed her gloves and straightened her hat.

Abandoning any pretense of boldness, she hoped against hope not to encounter J. Rothenburg as she walked, head down, to the front of the store. She hoped so fervently that when he spoke to her it was as if she encountered him with no preparation at all. Charlotte was shocked, but she didn't think she had recoiled visibly.

"Did you find what you were looking for?" he asked. She looked at him sitting at his desk with his napkin tucked into his collar, and a half-eaten corned beef sandwich and pickles on the wax paper spread in front of him. She forced herself to regroup. She would never see J. Rothenburg again. *Did you find what you were looking for?* She reminded herself that this was a shopkeeper's question and not a philosophical one. She hadn't been truthful with him, and she didn't have to start now.

Glass

n the kitchen of the house where Shayna grew up, Mother waves a lipstick tube at Shayna's mouth. "Make an O."

Shayna shuts her eyes and puckers. In that dark hangs a negative of Mother's face, closing over Shayna like a lid: vertical wrinkle between the brows, faint beginning of a second chin.

"Tighten your lips up like that and there'll be cracks. You want cracks on your wedding day?"

Shayna takes a deep breath, relaxes her lips, folds her hands in the lap of her white dress.

"That's a girl," Mother says, and applies pressure.

Shayna slips away to the public garden alone. She is early for photographs. She senses Vic will find her there. Tells herself she wishes he wouldn't. He is not the groom. But here he is on the bench, waiting for her. "It isn't bad luck for me to see you," he says.

He is also not a guest. "You shouldn't have come," says Shayna. "My bridesmaids will be here any minute."

"One last look. All right?" Vic stands. Smiles. "That kosher?"

"Ha ha," says Shayna.

He touches her arm.

She doesn't smile. She wants to lean her cheek on his collarbone. There are little holes in his T-shirt. She stares down at her shoes, shiny white straps crisscrossing, binding her toes. "In a year, you won't remember me," she says.

"That's not fair."

"Six months, I'll bet." She wants to touch his T-shirt. She loves the holes.

"There's still time," he whispers. "We could still . . ." She shakes her head, squeezes his fingers. She's not sure whose heartbeat she feels. Or whose hand it's in.

Now Shayna sits on that bench in the garden. Nearby, three bridesmaids wear yellow. Heat bears down on the bushes and grass. Shayna hikes her skirts to her thighs and wishes for a breeze. "It hasn't rained in weeks," she says.

"Lucky Shayna."

"What do you want with rain?"

Shayna sees the men coming, filing over the footbridge like soldiers in black-and-white uniforms, Isaac in the front; she can see his scar, the neat pink curve from chin to cheek, a souvenir from some childhood accident, from back before he could make safe decisions. She used to trace that scar with her finger. It used to feel like a roadmap home. Shayna pushes her skirts back down. Crinoline drops over her legs like a stage curtain.

Eighteen months ago, one month after Isaac proposed and Shayna said yes, she met Vic at the aquarium.

He was the new shark feeder. Shayna sold tickets from a booth. A right-after-college job. Nothing that ever felt permanent.

One evening at closing time, he stood on the other side of her glass window. Pressed his fingertips to it. Asked, "Can you come out?"

"Maybe," Shayna said into her microphone.

He came around the side to her little door and opened it, grabbed her wrist and pulled her right into the lobby. "It's worth your while," he said. He took her upstairs to the top of a huge tank. All blue water and no fish. They looked down on it.

He wove his fingers through hers. "Hop in," he said, and they jumped.

"A little to the left . . . that's it. Now just the groom's family . . . Just the bride's family. That's perfect. Perfect."

The flashbulb explodes and recovers, explodes and recovers. Isaac smiles. The scar smiles, too. Like a back-up smile. A just-in-case. He's smiling for both of us, thinks Shayna.

At the doorway of her apartment, weeks after that first swim with Vic, Shayna said, "Like this. Then kiss your fingers."

"Kiss my fingers?" Vic squinted his blue eyes at the mezuzah. "I'll just kiss *you*," he said. "All right?" Vic gathered her hair in his fist.

She rested her forehead on his shoulder. He smelled like peppermint.

"All right, Shayna?"

Shayna says now, "Something isn't right." She is on that bench again, her face in her hands.

"Cold feet," says Mother. "But they'll warm right up. Think. You'll make a nice Jewish home. So beautiful. And Isaac from such a nice family. Think of it." She fastens a pearl choker at Shayna's nape. It pinches the fine hairs there.

"Ow!" Shayna lifts her head.

"Stay still!" Mother unfastens. Refastens. Squeezes Shayna's shoulders, then goes to sit beside her.

Shayna squints in the sunlight.

"I'm sorry, Baby." Mother touches Shayna's cheek with the backs of her fingers.

Shayna wishes she were sick in bed and seven years old. Wishes her cheeks were burning up from fever. She leans into Mother. "It was my fault," she says. "I shouldn't have moved."

One day, the aquarium closed because of a blizzard and Shayna didn't call Isaac to tell him.

"I love hiking," she told Vic, strapping herself into snowshoes. She thought, Maybe I will love hiking. She remembers now that endless stretch of snow, the way her calves ached. Remembers watching Vic's backpack move ahead of her, his green wool hat, his face, pink, now and then glancing over his shoulder.

"You're not fading on me, are you?"

You love this, you love this, because he loves this, Shayna told herself. She followed the green wool. "I'm one hundred percent right with you," she said. She held her breath so she wouldn't pant.

"Cold?"

"Nope."

"Bored?"

She shook her head. She wanted so much to impress him. When he stopped suddenly, cutting off the steady crunch of boots to snow, and held up a gloved finger, Shayna stopped, too.

Behind a skeletal tree, a deer paused, its muscles strong beneath its brown coat, its eyes dark and wary. And watching. For no clear reason, Shayna thought of her parents. She took a step forward. The deer flipped its white tail up and ran.

"Did I do that?" Shayna asked.

Vic shrugged his shoulders. "Probably thought you were a bear," he said. He yanked Shayna's hat down over her eyes. Shayna readjusted the hat. "I didn't mean to . . ." "She was just being cautious. She might have babies nearby. Didn't want us getting too close." Vic touched her face. "What's wrong?" he asked. "Why are you crying?" Rabbi lifts Shayna's veil. "Is this your bride?"

"Who else's would it be?"

The veil lowers.

Shayna liked watching Vic swim with sharks. He wore an air tank strapped to his back and breathed bubbles. Shayna watched for the bubbles. Breathed when he breathed. And when he was finished, when he climbed out of the water and the sharks were alone, Shayna every time had to remind herself to exhale.

It was silly, really. She'd breathed on her own for so many years.

Father hooks Shayna to his arm. "Ready?" He squeezes her hand.

Shayna doesn't answer. She is sweating, but everything is white. She is bathed in white. The white gardenias smell so strong, they make her dizzy.

The *chuppah* is white satin, draped over bamboo poles. The white grows clearer and larger as Shayna approaches. Father lets go. The garden is hushed, pulsing with heat. But the satin looks like snow, looks white enough to melt a fever.

After Shayna told Vic, "It's because of religion, Vic. My parents. My family. I'm engaged. We just can't," she still liked to watch him feed sharks.

He said, "You've never taken a risk in your whole life."

"You're not hearing me," she said. "This isn't about risk."

"You don't always get hurt," he told her, "taking risks."

When she watched him then, from the dry side of the glass, as he swam weightlessly, his body draped in chain mail like something off-limits, she silently begged the sharks, *attack him, bite him, make him see.*

"I might be sick," Shayna whispers.

"Four more."

"I don't know if I can."

"Of course you can." Isaac and his scar smile uneasily. "Since when are there things you can't do?"

The sensation of spiraling. Gaining speed. One bridesmaid holds Shayna's train. Four Five, Six. Seven rings around Isaac. Rabbi cloaks Bride and Groom in a tallit, Isaac's shoulder against hers feels like something from a dream. She feels like a mummy. Pictures herself unwinding, away from Isaac, away from Rabbi, spinning and spinning down the grass aisle and out of the garden, like an ace bandage, unraveling.

Rabbi wraps a wine glass in linen, Shayna irrelevantly thinks of a guillotine, a hovering blade. The thought and the heat make her stomach lurch. Rabbi says, "Even in our joy, we remember destruction."

Shayna hears the shattering, the uproar: *Mazal Tov!* She is racing down the aisle, Isaac at her side, leaving behind a napkin full of shards.

Shayna knows this: if she still spent her days in that little booth at the aquarium, if she hadn't quit three months ago because of jealousy—she'd grown jealous of the sharks who circled Vic, who depended on Vic, who accepted Vic as though he, too, were a shark—she would still, after all this time, look for Vic's fingerprints from that day he tried to touch her through the glass.

"Your parents have made a good match," a face tells Shayna.

Another face says, "May you both live to a hundred and twenty."

There is dancing: concentric circles cluster and widen, widen and cluster. From her chair above the crowd, Shayna hears her mother: "I'm so happy. I'm so happy."

Shayna, bouncing, smiles despite things. Smiles because of things. Isaac tries to reach her with a handkerchief. She leans toward him and takes it.

Later, Shayna wanders over the footbridge. She feels like she just came through something. Like a warrior, she thinks. She feels very, very brave. Below her, the creek runs and doesn't look back. She thinks of jumping in, of letting it pull her away in her wedding dress, but even from above, she can see the sharp rocks.

The Wedding Photographer's Assistant

" I can't stand a bride who won't wear white," Lydia told Dina, flipping through show albums with well-manicured hands. "Watch how these brides cast space—how that dress makes her stand apart, almost above the crowd. When a bride's not in white it's impossible to follow her; she becomes just another woman, she disappears on the dance floor."

Dina wanted to respond that it was exactly the role of a white wedding dress to make women disappear, but stopped herself.

"There's no question about white. If they ask me I tell them, 'That's it, we're not even discussing this.'"

Dina nodded solemnly. She didn't mention what she'd said to Andrea the night before, while debating whether to leave the world of temp agencies for that of wedding photography. "The thing is," Dina had told her, "I hate weddings. It's all such rehearsed, performed happiness. Photography should be about capturing something real and true—real emotion, real despair."

"Dina," Andrea said, "you're the least romantic person I know. For you to be a wedding photographer is too hilarious to pass up." Dina had grinned, immediately liking this smart, tough image. For months she'd been waking up anxious, aware of all she had not yet accomplished; successes other women her age, just a few years out of college, had already achieved: connections made, awards won, future plans secured. Finally, she'd have her own impressive story to tell. She could see herself sitting in a hip bar with some tall boy, laughing about the weddings, cynical and sharp.

Lydia closed a white leather-bound album, looked up at Dina.

"These pictures," she told her, gesturing to the brides blushing past their dark wood frames, "will never hang in a museum. But they'll be treasured more than those museum photos could ever be. There's an old Jewish saying,

'Every time a man takes a wife, a new world is created.' These photographs are the first images of that new world."

Dina quickly learned that Lydia's lecture was repeated to every anxious pair who came to the studio. Her first day on the job she ate cake and sipped coffee while Lydia showed the albums to a young couple. The bride twisted thin dark hair around her finger; the groom turned pages dutifully. When Lydia told them how those albums would accompany them on future family picnics, how their children would clamor to see "Mommy and Daddy's wedding album," Dina was surprised to see both the groom and his bride smile shyly. All the talk of future and children and love; it felt too heavy a promise for the tiny suburban shop.

Dina wanted to laugh it off—who brings wedding albums on picnics? Yet watching the couple shift in their seats, earnestly flipping through albums filled with photographs—the first dance cast in a pink light, close-up of the best man offering his toast, aerial view of the bride throwing the bouquet—she felt only a confusion of superiority and shame.

From the beginning Lydia allowed Dina to photograph the weddings on her own. Dina always aimed for the outtakes—the moments when the bride reached for the lip balm or the groom nervously combed back his hair with a still-unringed hand and everyone made small jokes and traded compliments. Lydia's only rule was that Dina had to stay out of the way. Dina, who tended toward quiet observation in most social situations, was particularly good at that.

What surprised Dina, though, was how the weddings made her weep.

It was exactly like cutting an onion.

She would begin the wedding thinking this is fine, I feel fine, this can't possibly make me cry. But somewhere along the way she'd find it cut too deeply, and the tears would come. At one wedding it was the father kissing his daughter before the altar, the way he held her arm gently between them. At another it was the couples' first clumsy dance as husband and wife—they had turned so slowly, clung so tightly to each other.

The weddings were so joyful and yet so sad. Had her own parents once been this way—turning white circles on a parquet floor, arms closed seriously about each other—before the divorce, before the photographs of her father in California, running the sprinkler on another woman's lawn?

The earnestness of the event, the dogged determination to declare true love in suburban catering halls, broke her heart every time.

Dina had worked for three weeks, six weddings, when Rachel arrived for her appointment, solo. Dina immediately noted her beauty—tall and thin with perfect waves of long black hair and a wide, serious smile—and her confidence. Most of the brides felt Lydia was judging their relationship, which of course she was, and would drag their fiancés in and caress them through the album-gazing process, but Rachel just said, unapologetically, "I left him at our place in New York. He couldn't care less about this, and someone had to stay and walk the dog." Rachel, on the other hand, had definite opinions about wedding photography. "No colored lights," she said. "No phony backdrops, no throwing the bouquet, no photographs of me looking into a mirror or contemplating my ring finger. I will not fix my father's boutonniere or allow my mother to brush my hair. Okay?"

Lydia nodded and poured more coffee. Dina beamed.

The wedding was in only two weeks. The previous photographer—Rachel's close friend —had just been given an opportunity to accompany a biological expedition to Bolivia. It impressed Dina that Rachel knew those kinds of people, said things like, "it was an offer she couldn't refuse," even if she was marrying in suburban Philadelphia.

Wedding mornings Dina usually woke up later than she'd intended, instantly tense. She'd rush to the studio to quickly review names, family relations, and requests for special pictures with Lydia over donuts and coffee. But on the morning of Rachel's wedding, the first Sunday in August, Dina awoke early, strangely excited. She even dressed up: a new blue silk shirt, along with eyeliner, mascara, and lipstick.

It was a hot, humid, gray day; they took the formal shots under the thin shade of two tall sycamore trees. "Bride, groom, just the two of you now. Smile." "Dina—fix the veil, yes, like that, so it swirls more." "Okay, turn slightly to the left and hold that, perfect." Rachel's dress was a soft cream color, curved close around her breasts and hips. Her groom was tall and thin and looked as though he would cry from joy, but kept laughing instead. Rachel's mother said "honey," every five words; her father was a fat pink man who clapped everyone on the back and danced around between pictures, practicing the steps he and his wife had rehearsed in class.

For the first time, Dina managed to get the photograph of the father kissing his daughter at the end of the aisle. A good shot; she felt it when she took it.

The dancing began directly after the hors d'oeuvres. The band played "Hava Nagila," two concentric circles formed, and Rachel and her mother, linking arms, spun around the center of the inner circle. The guests shined, then sweated, as the music moved them faster. Someone brought two chairs and a small group gathered to lift Rachel and her husband above the crowd. Like make-believe royalty they rose, each clenching the chair with one pale-knuckled hand and a white napkin, buoyed up between them, with the other. The guests continued to dance circles around them.

Dina stood on a chair to get the picture, and stayed there while guests lifted up the groom's parents and then the bride's. She photographed Rachel's father as he stepped off the chair; he swayed, his face moist with sweat and his smile strained. Something in his expression made her pause with her finger above the shutter button, but then he took the hand of his wife, continued dancing.

When Dina looked over again the father had paused. He was clapping, but his eyes looked distant and his face red. Still, his smile was so sincere that Dina photographed him. And then again, because he was holding his chest. And then again, because he went, impossibly, from red to ash gray. And then again, as someone cried, "Give him space!" and he crumpled to the ground in his tuxedo and curled around the pain.

Several women ran for their purses, fished out cell phones with nervous hands. Two guests, transforming back into doctors, stepped forward and barked orders: "Stand back, remain calm!" The older doctor, gray hair at his temples, bent down to the father, spoke loudly: "Are you okay? Can you hear me?" Barely pausing to listen to the silence, the doctors rolled Rachel's father onto his back, four arms wrapping around his body, pulling him flat like a carpet.

Dina focused her lens while the older doctor bent his ear to the father's nose and mouth, watched the still chest with a creased forehead. Dina checked the light meter as he placed two fingers on the father's neck, paused, frowned. As he tipped back the father's head, opened the mouth and breathed—one, two—into the body, Dina took a picture. Then another and another while the younger doctor crouched over the chest, locked her elbows over the heart and began pumping—one, two, three, four, five. Pause. One, two, three, four, five. Pause. Again. Pause, two breaths, check pulse. Repeat.

By the time the paramedics arrived—five, ten minutes later; Dina wasn't thinking of time—the guests had grouped themselves into small whispering circles. Most tried to watch while pretending not to look, a few brought over water, juice. Dina photographed Rachel and her mother kneeling on the floor, holding each other, the untouched glasses lined up beside them.

The paramedics lifted the body onto the gurney and rubbed the defibrillators together. Electric currents searched for the heart; the body heaved while they quickly pushed it out the door. Dina captured Rachel's mother as she stumbled to touch the father's hand; Rachel stayed near the moving gurney while her new husband pressed ahead, seeking out doors to open, ways to help.

The catering staff slunk into the kitchen. The hall manager spoke with two policemen in the doorway, assured them that everything had been done properly. The guests remained in the room, devastated. At one table a woman sat with her head in her hands, sobbing; Dina photographed the woman's pale face behind her clasped-hand veil. Dina moved softly round the room, drawn to the way those left behind touched each other, knowing death had claimed someone from among them.

If the guests noticed her they ignored her; she was camouflaged in the confusion. But Lydia, who had been waiting in the lobby for Dina to join her, was horrified to find Dina roaming about, taking pictures. With a strong arm Lydia led Dina from the room, as if she'd disciplined generations of errant photographers. Without speaking, she drove Dina home. In the car Dina rewound the roll and removed it, pressing it safe to her stomach. She left the camera on the seat when she got out. "Give me the film," Lydia said. Dina shook her head no, and fled into her apartment.

Dina read the obituary in the paper the next morning. Rachel's father had been a successful car salesman, owned three suburban dealerships, and served on the local school board. "He is survived," the paper read, "by his wife, Rose Levine, his daughter, Rachel Levine, and her husband, Mathew Loeb."

In another section, the wedding announcement: "Rachel Levine, daughter of Rose and Arthur Levine, was married yesterday to Mathew Loeb."

How many people, she wondered, would connect the two, call over co-workers to shake their heads at the horror of it?

Dina developed the film, bit her lip to keep from grinning.

She brought the photos to a local gallery. "Tell me they're faked," the director said. When Dina shook her head no, he whistled low, then offered her a group show in October.

Dina found a job with the Philadelphia mural commission. She met with painters and community residents, reviewed mural proposals, photographed the painting process. The job took her to neighborhoods all across the city; she brought her camera on each assignment. Returning home from work each evening she'd survey her apartment, third floor of a red brick row house, bathed in yellow early autumn light. She felt like a character in a movie: young, urban, talented.

And then, three and a half months after the wedding, Rachel called.

"How are you?" Dina asked, too loudly, too strained.

Rachel ignored the question. When Lydia had paid a shiva call, Rachel told her, she said that she would have Dina destroy the wedding photographs.

"I've thought about it since," said Rachel. "Do you still have them?"

Dina paused. She could lie, say no, and pray that Rachel never saw the images. But Dina couldn't lie. "Yes," she answered, "I have them."

"Good," said Rachel. "I want to see them."

Dina didn't think to protest—this wasn't her obligation, her responsibility. Yes, yes of course Rachel could see them.

"I'm back in New York now," Rachel told her, "and I don't have time to go home this month, but I could meet you halfway, if that's alright, at one of those rest stops off the Jersey Turnpike. This weekend sound okay?"

Hanging up the phone, Dina placed her arms on the table, her head in her arms. When she'd looked back on that afternoon, days and weeks and now months later, she couldn't answer for why she'd done it. Why hadn't she put down her camera, showed respect for the dying? Even Andrea had been shocked to see the pictures. "Dina, you didn't, you couldn't have . . ." she'd said, while Dina had hoped her flushed skin looked like shame rather than the pride she felt. "It was," Dina told her, "just too good a picture. I couldn't resist, I just couldn't."

Dina pulled into the Molly Pitcher rest stop that Sunday at noon. The sky and the parking lot were the same shade of gray; the wind stirred paper cups and plastic straws in small circles. Outside the rest stop cars were lined up for gas; inside were the usual stores, arranged over brown tile: a coffee pavilion that almost looked like Starbucks; a Roy Rogers and a Home Country Cooking; a store that sold automobile products, souvenirs, sunglasses, and candy. Dina found Rachel seated at a red table next to a large window, watching for her. They smiled at each other and Dina sat down, placing her green canvas bag on her lap.

Rachel spoke first. "Listen," she said, "I want to see them. I don't know why, but I do."

Dina nodded, suddenly important, a real photographer on a grave mission.

"No one knows I'm here. Not even my husband. But I've felt it's so unreal—maybe everyone always feels that, but I'd looked forward to that wedding so damn long and then it was, stolen, you know?"

Dina nodded again, noticing the dark of Rachel's eyes.

"So I thought, that since you had these pictures and I had no real memory of the whole thing happening, that if I saw them . . ."

Dina reached into her canvas bag. She pulled out a manila envelope and pushed it across the table toward Rachel. "You can keep them if you want to," she said, half standing up.

Rachel placed her hands on the envelope, looked up at Dina. "No, stay. Please stay," Rachel said. "I don't think I can do this alone."

Dina sat down. She kept her hands clasped quietly on the table, crossed her legs to keep still.

Rachel carefully unwound the thread that held the envelope closed. Dina felt Rachel's eyes on her, but kept her own head turned to the window, watched a young girl in a yellow jumpsuit run after her father, try to reach the car first.

Rachel pulled out a stack of photos. She took a long time to lower her eyes to look, but, when she did, she smiled at the picture of her kissing her three-year-old cousin. It wasn't the wide, perfect smile Dina had seen before. It was a sad smile, slightly wavering.

"Oh," Rachel said. Tears came to her eyes. "Oh."

Dina's hands stirred when she saw Rachel cry. She could have stroked her face, but placed her hands flat on the table instead.

The next picture was of Rachel and her husband, discussing something intently during a short photo break. The next of her motioning to her mother, "Over here, come join us." Her mother was shading her eyes from the sun.

The procession began. Here was the groom between his mother and his father, all three delighted and tense. The groom's brother with his wife: she, six months pregnant, one hand on her stomach. Pairs of friends, arms linked, smiling down the aisle. And then Rachel herself, veiled, one parent on each side.

Rachel looked for a long time, a small wrinkle forming between her brows, her hair tucked behind her ears. "I haven't seen any pictures," she said. "Guests who brought cameras didn't send the film over, and I didn't want to see Lydia's. But I knew yours would be different." She reached toward Dina's hand, gently, but absently, covering it with her own.

Dina felt the touch inside; kept still. But Rachel drew lightly away, returned to the photographs.

Rachel's father lifted her veil and kissed her cheek.

"I want to frame this one," Rachel said, holding the photo with both hands. "Is that wrong? It's what I have."

Dina smiled. "I think that's okay," she told her, "I think you can do that."

Under the wedding canopy Rachel turned seven circles around her groom. Each sipped wine out of a silver cup, recited vows, placed gold bands upon pale fingers. The rabbi read the wedding contract aloud; the groom smashed the glass; the bride and groom embraced.

Rachel smiled as she looked through them, and Dina ached to see that sadness.

There was Rachel, held up on a chair, grinning, linked to her husband by a white napkin.

And then there were her parents, red faced and laughing, doing the same.

Rachel paused. Looked up at Dina. Again the bright, steady eyes. "Have you shown these to anyone?" she asked.

Dina nodded.

"Which picture is the most, you know, tough?"

Dina fished a picture out from the pile. A man was lying on the floor. Above him, a woman was screaming and clinging to a bride. A blur in the corner was the doctors rushing to the scene. The woman's eyes were on the body, the bride's on the doctors.

"I thought they would save him," Rachel said. "But I shouldn't have looked away."

She went in reverse now, back to the beginning of the death. And then forward, to the place where the paramedics came and he disappeared.

"He was dead when they arrived at the hospital," Rachel said, now staring so intently that Dina found it difficult to return the gaze, longed to blink away the intimacy. "He was dead right there," pointing to a picture. "That's my father dead. I can't believe it—all those cliché things—he looks as if he's asleep."

Rachel walked Dina to her car, gave her back all the pictures except the few of the ceremony. They stood for a moment, looking at each other. The wind lifted strands of Rachel's hair across her face, and Dina, without thinking, brought her fingers up to brush them away. And then Rachel was catching Dina's hand in her own, and then holding it. They stood another moment like that, while Dina's mouth went dry. Rachel dipped forward, placed her other hand around the back of Dina's head, pulled Dina toward her.

Dina was just recognizing Rachel's scent—something soapy, familiar— when Rachel drew back, kissed Dina quickly, and then stepped away, smiling. She stroked Dina's hair a few times; her eyes were red.

"Thank you." Rachel said, her car keys clutched in one hand and the photos in the other. "These . . ." she lifted them up, paused. "They give me something of my father back." Her voice was just a little high with sadness. "Thank you so much for that." Rachel lifted a hand goodbye, then walked away.

Dina leaned against her car. She waited two, five minutes. It grew colder, windier.

She wrapped her arms around herself, feeling warm despite the weather, and grinned.

AUDREY FERBER

The List of Plagues

The husband sits on the curb of a wide, four-laned San Francisco boulevard. The air is crisp but he wears no jacket, no socks. His old slippers, the leather scuffed colorless, splay out in front of him, half off his feet. He's still holding his cell phone. He's called his wife.

She arrives in minutes. "What happened? Are you okay?" Her mouth's a slash of lipstick red.

"I'm okay. The car's not so good." He gestures in the direction of his Jeep, the wheel, the axle, one whole side sheared off. "First rain of the season. Spun out."

His car faces the wrong way nosed into a concrete wall. Miraculously, no other cars are involved. Miraculously, he seems unhurt. The usually busy street is hushed in wadded quiet.

A tow truck arrives.

"How youse two doin'?" The driver's accent is heavy New York, and for a moment, although she left more than forty years ago, the wife wants nothing more than to be a child back in Brooklyn again.

The husband tries to get to his feet but he falls backwards. "First rain. God-damned slick roads."

The wife, on one side, the driver on the other, help him up.

"You can go home," the husband tells her, shaky and gray. "He'll drive me to the mechanic."

"Can't do," the driver says gently. "This car's totaled. It's going to the Yard."

The husband's ribs hurt. They wait in the emergency room for hours for x-rays and an EKG.

"His ribs are either bruised or cracked," the nurse says when they're finally in their cubicle. She pushes morphine into his line.

The wife sits in a low-backed chair and watches him sleep. She still finds him handsome. They'd met thirty years ago, when he was fifty, and she thirty-two. He was acting in a play, a mixed-media collage in which he'd rolled shirtless atop a map of the world, his chest hair electric under the lights. He'd been so vibrant and charming before the diabetes, heart disease, spine surgeries, depression, nerve damage in his hands, she'd barely noticed their age difference at all.

A few days later they go to the Yard to clean out the Jeep. On the crash side, jagged metal teeth outline the door and broken glass fills the seat. The other side is wedged so tightly next to another car, she can only open the door part way. The husband tries to squeeze in but he drops his cane. When she bends to get it something metal catches her sweater and pulls a hole.

"Shit! Let me in there." She pushes roughly between him and the car. "Tell me what you want. I'll pass it to you."

"I want everything!" He is angry too.

She hands him three pairs of sunglasses tangled, two faded baseball caps, and a saggy cardboard box. He limps the box, filled with coins, screws, earplugs, a shoe horn, screw tops from bottles, toothpicks, a screwdriver, two hammers and two retractable metal measuring tapes, trailing pennies, over to her car. At this rate, they'll be there all day.

They fill canvas shopping bags with theater programs, Sudoku books, bags of chips, boxes of sugar-free cookies and a six-pack of Diet Coke. She opens the glove compartment: a jar of melted candies, a jar of paper clips, a crushed box of tissues, a ball of string.

"You really want all this?" she asks.

"And those." He points his cane at the Betty Boop floor mats.

He'd originally bought them for her. She hates Betty's tiny skirt and push-up boobs. She'd liked Betty Boop when she was eight years old.

From the back of his car, she piles yellow waders, toilet paper, paper towels, flashlights, flares, cans of nuts and two gallons of water on the ground. He used to be ready for anything. He used to take care of her.

"I bought that for you." He taps a hardback in a pretty flowered jacket with the tip of his cane. *The Collected Poems of Emily Dickinson*.

She snatches the book and puts it in her purse.

"Not those," she mutters, when he dislodges the box of worn file folders and stained envelopes she'd purposely left behind.

"It's my stuff," he bellows, as if he's been waiting for just such an opening. "You don't get to decide what I can have!"

"What happened to you? You used to like beautiful things!"

"You used to like anal sex!"

The jumper cables she throws land rattling at his feet like snakes.

But they have to eat. And because they are married and because ending a marriage is more complicated than screaming in a junkyard, they stop at a Mexican restaurant they both like in that part of town.

"Let's just get burritos to go," he says.

"I don't eat burritos." She's been on Weight Watchers for years. He neither notices nor remembers.

"You're beautiful," was all he'd say when he was still the person she went to for reassurance. The kind of unconditional acceptance he probably wants from her now.

She orders the enormous Juarez Salad, beans, cheese, chicken, corn, avocado, a fried tortilla hidden under the greens. As many calories as a burrito, at least.

"I can't believe I wrecked my car," he says.

His sadness unfreezes her for a moment. She almost reaches across the table and touches his hand but she's too angry to give.

The cherry trees in their neighborhood bloom a riot of pink. The wife has her toenails polished Cha-Cha Coral. But spring is lost on the husband. He sleeps more hours a day than he is awake. Breakfast at noon, followed by reading the newspaper, then back to bed. He leaves a sticky trail of eggshells on the kitchen counter, muffins forgotten in the toaster, and on the dining room table, the newspaper flung open, as if he's been suddenly called away. Early in their marriage, they cleaned up after meals together. Now she does everything alone.

Her cousin calls to invite them to seder.

"Yes, we'll be there. Or maybe just me," the wife says.

"How is he?" the cousin asks cautiously.

"His ribs are healing."

The wife doesn't mention the Memory Center diagnosis of "cognitive changes" or the doctor's observation that in the elderly, it was difficult to pick the strands of depression and dementia apart.

When he sleeps so much, she is sure he is dying. What she wants to know is when. She might try to repair their relationship, be nicer to him, get back to the early days of attraction and laughs.

On the fifth day of the big sleep, she goes into his room at noon. It smells of moldy paper and unwashed hair.

"You need to get up," she says softly.

They have slept in separate rooms for years. Sometimes, he shouts in his sleep. Sometimes he stays up all night watching movies. She needs time to herself without the television blaring. She rests better alone, moisturized, high in a nest of plump pillows.

"You have to eat something. I'm worried about your blood sugar." She touches his hair.

His eyes open slowly. She imagines a tearing sound, his sparse eyelashes caught in the crust around his eyes. He blinks. She raises the shades. Sunlight floods the room and catches the scar on the side of his nose where a cancer was removed. A flight of wild green parrots call and swoop outside the window.

"Come have breakfast." The wife pulls back the corner of his blanket. "We can sit on the deck. The parrots are back."

He blinks again, more prehistoric creature than man. He will probably die first, but she's afraid that by the time it happens her hair will have lost its luster, that she'll be too tired to try again. He pulls the blanket up to his chin and closes his eyes.

The next day the husband is too dizzy to walk. The geriatrician agrees to see them. She declares a "diabetes emergency" and institutes stricter rules: Breakfast every morning between seven and eight. No chips, cakes, or cookies. Protein at every meal.

"Eggs, lox, cheese, meat," the wife adds, for although the husband has a genius IQ, he no longer knows which foods contain protein.

"Finger pricked, blood tested, before every meal," the doctor continues. "What is the one food you can't live without?"

"Hershey's chocolate," the husband replies immediately. Not even good dark chocolate, the wife thinks.

"Then you may have three Hershey's kisses a day," the doctor says.

"I miss my Jeep!" The husband bangs his cane on the floor.

The next day, the wife makes charts on a yellow pad. Blood sugar and foods consumed on one page, medications and dosages on another. The husband hates rules and schedules. Every story he tells about himself—smuggling snakes back from Mexico, visiting Mount Athos without a permit—show him defying authority. When they met, the wife found this attractive.

She removes his diabetes equipment from hiding in a decorative box and places the lancets, glucometer, insulin pen and the red plastic disposal bin on the dining room table. She is energized by the new regimen. Action gives her hope.

They have a good week. Most days, the husband follows the rules. Her fantasies begin. They will hire a personal trainer. They'll take long walks, travel again.

He leaves his bloody tissues and alcohol wipes on the table. She stifles her resentment and cleans up the mess.

"I still don't have a car," he says.

"You haven't been leaving the house much," she understates politely. "Maybe we can share mine?"

"I want my own car!" He pounds the table for emphasis. The wife is relieved. She hates couples that share one email address.

Banners billow on auto row: "March Madness!" "Our Prices are Insane!!!" But at the first dealership, the husband declines a test drive. At the next, he's too tired to get out of their car.

"Why are we here?" He sounds so fuzzy she decides they should go home.

But when they pass a used-car lot at the end of Auto Row, he grabs her arm.

"Pull in," he shouts.

"We don't want to buy a used car on a lot," she yells as they veer violently to the right.

"Pull in," he screams.

He starts opening the door before she has stopped the car. A salesman sidles over. Close up, he is frightening, his hair dyed with what looks like a smear of black shoe polish, his skin an artificial shade of orange tan. He looks at least seventy, with small gray-green eyes and teeth to match.

He leads the husband to a car she's read described as "the worst of the hybrids," notable for "poor visibility" and "sloppy handling." He opens the door for the wife. The inside reeks of air freshener, the leather seats wrinkled like old skin.

"I'm going," she tells her husband, and stomps away.

The husband takes his time chatting with the salesman. Just as she's about to leave, just as she's about to explode, he totters to their car.

"You're acting crazy," she screams. "And don't grab my arm when I'm driving. You could have gotten us killed."

"Shut up," he shouts. "Stop telling me what to do."

She pulls onto the freeway and in a moment, the motion lulls him to sleep.

Over the next few days, he decides he wants a new SUV, then a used wreck, then a luxury hybrid. The wife wearies of the circular discussions and of jollying him along. She suggests that he take her aging car and that she get the new one. She names a luxury car she's always admired.

"You're greedy!" he yells.

"And you're a stingy old tightwad!"

They stop talking about cars.

They stop talking.

On Monday, the geriatrician is ill and cancels the husband's follow-up appointment. The wife is despondent. She's lost her only ally. The bathmat slides as she steps out of the shower and yanks her legs apart. She sinks to the floor, gripping her knee. The garage door grinds open, the old motor shaking the house like an angry beast. The husband takes her car.

He returns with pink iced doughnuts, a gallon of ice cream, two mini fruit pies and two boxes of cookies. He dumps it all on the kitchen counter.

"How could you? We were doing so well." She follows him into the dining room.

He opens the newspaper.

"Why are you doing this to yourself? Answer me!" she pleads.

He raises the paper around his face.

She flies at the kitchen counter, squishes the donuts between her fingers, grinds the cookies with the heel of her hand, pounds the pies into mush. She throws it all in the trash.

Upstairs, she slams the bathroom door. She scrubs and brushes but can't get the oil-and-sugar stink out from under her nails. Her hand throbs from pounding. She takes a Xanax. Numbs out to *Law and Order SVU* reruns. Child prostitution, rape by a stepfather—lives worse than her own.

Later, she comes downstairs and checks the garbage. The husband still reads at the dining room table, quiet as a cat. "Where's all that crap?"

"I ate it."

"You ate out of the trash?" Pulses explode in her ears. She ticks like a bomb. "I'm not wheeling you around when you have to have your feet amputated! I'm not!"

"Leave me alone," he booms. "Stop hovering. You can't control my life!"

The next day, she does not wake him for breakfast. When he comes downstairs, she goes up.

This is the end, she thinks, not for the first time. They will live apart. She will spend Thanksgiving, Chanukah, Christmas, Passover, her birthday, even Valentine's Day, alone.

The next day, she does not wake him for breakfast again. Anger propels her around the lake in the park. Her knee hurts, a hot ominous grind, but she powers past a hunched old couple, the man leaning on a walker. The woman shuffles on a three-footed cane, holding his arm. Tears start in the wife's eyes. At least they're trying.

Overhead, the parrots appear. Raucous, acid green. Fucking birds!

She goes to Pilates and strengthens her core. She goes to book group. She looks at apartments online and imagines a small quiet space without urine on the bathroom floor.

But after a few days, she feels shaky. The silences she initiates are always harder for her.

"So what are we doing about a car?" she finally asks.

"I thought you wanted a . . ." He names the luxury car. "Haven't you bought it yet?"

"I do want it, but you said I was greedy."

"I might have said that but so what? Get what you want." What does she want? She is not the kind of person who leaves a spouse because they're old and decrepit. Is she?

She chooses a spunky brown car, the color of a chimp, her favorite animal. The ride is tight. It wraps her in luxury, but she wishes she were happier. She wishes the purchase wasn't layered with conflict. She wishes her salesman wasn't a Republican. She wishes she looked better, not sag-faced with sleep drugs and sadness, as she writes the check.

The next day, the husband comes downstairs early. They eat breakfast together.

"Here's a story about those parrots." He passes her an article clipped from the newspaper.

So he was listening. He can still surprise her. She abandons the idea of going to the seder without him. She has reached the point where it is taking more energy to be angry than to let it go. She remembers their first dance at their wedding, the sweet, open passion in his eyes. She remembers how he allowed her father to instruct him in the art of bonsai for hours at a time.

A small group gathers at the home of the wife's cousin for the seder.

The husband affects a stagey *Fiddler on the Roof* voice while reading from the Haggadah, a performance of being Jewish, that puts the wife on edge. The cousin leads them in a responsive reading, but the husband reads faster or slower than everyone else, never blending with the group. His originality charmed her at first. Now, he just seems incapable of unison.

"Blood." "Frogs." "Lice." The plagues are read, and after each they dunk their fingers in their glasses and flick the dark red wine at their plates.

Marriage, she adds silently to the list.

"Boils." "Cattle disease." "Death of the first-born."

The husband stiffens. Or she imagines that he stiffens. His son from his first marriage, his first born, a little boy killed so long ago.

She stiffens too. Her, their, one, two, three, four miscarriages, many years ago.

On Sunday morning, the wife wakes the husband. The night before, he had agreed to join her for brunch. She carries plates of smoked salmon, capers, tomatoes, toasted sourdough bread, fresh orange juice and coffee out to the deck.

When the husband does not appear, she goes back upstairs. He is sleeping again. She rocks his shoulder, kisses a tender place on his neck.

"Do you want to have sex?" He tries to pull her toward him, his damaged hand as blunt as a club.

"No. I want to have brunch."

Finally, he appears on the deck in floppy jeans cinched with a tired belt, a torn straw hat, and shoes with no socks, a diabetes no-no. The coffee is cold but he is there.

"To my beautiful wife," he toasts with his juice. "Who loves and takes care of me."

She scans the sky. Now is when she wants the parrots to appear. She needs to see them with her husband, to share a moment of joy, wring hope, encouragement from tropical plumage and flight.

The sky remains a bright empty blue.

Road Kill

F irst it was hit then thrown forward. Up and quickly down under the car in front before it rolled under mine. I could feel the body hit the chassis. I heard the impact. Driving north, toward Golan, not knowing where I was going, simply going. The border would stop me soon enough. I had to leave. Just that. What, I wasn't sure, though all these were afterthoughts. The first and only compulsion was to get out, to be other than there. That flat was cannibalizing my pain. A baby's waiting bedroom; unhung curtains, an unassembled crib. Six months of expectant life suffocated by a tumor determined to get me next.

My hands are red with blood. The dog is in my arms. Though no longer alive, at least, I think, technically, she is still bleeding slowly from her mouth, from her skull. She died while I held her, sang to her, and finally closed my fingers over her windpipe to stop the pain. How quickly she stilled. There is only so much pain that one should be expected to bear. Cars cruise by me. The drive-till-you-drop style Israelis don like a dark cloak, vampires all of them. Baring their teeth, they lean hard against the car in front, taking no prisoners, passing recklessly, hounds for blood. There is the unreality of feeling healthy in a world that is propelled toward decay and death. And there is the unreality of being sick in a world buoyed by the lie of life. I watch the drivers. Some listen to music. Some to the inescapable drone of political blather. Days float by, one becoming another, and there is no way to tell them otherwise.

I am there, not here, sitting on the side of the road, red bloodied hands folded quietly in my lap now, the carcass of a large brown dog beside me, her blood being drunk by the dry ground. No one pauses to see. Or so it seems. No one actually stops. No one wants to hear the story of Ella and the dog run over. Or the one about Ella and her unborn boy. There could be lots to tell in the latest chapter of Ella and Gil. But who wants to hear the usual crap about marriage, though Ella would like to tell her story. She would like to have someone enclose her in strong arms and assure her—and make her believe—that everything was going to be all right. She would like to try and understand what all right means.

She should stay home another two weeks, above the mandatory six, after such an operation. And if she needs more, hell, that's fine too, she was told over and over. Her boss and colleagues at the factory, so understanding. The surgeon, straining through his callousness, playing at concern. She knows they are all trying to be extra nice because of the baby. To have a uterus and a dead baby taken out at the very same time is the kind of blow that can elicit the best in people. (Whatever that means. Ella just reads relief on their faces: it's not them.) "And now six months of chemotherapy." My voice rises to a quiet croak as I tell the dead dog the forecast. "They hope they got it all, but just to make sure, the poison."

Of course I don't agree with the doctors. I don't necessarily disagree either, but I'm not rushing to having an intravenous drip toxic waters into me, drop by drop, that are not, like anti-missile missiles, sophisticated enough to attack only cancer cells. I watched my father's veins turn black from this stuff. I know all about the headaches, the nausea, the metallic taste in the mouth. Alternatives? Unsure. When I reach the border I might know more.

Ella had never looked so good, everyone, absolutely everyone kept telling her. Not that she wasn't attractive before, but something lit up in her and like the most time-worn cliché about pregnancy, she glowed. Women on the factory floor made dresses for her, deliberately using fabrics that Ella had designed for that season's fashions. Ella and Gil. High powered, fast living, a fashionable Tel Aviv pair. From their back balcony in the right neighborhood they could see a sliver of sea. Concerts, pubs, regular travels to Europe, Asia, and Africa. Everywhere, Ella sketched and collected. Shapes, colors, fabric swatches. The baby would slow them down, of course. But it was time now.

She had married at thirty, had had five years of play with Gil. Time had come to give to the future. A child. A namesake. A kaddish. Yet with one flash of the ultrasound screen, Ella had gone from being a forward-looking Madonna, doyenne of the fashion world, to a woman cloaked in death.

A rapid-fire transformation. From shifts to shrouds, hue to tonelessness, foresight to oblivion.

When I said to Gil, we were sitting in the hospital waiting room after that last ultrasound, that something was very wrong, that it never took so long to read the images of the baby and that I had never before seen three doctors converge around a printout from one of those machines, he said casually (to offset the moan that was beginning to rise in me) that no matter what they found out, I'd survive. He's still eating those words.

I begin to laugh out loud and can't stop for a good minute. The cars garble the sound. My arms wrap around my waist. I feel the blood stickiness on my fingers as they hold on to each other. I hope that glibness stays stuck in his throat forever. "Remember the sequence," this time I include the cars in my hearing audience, and scan the approaching headlights for a bright moment. "The doctors come out, we all go into a little cubby with the main man, he says, the baby is dead, no heartbeat, and there is a tumor the size of a grapefruit lying alongside. They are sharing a bed." Okay, he wasn't so poetic. My words. My body created and killed a baby. Cancer found us both. Him first. I get to sit through another act.

"Gil was green as the doctor's scrubs," I stroke the dog's muzzle, her black nose is almost dry, "an awful color to use for fabric. Doctor said I needed an immediate hysterectomy followed by chemotherapy. Life expectancy dependent on how far the cancer's travelled. Been down this road before— eh, what's up Doc?—something they'll see when I'm opened. Great, I say to the all-knowing, not-knowing doctor, I'm free after lunch. I wanted the baby out of me as soon as possible. I couldn't bear not feeling him kick and roll around and for the first time in the week that I noticed this quiet, know why. And with this episode, would end my short tenure as a mother, and possibly as a living being. Gil, when he finally found himself, started to scowl and went and sat in a corner. I didn't move. The doctor came back to tell me that I would have to return in four days and to stop by the nurse's station on my way out for the pre-op instructions.

Drank lots of vodka and orange juice that night, they're called screwdrivers in the States, and waited for them to bore a hole into me. I felt nothing for a little while then. The next day on a cheerier note drank vodka and lemonade. By the third day I was out shopping at the supermarket so Gil would have food in the house while I was in the hospital. I felt better, which was almost unbelievable and I thought, well I can handle this, and went on, stoic and resigned, I guess, couldn't call it exactly hopeful, until this morning, no it began already yesterday. Out of nowhere, I was folding the laundry, warm from the dryer, and then there was nothing in front of me. No images, no senses, no hope, a vast, or even dense, *is that possible*, emptiness. I knew I had reached the end of possibility. No matter what the official prognosis, and to inject something upbeat into this dank monologue, they, the all-important doctors, are hopeful and confident that they have "gotten it all," my life is over. Or, at the very least, this life I've been living is over. So how can I have left what no longer exists?

"Good question." I stroke the dog's long thick fur and feel my legs under her head begin to tingle from the "dead weight of her," I say out loud, as if drunk, my thoughts suddenly transformed into words erupting into the outer world. I thought long and hard about Gil's gun, the one he straps to his leg during the day. It would have to be at night or on a Saturday when he's not at work. Easy enough to go into the dead baby's room to blow my brains out. Messy but efficient. Gil will hire someone to scrub down the walls. But part of me still wants to live, though I can't say why. I certainly don't want to hurt anyone else, though sometimes I wish Gil would go away, very, extremely, permanently. He either denies or submits to his pain—either way, there's no place for me in it.

"The anesthesiologist was held up," I begin to tell the highway the story anyway. Who gives a fuck if it's listening. "The operation was scheduled for 10 and it was already noon. First Gil scolded the nurse who had prepped me for not getting the department head involved. Then when he found the doctor he hammered at him, his words relentless and cold, for the hospital's gross insensitivity and mismanagement. And you could understand his point of view." I allow myself a few hand motions to accentuate the narrative. "We had suffered enough already. Delays were unendurable. And the nurse who was replacing my IV bag agreed with him. But, she added, he should keep the anxiety and troubleshooting to himself. 'Out there,' she spoke firmly and kindly to him, but pointed hard toward the hospital corridor, 'not in here. She's going through enough. Here you speak softly, tell her everything'll be all right.' And she stroked the blanket under which I lay quietly. Gil smiled sheepishly, a little boy reprimanded." Oh, it was grand.

I had no intention of killing this dog today. I am not that out of control. I saw her from a distance. She was standing by the side of the road, head held high, tail alert, like Lassie scanning the horizon for Timmy. I loved that dog and watched her daily on TV. I longed for one of my own. Not a collie necessarily, but a relationship with a loyal and brave dog. When I saw this large brown dog, standing roadside, an overriding anxiety punched at my gut. I always feel this whenever I see a dog near moving cars. Move away, I said aloud. Don't come closer. And then she bounded across the two-lane highway, hitting the car in front of me and then rolling under mine.

When I was seven, my parents gave in and bought my brother and me our own puppy, a small terrier for Manhattan apartment living. Then too silly and small to know better, Toto ran onto the West Side Highway and into a car as if into the arms of a loving child. My father wouldn't let us see the broken body when we went to the ASPCA on 92nd Street. He identified Toto's remains and gave me the blue metal tag. My desperate prayers as we rode crosstown to the East River had gone unanswered. There had not been a mistake. Toto was dead. Devastated by this betrayal, though again, not permanently put off, I found myself again praying like hell, begging a phenomenon I had come to call God, to not make this ultrasound reading a tragedy. Unanswered prayers are haunting. The void I hurl my wishes into. Toto. *Todo.*

I drag the dog's broken body off the shoulder and look for something to dig a grave with. I cannot possibly drive off and leave her to become a diminishing mound of fur and bones in the undignified open. There's already way too much road kill: cats, dogs, foxes, mole rats, birds, jackals. I see them daily on my way to work; the slow transformation into dust. The work of the grave displayed. It is taking me a long time with the sharp stone I've chosen for this work, but I don't care. I'm not rushing anywhere. It's already very hot at ten in the morning and I'm panting hard, flushed from exertion, with inertia. The radio announcer may have mentioned a sandstorm from the Sahara. Maybe that's why the day is yellow. I do not hear a car stopping. "I can help you," a voice says to me, and I am surprised at how unsurprised I am. I turn slowly and see a man in an army uniform standing beside his car, trunk popped open, a shovel in his hand.

"Thanks," I say and reach out to take the shovel.

"Rest, and drink some water." He hands me the water bottle in his other hand. "Look how red you are."

I take the water bottle automatically, drink two long sips. Water dribbles down my chin and onto my chest. It cools me a little. I am sweating so much my shirt swaddles me, advertising my distended belly. I sit down in the shade of his car and watch how he methodically digs into the dry earth. With minimal, graceful movements he moves the dirt from the emerging pit to one side. A few moments later, his uniform too is stuck to him and the grave is nearly done. "Here, now you rest," I rise and place my hand on the handle of the shovel. I want to finish the job. I need to. But he resists. We look at each other directly for the first time and I see myself vaguely in the reflection of his black eyes. "Please, let me finish. It's important to me." I turn my head slightly, uncomfortable in his steady gaze. But still he resists. I let go, self-conscious and horrified by the image of me in his eyes: mad, flushed frizzy-haired, a sweaty shirt against a swollen form. He wears his stinking shirt so well. He is young and still calm. Eyes like midnight. Hair like cropped wheat. A body that digs graves in minutes, a mouth that might kiss some of the pain away.

I turn abruptly and walk toward his car, murmuring. "Desire. And shame." I'm ill. Withering. More than a decade older than this GI Joe. He's the fucking boy scout helping the old woman cross the street. I walk past his car and along the shoulder's edge, afraid the rage in me will erupt and I'll be vicious when he's trying to be kind.

"You want to help fill?" His voice breaks me.

"Certainly," I say, more shame burning me up. Of course he has seen me speaking to myself. I want to cut at the soft patience in his voice. Am I so pathetic and he so the mitzvah-loving Rambo? Am I the good deed of the day: helping this wacko bury a dog she ran over? With too much gusto I take the shovel and push dirt in over the dog's body. It doesn't thud the way I expect it to. I start at one side and methodically watch as the back, the tail and then the legs, torso, and finally the head are covered with a thin layer of earth. Humbled, my rage subsides some.

"I still expect a reaction from her, a shaking free, a what-the-hell-do-you-think-you're-doing-covering-me-with-dirt yowl, you know what I mean. It's that stillness that's awful." I look at him, I can't help myself, I feel the look, the words, they're coming out, I'm erupting and the lava is scorching.

Where was the baby buried, was it buried, why wouldn't they let me bury him near my father in Jerusalem? Children of the dead, in the Hasidic sections of Jerusalem's cemeteries, are not allowed to stand by the open grave, the man in charge told me and my brother at our father's funeral. So I never got a chance to cover him with dirt, tuck him in for a long good night. And I didn't argue. I didn't want to hear the thud I expected to hear when the dirt hit bottom. Enough that I had seen the body being lowered. Which is why they wouldn't let me see the baby. Drugged me and told Gil, too traumatic. But even on my morphine cloud I screamed that I wanted to see him.

"I helped bury my best friend last month," the young man says. I think I see tears rim his eyes. Saccharine clichés molest me. But his eyes do look like dark pools I want to swim in. "He was killed near the Lebanese border on a day when they gave me leave. Just for twenty-four hours. And I was supposed to be with him that day." He stares down at the covered dog.

"I know that supposed to." He takes the shovel from me and in a few deliberate strokes, furious and grievous, finishes with the grave. He throws the shovel into the car and slams the trunk closed.

"Now what?" he asks me.

"What do you mean what?" I cannot imagine what more there is.

"We're both soaked, stinking, and I can't just bury a dog with someone and say goodbye."

"Why not?" I say, feeling the lava lap at my mouth and I have to laugh at it. "I just buried a baby and said goodbye to a husband." I begin to laugh harder. I even burst out with laughter. I am not crazy, not yet, and the pain is stalking me. And I can't cry. He looks at me, shocked is it? "You serious? You're not pregnant? So casual about it, God, what's wrong with you then?"

"Hell, I'm going to die. We all are, to let you in on a little secret that was just broadcast to me on my own private cosmic earphones. Anyway, who asked you to stop . . . and help and who knows what the fuck you expect from me now and what you think we just did beyond bury an ugly dog that was stupid enough to run into the middle of the road with tons of metal flying in her direction at 120 kilometers an hour." I want to hit this man,

I want to bite him, piss on him, and fuck him. I run into my car and start the engine. He follows, looking like some shit-kicking cop in Mississippi (I have been on too many Southern back roads to resist the temptation of this image). He places his hands on the open window.

"I want you to follow me. I'm going to turn left at the next intersection and then right, toward the beach."

He is missing the mirrored sunglasses, but I see myself when I look at him anyway. He backs away slowly and I notice how the crease in his fatigues is gone, the dark boots dull, the belt on his hips slung a bit too low. When he starts driving, I follow, a metal shard directed by a magnet. We drive in procession, slowly, cautiously, past Nahariya's one-light intersection and on to a small road along the beach. He turns off to Achziv and I realize I don't have to continue but do anyway. I pull up next to him in the empty parking area. I don't know what I am doing, but I haven't known that for days already.

He comes out of the car wearing a clean T-shirt and I can't not notice how beautiful he is. Am I too old to be longing for youth this way? Probably not at thirty-five, but I am bloated like an aged crone, and feel bitter and brittle. Just missing a few warts, the cackle's already begun.

"Let's go to the water," he says, taking my elbow and guiding me over the rocks and the sand. I am limp and tense and don't know how else to understand the strain and longing for oblivion engulfing me. The sea is so clear it is unsettling. The sand ripples symmetrically on the bottom. The water takes me and I keep walking. My clothes pull away and fill with water which eddies around me, chilly and light. Not to drown, but to feel my smallness in each wave. I lay on my back and float like my grandmother, lulled by the waves during an acute attack of pain, only her heart broke, the springs popped, and it was over. Mine breaks with each moment, again and again, with every breath. I think of her lying face up to the sun in the water at Gordon beach, in Tel Aviv, the lifeguard watching her morph into inanimation. This is the same water, the same shoreline 150 kilometers north. In many other places in the world, this distance wouldn't be the other end of the country, but considered the same beach. And for me, raised with the Eastern Seaboard as a reference, it is the same beach.

My baby died in saltwater. My grandmother died in saltwater. It is good enough for me. I feel I am drifting quickly and it takes a moment to realize the man is pulling me to shore by my heel. I do not resist. I don't care to live but I can't deny his need to rescue. When I feel the sand against my shoulders, I sit up briefly. The beach is empty, midweek in May, and like always, is magnificent. The gravelly sand runs up to the Phoenician ruins, that forgotten port of call. At the waterline, and for the first time in weeks, I lie on my stomach. He sits beside me. What's there to say? Mercifully he knows this. He begins to untangle my hair, to lift it from my neck where it has become knotted in the thick rubber band. His hands are cool and clever and I wonder if he is a medic. But I won't ask. I don't want to know. Maybe this is my last tango, and no name is a crucial element. No biography. No words, just one body with the other, giving form to pain. Have I already ruined it by telling him about the baby? But I was vague enough about the cancer and didn't mention Gil by name.

I roll over on my back. The man lifts his hands and places them quietly in his lap. "Where was your friend from?" I ask.

"You wouldn't know him," he answers matter-of-factly. "You're not from here."

I want to protest, but don't have the energy to. I am from here, just not originally. I sat, gas mask ready, in my sealed room during the Gulf War. I say goodbye twice a year to a husband who still has an active reserve duty. I am at the same risk as everyone else that the next bomb will go off near me, on the bus, in a café. I was hoping to bring a baby boy into this world, my destiny bound to that of the place.

I watch the cloudless sky move. Bands of blue headed in the same direction. "You know," I sit up, "about the submarines that patrol the coast? Soldiers know things like that." I notice that his dog tags have fallen to the side. I wonder if they are hot like the sand. I want to lift them and do after a moment. Like a blind person my fingertips feel the letters in relief. I will not look at his name. He tugs at my hand and I lay back down beside him. Not touching. Not not touching. I can feel when he begins to cry. Hesitantly, but not quietly. I put my arms around him and despite the anguish suffocating me, know this man, fifteen years my junior, this boy really, still needs to feel there is something worth breathing for. I hold him closer, rock him, and like a puppy he nuzzles his head into my neck. I hold him even tighter and lick tears from the corners of his eyes.

"I'm going to the border," I whisper. "I'm going until I'm stopped."

"Don't stop," he breathes out and covers my mouth with his. I am lost, I am found, I am falling into warmth. He reaches under me and wraps my legs around him. This is not a prelude to penetration. This is bind me, this is shield me. I squeeze as hard as I can, wondering if the periscope of a submarine has us in the viewfinder, and with fingers desperate to enclose, grasp his metal dog tags. I cover his name with my fist and his mouth with mine. His tears don't stop. "Don't stop," I breathe out, "don't stop," and he wets us with loss, we are lost in the saltwater of beginnings, of ends. I open my shirt so he can suckle, a mother's son on his way to battle.

Probabilities

R yan proposed on Valentine's Day, 2009, arriving home with his lunch pail and one red rose, the twins jumping and giggling and clapping. Did the girls attach some significance to one red rose? Had he been watching reality TV with them on those nights when Jane was at the high school trying to teach color theory and abstract interpretation to folks who wouldn't paint a rose without first counting every petal? Even with Ryan's income from his plumbing business, his pickup truck now parked in her driveway, Jane couldn't quit working, at the very least to remind herself that he wasn't her husband, wasn't the girls' father, she was still responsible. But if his idea of watching them while she taught adult-ed evening classes was to turn on *The Bachelor* (or was it *The Bachelorette*?), then she might not, in fact, be very responsible in the choosing-a-new-father department.

Hadassah stage-whispered, "The box, where's the box?" And Esther actually reached her hands into Ryan's pants pockets from behind, while he stood at the kitchen sink scrubbing fingers black with grease from installing toilets all day at the new over-fifty-five condos across town. Valentine's Day, 2009, was a Saturday, but plumbers work on Saturdays, and Jane had taken her girls to ballet that morning, not to Shabbat at shul. They were still in their tutus, pushing and shoving in an un-ballerina-like way for a turn at Ryan's pockets. So, they knew what was coming. He'd apparently brought them in on his plan. Sweet and simultaneously scary, as if they were ganging up on her.

The box proved to hold a ring from one of Ryan's Irish great-grandmothers, a speck of a diamond set in Art Deco filigree. The box itself looked as old as the ring, black velvet worn bare by generations of fingers opening and closing. Inside, Ryan showed her a matching wedding band, a thin circle scattered with tiny diamond chips. Jane's immigrant great-grandmothers hadn't owned diamonds, certainly no engagement rings, and only solid (although equally thin) gold wedding bands, like Jane's first wedding ring, the one Brian had bought her, as per Jewish law, no stones to interrupt the unbroken circle, meant to represent the unbroken course of a marriage.

That ring, Brian's solid wedding band, Jane had finally twisted off one day just this past fall, after Ryan had moved in, October, Yom Kippur actually, blaming swollen fingers from traditional Yom Kippur Indian summer heat. On that day, when she was supposed to have been fasting as the final step toward atonement before being sealed in the so-called Book of Life, she'd been in the kitchen, feeding the girls lunch (bagel with butter for Estee, with cream cheese for Das), unwrapping lox and smoked whitefish in preparation for the evening's traditional break-fast meal (which would have to wait until after sunset, when her mother would arrive from concluding services at synagogue). Ryan had made his own sandwich and eaten it somewhere out of sight, so as not to tempt her, muttering something about the temptations of Christ as he'd left the kitchen. To Ryan, all religion was malarkey.

Brian's ring must still be somewhere in this kitchen right now, as Ryan slipped his new/old engagement ring on Jane's finger. "Does it fit?" "I told you it'd fit." The girls clamored, with giggling and shushing and conspiratorial tugging at Ryan's shirtsleeves. There had apparently been secretive sizing of this ring via stealthy matching with one of Jane's old rings, maybe that very gold band from Brian, which she was sure still lay in the custard cup where she'd left it, in one of these kitchen cabinets, behind a closed door.

Jane had a steak marinating on the counter, instead of the mac-and-cheese or spaghetti that she and the girls had grown used to, before Ryan. It was, after all, Valentine's Day. But he said to put it back in the fridge for tomorrow. "No cooking for you tonight," he said, squeezing her hand with the ring that fit perfectly. "We could go out, but I thought pizza with the girls?" So the girls snacked on his organic blue corn chips that now lived in Jane's pantry, while he showered and headed back out into the bitter February night with damp hair (risking pneumonia, her mother would say) and a fresh shave (an evening shave, don't think what her mother would say about that, the same thing Jane was thinking, anticipating).

He returned with a veggie pizza plus one small plain pizza (in case the girls weren't in the mood for vegetables) and one small white pizza (in case Estee wasn't in the mood for sauce). Also, balloons, which were pink, with *Strawberry Shortcake* and *Happy Birthday!*—not because the store was sold out of Valentine's Day balloons, but because the next day the girls would turn eight.

Brian and Jane had planned to ignore Valentine's Day, after the girls, not to detract from their February 15th birthday, although Brian had never trusted that was really their birthday. "How do we know for sure?" he'd said. "How do they know?" referring to the Korean orphanage and the mystery of the girls' birth halfway around the world. They were six months old when they'd arrived, or were they? "When my great-grandfather came from Russia," Brian had said, "he picked Christmas for his birthday. And his name was Jacob, not Jesus." Despite his doubts, Brian had insisted, "Let it be their day, their week. We can celebrate Valentine's Day any time, maybe in August, like a half birthday. Who's Saint Valentine to us, anyway?" By the following August, Jane had found herself preparing not for a summer Valentine's Day but for her first annual public kaddish in shul.

Ryan thought the same as Brian, but different (like their names), figuring out how to make Valentine's Day—and his proposal—about Jane, but also about the girls. "A birthday gift," he whispered in bed that night, reaching around, in the dark, to feel for the ring on her finger, "for all of us." Then he ran his hand up the length of her arm, her shoulder, the bumps of her spine. They'd learned how to make love, quietly, with Esther and Hadassah asleep across the hall.

"That's the same name, you know," Brian had said way back when those first photos had arrived from Korea, scrawny twins wrapped in one blanket, like a tiny two-headed Janus, God of beginnings. "Doesn't Hadassah mean Esther in Hebrew?"

"I know," Jane had said. "From the Hebrew for myrtle." She'd recited from the midrash in her baby-name book. "Just as a myrtle has a sweet taste and a bitter smell, so too the biblical Esther was good and listened ('sweet') to the righteous Mordechai but was also strong and fierce ('bitter') against the evil Haman." The best of both worlds for those girls. And they'd needed it, the sweetness and the strength.

"You like him because of his name," her mother had said, only once, about Ryan, who carried a toolbox instead of a laptop. "It reminds you of Brian." Ryan had no idea that Hadassah meant Esther in Hebrew, and if he thought about the Ryan/Brian similarity, he was careful never to mention it.

The phone startled Jane at 6:30 the next morning. "You didn't know it would be me?" her mother said. "As if I wouldn't call on their birthday?" Jane's mother often called early on Sundays, her way of reminding, without saying, that Jane ought to enroll the girls in Sunday school.

"I didn't know anything, Mom," Jane said. "I was asleep." The girls came running in their pajamas, squealing "Grandma!" They knew who would call on their birthday morning. The ringing of the phone didn't frighten them.

"Do you love him?" her mother asked when she called back later that day.

"What is this, *Fiddler on the Roof*?" Jane replied.

"Can I help with dinner?" her mother changed the subject. She always came for the girls' birthday.

"Could you pick up the cake at Stop & Shop? I ordered it for after 3:00, so they'd be sure to bake it fresh today."

"I'm making babka," her mother said. "Chocolate, their favorite. Already on the second rise." Then, "Oh well, never mind. Two girls, two cakes. It'll be perfect." Jane's mother sometimes forgot to be careful with Jane, but then she remembered.

In the early years, before Ryan, maybe even before that first kaddish, her mother had held secret conversations with the rabbi, secret until she'd started dropping tidbits of his advice into otherwise casual conversations with Jane about the price of cornflakes or weren't the girls old enough for potty training. To remarry ("Someday," her mother had always stressed, "I'm only imagining, it never hurts to think ahead"), she would need a beit din, a Jewish court, to certify that her husband was no longer alive. This was a problem for the 9/11 widows. The beit din could not rely on probabilities. Lacking a body, a "corporeal body" (Had the rabbi really said those words? Had her mother really repeated them to Jane?), the judges would need witnesses, evidence, proof beyond supposition that Brian was dead.

He had, after all, escaped once. Of that, Jane had evidence, one phone call, Brian's I'm okay phone call, his I'm okay recorded inside a machine that she would never throw out, although the technology to replay it would surely someday be as extinct as Brian. And what of the second phone call, Brian's I'm going back up call, the call she had answered, the call she'd waited frantically by the phone to be sure not to miss? Of that Jane had no corroborating evidence.

Maybe those rabbis, surely all men, would think she should have let the machine pick up that second call, too, should have heard Brian's final words only through the distance of magnetic tape, just so that now she'd have proof. But proof of what? Proof he'd started back up, proof he'd said he was starting back up, still not enough to prove he had actually died, been disintegrated, disappeared into what most people referred to as thin air, a sickeningly wrong cliché.

As if Jane hadn't wished, night after night after sleepless night, that the opposite could somehow be proven true. That he hadn't gone back up. That he was lying unconscious or amnesiac in a hospital somewhere, would one day awaken like Sleeping Beauty and walk back through her door. Or maybe he'd had second thoughts about parenthood, even about marriage, had grabbed his chance, fled to South America, anywhere, somewhere alive. She'd forced herself to figure out this new Facebook, had posted pictures of the girls—maybe he'd see what he was missing and come home—until her mother pointed out the risk of exposing her girls to the public. "They're rich girls now," her mother had said, "or at least that's what people think. And there are a lot of crazies out there." Jane could never imagine suddenly reversing course, concentrating all her energy on wishing to prove Brian dead.

Of course, all this was only relevant if she were to remarry a Jew. Even then, would she bother with a *beit din*? Jewish law hadn't exactly kept its promises to her in the past.

After carrying in both cakes from the car in winter's dark that made late afternoon feel like midnight, before even kissing the girls and giving them their presents, Jane's mother pulled off her gloves, took Jane's warm hand in her two cold ones, to admire the ring. "It's lovely," she said. "Just let me get my glasses. Where did I put my purse?"

"It's still on your shoulder, Mom," Jane said, reclaiming her hand. "I've gotta put on my boots." She'd shoveled a path to the patio grill, for the steak, which would suffice for the three adults, since the girls wanted their favorite spaghetti (plain for Estee, with Ragu for Das). Jane never broiled in her kitchen, not even in February, not even with the exhaust fan on for the smoke.

"You should only be happy," her mother soothed.

The girls ate in the Disney princess dresses her mother had brought for their birthday. Then they blew out candles on both cakes. "I thought for Purim," her mother said. "The dresses. They could both be Queen Esther."

"Hadassah's working on her own costume," Jane said, "binoculars out of toilet-paper tubes. I think she's going as a bird watcher." Jane had never admitted to Brian that she'd picked the names Esther/Hadassah at least in part because of her memories of dressing up as Queen Esther on Purim. Her mother had once found an old wedding dress at a thrift shop, and, with tucking and hemming, that dress had lasted through years of Sunday-school Purim parades. One year, Jane had been allowed to add one of her mother's old pillbox hats, once her pearls.

After dinner, while her mother tried to wash off green, possibly dangerous supermarket frosting from the girls' fingers, and lips and tongues, Jane and Ryan brought out their gifts—art supplies, grown-up art supplies, selected by Jane with care, paints and oil pastels and watercolor pencils, all organized in fishing-tackle boxes, just like hers. Her fishing-tackle box had been Ryan's suggestion, one day after he'd first moved in, when he'd been moving around her art stuff in the basement, looking for a place for his tools and table saw.

"Let's paint," they insisted. "Now."

"Just one," Jane said. "In the basement, then bed. There are new easels, wait 'til you see. Kiss Grandma goodbye first."

"I'll help with the dishes," her mother said, carrying plates to the sink. "Tell me about those condos of yours, Ryan. Should I sell the house and buy one?" At least she didn't call him Brian.

Esther, who refused to take off her new Cinderella dress, but also didn't want to get it dirty, drew a flower garden with watercolor pencils, to be brushed over with water tomorrow. And Hadassah, back in jeans and a polo, sleeves pushed up to reveal golden brown arms even in February, painted a family: a mother, a father, and two children, both girls. Without help from Jane, she rummaged through her box and found the tube of raw sienna Jane had bought—not perfect, but better than any kids-paint-set color for painting the girls' faces and also their hands sticking out from their princess dresses.

After Jane's mother finally went home, while Ryan emptied the dishwasher, Jane tucked the girls into bed, too late for a bath, Estee's hands still green from frosting, Das's streaked with every color of paint, what would the teacher say tomorrow? Later, in her own bed with Ryan, after one more midnight tuck-in and whispered happy birthday, she lay awake wondering where their mother was tonight, their other mother, wishing she was the one who could remember the day of their birth.

"We'll go shopping on Saturday," Ryan interrupted, his arms encircling her.

"Huh?"

"For a solid gold band, for the wedding."

"When did she get to you?"

"Who?"

"My mother." Jane rolled over to face him in the dark. "When did she talk to you? I should've known why she stayed to help with the dishes."

"Don't," he said, putting one finger to her lips. The backs of his hands were smooth and hairless from all the time they spent in water, but his fingertips were calloused. He wouldn't be wearing a wedding ring, as Brian had, too dangerous in his line of work—he'd once known a man who'd somehow snagged his wedding ring on a power snake and nearly lost a finger.

"Rabbis and their rules," Jane said. "If I don't care, why should you?"

"It's a nice idea," he said, "the circle of life."

"First *Fiddler on the Roof*, now a Disney movie?"

"Huh? I'm serious," he said, tightening the circle of his arms around her body. "Forever."

Ryan wasn't her mother, and he wasn't Brian. He was himself. He rotated her tires and cleaned her gutters and taught her girls to flip pancakes. He'd built the girls' new easels from scratch, in her basement, their basement—professional-looking A-frame wooden easels measured to just the right height for eight-year-olds. And in bed, after making love, he hummed, sometimes "Total Eclipse of the Heart," as if he'd known Jane since she was twelve. He would be as foreign to those *beit din* judges, in their long beards and side curls, as they were to Jane. But he wasn't foreign to Jane, not anymore.

"Okay," she said, recognizing the contours of his face in the shadows, "but your ring, too." She would wear his great-grandmother's wedding band, with its diamonds so tiny maybe her mother wouldn't notice. But if a solid gold band, for the ceremony, might give them a chance at forever, who was she to say no?

Sound Effects

D espite her best effort to open them soundlessly, the carved wooden doors to the sanctuary announced Lila's late arrival with a squeal that would have done the ram's horn proud. Rosh Hashanah services were well under way. People looked up, glad for the distraction or annoyed by it. Lila made her way between the crowded rows, past knees and ankles and purses, mouthing "Excuse me" on her way to the empty seat next to her husband, Gary. Saving seats was frowned upon, and now her husband frowned upon her.

Lila was late to the evening service because she'd been to rehearsal first and hadn't left as early as she'd promised she would. She'd been offered a small but juicy role as a daffy nanny in a creaky British mystery. The theater company was semiprofessional, a notch above her previous associations, and she wanted to prove herself. Gary had started bugging her about getting a grown-up job in the real world, and this company was going to pay her—in actual money, rather than comp tickets. Lila wanted to appear professional. Intimidated by the director, she hadn't wanted to leave in mid-scene, so she'd waited until a break in the rehearsal. No sense getting to services on time, anyway. That would mean even more chair time, more boredom, more attention-deficit comments from Gary. Now she had to gear down from her rush from the theater to the synagogue—had that last traffic light been yellow? Perhaps yellowish-red? She'd been rehearsing a poor-me spiel in case a cop stopped her. (Your objective for this scene is to get the cop not to write the ticket. She'd done it in acting class. She was just the tiniest bit disappointed that she hadn't gotten the opportunity to try it out live.) She should have taken her time. Gary was just as annoyed as he would have been five minutes later.

Lila was late to everything but performances. She'd been late to most

of her tutoring appointments with Gary, back when he was a serious engineering major who waited patiently, explained the math, told her what to study and how to study, and then called her the morning of the exam to make sure she hadn't overslept. She had. Heard in bed, Gary's voice had an intimacy over the phone that it rarely had in person. She liked being the only one privy to that voice, so she married it. She'd been just a half a minute late to her own wedding, having lost a shoe just before she set off down the aisle. Under her wedding gown, one nervous foot had slipped its *peau de soie* pump off and on and off again. It was the only cue she'd ever missed. Gary's eyes had held fear, relief, and annoyance in equal measure, the emotion coloring them a deeper green. Halfway down the aisle, she'd blown him a barely perceptible kiss. He'd smiled a barely perceptible smile.

Lila opened her prayer book and assumed the glazed expression of a congregant who'd been there all hour. This, too, was an acting exercise she'd done before—a little concentration and she was in character. She avoided meeting Gary's eyes. She ignored his predictable tapping on his watch—three times with a teacherly forefinger. She even managed to resent his intrusion into her character's psychic space, where prayer might otherwise be happening. Her character, the congregant, might well resent his bristling indignation. She continued the exercise by giving the congregant a name—Shirley Glasstone—and a history—newly arrived from out of town—maybe St. Louis. Fortyish. About a decade and some older than Lila. Divorced. A lawyer. An urbane woman suspicious of this southern synagogue with its small congregation and its disheveled rabbi. Lila sat up straighter—Shirley's power suit was structured, after all—and crossed her legs as if they ended in pumps instead of in Lila's inappropriate sandals. Shirley's movements were purposeful and clean. When the congregation read responsively, Lila gave Shirley the director's voice. Every statement sounded like a command. "May my prayer find favor with You" was not a supplication in Shirley's confident reading of it. "Blessed are You" sounded as if she was conferring the blessing rather than describing it. Ah. The text said You, not Him. Shirley approved of the gender-neutral language in the new prayer book. Not such a backwater after all. Shirley glanced at the serious man sitting next to her, took in his dark hair, carefully arranged to minimize the prematurely receding hairline, his erect posture, the intensity of his focus on the service. Not bad looking—broad shoulders, strong jawline, nice green eyes. But that frown. Shirley assumed with a mental *tsk* that he resisted the modernization of the prayers. Actually, that was cheating; Lila knew that Gary hated the gender-neutral language, but would Shirley guess that? What would Shirley see? Shirley saw a young man who had never really been young. Not someone who'd welcome her into this new town, this new synagogue. As if to confirm Shirley's assumption, Gary glared at Lila.

Lila tired of Shirley and let her go. Lila fidgeted and marked time, doing the arithmetic necessary to ascertain when they were a third of the way through the service and which page was the halfway point, taking into account that the sermon was a variable. She ran her thumb along the page edges, creating a quiet rustle. Her foot bobbled at the end of her crossed leg, missing the cuff of Gary's pants by an inch or so. Like a child, she weighed her chances of slipping away to the bathroom against Gary's disdain or his anger.

She was here as a concession to her husband, whose observance of his religion was a formal occasion rather than a come-as-you-were. He hadn't been particularly religious when she married him four years ago, but the death of his father last year had created a vacuum that Gary filled by trying to become his father. He started going to services regularly. He stopped eating moo shoo pork and BLTs. He wangled a nomination to the synagogue board and carefully planned his route to its presidency, a post his father had filled more than once. Lila was not an asset in this campaign. She came to services late. She didn't pay attention. She didn't schmooze with the right people. She was cast against type. Lila considered Gary's newfound reverence a regrettable instance of bait and switch. Lila hadn't liked Gary's father.

Before his father died, Gary had been fun. Well, more fun. He indulged her appetites for bad science fiction flicks, White Castle, picnics in bed, morning sex. He ran her lines with her. He gave her unusual flowers on opening nights—a spiky Asian mum, a single bird-of-paradise. He went with her to ballroom dance lessons. He was amused by her stories of backstage disasters. He called her "Lollygag" or "La-la." Now, he started every conversation with "Grow up, Lila" and worked the Sunday crossword by himself.

Gary nudged Lila back into the service. The congregation had begun a page of responsive reading in English. Responsive readings annoyed Lila. She didn't like joining in the plodding cadence of the congregation. She felt herded, forced into choices not her own. Sometimes she tried to imagine herself as part of a Greek chorus, but even then, she found the congregation's phrasing uninspired. So Lila read at her own pace, pausing to accent a word, speeding up to energize a phrase, varying her volume to create drama.

"Behave yourself," Gary whispered. "People will hear you. It's not a performance."

Lila tapped her prayer book three times, mimicking Gary's impatience. She kept reading aloud in her own rhythm but she reduced her volume. It was probably extra-sacrilegious to piss off your husband intentionally during the High Holy Days.

The congregation's previous rabbi had barked and yapped, sounding like a border collie rounding up the congregants' attention and guiding it to the front. The new rabbi didn't bully them into paying attention. Lila regarded her—her unruly gray hair, the screen of tan over a kind but unpampered face, her motherly patience. Her robes and tallis hung awkwardly on her tall, gaunt frame. She reminded Lila of a windblown scarecrow. The rabbi seemed to be an old woman with a young woman's voice. It was lively, with an accent of some sort. Maybe Canadian. Maybe British or Australian; if so, she'd been in this country for a while. Her vowels were flat and she hit her consonants crisply and quickly, but she slurred her Ss a bit. A good voice, a voice like sparkling water. For the next congregational response, Lila read with flatter vowels, crisper consonants, slurred Ss. She listened carefully to the rabbi's forceful delivery and matched her own pace to the rabbi's. Each succeeding response bore a closer resemblance to the rabbi's voice.

Gary hissed at her between his teeth. "Stop that! People will hear you making fun of the rabbi."

Lila wasn't making fun of the rabbi. She was studying her. She liked the energetic pace of her voice, the sigh of her Ss seeming to linger after she had moved on to other sounds. Once she had matched her voice to the rabbi's, she could ride it, carried along as if she had mounted a swift, smooth-gaited horse. It was a little dizzying, but exhilarating, too, this ride on the rabbi's voice. When it was over, Lila felt windblown and clean and calm. The hour had swept by.

Afterwards, in the parking lot, Gary started in. "Just what do you think you were doing in there? People were staring. Immature. Inappropriate. Typical." Without waiting for her answer, Gary took off across the parking lot to buttonhole Ron Spielman, the current synagogue president. Lila pitied the older man, who would get an earful about some trivial synagogue matter, which Gary would present with the detail of a mechanical proof. Lila got into her car and just to spite Gary, peeled out with a squeal of her tires. One more thing to atone for.

Lila was deep into a script, armored with industriousness, when Gary got home. The crunch of his wheels on the driveway had been her cue: Back door slams. Enter husband. "We've been on a bit of a foray—I took the children belly dancing," she offered Gary in her best British nanny accent. Gary, however, intended to finish the parking-lot scene, a scene for which she had not rehearsed.

"Put down that ridiculous script and listen. This is serious. You ought to be ashamed of yourself, making fun of the rabbi! During Rosh Hashanah, no less." No less was a phrase Gary's father had favored, proof that two negatives didn't always cancel each other out.

"Don't tell me how to worship." Lila summoned Shirley to borrow her confidence, her resolve.

"You're not worshipping. You're playing. It's embarrassing and rude. You're disturbing people. You're disturbing me."

"It was a kind of worship." Lila was startled; this assertion seemed to be a gleaming truth, something to treasure. "That was the first time I ever felt anything in synagogue, anything besides restlessness. I felt connected. I felt part of it. I wasn't making fun of the rabbi. I was being her."

"I cannot deal with you when you're like this," Gary said slowly, each word ringing like a distant gong.

"Like what?" Lila yelled. "Like myself?" The angrier Gary got, the quieter he got. His calm thickened the air until she couldn't breathe. Why couldn't he just yell like other people? Instead, he walked out of the room, a dramatic exit worthy of an actor. He had stolen the scene.

Lila returned to her script—isn't that what Shirley would have done? She raised her volume at his footsteps on the stairs, throwing her voice against the closed door of their bedroom, but she got no response. It was surprisingly taxing to be daffy and British just now. She found herself in the rabbi's voice rather than in her nanny character's, and just because it felt good, she finished her scene in flat vowels and Canadian consonants. A rabbi was sort of a nanny for the congregation, wasn't she? She could use that notion to build her nanny character. Eventually, she fell asleep curled in the chair with the script on her lap. She crept upstairs to bed in the half light of early dawn.

Lila awoke the next morning to a silent house, and leapt up, heart pounding. She called, "Gary?" once in her own voice, once in the nanny's voice, once in the rabbi's voice, and finally in her own voice again. No answer. It was just past ten; the morning service for the New Year had already started. Lila sped through the task of getting ready—a quick change backstage between scenes. The only thing that slowed her down was her search for her pumps. Her sandals languished under the couch.

At the sanctuary entrance, she waited until another latecomer creaked the heavy door open. Lila slipped in just behind him. Gary was an upright presence in the second row, sitting next to Ron Spielman. He did not turn at the sound of the creaking door. There was no empty seat beside him. Lila was free to leave—Exit, synagogue left. Instead, she took a seat in the back, with the other strays. She opened her prayer book, dismissed Shirley and the nanny, and waited for the rabbi to begin.

Today the rabbi's voice soothed Lila, like a mother's hand across her brow. Calm and still, Lila was carried through the service and on into the sermon. She didn't cross and uncross and recross her legs. She didn't dangle her shoe from her foot. She didn't riffle the pages of the prayer book. She just sat and listened, and eventually Lila heard the rabbi's words as well as her voice. "Make it right" was woven through the sermon. She had the week between Rosh Hashanah and Yom Kippur to make things right. "Use your gifts" was another of the sermon's admonitions. And suddenly Lila knew what to do.

She moved silently up the aisle and slipped into a lone unoccupied seat two rows behind Gary. As the congregation moved into prayer, Lila concentrated and found Gary's voice. She matched her pitch to his, her cadence to his, her phrasing to his. It was not a smooth entry, not at all like riding the rabbi's voice, but she managed, despite feeling like a trespasser. Gary's voice was heavy and slow. He forced it forward through the words, but Lila could feel it moving back, back to kaddish, back to his father's funeral, back to the moment when he swallowed his unshed tears. The weight of Gary's grief was crushing and Lila dropped out of his voice.

Back in her seat in the sanctuary, Lila took a deep breath. The intimacy of the experience stunned her, and in its aftermath, she felt her resentment loosen its knot. If Gary were a character she was playing, she would have studied him, known his backstory, built into her characterization the undertow of grief. She would have understood his irritability and impatience as a coat he wore that was never warm enough. Just as the rabbi had done for her, Lila could wrap her voice around Gary and warm him. She thought it might still be possible.

The A-Train to Scotland

L izzie noticed her shoes first. Dr. Karen Brown, fiftyish, wiry gray hair cut into a pageboy, no-nonsense dark shirt and trousers, greeted her at the door of her tiny office, offering a hand and a seat. Her open-toed heels were surprisingly stylish, a bright canary yellow peeking out beneath those sensible trousers. Lizzie immediately fell in love with those shoes. She decided this was a good sign.

"I'm going to ask you some questions about your family history," Dr. Brown said in a kind but not overly familiar tone. "Let's start with your parents."

"My mother died of breast cancer, young."

"How young?"

"Forty-one. Well, almost forty-two. She died three weeks before her birthday," she added, a distinction that was becoming increasingly important to her. Though she had always been horrible at math and vastly preferred that someone else figure out the restaurant check, it took Lizzie a nanosecond to tell how many years she was away from turning forty-one.

"That is young," Dr. Brown murmured. She was sketching a family tree on a pad of paper over a cluttered desk—a collection of framed photos sat next to a high, precarious pile of folders (patients' files? containing what sort of news? Lizzie wondered). She gazed out the window onto the fat silver tubes of the ventilation system, spouting smoke, looking menacing, practically medieval. Dr. Brown's office was located in the Atran building of Mt. Sinai, which Lizzie well knew how to pronounce, but privately, she called the A-train, greatly preferring this jaunty, jazzy variation.

It had been Lizzie's idea to test for the BRCA mutation. She had read an op-ed in the *New York Times* on the subject. Lizzie had heard of the genetic test before—the knowledge floated in the recesses of her brain along with so many scraps, like how to change a flat tire or how the word "corn" technically referred to a country's biggest import—but she had never considered taking it. Reading the piece in the *Times*, written by a woman who had also watched her mother die of breast cancer, a woman, bone-chillingly to Lizzie, very much like herself—Ashkenazi Jew, mid-thirties, single, professionally successful, wanting a family—well, that factoid shot to the front of her brain and refused to budge. She read the article again and again—phrases like "genetic legacy" and "predisposition to cancer" and "preventative mastectomy" lodged tightly beneath her rib cage. She reminded herself that she was a lawyer; her livelihood depended on facts. She had always placed her faith in them, professionally and personally. If a mutation was found in the 39th amino acid position of a protein of hers—if this indeed was her genetic inheritance—well, then. Unlike her mother (dead at forty-one) or her great-aunt (fifty-three), she could be the first woman in her family who could actually do something about it.

Lizzie's gynecologist had given her two names of genetics counselors—Karen Brown at Mt. Sinai and someone at Sloan-Kettering. But Sloan was where her mother had been treated, and for the more than fifteen years that Lizzie had been living in Manhattan, she had done her best to avoid York Avenue and 68th Street, the site of the cancer center, so forget about walking through its doors. Plus: how could bad news be delivered by someone whose name was as unmemorable and innocuous-sounding as Dr. Karen Brown?

So she had called Dr. Brown's office. Close to two years ago.

The cancellation of her first appointment was legitimate, Lizzie liked to think. It came during a mad crush at work—a dizzying close where she and a handful of other associates lived in the conference room around the clock. By the time she came around to rescheduling, it was autumn, what she later dubbed the fall of her fall from Ben, a time during which they were still engaged, but all she could think about was: *Oh God, I'm making a mistake. This is no time for more bad news.* Then suddenly she was single and then she turned thirty-five and then it was her mother's birthday and then the anniversary of her death, and all of those times felt so horribly wrong too.

Now here she finally was, after the fourth rescheduling. Dr. Brown was explaining about percentages and probabilities. Lizzie's chest hurt.

She glanced at the photos on Dr. Brown's desk. Two little girls, one light haired, one dark, yet unmistakably similar, clearly sisters, mugging for the camera, dressed in fuzzy monkey costumes. They must be her grandkids, Lizzie thought. Dr. Brown must have had kids in her twenties, the age you're *supposed* to have them.

She found herself asking, "What about children?"

"What about them?" Karen Brown asked, although now she was the one nodding.

"I want children," Lizzie said. "I want to have children," she clarified absurdly.

"Then you will," Karen Brown said, in such a crisp authoritative voice that Lizzie felt, if only for a moment, reassured. "We're getting ahead of ourselves. You'll have your bloods drawn; you'll come back for the results; we'll talk more then."

But when Lizzie did indeed return, there was no need for conversation. Karen Brown looked at her file, and cocked her head to the side. Thankfully, she did not sigh. "I'm sorry," she said, looking at Lizzie with startlingly limpid brown eyes.

On Tuesday she flew to Chicago for the day for a meeting. Wednesday found her in Boston. On Friday she left again, this time for Maddy's wedding in Scotland. All this travel was more than fine with Lizzie. She wanted to keep moving.

After a four-hour delay at Heathrow, she finally got off the plane in Aberdeen, as north as north could get ("the Scottish 'sticks,'" her ex-stepmother had cheerfully had called it). In the cab, she passed stolid oil rigs presiding over a glum, graying sea, and undistinguished apartment complexes and squat shopping centers, nothing like the Scotland of her imagination.

She was hungry—well, she was tired, which always made her hungry— and she was tempted to tap the squat-necked driver on the shoulder, ask him to turn around and pull into the Pizza Hut they'd just flown past, and devour several pies on the spot.

Out the window, the Aberdeen streets turned curvier and narrower, more picturesque. Soon the taxi pulled into a cobblestone driveway, leading to an old stone house that might have looked imposing, save for the front double doors painted a bright shade of blue. She paid the driver, collected her things. She headed up the walkway, curtained by blooming roses. The air smelled fragrant and clean. It was past 9 p.m., but it remained light outside, the sky a lovely silvery glow.

She checked into the inn, and the fair-headed porter who looked twelve led her up the polished, uneven stone steps, telling her about the daily tea and the small bar just downstairs. Her room was small, but nicely appointed, with high ceilings and a beautifully carved bed facing a small fireplace. Charming but tasteful, Maddy's taste through and through.

Lizzie kicked off her shoes, a pair of Italian round-toed heels she'd bought on eBay in a fit of panic post-Karen Brown. She lay stomach-down on the bed. She couldn't believe she was here. She couldn't believe much of anything these days.

For nine days she had been nursing the fantasy: Maybe it was a ludicrous mistake at the lab somehow? For nine days, she had told no one of the results: not her father; not Claudia, to whom she used to declare as a teenager, "I'll just cut them off by the time I'm thirty; I'm not going through what my mother went through"; not her sister, who had a 50 percent chance of carrying the faulty gene too. How was she supposed to discuss the matter when the thought of that mutant gene made her feel as if she were being buried alive?

Though her entire body buzzed with exhaustion, she forced herself off the bed, splashed water on her face, crammed her tired feet back in her heels. Time to keep moving.

The small bar off the lobby looked more like a study than a watering hole. It sported a gold patterned carpet that was too soiled to be cheerful and a handful of leather seats beneath a neon sign heralding Woodpecker cider. Lizzie ordered a beer and, from the few food options, an egg salad sandwich. She took up residence at a small table that enabled her to gaze at that enormous, implacable sky, which still hadn't turned to night. The place was empty save two older women, one pear shaped and short, the other tall and hardened, drinking pints of lager.

"You've always been much too hard on Tom," she heard the taller one say.

"Easy for you to say."

A young guy ambled in then, thin and wiry, gingery hair clipped short, wearing dark pants and a wrinkled white shirt. For a moment, Lizzie assumed he was a waiter, but he went up to the bar and ordered a drink in a brogue she barely understood.

Lizzie was about halfway done with her beer and her sandwich that tasted much better than it looked when she heard the shorter woman say, "He's been like this for years, Nicola—*years!*"

"Why can't you be on my side?"

"I am on your side."

"No, you're not; you've never been. It was like this with Michael. Your own sister. It's like Skye all over again."

"Jesus, I was eight years old!" She glared at her sister, her face heavy with recrimination, a lifetime of it, it seemed to Lizzie. *They were sisters?* Lizzie thought as she watched the women hurry out of the bar.

"Watch out for women with too much time on their hands," Lizzie now heard a voice say. It was the ginger-headed guy, the only person left in the bar, looking right at her.

"Really?" Lizzie said into her empty pint glass. She felt like it was men who were always stirring up trouble.

He walked over to her tiny table as if she had offered up the most gracious of invitations. "May I?"

She nodded. He seemed far too young to be so confident.

"You're not from around here, yeah?"

"A real detective." But she was looking at him when she said it, looking at his hands in particular. She had always been a sucker for nice hands. His were strong, expressive, with tapering fingers and clean squared-off nails cut so short she could barely make them out at all. She was looking at his hands too, to avoid looking at his attractive face. He was so young! A good ten years younger than she.

"Neither am I."

"Really? Now that I wouldn't have guessed." And this she meant. He had a thick brogue that to her ear sounded undeniably Scottish, undeniably of this place.

"You think all Scots are alike, yeah? I grew up outside of Glasgow. Nowhere near here. It's as if I assumed that you knew New Mexico just as well as New York, where I'm guessing you're from."

"I am. And I've never been to New Mexico."

"You should go, if only for the sky. I was there last winter, and I fell in love with the sky."

For some reason, this made her blush, this simple declaration of love by a Scotsman for a part of her native land she'd never seen. But instead of asking *why the sky*, which was what she really wanted to know, she asked, "What were you doing in America?"

"I was in New York, yeah, apprenticing, supposedly, to this cabinetmaker who makes these intricate pieces . . ." He trailed off, looking at her. "What brings you to Aberdeen?"

"A wedding, a friend's wedding." At this point, who was Maddy if not a friend?

He simply nodded, murmured something about being here for a celebration too. Could he be here for Maddy's wedding? Could her luck be that good? But when she asked what kind of celebration, he seemed not to hear—or at least pretended he hadn't—and she didn't press the matter. He wasn't asking her questions, for which she was glad. Soon they ordered whiskey. He told her how much he liked New York and Queens in particular, not Woodside, where he lived ("a shit, kind of boring neighborhood"), but places like Long Island City. The guy he apprenticed with was a real asshole, who constantly sent him out to pick up his dry cleaning. But he biked all over and he got to know New York that way, the exhaust mingling with the smell of the water, even fish, as he went over the Brooklyn Bridge . . .

Maybe it was this reference to biking, maybe it was this small flash of Ben who loved to do the same that fueled Lizzie on, or maybe it was the fact that she was older, more seasoned—there were things she simply wanted to know. She reached out, brushing his knuckles. "Wait," she said, as if he were just out the door. "What's your name?"

"Rory." This made him color, ducking his head. "I'm Rory. And you?"

"Lizzie." She held out her hand like the direct American that she was.

"And where do you live, Lizzie?" He dropped her hand and downed the last of his whiskey. Now he was looking out the window.

"Manhattan, the Upper Upper West Side."

"I didn't spend much time there," Rory was now saying, "went to Central Park, biked through it, went up to the Cloisters, that type of thing. But Long Island City—for some reason, I just fell in love with Long Island City. It reminded me of Glasgow, all those factories and the industrial look of it, the empty streets. There's a beauty to it, a ferocious unkind beauty—" He looked up at her now, his pale eyebrows arching high, his wide fresh face so animated. "Have you been to the Noguchi museum, the sculpture museum? That has got to be my favorite place."

Lizzie nodded. "Yeah, I've been there, once." She tried to say it lightly. She and Ben were supposed to get married nearby, in a loft, an airy space run by a charmingly odd woman. The first time they saw the space, they went to the Noguchi museum afterwards. There they had an epic fight. "Why would we get married somewhere so out of the way?" Ben had asked, adding (in a strategic error, Lizzie had thought, if only from a pugilistic point of view) that his mother was going to freak out that her friends would have to find their way to Queens. Lizzie was embarrassed to recall how she'd lost it, saying shrilly, who cares what their parents thought; they were getting married for themselves, who wanted a lot of their parents' friends there whom they barely knew? Blah blah blah. Finally, Ben had sighed and said, "If this is where you want to do it, let's do it here. I just want to marry you." It was a sweet, simple statement, the type of thing she had always longed to hear. And yet, it made her jaw tighten as if she were in imminent danger. They had been together almost two years at that point; Lizzie loved him, she knew that. They were nearly thirty-three, old by many people's standards. (Her grandmother loved to remind Lizzie, "When your mother was your age, she already had two children." Lizzie considered it a triumph that she didn't respond: "Yes, but she was also on the cusp of divorcing.")

Still: Lizzie couldn't breathe. Not when they talked to wedding photographers, not when she tried on dresses, not when they tried to decide if they should hire a DJ or a band. As the wedding date drew closer, Lizzie felt worse. She began to resent Ben's loud, boisterous way of telling stories, the way he constantly had to be the center of attention (God, like her father!). She began to hate the way he overseasoned and put garlic in nearly everything. She went running late at night, offered to be put on a closing at work. Even his hand on the small of her back made her want to scream. (Was this how her mother had felt?) That afternoon, at the Noguchi museum, walking among those strange, monumental forms of polished stone, Lizzie could remember thinking, distinctly and with clarity, *I don't want to be in this relationship anymore. I don't want to be on this planet anymore.* Two months later, after the engagement party on the sixteenth floor of his parents' lakeshore apartment, but before the invitations had gone out, she had ended it altogether.

Now Lizzie was looking at the freckles scattered across Rory's eager face, the blond wisps of eyebrows, the few light hairs above his left cheekbone he'd missed shaving. Ostensibly this was the reason she had called off the engagement, wasn't it? For the freedom to do what she wanted? But it was exhausting, the prospect of starting over, the thought of learning someone else's history. This had been the lesson of the past year, the dates that went nowhere and hook-ups not regretful, exactly, but unsatisfying. The few that charmed her weren't charmed *by* her. No one was as funny as Ben.

Just then a passel of well-dressed people came into the bar, laughing, chatting, ordering drinks, bringing with them a loud welcoming heat. It took Lizzie a moment to realize that Maddy, in a silky green top, pulsed at the center.

"Excuse me," she said to Rory, rising, "I have to—" but as she was saying this, as Maddy was enfolding her in a tight hug, she saw that Rory too was being exclaimed over and hugged, Rory was being clapped on the back by Graham, Maddy's fiancé, of all people.

"You made it!" Maddy exclaimed. "I can't believe you actually came!"

"I wouldn't have missed it," she said, as she watched Graham smile and laugh at something Rory said.

Maddy took note too. "Oh, so you've met Graham's nephew Rory?"

"That I did," Lizzie said, still processing. She would see him tomorrow then; this was not the end.

"He's a sweetheart," Maddy said, and Lizzie was moved to hug her again. It had been more than a year since she had seen her ex-stepmother, and it heartened her, suddenly, to see such a familiar presence in such unfamiliar surroundings, so clearly besotted. She told Maddy about her flight delays, she apologized for missing the rehearsal dinner.

"I'm just so glad you made it. You look gorgeous! I like your hair—it's shorter, isn't it? And your shoes!"

"Thanks," she said, grinning. "eBay." She *knew* Maddy would appreciate them. She still thought of her when she went shopping, tried to imagine, when she was hemming and hawing over a purchase, whether Maddy would approve.

Maddy asked her how long she was staying. "Only until Sunday? But you've come all this way!"

"I've got to get back to work," Lizzie said, not thinking of work at all, but running in Riverside Park. It had been a mild June so far, but Lizzie found herself longing for the feel of a good humid New York summer evening, the pale glow of the river, the lush canopy of the trees above, as her feet hit stone after uneven stone and she concentrated so hard that breathing was all that mattered.

"Ah yes, work," Maddy gave her a gentle smile, touched the beads of the choker nestled at her throat. "You've been working hard, haven't you?"

Lizzie only nodded, gazing at Maddy's necklace. It was gorgeous, Lizzie thought, nearly painstakingly so, the ivory beads delicately etched and punctuated by tiny silver nubs. It seemed, suddenly to Lizzie, the way it grazed Maddy's neck, nicely offsetting her silky green top, like the epitome of style.

"Too hard."

Lizzie nodded again, flushing under the attention of Maddy's steady eye. Her ex-stepmother didn't miss a thing. If Lizzie spoke, she might cry. The necklace was nothing. She found herself on the verge of telling Maddy the news that she had been trying so hard to tamp down for more than a week now. I don't know what to do, she wanted to whisper: *Please. Tell me what I should do.*

But instead, Lizzie found herself saying: "You look so beautiful, so happy." And she didn't try to cover the wistfulness that crept into her voice.

Maddy laughed, hugged her again. "Well, I am happy, I am."

Lizzie kissed her cheek, feeling so tired and raw, feeling as if the roles were reversed: She was the older, divorced one, and her ex-stepmother a woman in her prime, with all the time in the world.

TRANSGRESSIONS

Jewish women, inspired both by the burgeoning women's movement of the 1970s and 1980s and by their own increasing knowledge, scholarship, and deep familiarity with classic Jewish text sources, took up writing midrash, or new takes on traditional tales. Bible stories are our introduction to Jewish gender concerns, with fathers betraying their daughters, and women's loyalties threatened but usually proving steadfast.

The finest reimaginings of biblical women's narratives, like the one here, do not attempt to alter the bleak outcomes of stories featuring women, but imagine what these women might actually have said and done between the setup and the traditional ending of the tale, giving women more opportunity and less passivity than their biblical originals. Lot's wife could save her daughters, rain fire upon evildoers of her neighborhood, and get away with treasure. Her end in this story is no better than in the Bible, but she gives her pursuers a run for their money.

These stories of transgression, from Bible women onward, show independent women in action. Even girls have some agency in these narratives, trying to wrest a modicum of power from the patriarchy to suit their own needs, whether it's learning to drive, learning to use their own strong voices, or refusing to cede their power to others. These are risk takers and rule breakers, a far cry from some ornamental and corseted Victorian-lady model of reticent womanly behavior. Some of the Jewish women you'll meet here represent a completely different type: outspoken females willing to push up against expectations, defy convention, and make change. Sometimes they are brave and filled with intention. Other times they stumble, uneasy with the consequences of their rebellion. Transgression can usher them into a new space, even a new reality, while courting self-destruction as they test their strength against rigid—and sometimes brutal—patriarchal family structures. The more "modern" of the women and girls in this section develop the courage to take charge of their own trajectories, testing boundaries and flying in the face of convention even when they're afraid of the consequences.

Lot's Wife

S he sat in a small patch of shade, churning the goat's milk to butter. The courtyard was quiet with work, one daughter at the oven baking bread, the other grinding flour for tomorrow's loaves. It was good to have these girls, she thought, who had learned their way and were of use to those around them.

Slowly, the butter started to come. They'd have it tonight with the bread her daughter was baking.

Good, clean food, but she would admit to counting down to the next feast day, when they'd offer up a ram if the year continued so well. Already preparing the juiciest parts in her mind, crushed figs to bring out the meat's succulence, cloves for pungency, she let her mind wander and didn't hear the men's voices until they were inside the house.

Her husband came to the doorway. *We have visitors. Traders from Egypt. One of the field hands will bring in a goat. We'll need a full meal.*

She already had a fire lit when the boy brought the plump animal. While the girls continued to bake and churn, their mother quickly slit its throat and hung it upside down to drain. Once it was skinned, she quartered and pounded it so it would grill quickly and stay tender, then ran her hands and eyes over red lentils she spread across the ground, picked out the tiny stones that would masquerade themselves in the pot and ruin the dish.

The courtyard rustled with activity. It smelled of death and fire, cumin and bread. The scents, she thought, of a good life.

Amid the bustle of work, she looked at her daughters, thirteen and fourteen, older than she'd been when she was married off, taken away from the tents to another land.

At least they lived in the city. She had this courtyard, with its round stove and barrel of flour. Women to sit with in the square at shearing time.

It was more than she ever expected. But she would keep her girls closer. She could feel her old age coming in the creases of her knees and shoulders. She needed her daughters.

Too bad we aren't preparing for a real feast, she thought, something to bring everyone together, especially after the recent infighting. Rich men are not to be trusted, she knew. A poor man might steal a donkey or goat. But a rich man will start a war over an entire herd.

Lot had gotten through these arguments before. This time, Pildash, who already had a bigger flock and more pasture than anyone else, accused him of taking the best grazing land. But they had to live together. Someone would slip some coins to the other. It would be taken care of.

The shouting began as the men settled down to eat. Muffled at first, but soon closer, and then someone banged on the door.

Let us see these strangers you have taken into your home, one yelled. Another jeered, *Bring them out so we can get to know them.* A howl of laughter went up from the crowd. She recognized some of the voices. Men with grudges against Lot, or the poor who resented his wealth.

She hurried up to the roof and peeked over the edge. Nearly twenty men, one egging them on. Usually, the other wealthy men in the town could be counted as Lot's closest friends, and his only peers. But here was Pildash, shouting encouragement. *So, this is how he'll get what he wants*, she thought, *embarrass my husband in public.* Make him look bad enough and he just might give up that pastureland without a fight. *Rich men and their pride*, she thought.

No one noticed her up there. But they wouldn't. Life happened horizontally in Sodom—everyone on an even plane, landowners and the shovelers of shit all living side by side. It meant nothing. Four men still paid everyone else's wages. But if you can see them sleeping and waking it's easy to overlook how much more they have than you ever will.

No one would pay attention to a woman anyway. So no one saw her as she watched Lot open their door and step out into the hostility and the evening.

Friends, what can I do for you? he asked, as if he hadn't heard their demands or anger.

Give us the strangers! the men called out.

Lot tried to speak, but they cut him off, closing in and poking him in the chest. *All this over some grass*, she thought, with a small twinge of worry.

But she pushed it out of her mind. Her husband would work it out. They'd all go back to their dinners.

She watched Lot grow scared. He raised his voice.

Friends. You know I deal honestly.

What are they paying you? one voice called out.

Why should you get all their bounty? yelled another.

Finally, Pildash spoke. *You shouldn't be the only one with the honor of hosting them. Bring them out. Let's see how tight their assholes are.*

Again, the crowd surged, but Lot continued, fear audible in every word. *I have offered them a meal and a bed for the night. That is all.*

It wasn't working. The men were getting more worked up. She heard the door slam as Lot rushed back in, and ran down to find him flustered, his cloak ripped at the neck.

I have to do something, he said to her. *They'll break into our house and drag these poor men into the street.*

They're a drunk and worked-up mob, she replied. *Throw them some coins and they'll be happy.*

They'll do unnatural things to those men. I cannot let my guests be raped by a bunch of drunken farmhands.

They don't want to do any harm, she said, with as much vehemence as she dared in the face of his overweening pride. *Go out with a few skins of wine, compliments of the visitors.*

You're not listening! What do you think "let us see how tight their assholes are" means?

It means they want to see if they have gold hidden under their clothes.

Lot didn't hear her. He paced, head bent in concentration. Finally he said, *Go get the girls.*

The girls?

My daughters. We'll give them instead.

You're going to throw our children to that mob? Are you crazy?

Finally, he looked at her. *I have no choice. Our family's honor is on the line.*

Fully hysterical now, she cried, *Those men will kill our girls. They will rip them apart from the inside and leave them for dead. How much honor can you have if you are willing to let that happen to your own children?*

They will do that to my guests! To men! You're the one who said they won't rape anyone.

I said they wouldn't rape the travelers. But our girls have only their bodies.

If, by some miracle, they survive what twenty grown men do to them, we'll never be able to marry them off. You'll ruin them forever.

In tears, she clawed at her husband's clothing. But Lot had heard enough.

Get them now. He turned and stepped out again. She only heard the first few words—*Friends! I've come with an offer*—before the door closed behind him.

She only had a few minutes. She ran back to the courtyard, grabbed whatever she could—tufts of goatskin, batches of raw wool, and a pot of oil cooling by the fire. All the while, she shouted to the girls, *Run up to the roof. Grab whatever valuables you see on your way. Gold coins, jewelry, anything.*

She stuffed the wool into a piece of still-bloody goatskin, grabbed an unlit torch and thrust it into the oven. After its end caught, she ran upstairs. When her daughters followed, each carrying a bulging saddlebag, she was already putting the torch to the hay pile in the corner.

Mama! they cried. *What are you doing? We'll burn up!*

We'll be long gone by the time this is big enough to harm us. Slowly, a wisp of smoke rose from the hay pile. Once it did, she started grabbing tufts of wool and shoving them at her children. *Start lighting them*, she directed.

Confused and scared, the girls did as they were told. She hopped from their roof to the neighbor's, grabbing a flaming ball of wool, hurling it down into the narrow street in front of her house. The girls followed, handing her their fiery missiles as they moved. They went from rooftop to rooftop, setting each hay pile alight, throwing more projectiles down to the city below.

Mama, panted the younger girl, *what are we doing? They'll kill us when they realize what we've done.*

They can't see us, she said. *If anyone thinks to look up, we'll already be gone.*

But what are we trying to do? cried the older girl. *I don't understand.*

I'm saving you, was the only answer she gave.

From below, they heard screaming as people noticed the cramped city was on fire. A few men near Lot's house had been hit. They rolled on the ground, screaming in fear and pain as they were consumed.

What vengeance is this? came the people's desperate cry. *Why does God rain down fire on us?*

Panic spread as people trampled others to save their own homes. By then, she and her daughters had reached a narrow patch of city wall. She was sure her daughters could jump down to the ground, but her body was already feeling the effects of the run across the city's rooftops. Just see them to safety, she thought. *They are all that matters.*

Throw away the wool, she told her daughters. She flung the still-burning torch as far as she could. *Now, jump.*

Once down, she shouted, *Head for the lake. Don't stop and don't turn around. There's nothing here for us anymore.*

The girls took off across the flat land. She followed as fast as she could, but her breasts pounded painfully against her chest. She struggled to find breath.

Eventually, she felt the ground change beneath her feet. She was closer to the lake. Up ahead, she saw the surface of the water wink behind her daughters. But she couldn't take another step. She was too tired. Her breath caught with every inhalation.

Bending over, her chest heaved painfully. Her arms and legs shook from the effort of getting this far.

Standing back up, the blood rushed away from her head, sent her reeling, turning her to face the way she'd come. In the distance, Sodom still burned, higher than she ever thought possible.

Only then did what she had done hit her with its full force. Images of the life she had led passed through her mind. It was all gone. Her husband, who would have whored his own daughters out to serve his pride, was in there too, and she felt, in that moment, what it was to lose an entire life's work, a history of love and loss.

For the first time, she saw what her hands had wrought. *I have killed and I have destroyed to save my own*, she thought.

It was then, her body struggling to reassert itself, her mind fighting to align her pride at saving her children with grief at losing her whole valued life and horror at what she had done, that she started to cry. Huge, dehydrated tears poured down her face, sobs wracked her body. She sank down, crying harder even than the morning her own mother had sent her away into her new marriage, into the long life ahead.

She didn't want her daughters to see her cry, but she couldn't stop. Something had opened within her. She could not close it.

Stand up, Mama, they said. *You have to keep moving or your muscles will cramp.*

She would get up. She would let her daughters half-carry her along the lake's shoreline and into the hills. She would find a cave for them, sleep with her girls curled around her like lambs. She would wake the next morning to explain they could never return to their home, would have to forget all they had ever known and look only to the future. She would calm them when their fear of God's wrath shook within them. She would explain that they had done God's work, or the work God should have done when a man would ask a mother to sacrifice her virgin daughters for his own stupid honor. She would tell them they were instruments of God's wrath, that God had guided their hands when they set their home alight.

And after they all slept again, she would face their anger when they accused her of making sure there would be no man alive who would have them. She would soothe them, say the riches they had stuffed into the saddlebags would buy them a new life. She would promise to find a way.

She would keep that promise, purchase land where they could live. She would buy sheep and goats, hire field hands and shepherds. When they had enough new wealth, she would find husbands for her daughters. She would see them grow large with child. She would hold her grandchildren on her lap and know she had done something good. But for all that she would go on to do, Lot's wife would never rise from that spot by the side of the moonlit lake. She would never stop crying fat, salty tears for the life she left behind in flames.

Paved with Gold

"What if the journey kills us?" she asks him night after night. "If we stay, surely they will put us in the ground," is what he answers her every time.

So they leave, two more huddled masses sailing from old world to new. The newlyweds carry their tightly bundled life on board: Candlesticks, prayer shawl, brown crusted bread, hand-stitched lace, a family ring tightly sewn into the band of her thick wool skirt.

On day three as she begins to form sky-blue and pickle-green dreams of home, the young wife is yanked awake by the sound of her name. "Anna," her new husband whispers before clutching his chest and taking in two shallow breaths. In that moment Anna understands that pleasantly shaded dreams will never visit her sleep again.

Up on deck she feels clean air on her face for the first time since setting sail. The salty spray stings her skin, turning her cheeks and the tip of her nose a raw, fiery red. Four queasy strangers hurl her husband into the deepest of graves. His eyes wide open. His shoes still on his feet. The ocean's rage dampens the sound his clothed body makes when it smacks the sea. Jagged waves use him for a watery game of catch. Finally to the bottom he sinks. "See," she wants to tell the man she'll never get to know. "They aren't putting you in the ground."

Man overboard. Woman journeying on.

Whenever she could, Anna made a point of detouring through this alley, an especially putrid one that others made a point of avoiding. The closeness of the buildings kept the space dark even at noon on the sunniest day and the narrow strip captured every odor that blew south of 10th Street and east of the Bowery. Anna, who rarely felt sorry for anyone, took pity on this forgotten strip. Perhaps because she understood what it felt like to gasp for fresh air and never get any. Mostly Anna came here to be alone, something that she missed from her old life more than almost anything else, more than her dead husband, more than her old lumpy feather bed, more than her sisters, her parents, and the life she left behind.

"Good enough," Anna thought as she dislodged a pebble from her shoe. She steadied herself against the dilapidated building's corner to relace it for the rest of the way home. As she lifted her foot she noticed her heel was loose.

"Two days early," Anna mumbled.

It was only Thursday. The glue usually gives out on Sunday, allowing her to fix it using the jar next to the table where she makes buttonholes sixty hours a week. She didn't know why the glue always sat there next to the two women who pieced together men's pant legs or, for that matter, if anyone else ever used it. What she did know was that if she got there early enough no one noticed her opening the jar with the German label. At home—at what used to be home—she wouldn't so much as pluck a blade of grass from ground that belonged to someone else. But that was before. Before the noise, before broken shoes, and before overcrowded rooms and sewing shops became her life.

Manhattan's Lower East Side following the turn of the century was packed tighter than the steamship that carried twenty-two-year-old Anna to it. The streets were like scenes from fever dreams she couldn't untangle, teeming with peddlers with their off-balance carts, pale children with their equally pasty families, wagons with their dirty horses that defecated at will in the street, and the occasional diseased chicken with its filthy feathers molting. It smelled as bad as it looked. The odor of uncontained sewage, rarely washed bodies, and the stink of survival clung to the entire neighborhood and permanently worked its way into her hair and clothes. But the worst part for Anna was the noise. Inescapable noise. High-pitched noise, deep booming noise, hissing noise, rhythmic noise, random noise. Noise that infiltrated her sleep. Noise that made it hard for her to eat. Noise that shot bullet holes through her best memories.

With all that noise, it was the constant beat of the sewing machine that she hated the most. The rapid fire of the needle piercing cloth wafted through every street, every apartment, every butcher shop, so no matter where you stood inside or outside you could hear the Singers cry. For

Anna, who found it to be the cruelest of the noises, the sounds of the stitching factories registered on her skin. Usually on her arms between her elbows and wrists. She swore she could feel each stitch being put down. It pounded on her every minute of every day. That is except for when she walked through this one nameless and otherwise horrible alley. Her arms and head quieted in this foul-smelling, dark shred of a place that couldn't fit three people across. In the alley she could hear herself hum. Anna didn't even know she liked to hum until she arrived in New York City.

But a loose heel on a Thursday was nothing to hum about. The same mud puddle that gifted her the pebble must have loosened her heel. She shook her head. Anna Gold's luck ran like that. It didn't know one day of the week from the next but always seemed to show up at the wrong time all the same. It got lost in muck and small bottles of forgotten glue in windowless apartments turned makeshift sewing factories so it never showed up for the big stuff. It might provide a place to scratch your back but only after it first led you to coarse wool or a cold stove. Still, she acknowledged that her luck at least bumped into her on occasion, unlike some of the women who didn't even have enough rough wool for a sweater or found themselves with gaping holes in the bottom of their shoes too big to be fixed with borrowed glue.

Footsteps took Anna out of her head. Someone else was in the alley. Her alley. Quickly she fixed her shoe, and took a step away from the wall before preparing to walk the rest of the way home on the screaming streets. At the moment the first set of footsteps passed her, another man rounded the corner so fast and so carelessly that it knocked her backwards.

"Sorry," he said. "My apologies, Ma'am," he offered his hand and looked at her eyes. "Oh, I mean, Miss."

Anna did not correct him. Anyway she wasn't sure if she qualified as a miss or ma'am anymore. She was used to people thinking she was younger. A lot younger. Her skin and figure were almost that of a girl. Only her hands, her feet, and her broken soul hinted at the truth. Anna refused his hand and steadied herself once again before carefully turning on her glued heels. Instead of stepping aside to let her navigate the tight passage the man moved closer to her face.

"I bet you have a pretty smile," he said with his stare fixed on her eyes. "When you smile."

He leaned in and ran his thumb across her jawline before turning his head.

"How much?" he whispered into her ear. His hot breath stung like forgotten onions rotting from the inside out.

How much, she thought. How much for what? For a hundred pair of shoes? For a hundred bottles of glue? For a hundred ways to reverse what she knew would be the fate of the people she left behind? For a hundred minutes of quiet in a row? For a hundred days of sleep? She knew he didn't have "how much." No one in the world had that "how much."

"Now, there, you don't have to play shy with me," he told her ear.

Anna made her mouth form the shape of a smile. His posture relaxed as her lips tilted upward. And, right at that moment she growled. He looked surprised but didn't move out of the way. He pressed his thumb down harder into the flesh of her cheek. It hurt. She opened her mouth, shook her head, and bit his finger. She was pleased to see that she had drawn blood. Before the shock of the bite and blood wore off, Anna ran home leaving both heels in the street. The downbeat of the Singers followed.

Months later when they meet again in her alley the rotten-on-ion-breathed man does not recognize Anna. Stolen German glue no longer holds her shoes together and her sweater has been replaced with a proper lady's coat. It's a deep brown, the color of early spring earth, and its soft velvet collar rests on the patch of skin on her back that once screamed from coarse wool. Anna's ear turns hot as she tells him the price for her best girl, three times the going rate. He doesn't flinch at the number and, this time, she does not smile.

"Be careful, some of us bite," Anna warned him as they walk away. She then watches the man and girl disappear into her alley and feels the pain of a hundred phantom pebbles lodged in her shoe.

Driving Lesson

C elia Sasson stopped the car. A dirt road twisted around tall pines. It
was morning, still cool, the sun just a glint of light on metal.

"Your turn," she said.

Seated next to her in the passenger seat, Sam ran his hands up and down
the front of his trousers.

"Are you sure about this?"

"I told you, Sam, I can't marry a man who doesn't drive."

It still shocked her. Here was the broad-shouldered boy who'd tended
his family's farm in Kokomo, Indiana. The man who was so good with
numbers, he became the bookkeeper at the largest lumberyard in Mobile,
Alabama. The man the Bank of Michigan had employed less than a week
after he moved to Detroit last year. He stood six-foot-one, dwarfing the
other Jewish boys she knew in brains as well as inches. And yet, he had
never driven an automobile.

He didn't have a father, he explained. There was nowhere to drive to,
where he was from. Still, it was unacceptable. And so, when he'd declared
his intentions, she'd set him straight. "Not until we fix your problem."

"Why does it matter so much to you?" he had asked.

It was like asking why wings mattered to doves. Celia remembered the
day, almost two years earlier, when she bought herself a Tin Lizzie. She had
saved six months' profit at her hat shop on Woodward. Then she went to the
Ford dealer's and placed a stack of bills on the counter. The sum was $825.

"Your husband didn't want to see it before he sent you?" asked the dealer,
a baldhead in a suit with a glass eye.

She smiled. "No husband. This motorcar is not for any man."

"Oh! Well, let me show you this fine electric automobile. Henry Ford
himself just got one for his wife."

"An electric car might be right for Mrs. Ford, but I'm here for a gas automobile." She had no intention of purchasing some dainty car for the "fairer sex." She wanted to feel the speed and smell the gasoline.

When the dealer hesitated, she held up her green wad.

She drove her Model T back to Hastings Street. How it pleased her—the horrified look on Papa's face. *Nafka*, he yelled. Tramp! The same slur he used when she told him she was opening her shop.

"Nu, Celia?" her mother lamented. "What kind of man will want you?"

Her parents didn't know about her nights dancing with a gambler named Alan. Alan went once a week to the whiskered *bubbe* who ran the numbers behind the Yiddish Playhouse.

His numbers never won, but he was as determined as he was unlucky. She didn't care. She adored his brown curls, his brawny frame. He loved to dance the Turkey Trot as much as she did. Most importantly, he didn't try to restrain her.

Mama and Papa wanted her to marry a man like Sam Perlman, someone who might save her from herself. Not unless the boy learned to drive. And even then, she'd made no promises.

Now, Sam wedged a cigarette between his lips and pulled a brass lighter out of his pocket. He turned to light hers first. So polite, this one! Alan would have leaned over and pressed his lips against hers.

Sam's hands—his large, smooth hands—were shaking. She let him take a drag and blow smoke into the crisp air.

"That's enough," she said. "I don't have all day."

He opened the door, letting one leg dangle off to the side as though he were testing the temperature of bathwater. He stepped out and extinguished his cigarette on the trunk of one of the great pines.

"Okay, I'm ready."

"So what are you standing over there for?"

She handed him her spare pair of goggles and buttoned her duster. It fastened at her neck and came down below her ankles. She had designed a veil that held her auto cap firmly in place. The sign in her shop window read: "*Becoming AND Practical—For the Well-Dressed Motorist*." She hadn't sold many—yet—but as more women drove, it was sure to be a hit. With Sam's eyes on her, she tied the ends under her chin.

"I hope you brought gloves, like I told you."

"Yes, ma'am." He reached inside his jacket and held up a leather pair.

He looked at her like a Labrador who'd fetched her a bone and now wanted a pat on the head.

She yanked open the door on the driver's side. He took slow strides toward her, put a foot on the running board. He might have looked elegant with his long legs and slender build, if only he weren't so stiff. She had noticed it the first time he showed up at her store.

"A man's here from the bank," Rachel, one of her shop girls, had whispered.

"The tall one with the serious face?" Celia had asked. Rachel nodded.

In an instant, she was cloaked in his cologne. He wore a blue tailored suit. He had the mouth of a pouting child, little, round, and puckered. She would come to learn that his expression rarely changed, even after sex.

"I'm up to date on my payments," she said.

He removed his bowler hat. "I'm not here about your payments. I'm Sam Perlman. Your sister Ethel sent me? I thought you might like to have dinner sometime."

"Oh." That was so like Ethel—her beautiful, blonde baby sister—to give Celia one of her throwaways. Ethel had so many suitors she could fill her dance card every Saturday for a year. Even the boys from the German families—the first Jews in Detroit who considered themselves superior to the later arrivals from Eastern Europe—wanted her. But Ethel couldn't marry until Celia did; their parents, still tied to the traditions of the *shtetl*, forbade it.

At night, in the bed they shared, Ethel would beg. "Come on, Cele, you're practically an old maid!"

"I'm twenty-two," Celia told her. "There's still time before my hair turns white."

She was prepared to turn him down, this Sam Perlman. She could tell right away he was too quiet, too intellectual. And yet there was the gold watch, the tailored suit, the promise of comfort. There was, too, the earnest way he looked at her. Unlike Alan, her partner in adventure, he was a *gutte neshuma*, a good soul.

She reminded herself of his goodness as she stood in front of the car. Why shouldn't she want a man like Sam Perlman? She had to overcome the uncertainty that stirred her awake at three o'clock in the morning. Every other night, she rose from bed and ran to the outhouse to scream where no one would hear.

She got in position to crank the engine, always a gamble with a possible broken arm. This was her brother Ernie's job on Sundays, when she made her weekly trip to Belle Isle. Last weekend, someone from the *Detroit Free Press* had snapped a photo of her on one of her jaunts around the island. "Young Milliner Drives Automobile on Belle Isle; Scares Horses," the headline read. Papa had nearly dropped dead.

"When I get in," she yelled, "move the hand brake forward and put your foot on the clutch pedal." He gave her a weak wave.

She cupped the crank with her left hand, grabbed the fender with her right. She was four-foot-eleven and barely ninety pounds. In her shop, she lifted boxes, built shelves, nailed wooden signs above displays. "Men's work," Papa said. He didn't see that so-called "women's work" was harder on the body. Just look at Mama, her youth gone at forty-three, already stooped over from chasing after her children, slitting chickens' throats to feed them, grinding soiled clothes against the washboard. Sometimes, when she stared down, Celia pictured Mama's hands—cracked and calloused—attached to her wrists. The vision made her shiver.

After one vigorous half-crank, the engine started and Celia climbed in. "Now, Sam. Go!"

The car lurched forward. With the sudden jerk, her shoulders knocked against the back of her seat.

He turned. "Are you alright?"

"Of course," she shouted. "Keep your eyes on the road."

Sam faced the path ahead, pressing onward. Dirt flew into their faces, and Celia brought her own goggles down over her eyes. Although he maneuvered the road's sharp turns, she felt him hesitating, even after she urged him to go faster or else the car could stall.

It was his first time, she reminded herself. He would grow more confident after another lesson or two. And yet, she couldn't forget what the Ford dealer told her before he handed her the keys to her brand-new Tin Lizzie: "People drive the way they live life." The man could tell Celia was the type to drive without inhibition. And he was right. She had pushed down the throttle lever—and the wind, the dust, the speed had been the most thrilling feeling of her life.

"Like flying," she told Alan later that night. They were parked behind the ballroom. It was pitch-black. There were stars in his eyes. And so, the day of her first drive was followed by another first: She had taken Alan's hand and guided him up her dress to stroke her breasts.

How those exhilarating moments contrasted with what she felt now, with Sam at the wheel. *He drives the way he lives his life*, she thought, *with no fire*.

There was nothing ablaze in this godforsaken place with its endless rows of pines. How could she live out here with him, miles away from the loud Yiddish bursting through the opened windows on Hastings Street, or the tumult of her shop on Woodward?

"Enough!" she yelled, placing her hands over her ears.

Sam pulled over. "My god, Celia, your face is white! Now, just breathe . . . That's it."

She did as she was told, following *his* instructions, this time.

"Just picture it," he whispered. "Where those trees are now, we'll build a beautiful brick home. Can't you see the fireplace and the mantle?"

She did like the sound of it. In fact, she could think of little else since meeting his mother just a week earlier, when Sam decided it was time to bring Celia home.

"Don't you know who his mama is?" Ethel had asked as Celia brushed her sister's hair. "Mrs. Greenberg, you know, the landlady who lives in the big house on Elliot Street?"

Of course, Celia had heard of her. The *Raycha* Mrs. Greenberg. The Rich Mrs. Greenberg. But Sam's name was Perlman, not Greenberg. Was she really his mother?

As they'd approached the stone steps of the landlady's home, Sam had told her the whole story: "My father died before we left the Old Country. She married a farmer and moved us to Kokomo. Then *he* died, so she married Greenberg and moved to Detroit. Now, Greenberg's dead, too."

"Did she kill all of them?" That was one way to deal with a husband who bored you.

Sam didn't laugh. He had no sense of humor, as far as she could tell.

They found the *Raycha* Mrs. Greenberg on a velvet seat, her own private throne, fox furs draped around her shoulders. On her pinky was a ring adorned with an enormous sapphire.

"Mother, this is Celia Sasson," Sam said.

The woman clucked in Polish, *A skinny little chicken, this one!*

"Even a little chicken has wings to fly," Celia said.

Mrs. Greenberg's eyes widened, surprised Celia had understood. She must have assumed the Sassons were a lower kind of Jew. In fact, they hailed from a village near Warsaw, though they retained the Sephardic name of their ancestors who'd been expelled from Spain long ago.

Sam's cheeks reddened, but he stood there without a word. A *kuni lemel*, he was. A fool. And Celia knew in that moment that she would never respect him, not because of his cowardice, but because he was simply incapable of outrage.

And yet, as she looked around at the paintings in their gilded frames, the polished silver candlesticks, the maid scurrying into the room with a china bowl filled with sugar cubes, she thought she might go through with it anyway. She was a milliner, after all. She had the taste for beautiful things. The possibilities tantalized her.

They tempted her still. She sat in the car with Sam, picturing the home Mrs. Greenberg would build them, imagining a life she wanted but didn't want.

She put her hand on Sam's arm.

"Would you like me to show you how it's done?"

He got out and she took her place at the wheel, her throne. She watched him bend over and place his handkerchief over the crank to protect his hands from the grease.

When the car started, she did not wait for Sam to join her. The moment he stepped back, she was "off to the races," as Alan would say, Alan who had shown up at Sam's office with a rifle. It was the last time she saw him, the day two Irish officers dragged him, beet faced, from the Bank of Michigan shouting, "Celia's *my girl!* Mine!" Alan, her love. But what good was love, really? She was never his. Celia Sasson belonged to no one.

She drove off, gaining speed until the pines were only streaks of green and Sam was a speck of dust in her mirror. With one hand, she loosened her veil.

She couldn't see the end of the road, but she could see her future hedging her in, her old life flying at her like pieces of dirt kicked up from the tires. What if she simply drove on to wherever this path led?

She could leave him there in the field, she thought. He got out of the car to relieve himself and disappeared in the woods, is what she would say. His death was an accident. Mrs. Greenberg, with her three husbands in the ground, might know a thing or two about spinning these kinds of yarns.

Reaching the clearing, she thought of what Mrs. Greenberg had said that night, when Sam left them to have "ladies' talk." Mrs. Greenberg was stunned to hear Celia had no intention of closing her Woodward store after she married, even though, with Sam, she wouldn't need the money.

She pointed at Celia with her pinky, the one with the sapphire ring. "I know your kind. You've been fighting your whole life, haven't you? But wouldn't it be nice to rest?"

Celia Sasson stopped. She considered her twelve-hour workdays. Difficult customers. Mama's calloused hands holding a pot of boiling water, trying to keep them warm in a house without heat or plumbing. Mrs. Greenberg leaving the Old Country with a baby, alone. And this: a house with a fireplace, silk curtains, a vase of fresh lilacs on top of a grand piano. And him. Every day, him.

Sam was sitting at the base of one of the pines, near the spot where she had left him. He was reading his pocket dictionary. His goal was to memorize every word, he had told her on one of their first outings to Belle Isle.

"Oh, there you are." His politeness exasperated her. What a *kuni lemel*.

The clouds had retreated, the sun unleashed. Celia took off her goggles, squinted at him.

He got into the car, handed her another cigarette. Before she could take one, he grabbed her wrist so hard it startled her. "Listen Celia," he said. "There's something I want you to know about me." His nails were too long. She felt them digging into her skin. "You know, I spent my childhood till I was eighteen working my stepfather's farm in Kokomo. It was my whole life, that farm."

"Yes, you've told me." She tried to wriggle free, but he tightened his grip.

"Well, my mother sold it behind my back after my stepfather died." Celia stared at him, surprised by the bite in his voice, and listened to his story:

When his mother told him the farm would never be his, Sam had kept quiet. But the next morning, at the rooster's crow, he'd packed a bag. He carried his boots by the laces, crept down the hall. His mother's door was left ajar and he found her snoring underneath her quilt. He lifted the mattress where he knew she kept a cloth pouch and took all the money inside. Then he made his way outside to the barn. He turned over an empty pail and began to milk Dora, his mother's favorite cow. He dipped two fingers in the pail and sucked them dry, and he knew he'd remember that sweet taste. But that didn't stop him from grabbing his rifle from behind the barn door and shooting Dora right between her large brown eyes. The sound of his shot, of animal screams, had surely reached the house, so he scribbled a note and left it on the blood-soaked floor where Dora lay: "*Your son is dead.*"

Heading south to Alabama, he let Mrs. Greenberg believe the worst for five years until he decided she'd been punished enough and showed up at her doorstep in Detroit.

Now it was Celia who couldn't speak. Even on the days when Mama had slapped her with a wet dishrag and Papa had called her a whore, she couldn't have dreamed of such an act. Sam Perlman, who knew? Maybe he had invented the tale, but still, he had more chutzpah than she realized. She was a little afraid of him, and this, she understood, was what he wanted. Or rather, what she wanted: an undercurrent of danger.

"Shall I try the drive again?" he asked, releasing her.

Celia Sasson gazed out at the road, scanned the treetops, the stranger's eyes.

For the rest of the afternoon, she did not let go of the wheel.

Little Hen

I n those weeks of waxing darkness, I worked at Anna's side, my fingers mimicking hers. We sat in the kitchen of my aunt's place. I told Anna of my first days in the city, five years before. Of the time, for instance, my aunt had sent me for chickens and I came back empty-handed, crying into my elbow like a small child, unwilling to haggle or even to open my mouth out on the street.

Anna snorted to hear of it. "What did you think would happen to you?" she said. "Afraid of a toothless chicken plucker," she said. She shook her head in pity and in disgust.

I wasn't brave enough to invite Anna's teasing more than once. There were so many ways to be wrong; at sixteen, I subsisted on a steady diet of small atonements. So I sat silently for hours at a time, those long evenings in the winter of 1912, while she taught me at my aunt's Singer. She showed me how to make French darts, vertical darts, side seams. The things I wasn't learning at the factory, where I made only sleeves, day in, day out. The lessons were Anna's idea. She must have seen some promise in me.

Anna spoke and I listened. She spoke of her early tangles with New York: schoolmarms, landlords, a litany of bosses. And then she spoke of Vilna, where she was born. Of the time before her father disappeared. "He was a tailor's assistant," Anna said, speaking of her father. "To begin with."

To Mama, Anna told me, she was Khanele, Little Anna. To Daddy: Hunele. Little Hen.

A new century. The workers in Vilna had been organizing. Jews. For who else made up the bulging undergrowth of needle-men, cutters, tinkerers, cobblers? In those days, the *shtarkers*—strapping Jews, too, not only Christians—were brought in, swinging pipes as well as fists. The small factory owners and the wholesalers paid to keep the striking workers in bandages. Her father used to say, Come, Hunele, we're going to the Kitchen.

The Kitchen was in the crumbling center of the city, not far from the university and not far, either, from the Jews' almshouse and the Jews' hospital and other rooms filled to bursting with Jews. The Kitchen was heated by a great tile oven and, in winter and in summer, it was too warm. It smelled of cabbage and mildew. Two long tables ran front to back atop the packed-earth floor. And along the benches sat men like Anna's father, elbows knocking those of their neighbors. She sat in her father's lap and ate her soup. The soup was the worst she had tasted in her short life, Anna said. She nearly gagged now, speaking of it.

"But the food didn't matter," Anna said to me. The food was not the point. For this was the Cooperative Kitchen of the Vilna Needleworkers' Union. Bowl by bowl, coin by coin, men like Anna's father would unite Vilna's workers. And after that, they would bring together all Lithuania's, and then, in time, all of Russia's. So Anna's father said. The Kitchen would be the beginning, he promised, the means to nourish the consciousness of all those who didn't set out for the West or land in Siberian prisons or (it still sometimes happened) wake up one morning as shop owners, may they rot in the earth. And in the meantime, you could get a bite to eat and dream of the future, when all men would be free.

Anna remembered the red-cheeked women stirring pots in the back. "They must have been the age then that we are now," she said to me. Working girls. Revolutionaries. When one spoke, the others would shush her, straining to follow threads of arguments that ran up and down the tables in the din, where the men sat. Anna's father called one over once, she told me. A girl with black braids and a pocked forehead. Galya, our comrade needs directions, Anna's father said. The girl had nodded then. I'll take him there myself, she said.

On her father's lap, Anna listened to men mumbling and to men shouting. She knew some of the phrases they used. She spoke them to me now. *Di natsyonale frage*: the national question. *Klasnbavustzayn*: class consciousness. *Ekonomishe teror*: economic terror. But at the time she didn't understand. Not truly.

"Now I understand," she said, making me look her in the eye, pressing her fingers to my elbow as if to imprint those words upon my skin. She pushed back then from the table and stood beside me, not going anywhere, but standing all the same. By now I had let my aunt's machine go idle. I didn't want to miss a word.

Anna recalled an afternoon of endless rain. A rivulet ran below her feet on the dirt floor, there in the Kitchen. She had sat at the table with her father for so long she feared that she had wet herself; she felt between her legs and understood it was only rain that trickled between her boots. We have fists, too, her father had said then to the man across from him, white spittle at the joints of his mouth. No more fearful little Jews, he said. Anna spoke her father's words to me.

"It was 1900," she said. She counted silently on her fingers and sat down again. "No: 1901. Do you see? You might be sent away for years, back then. Over there. You might be killed. Shot and thrown into the river. Just for organizing. For educating the workers. And my father was in the thick of it."

You can go to jail here, too, I thought—but didn't say. Thrown in with prostitutes and drunks. For picketing. Outside the factory where we sewed sleeves all day, a woman had lately been passing circulars among us: All for One, All for Union at the top of the paper, in black letters that shouted. You can die here, too, I thought. Jumping from fiery windows. Like the Triangle Shirtwaist girls had done the year before, trying to save themselves. Offerings to Moloch.

"But didn't he worry, bringing you along?" I asked. Stupid. A question like a child's tug at a mother's sleeve. But I couldn't help myself. "That you'd be swept up by the tsar's men, too? That you'd get hurt?"

Anna looked at me, uncomprehending.

"You were only six," I said.

"My father," she said, "knew exactly what he was doing."

I didn't argue. Why provoke her? Anna, in my aunt's kitchen, teaching me to make a one-piece dress, telling me the things you said only to a bosom friend. I told myself to keep my mouth shut; anything to hold her there, beside me.

"And once, my father did this," she said. Anna lifted an imaginary piece of paper and mimed ripping it to tiny pieces. Her hands moved, dropping their invisible freight: plunk, plunk, plunk. "He dropped the pieces into each one of the bowls around him. Who knows what was on the scraps of paper? And the men around him, they ate the pieces. Ate them up, with their soup. Every bit of it. So the police would never find a written trace. Fiends," she said. "Scum."

"Who? The police, you mean?"

I reached for Anna's hand; she batted me away, crossed her arms over her chest.

"He was the bravest of them all," she said. "Now it's our turn," she said. "It's our turn now."

And in that moment something in her moved from depth to surface, something I had sensed but from which she had shielded me, till then. My heart raced and my hands shook to see it so nakedly. Her anger: a blue flame of pleasure.

I stood. "There's work tomorrow," I said. "It's time we went to sleep."

She laughed then. Not unkindly. But she had reached a verdict all the same.

"Always afraid," she said. "That's you. Always afraid."

I knew even at the time that Anna had taught me well; I was hired as a sample maker one year later, not long after Anna vanished.

I collected rumors: Anna had been among those hauled off to jail to molder during the February strike. Anna had boarded a boat at New York Harbor, she was sailing back to Russia to find her father, she was shipping off to Palestine to build a new world with her own two hands. Anna had poisoned herself by eating matches. Anna had suffocated herself with gas. No one had any real news of her.

The Kitchen, Anna told me that night at my aunt's table, lasted only ten months. Anna's father went missing even before the place was ransacked by the tsar's police.

Of course I understand it now: Anna fighting her father's battle—as she understood it—in the time I knew her. Following the revolution where and when it leapt to life.

But those were the days before I grasped, in full, what Anna had shown me. That some of us are made to burn, animal into smoke. And that some of us are made to gather the ashes.

The Proper Care of Silver

M arianne wonders if people still say housekeeper. Maid sounds too Southern, and cleaner sounds industrial and it's just the two of them here today, so without knowing the terminology—despite years together—they empty the sideboard of Marianne's grandmother's silver. Nana had used her oven to store shoes but owned a silver service for twenty-two, including large wine holders cleverly designed to store ice in a hidden compartment. Nana had come to Washington Heights in 1939 with money rolled up and stashed in her vagina. Right in the hoo-ha, she'd told Marianne. Not once had Marianne seen the service used.

"What was she thinking, bringing it all here?" Marianne says aloud to Zelia. Despite knowing Zelia won't understand, Marianne explains how sad it is, having such pieces all go untouched. Marianne pictures Nana, spidery hands clasped in her lap, waiting for partygoers who never show up. How tragic, she thinks, but then, just as quickly, she thinks how well preserved the set is now, right there in her sideboard. "See," she points out to Zelia, "it's like new!"

Zelia, perched on a folding ladder, passes a silver wine holder to Marianne who places it next to its pair on the empty dining room table. Small, decorative lions on the holders gaze out at them as though they, too, are baffled as to why this massive cleaning effort when both Lily and Daniel declared they aren't coming for Passover this year; Lily because she is celebrating Easter with Mark's father who has no one else with whom to eat lamb and mint, and Daniel because William's parents asked them first, which only makes Marianne feel she—the mother—should have asked at Thanksgiving although if she had she's sure to have been scolded for thinking too far ahead. "It's not a competition," Daniel had told her, his voice sounding interplanetary with his hands free of the phone. "That's exactly what it is," she'd said. "Well," Daniel had said, "Maybe we'll show up. Who knows."

"Ohmygod." Zelia, unsteady on the ladder, drops Nana's teapot and it lands with a muffled thud on the carpet. "Ohmygod."

Zelia knows only a few scattered words of English. Oh my god is all-purpose—torrential rain ohmygod; Marianne's father has lymphoma ohmygod. If Marianne needs to convey anything she has to act it out—wipe the shades in exaggerated motions or mime mopping the bathroom floor all the way to the grimy corners. Anything serious and she emails Zelia's fifth-grade daughter to translate.

Marianne had written the instructions for today because it was crucial that the silver be handled gently, that Zelia not scratch it or put it in the dishwasher as she'd done the year before. Marianne doesn't criticize Zelia for living in this country eight years and knowing basically nothing, but when Zelia's sister visited from New York and demonstrated her fluency (and sisterly love by splitting the housework that week) it did make Marianne think that if only Zelia would force herself to learn she'd be so much better off. She could negotiate more hours or apply for positions with people who had child-care needs or have a job that didn't require counting forks, though it was possible Zelia liked counting the utensils, proving they were all still there, not stashed in her lunch bag and brought home to sell or to melt down and then sell.

"Oh, it's okay!" Marianne picks up the teapot, overly cheerful to hide her disappointment. The thin spout is dented and the lid dinged. The thing survived Nazis and seventy years of tarnish and hiding in Washington Heights but can't survive four seconds with the Brazilian housekeeper.

"Never mind," Marianne tells her and makes a big show of putting it with its imperfect lid next to the wine holders. If Daniel shows up he will certainly notice the ding. Martin will not.

Marianne will have to show her husband, displaying for Martin the small lid on her palm like a game-show hostess with a tiny hummingbird prize, and narrate what happened. The ladder, the cleaning. Martin will shake his head and examine the spout as though a) he were a silversmith rather than a radiologist who spends his days in the dark, and b) this mishap opens the door for him to have his biweekly whinge session about Zelia. "If I can't find my socks I guess I should look in the produce drawer . . ."

"Okay," Zelia says and hops down from the ladder. Marianne sticks her hand out to steady the cleaner, both of them working together to fold the stubborn ladder and begin on the silverware drawer, which is a chaos of cutlery, knives wedged into fork tines. Zelia is speedy at organizing these and Marianne takes a moment to marvel at her delicate fingers, the gentle ting of each item as she fits it in exactly the correct spot.

"That looks good," Marianne tells her and Zelia beams, the one dead and slightly gray tooth of hers prominent in the late morning sun.

Marianne chose this room for its light, bought the house without Martin even seeing it. She was pregnant with Lily then, Daniel age four or nearly so she remembers, because he used the bathroom all on his own as she wrote a deposit check. Martin didn't mind. He praised her, actually. We have the kind of marriage, she'd bragged to friends, where we don't have to even talk about things. She'd meant she had jurisdiction, unlike one friend who couldn't even buy a mug—a single coffee cup—without her husband's approval of color, design. But perhaps in the end those small conversations were necessary, crucial in a marriage—who buys a house without even discussing it?

Zelia fits the final knife into its slot in the blue velvet holder, points to the empty space where knife number twelve should be. "I don't know." Her voice is lyrical, music in the vowels. Iiiidunnnoooo. She doesn't know.

She could have walked off with spoons stuck into her bra and Victoria's Secret sweatpants and Marianne probably wouldn't have said anything. Even when Martin's wallet went missing for two weeks and he was driving to the hospital without an ID and having to ask the attractive night nurse to buzz him in, Marianne didn't accuse Zelia of any wrongdoing. And, sure enough, it turned up when Marianne went to get Martin's car inspected. He'd locked it in the glove compartment before the trip to Marrakesh, taking only a single credit card and his passport. "There are other cleaners," he'd said.

And there are. Lois has a housekeeper who bakes tortillas when her grandchildren are visiting. And there are certainly services that come in, speak English, and don't leave the scrub brush in the bathroom sink or rearrange the living room furniture because they feel it's better that way. There are better cleaners. But if Marianne lets Zelia go and this new, miraculously efficient and bilingual woman comes, and she leaves the house tidier and—this would be the key—orderly in a way that is rational, meaning their clothes are segregated by owner not color and the golf clubs are not with the similarly sized standing dustpan—well, then what in God's name would Marianne talk to Martin about?

Because the sad truth of it is that Zelia's foibles are some of their best conversations these days. Martin will listen—with his eyes and face and ears—as Marianne recounts today's escapades and she will be rapt as he flings open drawers and closet doors to reveal the latest gross injustice with his dress shirts or the wrapping paper saved from Lily's engagement shower to which she had only been invited by phone. Martin's fingers might accidentally lose themselves over her knuckles and maybe he'd have taken Cialis and maybe. Well.

Zelia and Marianne have a generous understanding. Marianne never criticizes her terrible cleaning or suspect organizational skills and Zelia can't—or doesn't—judge her employer for a) Marianne's messy house, jam rings on the fridge's glass shelves, hair in the soap, or b) having a cleaner when it's just her and Martin now, or c) the fact that Marianne gives Zelia's daughter presents on birthdays and Christmases even though she never asked if this was okay and, as Daniel pointed out, speaks more to Marianne's needs than to the girl's.

Under the silverware caddy are ripple-edged Haggadahs that haven't been used in years but which Marianne refuses to recycle because they might be used again (they won't) and they were her mother's (they weren't used then, either) and since Daniel and William were already exploring birth options, they might want them (they don't—Daniel will make his own). "I just can't be free of them," Marianne says, fully aware that Zelia won't get her Passover joke. She points to the Hebrew text. "Prayers." Zelia smiles. Last year, Marianne had made a vat of matzoh ball soup, and presented Zelia with a bowl. Marianne thought Zelia would try it and understand something about Judaism or at least have a snack that wasn't the Coke and Filet-o-fish she normally brought for lunch, but Zelia dumped the soup into the farmhouse sink, assuming Marianne wanted her to wash the bowl.

"I wash?" Zelia reaches for a small silver cup.

"Polish," Marianne says, miming scrubbing and immediately wondering if she still has silver cleaner. "You have to do it gently, like this." She leads her to the sink. Zelia watches as Marianne finds the polish, uses the pads of her fingers to apply the blue-gray goop and with the smallest trickle of tepid water, rinses while scrubbing with a paper towel. "It's Elijah's cup. You put it on the table and wait for him."

Later, Marianne can hear Zelia on the floor above—putting laundry away in the wrong place, arranging pillows in a way that would make sleep or getting into bed impractical at best, possibly scraping the hardwood with the new vacuum.

Marianne, ripe from the success of polishing the chalice, has a pile of silver, even the dented teapot, by the sink, her hands slicked with tarnish. You won't believe it, she will tell Martin, I had to do the silver myself. Imagine paying twenty dollars an hour to clean your own house!

Zelia gathers her lunch from the fridge and slings on a coat the color and texture of abandoned tires; it once belonged to Marianne. "I go."

"Okay," Marianne says, her fingers puckered in the water. Isn't it early for Zelia to leave? Has she done all she can? She should say something.

"No. I go . . ." Zelia holds her arms, the Target lunch bag swinging and crackling as she appears to do yoga or swim.

Then Marianne understands, Zelia miming an ocean wave now, flying. "Vacation?"

"Noo. I sorry. Back to Brazil." She said this before once and then came back because it had been a six-week leave. Marianne felt her insides fold up. Zelia wouldn't even need the handed-down coat in Brazil.

Marianne stood looking for something to give Zelia for her trip—because it could be just that, a misunderstanding or language error, right? This Brazil trip could be just a holiday, nothing permanent. She'd just open the door with her key and come right back into Marianne's life as though there had just been simple miscommunication.

Or maybe Marianne wouldn't lock the door and she'd find Zelia right there having milky coffee at the kitchen table. Wasn't that possible? Nana or the kids or Martin and the cleaner all sipping and waiting for her to find them, almost as though the door had been propped open the entire time.

Boundaries

R ennie Josephs entered Lily Manheim's office for therapy via a personal referral. He knew one of Lily's former patients, although he didn't want to tell her which one. That was fine with Lily, but it did make her wonder what else he might be hiding.

Tall, with broad shoulders, long legs, and flyaway grey-blond hair, Rennie talked of himself with a disparaging humor: he said he was a terrible-yet-aspiring songwriter, a not-so-successful businessman, and a failed husband. Lily chalked this up to insecurity and his still-evolving divorce; it was clear to her that he was a talented storyteller and a bit of a comic. She figured it would take a while to get underneath why he felt he had to apologize for his very existence, but all in all, he seemed like someone who might be helped by therapy.

Rennie's appointment started at 1:00; they finished at 1:50 and agreed to meet the same time the following week. Lily worked her way through the rest of her afternoon—a divorcée who was having trouble believing what was her life was now her life; a teenager subject to depressive episodes and cutting; a grandmother frantic about one of her grandchildren who was "running wild." Lily listened, offered an occasional question and bits of carefully worded advice, wrote out billing sheets, and left the office shortly after five. On her way out, she told the office secretary that she'd see her Monday, wished the guard at the parking lot a good evening, then reached her Prius where she found a note tucked under the right windshield wiper.

"I know this is awkward," it read. "But would you like to go for a drink, sometime?" It was signed, "Rennie."

"Oh no," Lily said out loud.

Not only was it awkward; it was extremely inappropriate. It meant rather than getting down to business during Rennie's next appointment, they would have to discuss this note. Lily had learned this the hard way: once she had offered a patient who had issues with enmeshment the green angora sweater that Lily kept on the back of her chair when she said she was cold. The patient, Nora, a narrow professor of Victorian literature with a long pale braid and childlike hands, had visibly shrunk into her seat, as though Lily had threatened to detach a limb. Later, when Lily asked her about it, Nora had been clear—what if wearing the sweater diminished the separateness that she had been working on all these years? What if Lily's sweater swallowed her alive? The implications turned out to be enormous. They had managed to make a joke of it, but it was a lesson Lily never quite forgot—one woman's sweater was another woman's worst nightmare.

In the parking garage, Lily stared at Rennie's note. How had he known this was her car? Had he followed her to work? Asked the secretary or the garage attendant? For a second Lily flashed on Rennie, tongue caught between his teeth, bent over the scrap of legal paper, forming each letter, one at a time. A tick of empathy rose in her: it struck her that this invitation could not have been easy to write. Still, as she plucked the note from its place and put it into her purse, she knew it was completely unacceptable; it could not stand.

At her regular Friday night dinner with Meghan and Barry Rosen, Lily put the note aside. As she welcomed the Sabbath, she let the worry of the week fade from her mind. At dinner, she drank an extra glass of sweet wine and headed home carrying a container of Meghan's chicken soup. About to get ready for bed, she heard her phone buzz, an unfamiliar number lighting up the screen. Sleepy, she answered without a thought.

"So what do you think?" he asked.

Lily drew a deep breath. Rennie Josephs. A spit of annoyance nudged her awake. She switched gears.

"I think you should not be calling my home number," Lily said. "How did you get this number anyway?"

"I'm not a stalker," Rennie said.

"You're doing a good impression of one," Lily said. She paused and took a breath. She worked on regaining the peace of the evening; anger never helped anything.

"Look," she began again. "I'm willing to talk about this in our next session. But if you think it's impossible for you to stop contacting me in inappropriate manners and accept that I am your therapist and only your therapist, I think you should . . ."

"See someone else," Rennie finished the sentence.

"Yes," she said. "I think that's where we are. We can talk about this . . ."

"Next week," Rennie said. "See you then?"

On the other end, Rennie clicked off the phone.

This was really too much. There was something familiar and disturbing in the way he jumped in and took over the conversation, barely leaving her room to breathe—a sort of blend of her ex-husband Del and her uber-rational daughter Natalie. Lily dropped the phone, went to the bathroom to wash her face, and wondered if she should have cut him off right away.

The phone buzzed again. This time she picked it up without reading the number, prepared to tell Rennie that they were through and that she could recommend several people he might see instead, when Del's voice popped on the line.

"What?" she asked.

"Good Shabbes to you, too," Del said.

"What do you want?"

"Have you spoken to Natalie?"

"Why?"

"She has news."

"What kind of news?"

Del paused. "Are you sitting down?"

"Jesus," Lily said.

"Okay," Del said. "She's getting married. Next month. She wants us to meet his parents. Soon."

Lily was not sitting down, but as soon as Del finished the sentence, she dropped to the bed. In the dim bedroom, she closed her eyes. Behind her lids flashed pictures of Natalie, as a teenager, as a child. At her bat mitzvah, her confirmation class. The pictures flipped by quickly to the present, the last time she saw her daughter when she left Philadelphia for Brooklyn, furious and screaming, off to live with Jonah Emmerling, whom she had known for a grand total of six weeks. The last thing Lily, who had married Del at twenty-three, had told her daughter was that she was throwing away her youth.

"I'm not you!" Natalie had cried.

They had not spoken since.

Lily parted her eyelids, realizing that Del was still on the other end. "Del," she asked. "Is this some kind of joke?"

"No," said Del. She waited for more; Del always had something to add. She waited for him to yell surprise or tell her that he made it up. That this was an elaborate prank, designed to make her what? Angry? Sad? Happy? All at once? She was ready to jump on him, to accuse him of all of these things and more when it suddenly came clear.

"Del," she screamed, "Why the hell did she tell you first?"

"You wouldn't approve?"

"Damn right," she said.

Lily hung up the phone. She thought of dialing Natalie, but it was close to midnight. Still, if her daughter had phoned Del with the news, she might be awake. She checked her own phone, but there were no messages.

When Britney Spears padded over to her, she leaned down, rubbing her head on the dog's neck, wondering how everything got so upside down and mixed up. She had nurtured Natalie while Del ran around. Natalie had not talked to Del for her entire senior year of college. Yet he had been the chosen one to tell what could be the most important decision of Natalie's young life. Or at least one of them.

You wouldn't approve. Damn right.

The words echoed in her head. She knew, with a sharp certainty, that any peace she had drawn from the Shabbat dinner was gone; she would not sleep that night. So instead she leashed up Britney Spears, and, in her nightgown and robe, took the Schnauzer down the steps to the front lawn. The dog, unused to being out at this hour, jumped forward, excited by the nighttime smells.

"Married," Lily said. "At twenty-three."

She knew it was unfair, that just because the wheels had come off her own marriage didn't mean that Natalie didn't have a chance. But the truth of it was that even if she had not been divorced she would have tried to stop her, to tell her to take it slow. She imagined Natalie under a chuppa, pledging herself to a man she hardly knew. It was a rerun of Lily's mistakes years ago. But who wanted to hear that when they had dropped into love, and thought that they had solved a riddle that had eluded everyone else? Certainly she and Del had not paused to think. If they had, there very well might not have been a Natalie at all.

Above her head, the moon hung, a totem to foolish romance. Lily sniffed, taking in a high scent of deer scat and exhaust fumes. She thought of Natalie, how they had stood on this front lawn a year ago and howled at the moon, how lost she had seemed. Was Natalie getting married to settle her life in some way? As a reaction to her parents' divorce? Lily didn't know. Lily, who had once known everything about her daughter, her shoe size, her birthday wishes, her silly childhood dreams, had lost the thread. It felt inconsolable, as though a membrane had been split, a tendon severed.

"Natalie," she called out, startling the dog. Her voice reached into the night. "What the hell?"

Ruth called at 9 a.m. Lily considered not taking the call, but there was always the chance that her mother had fallen, broken a hip, was headed toward the emergency room. Or worse. Eighty-five, as her mother often said, was no picnic.

"Mazal Tov!"

Lily didn't answer but her mother barreled on.

"I heard from Del," she said. "He called me late last night, where were you?"

Lily stared out the window, contemplating the many answers to that question, then said:

"Apparently out of the loop."

"Don't talk in riddles," Ruth told her daughter. "It's a wonderful thing. Your only child getting married. He wanted to share."

"I suppose," Lily said.

"Lily," her mother said. "This is your little girl."

"I know that," Lily said. "It's just that somehow, she hasn't gotten around to telling me."

"Oh," her mother said. "Well, maybe she . . ."

"Thought I might not approve," Lily finished.

"Do you?" her mother asked.

Lily thought for a second.

"Mom," she said. "I'm hanging up."

"Lily," her mother said, "don't do anything you might regret."

"Too late," Lily told her. "That train left the station long ago."

Two days later, and she had still not talked to Natalie. Lily had lifted the phone to call her several times, but a kind of angry shyness came over her. She was afraid of what she might say. She questioned herself: Was she so bitter? She had moved on, or so she thought until Del's call. But now, she wasn't so sure. All of her anger at Del seemed to have crystalized in her response to Natalie's plans. Or, her so-called plans. After all, the only source of the news about the marriage was Del, hardly a reliable source. Upset, for the rest of the weekend, Lily had let the office answering service take her messages, with instructions to alert her only in an emergency.

And if her daughter, Natalie, called.

By the time Rennie arrived on Friday at 1:00 for his appointment, he and his note were the last things on Lily's mind. Lily had spent the week debating what she might say to Natalie. How to employ her wisdom vs. scaring her daughter away. Lily ran arguments over and over again in her mind. Couldn't they wait? She wanted to ask her daughter, practicing an even tone of voice. Maybe a long engagement, while everyone involved could go to counseling? After Lily and Del's separation and divorce, Natalie had chosen sides: first Lily; now, apparently, Del. And why not Del? He had celebrated Natalie's new love, while Lily urged her to slow down. Of course Lily could dissemble and tell Natalie everything was fine, but what about passing along a disappointed mother's own hard-won wisdom concerning love? How could she stop Natalie from making the same mistakes she had made? Or should she just sit mum on the sidelines while Natalie made mistakes on her own?

She pushed her questions down, as she had been pushing all of her feelings down over the last few days. As far as her patients were concerned, nothing had changed since she last saw them the week before. Her job was to remain inviolable, immutable as a figure on Mt. Rushmore, a figure they could post their visions of themselves upon, not the other way around. They were not supposed to know anything of her personal life. In fact, part of her job was to carefully conceal the fact that she had a life, at all. The patients might know one or two facts on occasion, as needed. A story about Britney Spears, the dog's name carefully edited out. The headline news that yes, indeed, she had a child. Or not. There were some patients with whom she had shared nothing, although she had known them for years and years.

"Hey there," Rennie said, poking his head around her office door. Lily looked up from his chart, and waved him in, swept by a little rush of annoyance, as the full memory of his indiscretions returned.

She indicated that he should sit, settled herself on her chair, faced him, and waited for him to begin. She saw them starting slow, then beginning to discuss boundaries, why he had left the note, what it meant to him, if he thought they should continue. If it were possible for her to trust him not to repeat such a gesture again. She opened her mouth, ready to proceed, when, suddenly, without forethought, she began to cry. Not little weepy tears, but full-throated squalls that left her throat and mouth raw, filling the office. It was hard to catch her breath.

She was appalled, ashamed. Yet she couldn't stop. Her chest heaved. What was she crying for? Natalie? Del? Herself? She tried to think of other things—what she might have for dinner, what route she had taken to get to work—but there was nothing she could do at that moment but sob.

On the chair across from her Rennie went pale. He stood. At first she thought he was going to flee—which was probably what she might have done had their roles been reversed—but then he said, "I promise I will never leave you a note again," and moved toward her chair and gently placed one hand on her shoulder. The inappropriateness of the note and the touch was nothing compared to her sobs; whatever hope there was of their continuing a therapeutic relationship as patient and doctor was done.

"I'm sorry . . ." she coughed, trying to get control. "I don't know . . ."

He held a finger to his lips. He looked into her eyes.

"Did someone die?" he asked softly.

"My daughter," she said. His face registered horror; she waved a hand in the air. "She's getting married."

"Ah," he said.

This is where Del might have jumped in, told her she was crazy and to calm down at once.

But Rennie did none of these things. Instead, he kept his hand on her shoulder. She looked up and saw that his eyes were damp.

"I'm a contagious crier," he said. He cleared his throat. "My mother died of MS when I was seven," he said. "My father was emotionally distant. He remarried when I was nine to a woman who didn't ever want children. I spent most of my time at my grandmother's, who had never liked my mother. I decided at ten I would be a stoic when I read about them in Greek tales. My ex-wife says I don't have feelings. And she's right. Nothing upsets me really," he said. Tears ran down his face.

Lily looked up.

"Is that why you're here?"

"Maybe," he said. "I really have no idea."

Lily reached over and handed him a tissue and took two. They both dabbed their eyes and cheeks and chins. Lily loudly blew her nose.

"I'm so sorry," Lily said. And then, "This is not how I operate."

"Me either." He looked around the office, taking in her therapy books, her computer, her plants. "Do you really think that any of this helps?"

She sniffed. "Sometimes. Yes."

Rennie reached over and lifted the green sweater from the back of the chair and dropped it around her shoulders. It was yet another boundary breaker, but to Lily it was the right thing, exactly what she needed. She stood up from her chair.

"What would you do if you were me?" Lily asked.

"Are you really asking my advice?"

Lily nodded.

"Call my daughter," he said. "And then say a prayer for recovering."

He tapped her shoulder one last time. And then he turned and left the office, closing the door behind him, probably forever.

Lily cancelled the remainder of her patients for the day, pleading allergies to cover her red nose and eyes, drove home and fell asleep at once, exhausted. At 5 a.m., she woke to the sound of Britney Spears, barking. "Britney," she called. The dog ignored her. Lily rose, dragging the green sweater that she had not taken off her shoulders to the window. Outside, beneath the balcony, stood two huge bucks. Each had full antlers, and heads bent, they were charging one another across the stretch of lot where she had walked Britney a week ago, locking horns then pulling apart over and over again. In the early morning light, they looked like dinosaurs, prehistoric creatures locked in a battle to the death. Britney and she watched, Britney barking, she spellbound.

Over and over again they crashed into one another, as though they were trying to break the boundaries of body that divided them, as though they were trying to merge into a single, powerful, awful being. Over and over again they proved it could not be done. And yet. At around 6:30, with thin sunlight breaking the dark, the bucks gave up at last. Snorting and stamping, they separated, several female deer materializing behind each of them, and charged down the main road that snaked toward the small patch of woods that remained in the overdeveloped neighborhood. Standing by the window, Britney whimpered. Around them, the rooms of the house loomed, empty and still. Without thinking of the time, Lily reached for her phone and dialed Natalie's number.

"Mom?" her daughter asked on the third ring. "Is something wrong?"

Lily didn't answer right away. Instead she thought of giving birth to Natalie twenty-three years ago, Del nowhere to be found, Lily feeling as though the baby had turned her inside out. Natalie didn't cry once except when she emerged; holding her after birth, the maternity nurse had called the baby's composure remarkable. The baby had opened her eyes and looked around, taking everything in, as though she somehow understood that like it or not, this was the planet where she was now going to reside.

Face Me

L ori follows Sharon down the sunlit hall and into the bathroom, dim as a cave. She wants the makeover Sharon promised, even though it's Shabbes and they're not supposed to touch makeup. Sharon's family doesn't snap electric switches on Shabbes, and using cosmetics, as far as Lori can tell, might potentially be even more forbidden than turning on a light. But Sharon says a lot of things you're not supposed to do on Shabbes you can do if it's to get a husband. In an hour their youth group starts. The younger kids play games and sing in the synagogue, but Sharon and Lori will stand out back, in the alley, talking to the seventh-grade boys. Sharon says Ronny G. will be there.

"Is makeup okay to get a boyfriend, or only for a husband?" Lori asks.

Sharon raises an eyebrow and says, "One thing leads to another," and they crack up. That's what the rebbetzins at their Orthodox day school say to their all-girls class about why they can't dance with boys: one thing leads to another.

The bathroom curtains are drawn across the windows on the far wall, and one small nightlight burns in the corner, a bulb behind a frosted glass shield that stays on from sundown Friday until Saturday night. The thick air smells of talc and potpourri roses and chlorine floating up the driveway from the pool in the backyard. As her eyes adjust, Lori walks up to the mirror that covers an entire wall of the bathroom, floor to ceiling. She is so tall the feeble light catches under her chin, showing her neck and jawbone and cheek on the right side, while her nose sends a dark shadow looping over her left eye and forehead.

The left side looks dark, hollow, maybe sexy. Lori isn't sure which side to like. She doesn't like either.

"You left the door open," Sharon says, going back to shut it. The lock clicks.

Lori is suddenly thirsty, drought-thirsty. She doesn't wear makeup, not really. Only lip gloss. She peers into the dimness and sees the sink; the nightlight glints off the chrome handles. At home she'd just drink from the faucet, but it seems tacky here. She can't do it in front of Sharon.

"C'mon," Sharon says. "What are you waiting for?"

Lori goes to the counter that spans the far wall, where plastic compacts and shiny tubes of mascara and lipstick fill a three-foot Lucite tray. The only places she has seen this much makeup are Robinson's and May Co. Perfume bottles, the ambers and caramels, stand at the back of the tray. A crystal bottle casts faint rainbows on the pink-and-gold wallpaper in the half light.

At Lori's house, her mom keeps all her makeup in one drawer. Weekdays, before her mom heads for work at the library, she puts two streaks of Sheer Apricot across her lips. On Friday nights, while Lori sits on the edge of the tub and watches, her mom unloads the drawer and puts on Cheryl Tiegs Covergirl Clean makeup. Then her mom and dad drive off for their weekly date. They don't care about Shabbes.

Sharon opens a drawer with brushes and combs, compartments for barrettes, hair bands, bobby pins. She quickly clips her bangs back, pinning loops of feathered brown hair to her scalp. Sharon's done this a million times before, including on Shabbes, no big deal.

Bobby pins slide right out of Lori's wispy hair. Jabbing one against her scalp, Lori grimaces in the wall mirror, taking in her head-to-toe wrongness. The straps on her new wraparound skirt tie at the waist in a protruding knot. Ridges have formed over her belly, and her skirt pockets bulge, where her blouse is tucked in. In the same reflection she sees Sharon lean across the counter, her long plaid skirt smooth across her hips. There is nothing lumpy on Sharon.

Sharon uses her thumb and index fingernails to wiggle the stopper out of a bottle of Chanel No. 5. It's a sample in a tiny glass tube, like something scientific. She positions the tube against her index finger and turns it over once, twice.

"Smell this," Sharon says. She holds her palm up, fingers extended as if she is giving Lori something. Lori breathes the air over Sharon's empty hand, careful not to let her nose touch. The scent is rich, dizzying, warm as another body in the room.

Lori pulls back. "Won't your mom be mad if we use her stuff?"

Sharon tilts her head so her long hair swings out of the way as she touches a place just under her right ear. "Nah," she says. She shifts her head to the left and dabs behind the other ear. "She won't know. We'll leave while my parents are asleep." She gives Lori a sly smile. "Or whatever they're doing."

"Ew," Lori giggles. "Gross."

Sharon's mom, dark haired and slender, shorter than Sharon, grew up in Morocco. She can yell at Sharon in French and English, and she doesn't care if Lori hears, but Sharon's dad is the scary one. He pinches Lori's cheek in greeting, or squeezes her hand so hard she can't feel her fingertips, and he keeps his blue eyes steady on hers the whole time, as if his eyes don't know what his hands are doing. He is tall and the fedora he wears on Shabbes makes him even taller, but he has no neck. His head sits right on top of his suit collar, over his round chest and belly, like a little ball on top of a big one. Before lunch he carefully hangs his hat and jacket, laying his tie over one shoulder. Then he cuffs his shirtsleeves as far as they will go around his thick forearms. He has numbers on one arm from when he was a boy, in Germany. Lori passes him the chicken and the spicy carrots without looking at his face, so she doesn't have to see his freaky blue eyes, but then she ends up staring at his arms instead. Which is still better than thinking about him with Sharon's mother during their Shabbes nap.

"You can't do makeup without perfume," Sharon says. She drags her index finger in a long line up the inside of Lori's right arm, wrist to elbow. It gives Lori a chill, like a fingernail on a blackboard, though there's no sound, just the feeling that shifts magically from her arm to her spine. "There," says Sharon. "Now we're ready."

Lori examines a compact with filigreed gold ribbons and pearls encrusted on the top. The white powder pressed inside is so fine it shimmers, as if it were made of pulverized glass. Sharon gets to work like a pro. Her elbow carves a sideways arc in the air as she applies mascara. She stands two inches from the mirror and paints black liquid eyeliner inside her lower lids. Isn't that going to smear on her eyeballs? Lori wonders, tapping the compact on the counter, making a small pile of white glitter dust. But of course the liner won't run. Everything stays where Sharon puts it.

"Crack that powder and you're dead," says Sharon, picking up a brush. "That's my mom's favorite." She shakes the brush to get rid of the extra blush before sweeping it across her cheeks. Under Sharon's olive skin the cheekbones show without rouge, but the added pink makes them seem to be moving, rippling. She takes the pad from the gold-and-pearl compact and sweeps up the powder Lori left on the counter. Then Sharon fake smiles with her teeth showing and circles the lipstick around her mouth. Twice. "Like it?" Sharon asks, pausing to judge.

Her face is a glowing oval of color. Her chin comes to a point like the bottom of a heart.

"Oh god," Lori says. "Totally gorgeous!"

"Thank you, dahling," Sharon says in her fake British accent. Then she appraises Lori.

"Let's do something about you." She opens a bottle of liquid foundation. Lori stares at the foam pad in Sharon's hand coming closer and closer to her face until her eyes cross, and the pad blurs to a white-and-grey blob. She smells the bouquet of perfume at Sharon's wrist, and under that Nivea hand cream, and something sharper, tangy—nail polish remover?

Sharon takes out the blue mascara. She stands on tiptoe. "You're such a giraffe," she says.

"Thanks a lot!" Lori huffs. "I love you, too!"

"Good for kissing tall boy-ohs," Sharon sings.

Lori snorts. "As if there were any at Ezra Academy!" But they both know there is one: Ronny G. How can Sharon be so sure he'll show up at their youth group today? She turns suddenly, wanting to ask Sharon, wanting to know, but the mascara wand stabs her eye. "Ow," she says, staggering away from Sharon, blinking madly.

"Stop fidgeting!" Sharon sighs. "There's only one way this is going to work." She pushes the makeup aside and sits on the counter.

"Now come here." Sharon takes Lori's wrists and pulls her close. Lori's belly bumps into Sharon's legs, and she sucks in her breath to make it flat.

"That's better," Sharon says. She stares at Lori, and Lori blinks. Where is she supposed to look? Until she realizes that Sharon isn't really gazing into her eyes. Sharon focuses somewhere north of Lori's eyeballs as she saturates the arc of skin between brow and lash with aquamarine. Lori can stare all she wants—Sharon doesn't notice. She studies Sharon's green irises, the threads of gold in them like tiny veins, the dilated pupils. There are whole maps of Sharon she's never seen, the slightly indented circles of skin around her nostrils, a tiny velvet mole that summits from Sharon's smooth, tanned cheek. But the truth about Ronny doesn't show.

Then Sharon grips the back of her head. "Hold steady," Sharon says, maneuvering a rollerball lip gloss around Lori's mouth, getting the syrupy color inside the line of lip pencil.

This is what Lori loves: Sharon knows exactly what to do.

"Go mwahh," Sharon says, and Lori smacks her lips.

Sharon opens a powder blush. She puts her hand under Lori's chin, tips her head back. Lori feels floaty with her head tilted. She closes her eyes and breathes in the smell of Sharon-Chanel. The nightlight makes a bright spot in the dark field behind her left eyelid. Her skin warms under the tickle of the blush brush. She can predict Sharon's butterfly strokes across her cheeks, anticipating the rhythm. Then Lori lets go. She lets go the bathroom, lets go time. Lets go her belly, which settles against Sharon's knees as the air rushes in. She pretends, for a moment, that the fingers on her chin are Ronny's, that he has tilted her head back to kiss her, that the light stream of breath blowing across her neck belongs to him. But she knows he won't smell as good as Sharon, as creamy and perfume-y. Sometimes Lori stands in line behind Ronny at the water fountain, or in the playground, waiting to play handball. He smells like pizza.

Sharon releases her chin. She hops off the counter and leads Lori to the mirror. "What do you think?"

Lori stares. She looks beautiful—is beautiful. She looks the way she dreams she looks.

It's not any one element, not the dark lashes that make her eyes pop out or the luminous cheeks or the outline of her pink mouth—though these items are essential, Lori sees, not one can be dispensed with—but the totality, the way the face has been taken apart and reassembled into something new.

Lori wheels around, giddy, and throws her arms around Sharon in a bear hug. Lori wants to say something, to say thank you, but the words aren't right so she kisses Sharon.

It's a fast kiss, a smooth lip-second, but long enough for Lori to taste the mineral flavor—is it her lipstick? Sharon's?—so delicious, like pennies but warm.

She likes the way Sharon feels, her slim shoulders, the softness of her breasts. All that is familiar from a hundred hugs before this one. What surprises Lori are the things she's never imagined. The swell of Sharon's bottom lip. How close Sharon's tongue is, its mobility and heat, just on the other side of her lips. What's surprising is that Sharon hasn't pulled back.

It's Lori who lets go. Her neck is hot. She turns to the counter where the makeup is scattered and hunts for something, peeking sideways to see if Sharon's eyes have narrowed to slits the way they do when she's mad. But in fact Sharon stands there, staring at her with curiosity, like Lori's in the middle of telling a story and Sharon's waiting to hear how it ends.

"Whadya do that for?" Sharon says.

"Um, nothing." Lori picks up the big gold compact again, thinks about sliding it into her pocket. Puts it down on the counter instead. "Sorry," she says, though she isn't.

"Whatever," Sharon says.

There's a knock on the door. "Sharon? Are you in there?" her father asks.

In a sweeping motion, arms colliding, both girls turn suddenly toward the door, as if it were about to open. Two lipsticks and the gold compact hit the floor with a clatter.

"What's going on?" her father asks. His W sounds like an ominous V.

"We're doing our hair," Sharon says. "Almost done."

"I want you out," he says.

"O-kay-ay," Sharon replies. "Be right out."

In the silence, breathing is impossible. Then the heavy footsteps fade down the hall. Instantly, Sharon is on the ground, tweezing shards of the glittering, compressed powder between her fingers as gently as broken glass. She deposits them in the bottom half of the gold case as if they were puzzle pieces, as if her mother wouldn't notice the jigsaw cracks. Who knocked it off the counter? Lori wonders. Not that it matters; even if she didn't do it, she did.

"Take off your makeup," Sharon hisses. "Hurry!"

Lori goes to the mirror. The wraparound skirt still doesn't work, her blouse is too tight, but it will be ok, she can talk to Ronny, if she can keep her face. She crosses her arms.

"No," she says, "I'm not taking it off."

"What do you mean?" Sharon's voice is high and strange, almost pleading. "You have to," she says. "You can't let my dad see you like that."

"I don't care," Lori says.

Sharon stares at her—not directly, but at the Lori in the mirror. Now

Sharon's eyes turn to slits. The mirror has some kind of magnifying effect, concentrating the beam of Sharon's rage so that it burns Lori.

"Fine," Sharon says, her voice hard. "I'll tell my parents the makeup was your idea."

"I don't care." Lori whispers it this time. Her stomach twists as she speaks.

Sharon arranges tubes on the pearly tray. "And I'm not going to youth group today. You go without me." The lipsticks click as she fits the halves together.

Lori feels the powdery air turn heavy. Moving at all is like walking through water, and she swims slowly to the counter. "I don't want to go without you," she says.

"Then go home."

Lori glances at the mirror again. The makeup is still on but her face looks different. Darker. "Where's the remover?"

Sharon passes her a bottle, and Lori puts some of the thick cream on a tissue. She makes slow, robotic circles on her cheeks, over her eyelids. The tissue is quickly sodden and her face turns a blur of blue and black, like a painting left in the rain.

"What are you doing?" Sharon says. "You can't take it off either, can you?" She holds the makeup remover upside down and shakes a blob of cream onto a fresh tissue.

"Face me," she says.

Lori turns right away. This is the sound of the usual Sharon, the bossy confidence, the Sharon she is used to. Sharon bends Lori's head forward and she keeps it there; she does what Sharon tells her. The first stroke of cream feels cool on her skin but Sharon wipes gruffly, over and over, till her cheeks begin to blaze. Sharon strips the blush, the foundation, the mascara, the shadow. Lori squeezes her eyes shut, telling herself don't.

Don't cry.

"Almost done," Sharon says, as she swipes at stray bits of color. Lori knows without looking that her old self is back in place. She keeps her eyes closed because if she doesn't open them she can still see her gorgeous reflection in her mind. The made-up face is truer than the plain. But that doesn't matter now. After they restack the compacts and stand the rows of lipsticks at attention, they will reemerge into Sharon's house, the world of Sharon's parents, the dazzling sunlight where Shabbes rules instead of the dim bathroom where it is suspended.

Sharon stops wiping. Lori opens her eyes. The only color left is at her lips and the contrast against the rest of her skin makes them look thicker, suffused with blood and turning red-gold in the nightlight glow. Sharon reaches for a fresh tissue. Fast, before Sharon can clear her lips, Lori licks them, top and bottom.

Zhid

M rs. Popovitch grew the most beautiful flowers in the neighborhood. Everyone said so. In the front yard she cultivated lilies, proud as princesses, white as snow.

Within their sheltering midst was a plaster sculpture of the Virgin Mary holding the Infant Jesus in the folds of her painted blue dress. Sonya wished the children didn't have to see this. But her husband Ben said, "Be glad it's not a crucifix."

In the backyard, Mrs. Popovitch tended dark red roses, heavy heads almost as big as the cabbages Ben peddled up and down Delmar Avenue. When the roses withered and dropped their velvety petals to the black earth below, Mrs. Popovitch gathered and then ground them into fragrant rose petal jam. Sonya had never been invited to try it, for she was a tenant in Mrs. Popovitch's house and therefore not deemed worthy of the delicacy, but she had seen the crimson-filled jelly jars lined up neatly on Mrs. Popovitch's pantry shelf.

Sonya had been renting the top floor of Mrs. Popovitch's three-story wooden house for almost two years. Mrs. Popovitch and her husband had the two spacious lower floors to themselves; Sonya, Ben, and their children Edith and Milton shared the rooms above. Though Sonya didn't like to admit it, she admired Mrs. Popovitch. Although just thirty, the landlady was capable and clever in a way that Sonya, only a little younger, could not imagine ever being. With her thin lips and cool gray eyes, Mrs. Popovitch was not beautiful, but she seemed aristocratic, even regal.

Sonya knew that Mrs. Popovitch had come from a poor family in Poland. Yet here she was with her own house, white storybook flowers growing out front, red ones out back. She had first come here as a maid for old Mr.

Popovitch. He married her and when he died, barely a year later, he had left her the house and most of his money.

Mrs. Popovitch married again, this time to a much younger, extremely handsome man. Sonya's mother, had she been alive, would have spit twice on the ground when she saw him. The man was an idler who spent the day in a green brocade armchair leafing through magazines and puffing silently on a cigar whose foul smoke always found its way into Sonya's clean kitchen. The one time Sonya saw him standing, it had been to comb his abundant, wavy hair before the mirror in the front hall.

But Sonya's mother would have conceded that Mrs. Popovitch was a *balebusta*, a housewife beyond reproach. When Sonya went downstairs to pay the rent, she had to acknowledge the shining floors that were swept and waxed daily, the pressed yellow gingham curtains, the white dish towels that Mrs. Popovitch made by slitting open and inverting empty flour sacks, then hemming the edges with her meticulous stitching that was as fine as embroidery, as unique as handwriting.

Sometimes, Mrs. Popovitch would take the handle of her broom and rap it sharply against the second-floor ceiling. Sonya understood that these knocks, coming up through the floor, were Mrs. Popovitch's way of summoning her downstairs, often to translate something she saw in the newspaper or to help her write a letter. Although Mrs. Popovitch spoke English well, her reading and writing lagged far behind and she relied on Sonya for assistance. Other times, Mrs. Popovitch would climb the stairs to Sonya's apartment on the pretext of borrowing a cup of sugar or some tea. How could the ever-provident Mrs. Popovitch have run out of anything? No, Sonya thought, she was coming up to snoop. She saw the way Mrs. Popovitch looked around the kitchen, taking in the well-scrubbed linoleum on the floor, the smooth oilcloth that covered the table because linen or even cotton was too dear. "I had no idea the *zhid* were so clean," she murmured admiringly. Sonya flinched. Though she was from Russia, not Poland, the word *zhid*—here they would have said *kike*—was the same in both languages.

Yet the woman could be kind; Ben was always pointing that out. Since they had no telephone, Mrs. Popovitch let them use hers. That way, Ben could call and let Sonya know when he would be coming home. When they were late with the rent, Mrs. Popovitch said, "You'll pay me when you can." And on Christmas Eve, she invited all the children on the block—including Edith and Milton—to join her and her husband for hot cider and cookies.

Sonya was of two minds about the Christmas visit. She felt uncomfortable about the tree and all it represented. But Edith and Milton begged, and she hated to deny them this small pleasure. "You're making too much of it," said Ben. "Juice and cookies. It's not like she's going to convert them or anything."

"That's how it starts," said Sonya, who relented anyway. Her one condition, however, was that they appear at Mrs. Popovitch's holly-wreathed door immaculate and shining, as if dressed for the High Holiday service at the shul on Burlingame Avenue.

"Ma, what difference does it make?" whined Edith as Sonya yanked her hair into smooth, tight braids. "She sees us every day in our regular clothes."

"It doesn't matter," said Sonya, using a dab of her own pomade to slick down some stray wisps. "If you want to go, you'll stand still." Only when they were bathed, coiffed, and dressed in their best clothes did Sonya allow them to descend the stairs. She wasn't going to give Mrs. Popovitch the opportunity to say that the zhid's children were dirty.

When they had gone, Sonya went quietly downstairs and out the door. It was snowing lightly, and standing there in only a housedress and an apron, she shivered. She could smell cinnamon, and through the wet, misted windowpane, she saw the tree presiding over the room like a queen. There were her beloved children—Edith with her round, dimpled face, Milton with his perpetual cowlick—eating and drinking with the goyim. Sonya was ashamed, not just of them, but also of herself, for envying them. When she finally went inside, her dress was soaked.

Later, Edith and Milton trudged upstairs too stuffed with cookies to want any supper.

"I think there should be Christmas for Jews," announced Milton.

It was some time after this that Sonya was summoned downstairs by the imperious rapping of Mrs. Popovitch's broom. It was too early in the day for Ben to be telephoning her so it must be something the landlady needed. Sonya had been making chicken soup and the front of her apron showed golden dots of grease and shreds of carrot. When she entered Mrs. Popovitch's kitchen, she was sorry she had not thought to take it off, as Mrs. Popovitch was not alone. Sonya recognized the heavyset woman with the curly hair, a friend of the landlady. The man was a stranger. But they, like Mrs. Popovitch, were so engrossed in examining the soft, shining pelts of fur that covered the table that after a quick nod in her direction, they didn't look at her again. Mrs. Popovitch's husband was nowhere in sight.

Sonya moved closer. She had never seen so much fur, so close up. There were shining brown stoles, a glossy black jacket, a silvery gray hat, a honey-colored muff. Some of the garments were made of fur that was long and fluffy; others, from fur that had been sheared and was now as soft and dense as velvet. Mrs. Popovitch was stroking the furs reverently. Finally, Sonya took a closer look at the man.

He was seated at the table, arm stretched out over the fur in a proprietary manner. He wore a navy-blue peacoat from which the buttons were missing and threadbare trousers of the same dark blue. Something about these clothes looked familiar; it took Sonya a moment to place them but then she realized he was dressed in a uniform from the Russian navy. Though it had been many years since she had left Russia, reminders of her homeland still brought on the urge to weep. She looked carefully at his face, which was very handsome. Unlike Mrs. Popovitch's husband, whose looks seemed overly groomed and almost feminine, this man's features were rougher. He had high, slanting cheekbones, full lips, and straight, thick blond hair that fell in a spray over his forehead. His eyes, Sonya saw, were a clear, light blue, like the sky that floated over their summer house, all those years ago.

Seeing him made it all come streaming back: the summer days with Mama and her sister Irena, sitting on the sun porch and eating the berries they had picked together. The maid washed and placed them in crystal dishes that she carried carefully on a heavy silver tray. Solemnly, she poured cream over the berries before setting the dishes down. Sonya dribbled cream all over the front of her linen dress but Mama only smiled. In winter, she and Irena were taken to a carnival, where there were Gypsy dancers, a puppet theater painted with gold stars, and a stall that sold bits of fried dough that were dipped in powdered sugar. She could still remember how steaming dough warmed her chilled hands and how the sugar drifted down and mingled with the snow.

Then all the other things came back too. In their rush to be remembered, they fell all over one another, like the game of dominoes Edith and Milton played. There was the talk of revolution that made all the grown-ups frown; Papa's sudden disappearance; Mama's hands laced so tightly together that the knuckles turned white as she waited for news; Papa's broken body coming home at last in a blood-stained mail sack; the burns around Mama's mouth after she had drunk the poison. Then came the time when windows of the house erupted in explosions of wood and glass and mattresses were stood on end in the places the windows had been, waiting alone with Irena for Mama to return with food, the agonizing boat trip with everyone vomiting and calling out to God for deliverance.

Sonya willed herself to look back at the furs. Seeing the way she gazed down at them, Mrs. Popovitch's friend said, "They are beautiful, no?" Her accent, when she spoke English, was thicker than either Mrs. Popovitch's or Sonya's own.

Before Sonya could reply, Mrs. Popovitch said, "I want you to write something for me. A contract."

"Of course," Sonya said. "What should it say?"

"That I, Anna Popovitch, am buying these furs—" she stopped to tick off on her fingers the number of stoles, jackets, hats, and muffs—"from this gentleman for the sum of five hundred dollars."

"Maybe we should say exactly how many of each, and what kind?" suggested Sonya.

"That's a very good idea," said Mrs. Popovitch. "Here, let me get you paper and a pen. You—" she pointed at the man, "get up so she can sit." He stood and stretched, running his fingers through the thick sheaf of his hair. Five hundred dollars! But the man hardly seemed excited; in fact he barely paid attention to what Mrs. Popovitch was now dictating to Sonya. He paced around the kitchen, stopping at the window to look out, and pressed his hands to the back of his neck.

"That's two stoles, both beaver," Mrs. Popovitch said. "Another of silver fox—"

"So many Anna!" murmured her friend. "What will you do with them? You can't wear them all at once."

"That shows how much you know," said Mrs. Popovitch. "I'll sell them. For a profit too. Do you want to buy one?"

"Me?" The woman patted her curls and smiled. "Oh no. But maybe your little friend here . . ." she said slyly, indicating Sonya.

"No, the zhid won't be buying this time," said Mrs. Popovitch as she counted out the bills into the man's open hand. Sonya's face burned but she kept writing.

When the contract was completed, Mrs. Popovitch, the blond man, and Sonya all signed their names to it. Sonya saw that his first name was Sergei but she was unable to make out the last. "You're the witness," Mrs. Popovitch said to Sonya. "Don't forget." Sonya was ready to leave but before she did, something made her turn around. The man was looking—no, staring—at her with those pale blue eyes. His expression was one of pure supplication. But what could he possibly want from her? Sonya averted her eyes and hurried upstairs.

"You should have seen them!" Sonya told Ben later that evening when the children were in bed and she was serving him supper. "The whole table covered with them. Dark ones, light ones. As many as in a furrier's shop!" Ben chewed his pot roast thoughtfully—even after hours of cooking the meat was still tough—and turned a page of the newspaper. "You're not listening to me," Sonya accused. "I wait all day long for you to come home so I can talk to someone and then you don't listen to me."

"I'm sorry," Ben said, pushing the paper aside. "I'm listening. You want a fur coat? A stole? Look, I'd like to buy it for you, Sonya. But how? With what?"

"I didn't ask you to buy it for me," Sonya said. "It was just something to see. Something to talk about."

"Why talk about what you can't have?" His eyes strayed toward the paper again. Sonya got up from the table.

"You don't understand," she said. And he didn't. Back in Russia, his family had been as poor as Mrs. Popovitch's. He didn't know what it was to want fine things not because of the things themselves, but because they reminded you of who you had been before so much had been taken from you.

Sonya didn't see Mrs. Popovitch for several days after that. The weather turned brutally cold and the strong winds that came off the lake went right through Sonya's thin winter coat. She thought of the furs she had seen but not touched.

Then she arrived home from the market one afternoon to see Mrs. Popovitch's flushed face peering out at her from the front window. "There you are!" she said, opening the door for Sonya to come in. "I've been waiting!" Sonya stepped into her landlady's kitchen without even going upstairs to drop off her bundles.

"Read this!" she commanded, thrusting a newspaper in front of Sonya's perplexed face. "I want to know what it says here!" Sonya set down her bags and began to read aloud.

"Fur Scam Sweeps Detroit Neighborhood. A man posing as a wholesale fur dealer has been swindling residents near Delmar Avenue, police have reported. Claiming to offer fox, beaver, mink, and raccoon at rock-bottom prices to unsuspecting clients, the man, a Russian emigre, has instead been peddling stolen furs that are believed to have come from . . ."

"How will I ever sell those furs now?" said Mrs. Popovitch. Her face had lost its flush and was now as pale as the lilies in the front yard. "I'll find him and when I do, I'll kill him with my own two hands."

"But you have a contract," Sonya reminded her. "I wrote it all out for you."

"Contract!" spat Mrs. Popovitch. "I don't want money. I want blood!"

"There's a number to call," Sonya said hesitantly. "If you have anything to report."

"Then read it to me!" Mrs. Popovitch said. She might have been giving a firing squad the command to shoot. Sonya's voice trembled slightly as she read the number aloud.

"Can you imagine, Ben? The whole thing was a fraud. That man, the one I told you about? He was selling stolen goods." Sonya spread the newspaper out in front of her husband that evening.

"Well," he chuckled as he leaned over to read the story. "So much for Mrs. Popovitch's get-rich-quick schemes. You don't get something for nothing."

"She did get this house, didn't she?"

"Yes, but she had to sleep with the alte cocker first."

Mrs. Popovitch wanted Sonya to accompany her to the police station to help make an identification. They set off together one morning after Ben had left for work and the children for school. The day was sunny though bitter. Under a blanket of snow and dark soil slept Mrs. Popovitch's red roses, her pallid lilies. Sonya wondered what had become of the furs, which the police had demanded and not returned. But Mrs. Popovitch said nothing about them. She walked briskly along in her black suede boots, her face composed, yet merciless. Sonya had to hurry to keep up.

At the police station, they were led into a large room that contained a raised dais and rows of wooden benches, almost, Sonya thought, like a shul. Or a church. Mrs. Popovitch took a seat in the front and Sonya sat beside her.

On the raised platform, several tables were lined up end to end. Metal chairs were placed behind the tables. "Okay, you can bring them in," called the sergeant. One by one, the men shuffled in, walking first past the tables and then behind them until they reached the chairs. Sonya watched carefully. The first man was too tall by a head, the next too dark, with brown hair and olive skin. Sonya felt she would know him anywhere, with that shock of gold hair and those pale, azure eyes. The third man was blond and the right height but his hair was wispy and thin. Mrs. Popovitch stirred nervously beside her. "Do you see him?" Sonya shook her head.

Then he walked onto the dais. At least Sonya thought it was him but he looked much thinner. His hair had been cut, nearly shaved off, his forehead was laid bare. Sonya had trouble seeing the color of his eyes.

"I think that's him," said Mrs. Popovitch, digging her sharp elbow into Sonya's side.

"I'm not sure," Sonya said. "His eyes . . ."

"Sergeant," Mrs. Popovitch said in a loud voice, "I think I see the man. Can I get closer?" The sergeant nodded and Mrs. Popovitch took Sonya's arm and moved right up to the dais.

It was the same man. Not only did Sonya recognize the face with its full, pouting lips and slanted bones, there was no mistaking the eyes. Without their golden cover of hair, they seemed naked and vulnerable. The man looked not at her, but into her. This time, however, Sonya steadily returned his gaze. And that was how she saw him mouth in Yiddish, "Have pity on a poor zhid." She sucked in her breath and shut her mouth.

"Now I'm not sure," said Mrs. Popovitch, as she continued to peer at him. "He looks different. The hair for one thing. I don't know. I want to identify him, but I have to be sure it is him." She turned to Sonya. "What do you think?" The man's eyes held Sonya's, blue as the skies of childhood summers, clear as tranquil water. Not even her babies' eyes had been so blue.

"No, it's not the same man," Sonya said in a bold voice she scarcely knew as her own. Mrs. Popovitch stared.

"You're sure then?" she asked tentatively, as if Sonya's sudden display of strength had leached dry her own.

"Positive."

"I didn't really think so . . . ," muttered Mrs. Popovitch. "Though I was hoping of course . . ." She allowed Sonya to lead her away.

"All right then, ladies. You'll have to come back next week. When we have some more suspects," said the officer.

"Next week," said Sonya confidently. "We'll come back."

Leaving the building, they walked in silence. Mrs. Popovitch was the first to speak. "You'll come again," she asked in a hesitant tone Sonya had never heard her use before. "To the lineup."

"I already said I would," Sonya said, allowing her impatience to seep through. But it wouldn't matter. The man would be long gone by then. Sonya imagined that he would choose some place warm: Florida, Mexico, Argentina.

"I'd like to thank you," Mrs. Popovitch said, her voice almost shy. "For coming with me."

"You're welcome," Sonya said.

"If there is something I could do for you. A favor perhaps . . . ," Mrs. Popovitch continued.

"A favor," repeated Sonya, thinking of the furs and their varying hues: chestnut, ebony, silver, wheat, honey. But the image drifted away like smoke, replaced by an image of roses, Mrs. Popovitch's roses, crimson and dark in the brilliant sunlight of a June morning.

"The petals," she said out loud.

"What?" asked Mrs. Popovitch.

"The rose petals from the garden. That you use to make jam. I'd like to taste them."

"But of course," said Mrs. Popovitch, still not understanding. "I'll bring you a jar tonight."

The two women arrived at the house, where Mrs. Popovitch opened the door. Sonya could see into the parlor, where Mrs. Popovitch's husband dozed in the armchair, mouth slightly open. She could feel the landlady's eyes on her as she ascended the stairs, but she kept her head high, high as the lilies.

She imagined herself seated at a table that was no table she had ever seen. There was a heavy white napkin in her lap, a silver spoon in her hand, and she was eating rose petal jam from a porcelain dish, the kind she had not touched or held for years. The taste of the jam was complex; along with its ineffable sweetness, she detected a hint of orange, of clove perhaps, and of vanilla. She kept it on her tongue for a long time before she swallowed. At her feet there was a carpet of broken blossoms, bright as blood, staining the floorboards below.

Deep in the Valley

It is Wednesday night and she drives to a motel deep in the valley. She has never been deep in the valley. The deep valley is far away. She loves the way *deep in the valley* sounds and she loves the thoughts she thinks about it. She thinks of the envelopes taped to the headboard of her single bed. She has slept in that single bed forever, since she was a child. There have been many other beds over the years, single beds in white rooms with black barred windows, common rooms where she sat with people who rubbed tabletops, watched games played, rules chucked aside, listened to piano keys plunked by cross-eyed women.

It is hot in October. It is humid in Los Angeles. It is not a regular night. It is the start of the Jewish New Year. It is the first night leading the Jews, she, and her mother and father, into days of repentance, collective guilt, and interior monologues.

Will you come to temple with Daddy and me tomorrow?

Maybe tomorrow I'll come with you and Daddy. But don't worry tonight. I'll be out late.

Her mother nods. Her father walks in. Her mother says, *She's not coming tonight. She'll be out late, but we aren't to worry. Right, honey? And she'll probably come with us tomorrow morning for services.*

Her mother and father are used to her late nights, her disappearances, her living at home in her childhood bedroom. She thinks it is strangely nice that the three of them had lived together for so many years.

They walk from her parents' bedroom down the stairs. She stops halfway and says, *Maybe I'll come tomorrow. Probably you can count on it.*

At the bottom of the stairs her mother calls up.

You could wear that new dress we bought. You look so pretty in purple.

From below, her parents wave goodbye. From above she waves back.

Her father opens the front door. The sun is still in the sky. The trees in the front yard frame her parents at the threshold. They look back at her. She floats on the stairs; her face scrubbed clean like her father prefers. Her hair, long and wavy, is still wet from the shower.

She stopped drying her hair in the first mirage. Over the years she has lived in rooms without locks along hallways that were always locked and required keys to enter and exit. She cannot remember those places, or her rooms in those places. Cords, electricity, shoelaces, belts, hairpins, razors, studded earrings, none of that was ever allowed in any of the mirages.

Her mother blows up a kiss.

I'm so glad we'll all be together tomorrow.

She blows back the kiss. Her delicate hands send her mother down the walk to her father. She sends her mother to pray. Her mother leaves believing they will all pray together in temple tomorrow leaning against flattened burgundy nap in seats that sort of rock, listening to the shofar blow while she twists her mother's wedding ring round and round and round on her mother's finger until, like always, her father takes her busy hand and smooths it, quiets it, laces his fingers in between hers, crooks her arm up into his elbow, and smiles down at her.

When the front door closes she walks up the stairs.

Her hair is dry now and she is in the car. Her bag is in the back seat, the contents winnowed. She has chosen her dead dog's favorite ball that she has kept for years, the latest issue of a fashion magazine, a pill bottle, and an undershirt she found in her father's drawer years back. She has worn it to a white softness finer than silk. There is a frayed hole at the collar. The hole makes her feel safe.

She stops at the red light at the bottom of the hill on the street that leads deep into the valley. She feels good. In the next car an older man smiles at her through his window, his hair rising and falling in the air conditioning. He smiles over like he is a Jew too and also avoiding temple. She smiles back and turns up the music. At the green light she presses hard on the gas and her hair whips behind her in the heat. It is still steamy though the sun is long gone.

She thinks of all the clicks and snaps and locks behind her. She can still hear them. But tonight there were only three: the solid click of the front door; the softer snap of her bedroom door, lockless for years; the back door lock when she left.

She thinks of her mother and father in temple, prayer books open. She sees them listening to the sermon. She sees them listening to appeals for contributions. She sees them listening to the schedule for morning services and the temple activities for the days of awe and atonement from Rosh Hashana until Yom Kippur comes to a close.

She thinks of those who will be inscribed for the coming year in the Book of Life. *Who shall live and who shall die* and she thinks about that sung incantation, that musical recitation of all the different ways people will die during the coming year. She thinks about those whose time has come. She thinks about those who will not be inscribed in the Book of Life.

She rents the motel room for a few days and pays with her new credit card. She was given the card after she avoided another mirage for a year. When her parents gave it to her they said they were proud she was handling the pressure. She agreed. She had been handling the pressure well. The clerk at the desk, a boy, is nice enough. He smiles but does not make dumb polite chatter. He does not ask to see her driver's license. She is used to showing her license because she looks young. She knows she looks older than a teenager but not quite a woman. She knows she looks perpetually suspended: otherworldly and not quite grown. She is thirty-three. This year her birthday falls during the Days of Awe, on the day Yom Kippur comes to a close. She signs the receipt in her tiny handwriting. The clerk's silence seems right to her. She is near now. Probably no one ought to talk to her.

The room is sort of okay, beiges and pinks, with a flat, king-size bed. It is a motel but the minibar is stocked. On top of the minibar is a binder filled with information about tourist attractions. The Bible is in one nightstand on sticky floral contact paper and a local phone book is in the other. Neither is quite the Book of Life, she thinks, and unpacks her bag.

She walks down the hall to fill the plastic ice bucket. The hallway is quiet. There is only the hum of the ice machine. The halls are not quite fresh, but she has lived in much worse. She has lived in places she tries to forget. She turns her head when memories of those mirages squiggle her brain.

She fills the ice bucket. She hangs the Do Not Disturb sign outside the door. The door clicks and she snaps the lock. She peels the plastic from the tall glass in the bathroom. She fills the glass from the tap. In the bedroom she strips naked and avoids the mirror. She pulls on her father's undershirt and sits cross-legged on the bed. The bedspread crackles. Squeezing her dog's ball, she slowly flips through the fashion magazine.

She knows what she hopes. She knows she floated her mother false hope. She feels badly about that false hope. But her final false hope is not as bad as other things she has put her mother and father through. She never wanted her mother and father to suffer. She just cannot do anything about anything when it all comes upon her. When it all comes upon her she wants to whirl and whirl. The faster she can whirl, the faster she will float, out there, up there, float to a place where it really does feel good, to a place where it is warm, buttery warm, and she is calm. That is where she wants to be. She wants to be in the warmth and calm. She wants to be cocooned and at peace. She is on the last page of the last chapter of last year's book. This year she does not want to be inscribed. This year she will not be inscribed. This year it will be done. This year is done. This year she is done. She knows that.

She knows where she is going. There is nowhere else to go. There is nothing else to try. There are no other beliefs to believe. She no longer imagines she possesses something everyone else seems to have. The box is too little now. The box she is in is too little. She has become clear in her thinking. She knows that the little box she is in will never expand. The little box has no doors. The little box has no windows. The little box only has walls that keep pressing in. The walls keep pressing in toward the center. She is standing in the center of the little box. She knows the walls of the little box will keep pressing in until the little box is a tiny white square, small and perfectly folded, perfectly folded like one of her father's handkerchiefs, like the handkerchiefs stacked in her father's top drawer, and she will be inside that little box, perfectly folded like a tiny handkerchief, and no one will be able to unfold her ever again.

She reads an article in the magazine about applying mascara in a new way. At the mirror she tries the new technique the article says will make her look like a star. She brushes mascara onto her lashes. She follows the directions in the article but her eyelashes look the same as always. New techniques are always overrated, she thinks.

She turns on the radio and finds a clear station. The station plays music without interruption. It is pretty music without words. Pretty music without words seems right to her too. She is near now. Probably she ought not hear the words of others.

She folds down the bedspread. She has drunk the water and fills the glass up with ice cubes. The ice cubes are cubed, perfectly cubed. The cubes are clear. The cubes are perfectly clear, not cloudy at all. She loves the tinkling pinging sound the ice cubes make when they hit each other and ping against the sides of the glass. She refills the glass from the tap.

The curtains are drawn and she pulls them open. The view is not great, and there is no moon, but looking at the dark sky is much better than looking at the faded cabbage roses on the curtains. On the bed she plumps the pillows behind her. She unscrews the bottle and pours into her palm all of the pills. She has hoarded all of the pills for a long time. She has hoarded the pills from her last visits to mirages, mirages with green bars and many guards. She hoarded the pills between visits and then for a year. She swallows the pills. She has learned that pills go down quicker if she snaps her fingers. Her fingers snap to the beat of the music. She takes a long drink of water. She clicks off the light. Through the open curtains the white light from distant constellations floats into the motel room. The white light is faint but makes the motel room look star dusted and almost romantic.

Her mother and father will not be home from temple yet. It will be an hour before services end and everyone has kissed everyone they know and wished strangers *a happy, yes and to you, a healthy new year, may we all be blessed. May we all be blessed* she can hear the strangers say while shaking hands awkwardly with those ahead and behind. She wonders when her mother and father will find the envelopes. She wonders which of them will pull the envelopes off her headboard and ball up the tape she used into a sticky nothing and throw the sticky nothing away.

She selected her words carefully. She wrote the letter several times. She wanted loving words. She wanted firm words. She wanted her words to tell her mother and father those other times they found her perhaps she had not taken the necessary steps to see it through; to see herself through it, though she thought she had. She wanted her words to tell her mother and father that maybe those times she had not been sure, or not as sure, but she had seemed sure on the inside where it counts. The words she selected about this time leave no doubt. She has no doubts. She selected words to tell her mother and father they cannot save her. She does not need their saving. She is saving herself. She selected words to tell them their repentance is not necessary, their atonement not required; they are absolved of their misplaced guilt. Her words tell them there is no belief called *just if.* Her words tell them she is freeing them, *just if* they will be freed.

She knows her mother and father will give the concert tickets to her boyfriend, a birthday present she bought with money earned at the pet store. Her boyfriend will not be prepared. She never told him a lot about herself. She just danced in and out of the light.

She hopes her mother and father have had enough time. She hopes they have prepared over the years. They should have prepared. They should have prepared for her, for the fact of her, for the fact of her core, of what is there, and what is not. Everyone sees her broken wings. Since she was young she knew she was different. She saw her difference. Everyone saw her difference. She saw her broken wings. Since she was young she knew she was a creature created differently. She knows she was created differently from everyone around her.

She hopes her mother understands the floated false hope and forgives her pretending that mother and father, and daughter, would pray together tomorrow. She hopes her father has the strength. She hopes that if her father does not have the strength, that he will find the strength. She hopes her mother and father find peace. She hopes finally they will be at peace. She hopes with that peace her mother and father will remember what it feels like to be fearless and brave. She has loathed herself for the fear she has made them feel. She just never had any choice. Now she is fearless and brave. Bravely she lies down deep in the valley.

WAR

If you're a Jew, there's always "The War," no matter the century. In the twentieth century, and now the twenty-first, there are still plenty to choose from. Females are trapped, in so many ways, by the ravages of war, whether tending the proverbial fires on the home front while males are doing the fighting; as couriers masquerading as members of the "other side," able to pass because they're not males; as prisoners of war; as Holocaust victims or survivors; or subject to the particular sexual ravages that enemies wreak on the most vulnerable on the other side.

For years, *Lilith* magazine had to counter critics who claimed there were no experiences during the Holocaust that were different for women. While of course all Jews, regardless of gender, were reviled and persecuted equally as Jews, nevertheless there were the common and horrific sufferings typically reserved for women: rape, forced abortions, forced pregnancies, sexual exploitation, and the particular anguish of women who decided not to attempt escape but instead remained with aged relatives who could not get out—usually their own mothers. And then . . . the toll taken on many female survivors afterward, when their experiences in hiding or in the camps left them with reproductive challenges. Finally in relative safety somewhere after the war, some survivors who decided that they wanted to bear children found they could not sustain a pregnancy.

This is not a competition over suffering, but a necessary grounding for the themes that motivate much of the fiction *Lilith* has considered for publication over the years. The Holocaust continues to loom large in the imagination of today's Jews, no matter what their ancestry, even two or three generations later.

While you won't see the actual horrors of war, in one story snapshots and studio photos of normal Jewish lives before devastation are potent reminders of hope destroyed. And anyone who has seen the tower of photographs at the core of the US Holocaust Memorial Museum in Washington, DC, will have flashes of those family photos as documentation of prewar Jewish life comes into focus.

The first stories in this section deal with women's particular experiences of war and persecution in Europe, and the last with the ongoing conflict between Israelis and Palestinians over land and rights. Women have been in the forefront of attempts to bridge differences and establish friendship circles, cooperative ventures linking Muslim and Christian Arabs and Jews, but the struggles between the peoples too often become armed battles.

The ways war transforms—and can deform—lives through multiple generations demonstrates again how the political is always, in the end, personal.

La Poussette

Sylvie Beauchard has been cooking since dawn. Her in-laws will be here shortly, so despite her fatigue, she is brisk in the dining room, snapping down the linens and cutlery. The wine glasses she places carefully by the plates. The green stems make her think of tulips and she wishes she had some for a vase. It is too early for flowers and besides, she chides herself, she has what she has most wished for.

She has planned the exact way to tell Charles' parents about their grandchild. Charles has agreed to her plan, though he'd prefer to tell them straight away. After the meal, Sylvie will suggest the front room for dessert. (The hazelnut torte is indeed the reason for rising before dawn. It has layers and filling and a frosting made glossy and smooth by her hand.) Once seated, she will take out her knitting—a tiny sweater in the palest blue. How long before they notice what she is making? With her father-in-law it could be hours. He'll start in with news of the Occupied Zone, then move on to the price of petrol in Nîmes, but Mother will notice. She will raise her eyebrows, gather her lips, a look Sylvie finds fearsome, though it is Mother's most common expression. She will demand to know what Sylvie is doing and why. And then they can tell her, watch her impatience and annoyance turn to pleasure, maybe even pride, who knows? But Sylvie has gotten ahead of herself. There is still work to be done before they arrive.

From the window over her sink, Sylvie can see the tenants in the next farm over out in the orchards. It had pleased her at first to think of the farm being inhabited again. Then she saw the tenants in town with their city clothes and manners. The woman's skirt had pleats in the back that flipped up when she walked. They weren't farmers, she thought then, and sure enough, Charles had found their cow in his pasture. When he took it back he'd found them reading books. Books about farming! Who knew such a thing existed? Were there also books about walking? he'd asked Sylvie. Taking a leak in the woods? That was weeks ago, and still Sylvie will hear him laughing in the other room.

And now, here he is, stomping his feet outside the door to get the dirt off them as she has taught him.

"The wine," she says when he is in.

"Yes, yes."

He is not one to be rushed, Sylvie knows, but he wants the dinner to go well, too. A son would make his life easier, but Sylvie cannot help herself; she wants a girl.

"I'm hungry," he says. "It is ready?"

He's been up for hours too. Outside the dogs—Sammi and Bruno—bark their excited welcome. They are good dogs, loyal and affectionate, fine company when Charles is gone. Over the barking she can hear the truck sputter and grind on its ascent. Sylvie tucks a loose strand of hair behind her ear. There isn't time to change into a fresh apron. Pity.

"*Bienvenue!*" Sylvie calls to her in-laws, "Come in!"

"Please," Mother Beauchard says, "I'm not the Queen, just an old woman." She pecks Charles on each cheek. Her fingers grip Sylvie's shoulders as she pulls her in for her kisses. There is nothing frail in her touch.

"Where is Papa?" Charles asks, taking her coat and kerchief.

"With your beasts," she says. "He brought them bones."

"He's sweet on those two," Charles says.

"Just two more mouths to feed, that's all they are," Mother says.

Sylvie knows where this conversation is going: they spoil the dogs, treat them like children. If they had children they'd see how foolish they look.

"That yarn is lovely," Sylvie says, reaching for Mother's arm in a new sweater.

"I traded plenty for the wool," Mother says.

"A good color on you."

Mother says nothing, but Sylvie can tell she is pleased. She puffs up like the tawny *poule* before she lays.

Father Beauchard has been drinking already. He's mild and affectionate when he drinks, no trouble. He might grow mushy at their news, but that isn't a crime, no not at all.

"Father," she says kissing him. She smells the wine on his breath—warm and briny against her cheek.

"Shall we sit down?"

"Yes, please."

"Such fuss for family," Mother says, taking in the tablecloth, the good glasses.

"Never mind," says Father, "never mind."

Charles tries to catch her eye. He'd like to blurt their news, to stave off his mother's relentless crabbing, but Sylvie won't look. She must get the roast from the stovetop where it cools. The juices will make a tasty gravy, thickened just a bit with flour, a touch of wine. And then the dogs are barking again.

"Such a nuisance," Mother says, smug, her opinion confirmed.

There is a rap at the door and through the kitchen window, Sylvie sees it is the neighbors. At this time? Everywhere families are sitting down to Sunday supper. Father is liable to invite them in, tell them the history of this house, the village. His favorite is the story about their region being the model for Heaven, such is its charm. Between her mother-in-law's sourness and this interruption, Sylvie's high hopes for the day plummet.

She opens the door. "*Oui?*" Two men stand before her, their round spectacles making their eyes look particularly inquisitive. With them is the woman in her pleated skirt. This time she has a baby carriage with her, and in the carriage, a little girl with wispy dark curls, the kind Sylvie would like to smooth with her hand. Sharply, the child turns her head from Sylvie's gaze.

"Good afternoon," the taller man says. His dark hair is brushed back from a high forehead. "We're your neighbors." Sylvie catches a whiff of something foreign in his speech.

"*Oui,*" Sylvie says again.

"We were hoping to speak with you regarding—"

But then Father Beauchard is calling from the other room, "Come in! *Bienvenue!*" Sylvie opens the door wider, so they can all enter. The shorter man lifts the carriage over the stone threshold, and then the child is removed. She goes to the woman, tugs on her skirt to be lifted. Once on her hip, she buries her face in the woman's shoulder. In the past, such a display would've pained Sylvie.

"We've interrupted you," the woman says, seeing the table. "We'll not bother you long."

"No bother, no bother," says Charles.

"We must inquire," says the shorter man. "If you have any food you would sell. You see, the farm isn't yet producing."

"No," says Sylvie, before Charles can answer. She wants them to leave *tout de suite* so she can resume her cooking, proceed to the announcement, the celebratory cake. She tries to usher the neighbors toward the door again. She sees that during this interruption, the potatoes have boiled over, leaving starchy ribbons down the side of the big pot.

"Potatoes," says the woman.

"For the pigs," Sylvie says.

"Would you consider for the child?" the woman says. "She is growing."

The child has round cheeks, legs like sausages. Even her fingers are pudgy. Is she pale? Perhaps, but it is that time of year. The child stares at her, her dark eyes appraising, it seems.

"We must take care of our own," Sylvie says, averting her eyes.

"You know about the market on Tuesday?" Charles says. "Some will barter there."

Sylvie watches the woman return the child to her stroller. It's a stylish little *poussette* with big wheels, a navy awning and seat with a sturdy basket beneath. She has seen these only in magazines. And though there are no sidewalks or gardens or parks in which to push a *poussette*, Sylvie must have it. Why should this baby have one and not hers?

"Wait," she says. "I've forgotten the barley." Neither she nor Charles care for it. But these people can't be choosy, even with their fancy ways.

"For the *poussette*," she says, "a hundred kilos."

"Ridiculous," says Mother Beauchard.

The child is being lifted out, her fat little legs kicking. From under the seat, a blanket is removed. "*Et voilà,*" says the shorter of the men.

"What do you need with that?" Mother Beauchard says.

Sylvie doesn't care what Mother thinks. She steers the *poussette* past her frowning mother-in-law, out of the kitchen smelling of burnt meat and into the front parlor.

Charles has brought up the barley. The men each lift a burlap sack, hoist it on their shoulders, and take off down the hill.

"I'll bring the rest around after *midi,*" Charles says.

"Well," says Father Beauchard, "where were we?"

"Mother," Sylvie says, cupping her belly, "have you not guessed it? We are having a child."

"Bravo!" says her father-in-law. "Congratulations to the both of you—and to us as well—a grandchild!"

When Sylvie looks to Mother Beauchard, she sees that she is smiling. Is it possible that her eyes are wet? Later, Sylvie will remember this door opening between them, approval like a light shining on her. This hadn't been her plan, but it has worked out. Even the meat is fine, not overcooked as she feared. They eat well, sopping up the juices with the crusty bread and nearly polishing off the cake.

Lise hasn't seen such plenty since before the war. There'd been a fat, golden loaf on the breadboard, meat crackling in the oven, a cake with chocolate frosting, hazelnuts circling the top. She had expected the woman to offer some to Eugénie. How long since the child has had a sweet? Where Lise is from, guests are a blessing. They are ushered in, fed the last morsel, given the best seat at the table.

But Palestine seems not just far away to her; it is from another time, some distant past. There is so much here that her parents would dislike or misunderstand—the young couples walking arm in arm, Lise's own calf-baring skirts, the crisp greetings in the shops and offices downtown.

March 13, 1941
Très chers,
At present, we are living in the Vaucluse region. The farm has cherry or-chards and almond trees already established and we have planted potatoes and wheat. Until then, we have barley, which our neighbors grow in abundance. Besides crops, we have chickens and a cow, so we have milk for the child and cheese and butter. Eugénie delights in the open space here and grows like a mushroom.
Kisses to all of you, from all of us.
Lise

Of barley, one can say this: it is versatile. Lise makes porridge with it for breakfast. She roasts the kernels and makes a kind of coffee. Adding the first scraggly vegetables and wild garlic, she makes soup. She grinds it into flour and makes bread and cake, adding cherries from the orchard once they ripen. They don't go hungry, but she will never eat barley again after the war. Just the smell of it cooking will turn her stomach.

By June, Alain and Jean have mapped the property and cleared a spot for planes to land. What they will bring or take away—food? Ammunitions? People? Her brother and husband speak of this after supper while she cleans, puts Eugénie to bed. So often, she thinks, since the war began, she can do nothing about what most troubles her. She can't bear not to act either, so she cleans the crumbling stone floor, tidies the shelves. This activity both occupies and distracts, though not indefinitely, not perfectly.

Sometimes she knits while they talk, counting stitches, rows. She hears them, but doesn't. This is the other discovery she makes during this time— the mind can know and not, hold apart certain facts where they aren't as bothersome.

She is making a cardigan for Eugénie from wool that was a sweater of Jean's before he tore the sleeve on a fence. It's rough yarn, too scratchy for a child, but it will keep out the cold. Eugénie is a good girl, as if she knows she mustn't complain. What will be the cost of all this early and necessary compliance? Lise wonders. There is too much to do for Lise to consider this long. And then her brother is gone to Lyon where he does God knows what. Each time he returns she is afraid it will be the last time she sees him. He and Jean speak late into the night, and she cannot bear their murmurs.

When it happens, Charles has gone to the mill in Avignon. Sylvie is in the pantry gathering ingredients for a tart when a cramp seizes her, a knife so sharp that she clutches that place she knows only as down there. Through the layers of dress and apron, she feels the dampness. It's too early for this. *Pas encore*, she whispers, as if hushing a baby back to sleep. *Pas encore*. She cannot remember when she last felt the baby moving inside her—was it last night? This morning before the milking? Then she can think of nothing but the hot, rude pain.

When Charles returns, it is over. The blood and mess have been disposed of, the floor mopped clean. He comes home smelling of wheat and wine and is slow to understand when Sylvie tells him the baby is gone.

As soon as he entered, the doctor gave Sylvie a tablet to swallow. She would like to sleep for a long time, but after the examination, the doctor insists on talking to her. Charles, in his muddy work boots, stands by the bed. When he leaves, there will be two discrete piles of dirt on the bedroom floor.

"The womb," the doctor says, "is a vessel." He picks up the glass beside the bed to illustrate. "Yours is tilted, Madame. Like this."

Sylvie turns her head into the pillow. The bedding smells sour to her.

"You must accept, Madame."

Sylvie can hear Charles shuffling, grinding the dirt into her floor. So much mess, she thinks.

"I recommend rest," the doctor says, "and quiet."

"Yes, yes, of course," Charles says.

Sylvie keeps her face in the pillow even after she hears the door click shut behind them. She hears their voices in the next room, but their words seem not to adhere one to another. Then it is quiet. A breeze comes through the open window.

How many days pass in this manner? Tea and bread, then sleep. Soup and more sleep. One day after the bleeding has at last stopped, she feels well enough to sit up and knit, but the discovery of the small yellow bonnet, nearly completed on her needles, sets her back. Should she unravel all her hard work? The yarn is good cotton, but what to do with it, she cannot imagine. She sets it on the pillow, lies down. Then from the window, happy shrieking, peals of laughter. It's the girl with the dark curls. Sylvie rises and goes to the window. She can see the child running from one of the men, laughing. The man sings as he scoops her up and she shrieks again. Sylvie shuts the window, pulls closed the curtain. Still the noise seeps in: piercing, ruinous. She knows what she must do. Hasn't the doctor insisted on quiet?

At Hôtel de Ville, Sylvie is made timid by all the movement, the brisk efficiency of high heels clacking over the tiled floor and the voices echoing up into the high ceiling. The entryway smells of rain and cigarettes. Thank goodness there is a placard by the entrance. What will she say to Monsieur Gilbert? How does she know they are Jews? Their speech, the dark hair, spectacles—don't Jews always have poor eyesight?

As it turns out, she needn't have proof. Any suspicion is sufficient. Monsieur Gilbert thanks her and moves her quickly along. He'd rather spend his time practicing *boule* than worrying about Jews, but there is pressure from Paris. Still, he thinks, he will play his match after lunch as he intended, before sending out the gendarmes.

Mid-morning, while Lise knits, there is a knock at the door. This could be any number of things—the cow in the neighbors' field again, or a peddler, but Lise knows it is something more. She watches Jean at the door, combing his hair back with his hand as he listens. The man who has been sent to warn them is no one she knows, but that is to be expected. "You must hurry," he says. Before the door is closed, she is gathering their things—clothes, books, papers. A sack of barley cakes and the first almonds from the trees. They're on a train to Lyon before dark.

August 12, 1941
Bien chers tous,
By the time you read this, we will be in our new town. Alain promises it is a good place. Jean will find work in a lab. Alain assures of this as well. I imagine there will be parks for Eugénie with paths we can wander.

She stops writing for a moment, remembering the stroller. Is it growing easier, this leaving and discarding? She cannot even remember all she has left or abandoned, so it's funny that she will remember the stroller for a long time. Beside her, Eugénie sleeps, her cloth doll in her arms. Lise leans her forehead against the glass. In the last light, the fields outside gleam. She must finish her letter, so she can post it at the next station.

Perhaps when you read this, we will be sitting down to supper in our new apartment. Think of us there—safe and together and missing you.
Lise

When Charles mentions the neighbors' sudden departure, Sylvie shrugs, continues her polishing. She tells no one what she has done—not Charles or her in-laws. Several times that warm fall when she opens the windows, she imagines she hears the girl calling out or singing. But no, it's only the wind sifting through the leaves on the larch trees, and farther off, Charles cutting hay.

The baby carriage and the layette of gowns and sweaters she'd assembled were taken away while she convalesced. For this, Sylvie is grateful. The dogs are gone, too, and though she doesn't ask about them, for a long time she will expect their sharp, energetic barks, the frantic swinging of their tails as she moves about the yard.

The Fronds of Knives

M anon Peren swallowed hard. The taste of stale bread filled her mouth, an ache that reminded her of flowers and the smell of baking bread in a Montmartre bakery in the spring. Fifteen years old, she dreamed of foamy milk and pastries, with neither to enjoy. Over the scent of bougainvillea from the open window, the air reeked of burnt toast from her attempts to make a birthday cake by melting preserved cheese over bits of bread. Back in Paris, she'd have set the elaborate triple burners on high. But this apartment—tucked away beside the Promenade des Anglais, near the Cours Saleya in the old town—only had a single burner, and no salt or olives, or anything for spice. Reeking of strangers and homesickness, the place felt like a foreign landscape, constructed from someone else's clothes, dusty furniture, and well-used pots and pans.

A light on the boulevard flashed off and on. In each flash: her father's wide silhouette. That low-brimmed hat covering his eyes. That inner energy that, no matter his pace, followed him. Three weeks back, soldiers had taken him to a Besancon work camp, leaving her weeping, her mother sleepless at the doorway till dawn. They said—lies, she knew—he'd be back.

At least they'd left Paris. Her grandmother had heard the rumors at her embassy job.

Nine at night. Her grandmother stood to clean their cups of hot water, not complaining about the lack of tea; a silence that struck Manon as sad. For years, complaining had been her grandmother's way of showing she was alive. Her mother, beside her, had lit a single short-wicked candle. It flamed on the table, weaker than their candles in their Montmartre apartment.

A knock on the front door. Her aunt Ava. One quick rap. With piled dark curls, wire-framed glasses, and a stare like a wintry bird's, Ava spoke in a way that implied constant drama. A dancer, she'd owned a salon on the rue de Miromesnil. Until the Occupation, she'd welcomed all manner of high society, in smoky salons that had lasted well into the night. Manon had been the youngest invited. To her mother's horror, she'd dressed up and gone out most weeks.

Relieved at the distraction, Manon stood and walked over. Blood rushed to her head.

"I've got news," Ava said, in a stage whisper. She hurried in, smelling of sweat and oranges. Her loose shirt and pants gave her a slovenly look. Back in Paris, she'd prided herself on her ironing skills. Her mother stumbled forward, and the two embraced clumsily.

"My father?" Manon asked, at the same moment as Ava exclaimed, "Matisse."

"Matisse?" Manon fumbled on the name. Breath short, she clutched the pilled dish towel. Each vertebra fired up in her back. Matisse. Who hadn't heard of him? Living in Cimiez, outside of Nice, high on a hill at the magisterial Hotel Regina. In his seventies at least. An international celebrity. Six months back, she'd studied his paintings. In her stuffy classroom, her teacher had passed the book through the rows, exclaiming at the power of those images. Such wild-bodied dancers, limbs packed with movement, like branches on windblown trees.

"He's wanting a substitute model," Ava said, taking the dish towel with a nervous energy. The air filled with the clack of her nails. "My gallerist friend called with the details. He's looking for someone delicate, not too practiced, with a soft face. Someone patient, discreet."

"I'm sure a man like him doesn't want for models," her mother said.

"You'd be surprised." Ava wrung out the dish towel. "Princess Nezy, his old model, turned twenty and got married. She went on a honeymoon, then returned, too sick to pose."

"Princess Nezy?" Manon asked. The name marbled in her mouth. Hazy, foreign. How dull the windows looked, how homely the baseboards, edged with green paint that had started to peel. A cruise ship princess, gobbling down boiled eggs and pears; she'd force off her jealousy.

"A perfect model," Ava said, clearing the table of crumbs. She wiped them to the floor, a habit her mother hated. "You've read the interviews? He called her a *natural flirt*, said she was *pert*, *seductive*. Dressed up in a robe, a silk scarf, a smart spotted veil."

"Who could live up to that?" Manon pulled her housedress tighter, catching Ava's gaze. From anyone other than her aunt, she would have dismissed this all as a fairy story. But her aunt had connections, and back in Paris, knew half the painters in the Marais. *Flighty*, her mother had always called Ava. Since childhood, the two sisters hadn't gotten along. Moving to Nice hadn't improved things. The women looked nothing alike, except for their turned-up lips.

"He started up with all these young, cosmopolitan women." Ava looked off. "Bored in Nice, they claimed, with nothing to do. Poor them, huh? But his latest model was detained, apparently. A Jewish girl from Moscow."

"Detained?" Manon sucked in breath. "Couldn't he have helped?"

"Suppose not." Outside, the cats started mewing, a flooding sound. "He's only barely started painting again." Ava squinted as if picturing the scene, then gestured with loose swoops. Manon envied her blustery fire. "One hour per day at his easel, and requiring frequent breaks. Probably he'll paint mostly from bed. So he especially needs inspiration. My friend asked if I knew anyone. He knows I've got taste. And I said of course. That's you."

She thrust out a yellowed paper. Manon took it, shaking. Modeling for an *artist*? How absurd, like telling her to ride an elephant.

"You should have asked me," her mother said, dropping her knitting, a purple mess of yarn. Losing her vision, each week more. Her mood had worsened with her sight. Stargardt Disease, diagnosed five years back. The central vision would go first, then the periphery, till she'd go blind. No matter how often Manon reminded herself, still she found it impossible to believe.

"But what if I could earn something?" Manon asked. "Wouldn't that help?"

With her father's departure, they'd lost their one source of income. How helpless she'd felt, not able to help her grandmother with her secretarial work, mailing letters, as she once had. Her grandmother had left so suddenly, she'd had no time to ask for extra funds, or for visas. Already her mother had pawned off her wedding ring. How her father had shouted.

"You are *not* modeling," her mother said, glancing over with a startled look. "It's not proper—and you're not the model type."

"I'm not pretty enough." Manon echoed what she assumed her mother thought. Since she'd turned twelve, her mother had remarked on her pointy chin, her high widow's peak, receding like an old woman's. *Visas*. If Matisse couldn't get them, no one could.

"It's not that." Her mother spoke without conviction, fingers at her temples.

"His paintings focus on inner beauty." Ava clacked her fingernails. "That you have. And it's not as if he has options." She didn't bother to hide her sarcasm.

"*Merci*." Manon ignored the slight. *Doe eyes*, her mother's nickname for her, given her round, almost lashless gaze, and her irises, one blue and one brown. An artist—inner beauty—the words seemed to come from a foreign language. "But he'll want me to pose—naked?"

"Well ... yes." Smirking, Ava looked away. "But it's not sexual. You'd be a working partner to him. With what we need, you shouldn't be picky."

"It's out of the question." Her mother's expression darkened. "To the Hotel Regina, like some common prostitute? What would he ask her to *do*? Plus, she's bound to be seen. Too much coming and going. It'll be just like in Paris. You know, they already took Rosa."

"*What?*" Manon jolted up. Her knees slammed into the table, rattling the legs, until the pain-jolt startled her back. Rosa? Her classmate. One month back, they'd played cards, gossiped over the latest fashions. Rosa—heart-shaped face, perfect handwriting—had always seemed more put-together than anyone. Manon wanted to cry but sensed her mother couldn't handle it.

"I didn't want to tell you." Her mother spoke sharply. "Her family was on their way here, but got stopped at Lalande. No one knows where they'll be sent to next. And rumor has it the Italians are coming. Madame C. told me. They won't treat us well."

"How long do we have?" Manon asked, biting her cheek. Madame C. ran the underground shop and knew everyone.

"Thirty days at best. Assuming we find a way to get food."

Plates clattered from the back room—her grandmother, cleaning—and a thin whistle of steam rose. That sound, once comforting, struck her as irritating, but she didn't feel like plugging her ears. On her dress hem, a loose thread dangled. She yanked it and drew up tight, tensing her calf muscles, as she had in her prerehearsal stretches. Thirty days. Not enough to see the change of seasons, to watch the blaze of summer light over the Promenade shift into an easy, endless fall.

"Listen." Ava leaned closer. Her eyes gleamed with that same fire she'd had, greeting guests in her salons. "You know his daughter's in the Resistance? You know they're close?"

"Yes?" Manon hadn't heard.

"He can't openly help, not with his international commitments." Ava stole a glance at her mother, who wiped her eyes. "But he can pull strings with the committee. I've heard he already has. It's by far our best shot. A few signatures, some handshakes, and we'll be on our way."

"Visas?" Her mother rubbed her hands together.

"I'll ask him," Manon said, before anyone could. Could she? In any case, she wanted something to say, or some way to keep her mother from her usual evening sobs.

"What's this all about?" her grandmother called from the back. Her voice, gone high with effort, had a ghostly air. The steaming kettle she carried in smelled of ginger. The stacked cups shook in her hands. Her narrow face, already thin as a child's, looked even more drawn.

Manon took a cup. "It's our only chance for visas," she said. "And food."

"He'll help us only if he likes you." Her grandmother clattered the cups down. Her mouth moved as if tasting preserves. "But if he does—that's the golden ticket. Visas for all of us, can you imagine? And soon? We'd be off to London. The States. You'd go back to school. Forget all those restrictions. Maybe even dance again."

"No man of his status would care for us." Her mother patted the table for a cup but came up bare. "We're like little ants, grabbing at sticks. He paints women on cushioned divans, lounging in harem pants. And can you imagine what the soldiers would say—a young Jewish girl, traipsing back and forth on the Promenade? A slap in their faces. Totally obscene."

"He's spent six months in bed." Ava pulled her bun tighter, a hint of her dancer's past. "I read the doctors say he won't survive a second operation. A liver problem. He needs rest and a change in diet. Even so, he'll probably be dead by year's end."

"I didn't realize," Manon said. Dead. She tried to imagine an artist near death but came up with only a white-haired man in a wheelchair, straining at a canvas, brush darting with mastery. *Matisse flirts with colors*, her art teacher had said, holding up a copy of *Still Life with Oranges*. A cluster of fruit inside a porcelain bowl. One orange cut in half, its juice so fresh she could taste. *A famous artist*. A quiet hunger lit in her, and a slow fire she hadn't expected herself to feel.

"Posing would bring him happiness." Ava's voice rose. "And happiness means visas. Haven't you read the papers? Not Jewish, himself, but sympathetic. Not like Derain. He didn't go to Germany with SS officers. Didn't take part in the German embassy parties. And, when he did show up with government officials, he didn't smile. Looked stone faced. You know his daughter's gotten herself into trouble. He's pulled strings to protect her."

"He's on our side," Manon interjected, chest filling with warmth. The scene at the Vélodrome d'Hiver, one month back, hung in her mind. Thousands of Jewish Parisians crowded in, forced to sleep on top of each other. Nowhere even to relieve themselves. Deporting thousands, including children—it had seemed impossible, even as she'd pinned on her yellow star. She'd hidden in her bedroom closet. Her Hungarian housekeeper Imre had claimed she'd gone out. But then—a guilt she couldn't forget—the soldiers had taken Imre instead of her.

"This *is* the option." Ava leaned over. "If we say no, it's only a matter of time. Everyone knows the Germans are closing in. Please."

"He wouldn't want me." Manon sipped. The ginger bite filled her throat. She'd lost the energy for tears. Still, the thought of wanting hung, proud and precious, a curtain not yet closed.

"He's invited you, if you accept." Her aunt flashed a smile. "I already asked."

"Oh?" Her grandmother jolted to stand, clattering the teapot. "Without permission?"

"You *what?*" Her mother took the ad and, with deft fingers, ripped it in half. She had the same look as when Manon had gone out in Paris past curfew. "You had no right."

"It's only a one-time trip." Her aunt hardly sounded sorry.

"A trip that could end in her death." Her mother dropped the ripped ad.

"Nicola," her grandmother whispered, "don't spit at the chance for help."

"So you'll let Manon do your dirty work?" her mother asked, sipping in sharp breaths. "Take a pretty girl and get us visas that way? Make her into a pawn?"

"Has anything else worked?" her grandmother asked, and Manon knew she was right.

"It's about her safety, and ours." Her mother slumped, silhouette sharp against the green printed tiles. "She'd attract attention. The soldiers would follow her here."

"*French soldiers.*" Ava craned her head back. "And she doesn't look foreign."

"Let Manon decide," her grandmother said, as if discussing groceries.

"It's not up to her." Her mother turned to Manon, blinking rapid-fire. "Are you all crazy? A fifteen-year-old girl, traipsing around Nice? Putting her—putting all of us—at risk?"

"Please." Manon spoke softly, sensing more words would make her mother lash out. Her grandmother laid a hand on her mother's arm. They sat in silence a long moment. On the far wall, their silhouettes merged. Two dark outlines, quaking, against the dim thrall of the sea.

"I wish I didn't have to forbid you." Her mother drew to her full height— taller than the others by half a head—and tossed her half-finished scarf on the ground. "But if you won't see the big picture, I must. You're too naïve. Straightening your hair won't trick the officers for long."

"I'd be careful." Manon picked up the scarf, fingered its soft folds. So her mother knew.

"Nicola," her grandmother whispered. "Please."

"Come," Ava said, leading her mother out down the hallway. Her grandmother followed. A flutter of whispering. Manon put on her mother's scarf, looping it three times. Its musty warmth felt heavy but didn't soothe her. Wanted by an artist; could she be? She wasn't pretty. An upturned nose, triangular chin, and pillowed lips, the butt of jokes among her school friends. Yet she walked straight-backed, with a strong edge.

And visas. They'd be off, away from this cleanly lit city, this trap. She no longer found the Promenade's white expanse welcoming, nor that outlandishly blue-green sea. But Matisse's rooms at the Hotel Regina must be elegant, filled with classical music, high on the hill.

In the next room, her grandmother and mother murmured, a quick patter with silences in between. An echo of those Montmartre evenings, one month back: the fleeting buzz of radio static, click-click of men playing *petanque*, birds cawing in alleyways, silverware clacking, waiters passing by, swiveling, taking bills. Her father's face in lamplight, eyes lifted, the gleam of the Sacre Coeur at his back. With a borrowed telescope, they'd found the Big Dipper and gazed out at the scattered stars. He'd bandaged all her scrapes so tenderly.

She rose and opened the window. Soldiers paced outside, guns slung at their hips. The air's sudden chill surprised her. Far chillier than she'd expected Nice to be. The sunset cast an almost purple glow onto the wire fence surrounding the terrace. The darkness, which had always made her feel safe, had a new edge. She'd always thought of herself as a girl who loved beauty—but how could she love a place of such danger? Even the palm trees had fronds like knives. She put her hand to her neck, where her Star of David necklace hung. It was warmer than her skin, with sharp points. Her father's last gift. The night before the soldiers had taken him, he'd opened his hands, revealing a small gold chain, then passed it to her, whispering, "Be brave."

Be brave. Thudding words. Her head, in a blood rush, seared.

"So?" Ava returned and gestured out. Her mother close behind. "Have you considered?"

"I have to." Manon had never made such a demand. "Let me go."

"I won't allow it." Her mother grabbed the chair edge. "I'm sorry."

Buoyed by her own words, Manon stood and walked to the window. Her mother kept talking, protesting, but she didn't turn. Out on the Promenade, under lampposts, those soldiers marched, heads pitched back, guns angular lines. How could they ever have been babies? What would their mothers say, if they could see? Outside, the mewing turned desperate. Sharp, angular cries. Every weeping palm tree cast small shade. Steeling herself, she dug her heels down, clenched her fists. Fear had never been a thing to stop her. She'd take the chance.

Street of the Deported

E dith played with her father's wooden leg like it was a horse on a carousel. He pedaled at the sewing machine with his other leg, singing to "Lakmé" on the radio. The wool of his pants scratched her cheek. Her mother, belly big with her sister, knelt and huffed around a crabby woman, who swiveled this way and that to catch herself in the mirror.

"Leave your father's leg alone," her mother said through the pins pressed between her lips.

So Edith crawled out from under the table and admired the woman's crocodile shoes and sang.

The woman in the crocodile shoes disappeared behind the green curtain and returned with freshened lipstick in a cupid's bow. Her cloche hat chic, her trench coat cinched. Edith's mother handed her the alterations ticket.

"Your child is lonely," said the woman.

"Not for long," her mother said.

Edith had one sister and then three years later another. Instead of playing with her father's wooden leg she asked him about the Revolution. He told her about the bullet wound in his shin and the gangrene. She imagined him a younger man, the year before her birth, 1919, hunched forward on a march. Rain and mud. Sparrows chirruping on bare trees. She braided the middle sister's hair and her mother nursed the baby. "Lakmé" came on the radio and now she knew all the words. With her father she sang. Her mother, off-pitch, hummed.

One night, Edith stood on a chair and dangled a candy on a string above her sisters on the ground, who hopped up and down trying to catch it in their mouths. They barked like puppies and clapped their hands. Tails of balled-up yarn bounced, pinned to the backs of their dresses.

Edith's father, Ludo was his name, limped home from a stroll.

"Thank god we're godless," he said, soberly, hanging his hat.

Edith laughed and dangled the candy string.

Laura, Edith's mother, said, "Don't laugh." Her round glasses flashed in the light. Her gaze said to Ludo, *speak*.

Adela caught the candy in her mouth and tugged. Eva, the youngest, pushed up on Adela's shoulders, yapped, growled.

Ludo eased into a chair. "Hooligans again."

Laura clutched the top of her blouse and muttered *Oy gevalt*. She drew Edith's sisters near. Uncomprehending, they pressed their faces into her skirt, little fists clutching the delicate floral print. Ludo locked the door.

Edith sang so well people stopped in the street to listen through the shop window. The woman in the crocodile shoes and the cupid-bow lips told Edith's parents she should have lessons. She could join her daughter Rita, she said, and split the cost.

Rita wore flouncy lacy things. The woman in the crocodile shoes, Mrs. Herzig, gave them linden tea with honey in delicate porcelain glasses. They lived in a stately apartment building, plaster curlicues on the ceiling. The teacher was a slender young man fresh out of school in Vienna with slicked-back hair and tortoise-shell glasses. He tuned Mrs. Herzig's warped piano. For him, Edith perfected her coloratura. After the lesson, more honeyed tea and poppy seed roulade. Rita and Edith squeezed in front of a mirror picking seeds out of their teeth. Before dark, Edith hurried home.

Once, the family went to a studio for portraits. They craned their heads this way and that and there was a click and a flash. Later, their likenesses appeared frozen in sepia. Edith asked her parents for a camera. Just a little simple one. A plastic box. She'd seen the models in the studio window. But even the simple little ones were costly.

"Singing or camera, not both," Laura said.

Ludo showed his gold-tooth smile.

Edith apprenticed with the studio photographer. He was a broad-shouldered man in suspenders. He explained to her all the vinegar-smelling chemicals. He explained to her how to catch the light. Rita sucked her tongue when Edith gave up her lessons. Mrs. Herzig said Edith wasted her talents.

Singing was just air. Good for the soul but hardly practical. Cameras made things, captured time. If you're good enough, they'll record your voice, Mrs. Herzig said. Edith shrugged. Nights she still sang with her father alongside the stutters of the sewing machine. At school she learned math and Russian and on Saturday afternoons she bathed photographic paper in chemicals until faces formed. Her fingers turned black.

The Herzigs threatened to leave Romania. Ludo said they were neither fascist nor communist, simply capitalist. Edith practiced wrinkling her nose in the mirror. She would capture her expressions on camera when she had one of her own. The Herzigs stayed. The laws changed. Ludo and Laura still worked. The laws affected those in higher professions. Attorneys, academics. The Herzigs thought again to leave. Instead, Mr. Herzig found work with a locksmith.

Edith became a woman. Laura fitted her into a brassiere and explained menstruation. Contrary to Laura's warning of pain and diminished energies, Edith's powers grew. She flit from school to home to the photography studio. She printed, dried, and filed family portraits large and small to be picked up in glassine envelopes. Soon she was shooting portraits too. She tossed little Eva up and down even though she was now a big girl. She followed the war on the radio and cheered on the Soviets. There were talks of deportations.

The photographer cornered her one day in the darkroom. His hands went everywhere. He said this is what men and women do. He said he would give her a camera. She thought about the singing teacher with his slender hands. She didn't think that's what he did. She upended a chemical bath and fled.

At home she packed her father's army rucksack.

"I'm joining the Soviets," she announced.

Laura said *you are not.*

Ludo clapped his daughter on the shoulder.

"I want to go too," Adela said. She looked at Edith with big stars in her eyes. Eva hugged her mother's knees.

"She is eighteen," Ludo said to Laura. "She can go if she wants. She can supervise Adela."

Laura's eyes rolled up to the god she didn't believe in.

They packed Adela a rucksack too. Ludo told Laura to stop blubbering and be proud of her good, brave girls. The family walked to the train station. They were going to work in a steel mill in the province of Voronezh. Steel for the war.

Edith's eyes felt sharper and newer. A fire propelled her, a hot-air balloon inflating in her torso. She hugged her parents and Eva. She grasped Adela around the shoulder, who leaned into her. Still smelled like a baby. Talcum and sugar. They climbed the train and the family stared at each other through the window, waving until it hissed and lurched, eastward.

Edith was in the factory kitchen when the news broke: war over. Adela had given up the endeavor long ago. Within a month of arriving in Voronezh, she wrote Ludo begging for money to come home. Silly Adela. Edith did easy tasks, boiling potatoes, ladling soup, while Adela's small nimble fingers had been put to use on the assembly line. Hard work. Since Adela left, Edith had not heard from her family. The war disrupted all communications. But Edith fell in love with a factory foreman. She wanted to write to her mother, tell her father Boris wanted to settle in Moscow. The letter sat, bundled with other letters, inside her father's rucksack. But the war was over. She would go home and tell them herself.

"I'll wait for you," Boris said.

She laced up her boots, lips pressed together. She put on her father's rucksack. She put on a jaunty hat.

What can we say about Satu Mare when Edith returned? The buildings were mostly the same. Red brick. Gray stone. Yet the claws of some great beast left the streets scraped.

Gaunt people wandered in a daze. Unrecognizable faces. From where? They appeared to drift in on gusts of dried leaves and ash. Windows boarded up, in splotches. Laura and Ludo and Adela and Eva were not in the shop in which they'd lived and worked. A strange woman stood in the window. Cheekbones like ledges. Edith knocked on the glass. The woman scowled, switched on a lamp and pulled down the shade.

Edith found herself at the Belle Epoque building in which the Herzigs lived. A line of people wound out of its black-and-white tiled lobby. They shifted side to side on tired feet. She studied their faces and they hers.

"What is this for?" she asked the man on the threshold.

"Redistribution of goods."

Edith's heart jumped.

The line snaked inside of a large ground-floor apartment. Edith waited her turn. Inside, the line split in two. One toward a back room with grand furniture: lion-clawed, mahogany, Chippendale. A slender spectacled man managed that room. Not many people in it. She squinted, tried to make out her former piano teacher. It wasn't him. But a piano (the Herzigs'?) sat there in the shadows. The longer line in the front room led to a woman who organized many boxes of small items. Spoons. Plates. Baby clothes. Fine, fine, baby clothes, with sweet embroideries, soft cotton eyelets. The woman's hair was colorless and shorn.

A person would make their case. The woman would look through the wares and provide. She kept inventory on a clipboard. It became apparent that the furniture was in less demand because many had not settled back into places of their own.

Edith strode up to the woman.

"What do you need?"

"Rita?"

Rita dropped the baby blanket she'd been fondling. They moved around the table and hugged, firmly. She grasped Edith by the face. Thumbs to ears' curves. Hearing blocked.

"Have you seen my family?"

Rita's thumbs were off her ears but everything muffled.

Rita shook her head. Her lip half drooped. "Not yet. Maybe—"

"18,000 gone," a hoarse voice said behind her. Edith turned to him. "And here I am, waiting for one of their spoons." Ringing ears. Warped words.

Edith dropped her father's rucksack. She sat directly on the floor. She ripped the bottom of her shirt.

"Edith, no. You don't know."

"18,000? It doesn't matter." She ripped the shirt further. "But you were there? With them?"

Rita crouched beside her. The waiting man sighed as if squeezing out the dregs of his soul. Rita's voice low. "A different deportation. A different camp."

"Death all the same," the man said.

"You're still standing," Rita said to him. "Edith, please. Wait for me in the other room." She turned back to the man.

"Here's your spoon. What else do you need?"

"My husband," Rita said to Edith, introducing her to the man in the furniture room. "Mattias."

"The question is," he said, as if mid-conversation, "do we talk all night or do we never speak again? I can't seem to find a balance." They all sat on the hardwood floor.

"We met—there."

"We're giving people basic things. Basic things they need, otherwise where do the things go? In a heap." Mattias darkened at the word heap.

"Your parents?" Edith ventured, gentle.

Rita shook her head. "Separated upon arrival." The newlyweds exchanged a slow glance. Spontaneously, Mattias broke out into the Kaddish. Over his prayers she said, "It's almost a sickness. He keeps saying it. He keeps saying it." She put her head in her hands. Edith's boots splayed out in front of her. The pain came strangely. Not in the chest but above it, in her shoulder. A push upwards. As if that essential organ wandered. Or as if her lungs, trying desperately to find new air, attempted escape.

Before she left, before she went back to Boris in Voronezh, utterly depleted, Edith rummaged through the boxes Rita had organized.

"You're married now," Rita said. "Take these baby clothes."

Edith pressed the little ruffled dress to her breast. The little footed suit. She folded them into her father's rucksack. The load was heavy.

Before she left without saying goodbye, before she left when Rita's back was turned, before she went back to Voronezh and was never heard from again, Edith rummaged through a box of photographs Rita had found in the back of the abandoned photography studio. Edith searched and searched among the faces. She studied them, slid them back into those same glassine envelopes. A fashionable woman with bobbed hair, dark and sleek. A children's birthday party gathering around a big sliced babka. A couple on a summer picnic, reclined in the grass, the voluptuous wife resplendent. Her family wasn't in there. Her family had their photos with them; she'd delivered them herself. She kept searching. There was one of a little blonde girl in braids, sitting in a flowering chestnut tree. She didn't know her. Just some girl. Bare kneed, legs dangling. She wasn't quite smiling. She was fierce. She squinted directly in the sunlight. Her cheeks were crinkled. Edith pretended she'd taken that photograph. She felt the warmth of the sun on her back. She heard the rustle of the leaves. On a gust, the scent of its blossoms. She felt as if the girl would hop off the tree and whistle. She felt the force of the girl's challenge. Take me home, she said. Her heart slid down from where it had bunched up in her shoulder. She slipped the photo against her sternum like a salve.

RUCHAMA FEUERMAN

Facts on the Ground

E inat gazes at her younger sister fiddling with the CD player, trying to find the right song to match the mood of the day. As if the right background music while your house is getting destroyed will make all the difference!

She stares out the window, past the greenhouses bare and stripped so that you can't even tell bug-free lettuce ever grew there, but no, she won't think about that. Her eyes fall on the boy soldiers and girl soldiers dressed in black, like they're bit players in some horror movie. If she squints her eyes, they look like black teeth. Or maybe, if she tilts her head, like a weird moving black wall. Hard to believe many of these soldiers are eighteen, like herself.

Her father over in the study is bent over a Talmud. She's used to seeing him with a spade or pruning shears or dealing with shipments of plastic bags. He rarely studies Torah and isn't much of a scholar, although he's the best chazzan in all of Nevei Dekalim. And Ima, the brains of the family, is saying psalms, not writing one of her usual sharp letters to the editor of *Ha'aretz* that never get printed. So today everything is upside down.

"I hate them," she hears her sister Meirav say, her face pressed against the window. "Trying to scare us like that with their black uniforms. Pathetic."

Einat lets out a short laugh. As if their uniforms are the worst of their crimes. Anyway, she won't waste her fury on the soldiers. And she doesn't think the uniforms are pathetic but a brilliant move. The familiar khaki-colored army uniforms are gone. The Soldier, the chayal—the one who normally is someone's own son, brother or sister—has now been replaced, turned into the Other.

She feels like an Other herself. Her bags are packed, unlike everyone else in her family. That one act separates her from them. There is no way she's going to leave her clothes, photo albums, books and jewelry behind to be destroyed by the claw machine! Is her family nuts? No, the whole community is! Even if she understands why.

The Prime Minister had given them a choice. Those who leave Nevei Dekalim beforehand will be compensated with jobs to make up for their destroyed livelihoods. With a place to live, and extra cash. Sure. Only idiots believe that. And those who wait for the last day will have everything they own destroyed by the bulldozers and the claw. But at least, the people tell themselves, they will have their self-respect and the company of their friends and neighbors. For months, that's all the neighbors talk about as they eye which family is packing, going, and which family is staying.

What a way to live, Einat thinks. She wants to shake them. What's wrong with everybody? Children rely on parents to show them the way, and all these years she let herself be guided by her parents. Wise, good, hard-working people, everyone says, and it's true. Her father came up with the smartest idea about how to market the bug-free lettuce overseas. And when Einat was suffering from a strange rash that no doctor could cure, it was Ima who spent hours Googling every night till she found the right treatment. But for the first time in Einat's eighteen years, she sees she can't rely on them. It's like her parents jumped off a high diving board and only halfway down checked if there was water in the pool. Do they have to be so honorable and stay till the bitter end?

So her bags are packed. At least she should salvage something from this whole mess. She has even secretly packed a luggage with Ima's bread machine and wedding albums, the nebulizer for her brother's asthma (they use it maybe once a year, but still . . .) and some of the better pieces of jewelry. If Ima knew, she might get angry, but later, Einat knows she'll thank her. Not now, but later, after the claw comes and everything is demolished. Her mother's precious computer, too.

"You will see, you will see, how much good there will be, next year . . ." Her sister listens to a few bars and then switches to another song.

Ach. Meirav and her fantasies. She has always been that way, writing her little poems about the flowers of Israel and soldiers who find God in a rainbow. Actually, some of the poems aren't bad. But today, Einat has no patience for dreamers or poets.

Through the open window, she can see the star-shaped synagogue—so cool, so retro. Her friends gather there in their garish orange T-shirts with slogans like "Disengagement Is Suicide," and "Never Again to Deportation." They are praying like it's Yom Kippur or something. Calling out in that open-souled way. Part of her longs to join them. But no—she shakes her head—it feels too phony. She isn't an idealist like them. Her faith is tainted by practicality.

The black wall of soldiers has moved closer. Is that smoke she sees in the distance? She hears muffled sounds coming from the study. It's her father moaning—or worse, crying? She can't stand to be close to her parents right now, to hear Ima's rants, see her finger jabbing into the air like a bullet as she makes her points—as if anyone cares—and Abba all uncomposed, his beard disheveled, the tabs of his collar twisted this way and that. Like a kid, she thinks in disgust. A kid!

The anger she has been sitting on for all these months rises up in her throat like indigested lumps of food. Her foolish, misguided, naïve family with their foolish ideologies, more precious to them than . . . than, she doesn't know what. She grew up on this ideology—it was their religious duty to create little villages, settlements, in the midst of Arab enclaves, and in this way ensure a Jewish presence that could not easily be dislodged—no matter what peace deal the Israeli government might broker.

"Facts on the ground!" Rabbi Even-Cheyn declared from the pulpit, Shabbat after Shabbat. "A Jewish town is a physical fact, a reality that cannot be changed! Only in this way, building communities in the midst of the Arabs, can we reclaim our ancient land!" Not only that, the rabbi explained, but this land in the middle of Gaza is a strategic asset to Israel, and holding onto it is a way to protect Sderot, Ashkelon, and many parts of Israel from Arab rocket fire. "You are the frontline soldiers in this battle!" he thundered, backed up by plentiful Torah sources, a flowing beard and burning brown eyes that made him look like a prophet of Israel. And when she listened, she felt pride and imbued with purpose, like Atlas, holding up the world.

The other day Einat went to the hothouses where Abba and Ima had built up their bug-free lettuce business. The place was totally dismantled. Empty. Thirty years' work gone down the tubes. Hundreds of livelihoods swallowed up, just like that. She kept circling the place, searching for something, a memento maybe. Finally, who should she bump into but Rabbi

Even-Cheyn. He walked over, to try to give inspiration; she could tell because he had that shiny, idealistic look in his eyes. She tried to turn away but he called out, "Einat, chazak v'amatz! Be strong—for all the Jewish nation."

She stared at him. What are you talking about? She wanted to yell: You let us down. You fed us slogans. Facts on the ground, facts on the ground. That's all I ever heard from you. You said a Jewish government would never kick out Jews from their own homes. Never. You promised! All she muttered now was "Chazak v'amatz," and got out of there fast.

Well, today, the Never is happening.

Einat peers out the window at a boy who is two years older than she is, crawling on the road, clawing at the dust, moaning like a woman in labor. She knows that boy. Doron. In fact, one summer she had a crush on him. But look at him now, like an animal. How's that for a fact on the ground? She snorts softly.

Meirav takes out her tiny book of psalms and begins to pray, her lips moving tautly, quickly. Einat can hear Ima in the study shouting into the phone, "My computer's not working. You don't understand, I have to send this email to the Prime Minister!" The intensity in her mother's voice makes Einat cringe. How will Ima leave the house when the soldiers come for her—with dignity, or screaming, refusing to budge, each one holding a limb? When she closes her eyes and sees that image her palms prickle with dread. Einat's Torah teacher, Gveret Shemer, says a religious woman should never draw attention to herself. Gveret Shemer who travels in from Bnei Brak to teach is the picture of self-containment and refinement in her short, black, side-parted sheitel.

Abba suddenly barges from the room, his big knitted yarmulke sloping to one side. "I'll be back," he calls to the girls. Einat sees him stride toward the soldiers, his speckled beard fluttering. What's he going to say to those soldiers that will change their minds? Her parents are dreamers. Dreamers! And now Ima has leapt up and is joining Abba outside.

Einat turns away—she can't bear to watch them make jokes of themselves—and goes to the kitchen. She pours herself some orange juice, their last carton. She sees the sandwich maker next to the toaster. Meirav begged Ima to buy it, but they rarely use it. No loss there. Her eyes drift toward the silhouette she drew of her father years ago, a pretty good likeness, considering she has no artistic ability. It always touched her that her parents hung it up for all these years. If it had been her child, it wouldn't have lasted more than a week. Clutter. But now the thought that her silly artwork will be destroyed by the claw makes her stomach bend in two.

She stares at the clock that makes funny bird sounds on the hour, at the terra cotta-colored backsplash that Abba set behind the sink with his own hands, doing the caulking and all. She can already picture the claw coming, can hear the horrible growling sound of stone giving way, the slow caving in of walls, dishes flying, the oven turning to metal pulp, the leather easy chair collapsing like mud, bricks flinging everywhere. The whole world is collapsing. She feels a tightness in her chest. It's hard to breathe, as if the claw has already done its work, filled her home with ash and smoke. Can a house disappear just like that? She lets out a groan. "All gone," she mumbles.

Meirav lifts her head from her psalms. "Stop it!" she implores, her wispy hair falling into her eyes. "Rabbi Even-Cheyn says a person should have faith even as he feels the sword on his neck."

Einat says nothing, just shakes her head. Who can she even talk to? Nobody's left. How come she's the only smart one? If she'd been the head of this whole Gush Katif movement, she would've focused on different things, instead of land, land, land. She would've tried to get the public on their side. Change people's minds and hearts. A movie could've done that with some famous actor. But whenever she suggested that, people just laughed at her.

Well, they won't laugh much when she decides to leave, Einat thinks. And then she straightens and rubs her eyes. Leave? But where will she go to? She and her friends are all signed up for National Service. She'd been hoping to get assigned to a school in some poor development town up north. But suddenly the idea of being together with all her friends who think just like her—or the way she used to, Eretz Yisrael Shleima—the Greater Israel and all that—makes her gag. Forget it. No way will she join them. Her bags are packed. She doesn't know where those bags will take her, though.

Meirav is now fiddling with the radio and lands on a Kotel classic. ". . . There are men with hearts of stone," it plays, ". . . there are stones with hearts of men."

"You know what?" Einat flings out, "I'm going to Bnos Devorah seminary in the fall."

Meirav squints at her. "What are you talking about? Where's that?"

"It's in Bnai Brak," she clarifies. Where Gveret Shemer, her Torah teacher, lives.

Meirav's eyes go round with shock. "You're kidding, right? A black-hat place? For hareidim?"

Yeah, she was kidding, but now suddenly it doesn't seem so crazy. She has seen the children who live over in Bnai Brak, boys with their swinging side curls, children who aren't complicated by the outside world, by politics, by foreign music. She has seen the girls her age who dress with a modesty of a different era, girls who strike her as complete. Einat shakes her head. "Our whole life, it's over." Her hand cuts sideways through the air, chopping all their slogans and ideology in half, and another chop—into quarters. "Obsolete," she says harshly.

"Hah, hah, sure," Meirav scoffs. "You'd last a week with the dossim. No, a day."

Einat shrugs. Her sister still thinks the world begins and ends with Gush Katif.

"Or who knows," Einat continues, playing with the curtain, something Ima always forbade because it gets smudged so easily, but now, who cares? "Maybe I'll go to journalism school." But of course there won't be money for such things. Or for anything. Overnight they'll be beggars.

Meirav merely flicks off the radio, no longer paying attention. "Ach, this song is too sad!" She saunters off into her bedroom.

Is that a sound of a luggage getting dragged out of her sister's closet? Einat wonders, just as she hears a woman's high-pitched scream from outside. The scream rises above all the noise and tumult. It is pitched so high, so powerfully loud, the entire village must hear its raw anguish. Einat swallows. A split second later she recognizes the voice.

Ima. Einat's hands and throat go cold. It's Ima, for sure. The shock of her mother's cry propels her toward the front door. Ima! I'm coming—the thought shoots through her brain as she flings open the screen door and runs outside. She cranes her neck, looks past the old petting zoo evacuated three weeks ago, looks here, there, beyond the claw machine waiting to begin its horrible work. She blinks and sees teenage boys crouching on a roof with buckets of red paint—as if they could stand up against an entire army!—she sees smoke rising from one of the houses, she sees crowds of people streaming past, the ones in orange, and always, always, the soldiers in black, but where is Ima, where oh where is her Ima? Her breathing comes in fits and starts. She runs toward the claw, and right there beyond the empty greenhouses she spots—yes!—her mother's straw hat and her blue peasant skirt. A crowd of girl soldiers surround her. One holds out a bottle of water toward her mother. Ima's hat is askew, her face blotchy and distorted with fury, her head is bobbing up and down, her arms are moving like a windmill, and she looks like . . . like a clown!

Ima is screaming at the top of her lungs: "You stole our cucumbers, our parsley, our dill! You cut off our feet." She shakes both arms wildly.

Einat covers her mouth. Is that Ima, truly? Her mouth goes dry as smoke. A shudder starts in her shoulders and travels down her arms and palms. So silly, so sad. Ridiculous, roars through her. She ducks behind a mailbox, crouches there, hidden—and then—hurry, fast, before anyone sees—she turns back, runs the other way, fast, faster, her shoes scuffing against each other in her speed to get away from that horrible spectacle. Silly and sad, silly and sad. The words repeat like the banging of a shovel against her head. Her chest is hurting so much, each breath pokes her like glass. She keeps running, but her lungs are closing and it's so so hard to breathe, until finally the earth rises and she trips and falls to the ground near a palm tree, and there she rubs her knees and whimpers, Ima.

BODY AND SOUL

Themes from Jewish law and lore can persist in consciousness, even for those who don't observe the dictates over what is permitted versus what is forbidden. These include constraints around blood of every sort, from a blood spot on an egg that would render it not kosher for consumption to the menstrual blood that means the menstruant cannot be touched, much less engage in sexual contact. The mikveh, or ritual bath in which a religiously observant (married) Jewish woman is supposed to immerse herself after the conclusion of her menstrual period each month, becomes the setting for women-only stories, for revealing secrets, for resetting the clock, for seeking absolution, or for entering into a new state (marriage, divorce, gender transition, healing after abuse, menopause, and more). Despite its origin as the locus of rituals for bodily purification, immersion in a mikveh today is used for spiritual changes as well.

Other physical markers of being Jewish and female evolve not from Jewish law but from the discrimination that marked Jews as "other," often by legislating distinctive garments like the yellow star enforced by the Nazis. Even in places without overtly antisemitic attacks, Jewish bodies can signal difference. Curly hair, or prominent noses, or full figures became unwelcome signals that a woman didn't fit mainstream (read WASP) models of pulchritude in the twentieth century and even today. This body-shaming is hard to resist, especially for anxious and insecure adolescents and young women. Yet these "corrections"—like straightening one's hair, nose, and body—can feel like gaining control.

Paradoxically, the flip side of being seen as an undesirable other is the *exoticization* of Jewish women, especially by non-Jewish men. Rembrandt painted a stunningly gorgeous "Jewess." And in "The Lives under the Stones," the Jewish concubine of a baron knew he was aroused when he would address her in their sex play as "My little Jewess."

In sharp contrast is the immediacy of vulnerable bodies in "The Comet Neowise Listens In," which blends the voice of the Black Jewish narrator with the imagined utterances of the comet calling us to justice.

The Lives under the Stones

To get to the Jewish cemetery, you have to go underground. This is true for the living as well as the dead, although it's been an eternity since fresh ground was broken here. Space was always at a premium; there are only so many bodies you can pack into two acres. They stacked them up like cheerleaders, one on top of the other, knees resting on shoulders or balanced precariously on skulls, but they still ran out of room. Gravestones cracked and toppled under the pressure. By the time the Emperor granted space outside the City, the skies were already darkening. When the storm was finally over, the handful of survivors floated away on floods of tears.

No matter how dry the day is, the stones sweat. Now that the rest of the City hovers a good five feet above, it's like standing below sea level. Once past the entrance, you spiral down a long, rickety stairway. With each step, the metal squeaks and groans. At the bottom, you're greeted by a ticket kiosk and a security guard. In the absence of live Jews, the local delinquents have taken to beating up dead ones. Keys, Swiss knives, even nail files are checked into tiny lockers to prevent further damage, although your presence, your mere breath, wreak havoc on the ancient stones. Stray sunbeams rain down, turning the dust mites and gnats into tiny, fluttering jewels, but for the most part, it's dusk-dark down here. You grab onto details to stay afloat: sculpted colonettes and triglyphs, curlicue arabesques and rolled scrolls, praying hands and lions and fish. Every stone tells a story. The stories press against each other, fighting to be heard, but you only have time for one or two:

Rachel Blumele, 1632–1674, her name spelled out in a flower. Beloved wife and mother. A life lived in kitchens and bedrooms and trips to the market. She spent most of her adulthood tucked inside a cotton apron that became tighter and tighter with each pregnancy. After her fifth lying in, the faded check pattern stuck to her like a second skin. She was a good cook, able to turn barley noodles and potatoes into a feast. A magician with liver dumplings, she could make less than a pound of meat feed seven. She saved her best tricks for the market, where she bargained down even the toughest vendors with a look or a plea.

"Here you go, ten zlotys for the apples."

"Fifteen."

"Really? I was sure you said ten. I only have twelve. Take two back." A sigh like an expiring bird. "I guess little Sarai will have to go without."

Unable to deprive little Sarai/Avram/Natan, the fruit seller/dairy man/butcher almost always gave Rachel her price.

In another age, Rachel might have been an accountant or a lawyer. Or not. Maybe she loved her kitchen-bedroom-market life. Rachel and her husband regularly made love on their single bed, their slippery bodies somehow managing to click into the right place at the right time, like the workings of a clock. Her wig slept on the shelf so her auburn hair could be free for a few hours. Loose strands framed her prematurely aged face. Dead at forty-two, she could have been sixty. Eight pregnancies had loosened her taut belly. At night, when the five who had survived infancy were asleep on their bed on the other side of the curtain that divided the room, Rachel's husband rolled over and massaged her stretched flesh. Stateless, this was his country, the only place he was at home. She smiled as his fingers slowly crept lower. Reluctant to intrude further, you move on.

Salome Karpele, 1744–1810. Like everyone else, the first thing you noticed was her beauty. Who could resist those pillowy, pink lips and heavy-lidded black eyes? Not the Baron of Ludlovy, who plucked her out of the ghetto at fifteen and installed her in a suite of rooms in the center of town. Her attractions were obvious, but her thoughts were harder to read. After years of playacting, it was possible that Salome no longer knew what she was about.

You check her surroundings for clues. After all, we are what we buy, and Salome was a connoisseur. Only the finest Meissen ware graced her table, although she rarely had more than one guest and the Baron couldn't distinguish Sevres from Chinese import. Her furniture was French, her pianoforte Italian. Tucked beneath her bed was the expensive magnifying glass she had ordered from the finest craftsmen in Amsterdam so she could check her diamantine face for any flaws. The shelves of her kitchen were lined with jars of the olive oil she used to soften her skin. The pantry was well stocked with bottles of the finest champagne, which kept her hair bubbly.

At the Baron's suggestion, she went to church every Sunday where she prayed for the preservation of her beauty, but the Mysteries remained a mystery. She took communion once, out of curiosity, but felt nothing. How could a tasteless wafer be the body of God? And if Christ died for our sins, what was the point of confession? Only limbo made sense to her; neither Jew nor Gentile, wife nor servant, she knew what it was to float between worlds. She refused to be baptized for fear that the water would wash away the otherness that was as much a part of her appeal as her dainty pointed chin, thin ankles, and torrents of wavy, red hair.

"Say something in Jewish," the Baron would whisper in bed on the nights when his little soldier refused to stand to.

"*Kush meer in toches.*"

"My little Jewess" was her cue to release the moans that assured her commander that the battle had been won. Since beauty turned as quickly as fine wine, she was determined to acquire other skills to hold onto her Baron. Veiled, she snuck back into the ghetto from time to time to learn how to make the chicken soup and stuffed cabbage that had glued her parents together for so long. Belgian lace failed to hide her charms and groups of boys, fresh out of cheder, would inevitably fall into line behind her, announcing the arrival of the Sabbath bride.

Once she was safely inside her old home, she slipped a stained smock over her silk finery and sank her hands into mounds of grainy chopped liver and squishy small intestines. For a few, brief hours, she breathed in the smells of her childhood and bathed in the comfort of knowing her place. When the late afternoon sun lit up the crumpled paper stuffed into the hole in the window and the chipped brown paint on the walls, she knew it was time to go. Her mother looked away as Salome reached into her bag for a small purse and tucked it under the challah cover. Bending down, she kissed the top of her mother's head and returned to the house that was not quite her home.

Kartoffeles and liver dumplings bought her some time, but as her thirties bore down on her like a rabid wolf, Salome knew the Baron would get restless. Since jealousy was the strongest aphrodisiac of all, she invented a lover. When she heard the tap of the Baron's walking stick climbing the stairs to her landing, she had her maid undo her bodice and refasten the buttons out of order. She imprinted the ghost of her ghostly lover in the furniture by spraying cologne on the chairs and divan. The Baron's nostrils flared the instant he stepped into the apartment. When he noticed the unhooked buttons on her bodice, he insisted on undoing the rest of them himself.

Hoping to catch her *in flagrante*, he increased his visits. And since no respectable patron arrived at his mistress' lair empty-handed, Salome became one of the wealthiest women in the quarter. When the Baron died and his heir ordered her to leave, it took a full week to pack up her things. Over time, her past was largely forgotten. To the new priest at St. Gundula, she was a respectable, gray-haired lady devoted to Christian charity, but her Jewish roots came out when she died and she was shoved into the old cemetery with the other members of her tribe.

You brush your fingers over the fish sculpted into Salome's headstone. The rectangular block is capped by a fancy gable. A pair of scrolls frame praying hands. Praying for what? you wonder. Your curiosity twists and turns on itself like an insomniac unable to sleep—did Salome love the Baron, what happened to Rachel's children?

Back on the crowded street above the cemetery, strangers bump into you, cursing you for getting in their way. "*Kush meer in toches*," you whisper in a language you don't speak as you head for a "kosher-style" deli that serves liver dumplings to a nonexistent Jewish community.

CHANA BLANKSHTEYN

translated from the Yiddish by Anita Norich

Do Not Punish Us

A group of doctors, mathematicians, and lawyers who had just completed their final exams celebrated by organizing a friendly gathering. In the morning they took a boat out to a small summering place famous for its historic castle and its large, lush park that stretched for several miles along the river. There was a small pavilion built in an antique Italian style, with a restaurant inside. Once upon a time, after a walk, lovely, proud ladies with powdered hair and laced-up bodices rested there. Cavalrymen, and black cuirassiers, and dragoons in clothing embroidered with gold and silver drank Burgundy from their silk shoes, rode horses at breakneck speed, tortured their slaves nearly to death in order to give their beloved, at the exact right moment, a note on perfumed rose paper with a royal coat of arms.

The long narrow table was set on the green meadow, encircled by old bushy fir trees and tall hundred-year-old oaks. Squirrels with golden-red tails were on the branches. One could imagine that, from behind a large tree that two people holding hands could not have encircled, a satyr with goat's feet would appear, looking at a wood nymph he desired.

About twenty people were sitting around the table, among them a few older friends who lived in the city. Quite a few bottles had already been emptied and lay on the grass. The group was heated by glasses of wine, happy that the difficult months had passed and excited to be in the crystal-clear air with its strong scent of earth and trees.

She sits at the end of the table and refreshes herself with frozen punch. Slowly, with a small spoon, she snacks on the cold, sweet dish, and with closed eyes breathes in the strong scent of rum.

"Pretty Max" stands up from his place next to his friend, the private tutor, and with measured steps approaches her. "A hot day," he says most earnestly, and waits for an answer. Pretty Max deals with everything in the world most earnestly, and most of all with himself. A young man without uncertainties: he never doubted that he would become a famous gynecologist and travel around in his own car; never doubted that all the female students were in love with him and he even pitied them a bit—clearly, he couldn't love all the women at the same time!

Since she is still silent, he moves a chair near her, sits down and stretches out one foot in its lavender sock, exactly the same color as his enormously wide handkerchief in the breast pocket of his elegant brown summer suit. Because Pretty Max takes everything so earnestly, everything about him is exaggerated: not simply well dressed, but elegant, not simply spoken, but orated—impressing even himself. Friends used to laugh at him, but in a good-natured way. To tell the truth, he never injured anyone by word or deed. The female students also laughed at him, but not really wholeheartedly—he was, after all, a handsome young man. Unusually handsome.

"I want to visit you before we all go our separate ways. Tomorrow, at two o'clock I'll have the honor to do so."

His brown velvety eyes claim her attention. She feels them on her skin, on her suddenly dry lips. It isn't the first time that she blushes when he speaks to her. She jokes about him just as the others do, but, still, she likes him. Raised in her grandfather's well-to-do household in the village, she is drawn to him with all of her healthy youthfulness. Whenever she meets him, her blood pulses faster and her heart beats more loudly. She thinks that he has the same effect on the other girls. They don't want to admit it, or they just don't say so aloud.

Pretty Max stands up:

"So, tomorrow at two o'clock. You won't be bored," he continues with ingenuous solemnity. His velvety eyes caress her. A bit of red pours over her cheeks, flares down her neck. She bows her head. "Good." Pretty Max returns to his place near the private tutor. He is calm and earnest.

It has become very hot. And she is also tired. She wants to lie down. At least for a quarter of an hour. Not more. With gentle, womanly gracefulness she stands up, takes her coat from amongst the clothing strewn about, and goes to sit under the trees. A friend calls. Someone laughs. She doesn't stop. She pretends not to hear. In the woods, it's not as hot. Here, under the old fir tree whose branches hang down to the ground, she stretches out.

She sees them all from afar, but here it's not as noisy. The thick branches swallow the cheerful voices.

She puts her coat under her head, stretches out. How nice it is here! An isolated, hidden corner. Over her head—an entwined green roof. It's just like in the old story about the beautiful queen whose husband, the wood nymph, cast a spell over her. She had seen illustrations of the story at the dentist's where she lived. She doesn't remember why and how the mean king cursed his wife. Her head is spinning . . . But in such an old thick forest there really could once have been all sorts of beings, good and bad spirits, nymphs and monsters. Only now does she feel how very tired she is. Deep in her bones, she still feels the weight of the last difficult exams. The professor drove the students hard. He had been especially angry today. Maybe he was on the verge of an attack of gallstones. Whenever that happens, he doesn't know what to do with himself or others. She isn't at all afraid of mathematics, but it's still good to know that everything went well. She can finally sleep peacefully . . . But what's so strange? He? Pretty Max?

Dry needles from the fir tree pour down. Someone is coming . . . Who can it be? Who? The tall trees move apart, the woodland king appears. Two pairs of gnomes, one pair following the other, carry his long green beard. In their free hands they hold tiny golden axes. Behind them walks the chief marshal, the old satyr with his goat's feet. The woodland king, with the yellow face of the mathematics professor, stops. She wants to flee, but behind her the satyr's horns emerge. He raises his scepter with its head of a dead owl. She feels faint. She feels his green beard on her cheeks. She knows—it is a great honor when the lord of the field and forest casts his eye upon a mortal girl, but, still, she has taken all her exams . . . Why does she deserve this? No, no! Suddenly the branches start to rustle, thousands of birds sing sweetly, the entire meadow is full of nymphs and sprites. They stand around the woodland queen. Golden hair bedecks her white back, redolent flowers circle her body. On her head she carries a crown of diamonds that the gnomes dug out of the depths of the mountains for her. She raises her hand.

"Aha! Caught! Lusting after a young nymph!"

Her mother of pearl bosom rises and all the birds emit a melodic sigh. The chief marshal lowers his horns and hides behind the king.

The girl under the tree jumps up on a wide tree branch. The thick growth hides her. No one sees her. The woodland king raises his nose, just like the professor.

"Foolish woman, are you jealous? Do you concern yourself with the women who creep around on the earth? They are born and disappear like dust under our feet. Don't you know that I cannot allow our godly generation to die out? Even you, immortal women, don't understand your men!"

A wild storm erupts. Tall trees bow down and tremble like torn leaves. Thunder splits the sky. All the living beings fall down. The woodland king's eyes burn like fire and his voice is louder than the thunder.

"Go, foolish woman. Because of your jealous curiosity I cast upon you my royal curse. Go!"

The queen lowers her head. A bejeweled tear falls from her diaphanous eyes. She departs slowly. Around her is her frightened retinue.

The golden axes resound in the hands of the gnomes. The earth shakes under the woodland king's heavy steps. He disappears.

As soon as the godly pair disappear the thunder is silenced, the birds once again begin to praise the day, and the sun in the clear heavens smiles down on the world.

She jumps down from the tree branch and heads through the forest. A clear river beckons her from afar. Heatedly, she throws herself into the cool stream, jumps out, dries herself in the golden sand on the shore, weaves a crown, and adorns herself with white lilies. A sweet melody is heard: the little lonesome shepherd is playing on his fife. She runs over, taps him on the forehead and hides among the bushes. But the shepherd finds her. She sits on a fallen tree trunk. She refreshes herself with the redolent honey of a green leaf that has stolen out of the hollow of an oak tree.

The old black billy goat gathers the white sheep. He knows that as soon as the young shepherd runs after a girl, he—the old billy goat—must guard the flock.

Suddenly two white doves fly by. They are blowing on narrow silver trumpets—the queen's messengers are summoning her nymphs. She reminds them that she, too, is in the king's retinue. She runs to where the silver trumpets beckon.

The entire court is already assembled on the flowery meadow. In the middle stands a tall brown jackass. Its coat shines like copper under the sun. The queen rises from her throne. The white swans at her feet spread their wings and fly after her. Two nymphs bring a wreath of roses. The queen puts it on the jackass's forehead. It turns around, looks at her with big brown eyes, stretches out its head and emits a long dreadful cry. The queen is delighted.

"Listen to how majestic and grand is his sweet voice. Listen!"

The sapphire eyes shine, the dainty hand with the coral nails stretches out. A contented sigh raises the buds on her mother-of-pearl breast. The evening stars of her crown, a gift from her sister the Night Queen, descend . . .

Tenderly she embraces the ass's thick mane . . . The queen's companions cover their faces with their hair and weep quietly. Others laugh. Behind the trees there are all sorts of creatures who live in the forest and make fun of their ruler whom the king, her husband, punished with the curse that she would bless an ass with her divine body. The old satyr, the chief marshal, leans on his scepter with its head of a dead owl. He shakes his horns gleefully. "Ha, ha, the proud and beautiful queen is in love with a fool."

The young woman under the tree trembles in sadness and pity. Shame has turned her face red. Frightened, she startles. Where is that laughter coming from? She leans on her hand. Where is she? And where is the angry king with the professor's yellow face? And who is there on the meadow? She stares. A tall man is standing near the table. She sees him through the branches. His straight, dark hair falls over his ear. His brown suit glistens like a pelt. Who is he? Whom does he resemble? And why are they laughing around the table? Oh my, whom does he resemble?

The strong, healthy young woman, the first female mathematician to graduate, sits under the bushy fir tree and sways, just like her old grandmother at home used to do when saying her prayers on the Sabbath. Swaying and murmuring and wringing her hands. "Protect and shield me, Master of the Universe! Do not let my foolish infatuation crown the ass in my heart. Grant mercy to your daughters. Do not punish us with a fool."

Cheerful voices call out:

"How much longer will you sleep? Get up, we're going swimming!"

AMY GOTTLIEB

Working the Mikveh

W e take turns: Yehudis, Miriam, Lillian and I. The mikveh is behind Miriam's house so she gets to staff it three nights a week; the rest of us take the other three and then rotate for Shabbes. In theory, no one wants to work the mikveh on Shabbes because it's better to be home greeting the Shabbes queen, making our homes into a little paradise. We'll set our tables with linen and flowers and then put paradise on our freshly bathed bodies with clean dresses and shiny shoes. And then later, after all the food and talk, pass the kugel and who wants tea, after all the singing and table banging, then it's time for paradise between our sheets.

The more kids you have, the less like paradise. Four baths by sunset, four changes of clothes, four picky eaters, four bedtimes, and four chances you'll be too tired for a hot and holy Friday night fuck. I wasn't born into this religious ethic of guarding one's tongue, but Rebbetzin Lazar says, "Don't sever who you are, Ruth," so this is how I talk, even now with all this sanctity. I'm working on it, though. I'm evolving.

I like working the mikveh on Shabbes. It's good to get away from the kids and have some quiet before dinner. In the stillness the mikveh looks less like a small tiled pool and more like a pond of sweet rainwater gathered together simply to make a person ritually pure. This is how it goes: menstruation equals dead egg, dead egg equals impurity, no more sex, count the days, visit the mikveh, soak off the world, stand before the attendant, dip once, say a blessing, dip twice more, and poof! Instant purity, body and soul. What better foreplay could there be?

I don't love immersing: the water is kind of scuzzy—but I enjoy watching each of my mikveh sisters take the plunge. When she is fully immersed, the splash of water turns to stillness and in that moment, her fingers loosen, lips part, and eyes open to all that holiness. When she's down deep, the surface of the water barely shimmers and I know she is in a womb-like embrace, no place untouched.

My mikveh sisters talk to me. After all, when someone is standing before you, dropping her towel for your inspecting eyes, she'll tell you anything. And that's how I know things, secrets I shouldn't even talk about because as Rebbetzin Lazar says, my tongue is my evil impulse. I'm working on it; I really am.

Here's what I know.

Batya cancels a lot because she can't wait. The law says count all the days of your menstruation, then check your underwear to make sure there are no more leaks, and then count seven more days till immersion. It's the rabbinic way, so we do it, no questions asked. Batya makes an appointment every month and then calls the answering machine and in a little sing-song voice, says, "I spotted." Now the other attendants don't know this but I saw: Batya has a tattoo on the inside of her thigh. You would think she had a wayward past like me, but she's *frum* from birth. For her, there was no summer adventure with a married man, no college years wearing sheer Indian broomstick skirts with nothing on underneath. Batya was a buttoned-up Young Israel girl from Queens who spent her teenage years in long-sleeved blouses with angel collars, learning Rashi and collecting kugel recipes. Her tattoo is very pretty; a small blue butterfly.

When Batya comes to shul she wears the biggest hats; that's how everyone knows her. Wide brims, white on black, feathers, a little black veil. She and her husband are big donors; this is not a secret. But here is what I know. Batya works for a man named Liam who owns a silk flower shop and she is in love with him. First, it was for his kindness, she said, because he let her take off for all the Jewish holidays. But then it was more. I once spied them on the BART, sitting side by side, knees touching, pinkies intertwined, her cheeks flushed. They got off the train in downtown Oakland and disappeared into a crowd. And now, when I watch Batya immerse three times, I wonder who she dips for, where her purity lives. I wonder about her often. Rebbetzin Lazar says curiosity is healthy, but to judge is only for God, so I just stay curious.

Now Chani is another story. Her heart is so pure that I think she must have a fresh bar of Ivory soap floating calmly through her frail, pale body. She spends her whole week doing mitzvos and preparing for Shabbes.

Monday she reads for a blind girl at the library, Tuesday she works at a soup kitchen, Wednesday she cleans her mother's house, Thursday she holds sick babies at the hospital, and Friday she wakes at dawn to iron her husband's clothes, change the sheets, bake challah, clean a chicken, and frost a sponge cake that reaches to heaven. Just before she gets herself ready for Shabbes, she inspects lettuce leaves on a slide tray, looking for the one single insect that could render a salad as *trayf* as a lobster bisque.

But Chani has been married for ten years, and she weeps every time she gets her period. She thinks she's not good enough to bear a child, not evolved enough. I tell her God is not judging her, but she thinks she is being punished because she and her husband touched before their wedding. "We really touched," she told me. "His fingers were inside me and I had my first orgasm. Surely this is my punishment. God heard my pleasure and made a decision."

"No way," I said. "Sin and punishment don't apply to sex. Not for us."

"You know what your problem is, Ruth? You were modern before you were religious and you have no idea how I think. Surely I am being punished."

Chani immerses so beautifully; she was born for this kind of holiness. First she dips once and I declare her immersion kosher. She mutters a blessing and catches her breath. Two more dips. Kosher. Kosher. Then I turn my back to give her some privacy as she dips seven more times for all of God's kabbalistic emanations and for the completion of the world. "My Ivory girl," I whisper to myself when she comes out, always averting my glance. With her pure face wet with mikveh drops, she goes back to the changing room, pulls on her tights, blouse, long skirt, beret, and wedding ring, and walks out to her husband's waiting car. Chani lives only two blocks from the mikveh, but her husband doesn't want her outside by herself in such a vulnerable state of purity.

Our mikveh is not some scummy Old World ritual bath like you'd find in Brooklyn or Jerusalem. This is California after all; our mikveh is in a heated log cabin set back in the woods. The buzzer on the door doesn't always work, so the mikveh sisters know that they can let themselves in and wander into the waiting room. It's a hippie mikveh in a hippie sort of town where mikveh attendants are women who listen to the Grateful Dead and bake vegan meatloaf. Many of us don't have such devout pasts, but you'd never know from looking at us now. Even the changing room checklist Lillian wrote is not your traditional litany.

Women: Bathe and soak, use a pumice stone to smooth your heels. Take a few minutes to do a breast exam. Know your body. Be sure to remove your nail polish, cut your nails, floss and brush. Use the cotton balls for earring holes and belly buttons. When you are ready, take a deep breath and relax. Find your kavannah. Remember, mikveh sisters, this is your time. Yours alone.

Believe me, this is not how it reads out there in the mainstream.

I'm not into hocus pocus. Some people say that if a great rabbi visits your town and immerses in your mikveh, the first woman to dip after him will absorb extra blessings and everything she prays for will come true. Every last wish. A certain Rabbi Yehuda immersed in Safed one morning, and the first woman who plunged that night had been infertile for twelve years and poof! Twins. Reb Yankelovich immersed in Cleveland on a Friday morning and the woman who immersed soon after learned that her orange-sized malignancy shrunk down to an olive, then a pea, then nothing. Clean as a newborn.

But I know myself. If I were the first one in, I would be down there in the tub with open eyes, wondering about the body that went in before mine. And thinking about some great rabbi's body is where I draw the line. But for others it's a different story. They want to open themselves to some kind of promise, closeness to God. And who am I to judge? Anything is possible. Sick bodies can be healed; empty wombs can be filled with hope and gestation. So when Rebbetzin Lazar left a message that Reb Gershon of Milwaukee, a direct descendent of Rabbi Loew of Prague, was coming through town on the second of Tammuz, I knew what to do. I called Miriam who called Lillian who called Yehudis and we all agreed: Chani.

"You'll be the first one in after nightfall," I told her "The second of Tammuz, in the dark."

"There must be someone needier than I," said Chani. "Yehudis knows someone with breast cancer, Lillian's little boy has that attention deficit problem—these women need help more than I do."

"You need a child," I said. "Your goodness has to be passed down."

Men immerse in daylight; they can frolic with each other in the mikveh water and enjoy pool parties before Shabbes. But women are commanded to immerse alone, and because no one should know the details of our intimate lives we go after dark, and only after dark. Lillian says it's romantic for her to sneak off to a cabin in the woods where she can peel off her clothes and go for a meaningful dip. "It gets me in the mood," she says.

About me, there is no secret. The mikveh doesn't arouse. I immerse because that's what the Torah says, right there on the parchment. No place is hidden from Jewish law, from the space between my teeth to the food in my cabinet; from the fibers on my jacket to the hair I keep covered. Three fingers of hair are permitted to stick out of my beret, so I have some tendrils of bangs. The rest of my hair is a secret only my husband knows. Call it another prop on the stage show of life, but everything matters.

"When you inspect them for loose hairs," asked Lillian, "don't you wonder about their sex lives?"

"Of course I do. We all do."

"But when does your wondering turn to judgment?"

"Only someone not born into this world would ask such a question."

"Well, what about Batya?" asked Lillian. "Don't you judge her?"

"No," I said, "even though we both know about Liam."

Lillian paused. "Do you think she comes to the mikveh when she has her period?"

"What? Just to trayf up the water?"

"God forbid, but anything is possible."

"She cancels all the time. Look, with two men to fuck—"

"Ruth!"

"I'm working on it. I really am."

"You could use to dunk after the rabbi."

"No," I said. "It's all about separation and purity. We don't dunk for speech."

After nightfall on the second of Tammuz, I unlocked the door to the mikveh and turned on the lights. There was a note from Rebbetzin Lazar, saying Reb Gershon had immersed that morning and the water was in a special state of holiness. I went to the mikveh pool and leaned down, pulling my hand through the water. It was clear as fresh rain, no dirt, no hairs. I looked at my watch: Chani would come for her plunge in fifteen minutes. Everything was ready: I only had to guard the expectant water. I could go down myself, I thought. Four children, a husband, my wayward tongue: life is a narrow bridge and it couldn't hurt. But hocus pocus or not, I would be searching the depths for the old flakes of skin off Gershon's body. The water belonged to Chani. Blessings were ripe for her immersion, suspended in the water like holy molecules waiting to purify every strand of her hair, surface of tooth, eardrum, armpit, cuticle. I thought about her body and got goose bumps.

I sat down in the waiting area and listened to the quiet, my eyes opening and closing in the soft light. A parade of women passed before me, first my friends from the past, then my religious friends. They passed in two different lines; no one looked at anyone in the other line. I watched my children as babies crawl along the floor between the lines of women, and then I saw them: Chani's babies, two little twin girls, pale like their mother. Chani picked them up and laid them in two wicker baskets the color of flax. She held one basket in each hand and walked in her line, perfectly balanced.

I woke to a loud splash and ran to the mikveh. The water was momentarily still but a sheath of black hair moved through the depths and a set of limbs fluttered like a jellyfish. The swimmer stayed down there for at least a minute and then popped up, gasping for air.

"I had to come. I couldn't wait," mumbled a dripping-wet woman. "It's a bad time, isn't it?"

I flicked on the light. Batya stood in the water with tears streaming down her face. "I don't know whether I'm coming or going," she mumbled. "My life is such an entanglement."

She stumbled out of the mikveh and brushed past me to the changing room. I waited for her to dress and go. From the window I watched her open a car door, and her eyes were puffy from crying.

The water was cloudy and stagnant, like an old abandoned swimming pool. I used a fishing net to scoop out strands of Batya's hair. There was a small scab floating on the surface and I scooped that out too. The pull of the net brought a small wave to the surface and I watched my reflection shimmer in the murky water. It was almost the end of the twentieth century, on the west coast of America. The second of Tammuz was also a day in the month of July. It was a hot summer and I was wearing a black wool beret on my head. Not so long ago I would have looked at someone like me and there would have been no recognition. I had become a woman whose hair was buried under a shapeless hat, who was standing silently at the edge of a pool that had something to do with holiness, with paradise, with love.

Chani was ready. I inspected her in the changing room where her wedding ring was nestled on top of her beret; dental floss and cotton balls lay in the garbage pail. Her nails were freshly trimmed, her skin faintly pink from having scrubbed off the dirt of ordinary living. I pulled a loose hair off her back and she shuddered.

"I feel different this time," she said. "Hopeful. Thank you, Ruth. My prayers will fly on the wings of your goodness."

Chani stepped down into the mikveh and sighed. "It's living water," she said. "Something happened here, I can feel it." She put her arms out in front of her, plunged deeply, and came up for air. "Kosher," I said, and Chani muttered the blessing. She dipped twice more for obligation. Kosher. Kosher. Then I turned my back on her as she dipped seven more times for God's emanations, for the completion of the unfinished world. And then it was very quiet, so quiet that I could hear the sound of my own breath as it received the air. I closed my eyes and felt my body surrounded by water, as if I were immersed also. After what felt like an eternity, I slowly turned to face the mikveh. Chani was floating in the center, poised like a lily pad, her face blushing and radiant.

Ironing

E sther watched Tennis Boy amble across the hotel lobby, racket slung
across his back, and decided on the spot he'd be her first boyfriend. He
wasn't noticeably handsome, but he was noticeably normal, and to Esther's
twelve-year-old eyes, that was everything.

The mirrors on the wall created four of him, no, six, each more polished
than the last. Esther's own family needed no multiplying, boisterous and
too many already; they monopolized the desk as they checked in for their
reunion in Puerto Rico, her uncle passing out room keys like prizes.

Given that Tennis Boy would be gallivanting past at regular intervals,
he was an obvious choice. He would fall for Esther's wholesome looks, a
contrast to the gussied-up falseness of his friends back home. He and she
would dive beneath the same surging wave. Impressed by her courage when
she rose in the surf's wake, he'd compliment her. Then as the sun sent light
skittering across the turquoise waters, he'd kiss her. She would soon be
transported by a momentous passion, leaving behind her squabbling clan,
the impending double doom of braces and bat mitzvah, the fact that her
best friend Lin had a date to the winter formal, and the terror that underlay
it all: a sense that each day since seventh grade began had colluded with
the day before it to shove Esther into a shackled crouch, to render her one
day less free.

Unfortunately for Esther's plans, the hotel's private beach was lake-like:
no waves. Even worse, the air above it was what the girls at school called
"bad hair day humid." Though she'd ignored her cousins' request to build
a sand fort so she might recline beneath the umbrella and alternate reading
a *Star Trek* novelization with conjuring Tennis Boy's lips brushing hers,
her curls still bloated.

Her cousins gave her a new nickname, after the expanding animals on

TV infomercials, those hideously mushrooming balls of greenery. "You know what Estie looks like? A Chia Pet!"

They sat at dinner at the resort's mediocre Italian restaurant, all in polo shirts. She'd already slathered in gobs of her brother's gel, so much that her scalp itched. But "LA Style 100 Extra Hold" had failed.

"Ch-ch-chia Pet!" Her brother's shoulders churned up and down with mirth, like engine parts. The adults gulped their amusement back, their throats constricting. Esther's mother, whose hair was cut close to her skull, ran a hand through the girl's massy locks, but was halted by thick, gel-caked snarls.

"Like me," she said softly.

"Like *your whole* family!" Her aunts, not Jewish, denied involvement in the travesty. "Esther honey, don't butter the bread. You're not getting taller."

"Well, she's certainly sprouting," said her uncle, and everyone tittered because Esther was a noticeable B-cup, which was something for a twelve-year-old, *not that it sent the boys running in her direction yet*, she had heard her father telling her aunt on the tarmac this morning, adding: *Thank God*.

Esther, who had been attempting to be a good sport at dinner, wondered suddenly what kept the boys from running. Did she want them to run? She squeezed a spongy curl, felt it rebound, and fantasized about impaling her family with a butter knife, then stabbing herself in the heart.

Tennis Boy and his family emerged from a corner table. Esther thrust her shoulders back and offered him a bold natural gaze, which he neither noticed nor returned. Yet he beckoned her into a better daydream; her T-shirt morphed into an evening dress, her hair softened and spread like wings and together they danced until dawn to Caribbean drums. She buttered her bread and floated away.

Esther's best friend Lin had met a boy on vacation in Mexico and gotten to second base, a relief because what else did you even *need* before high school? Esther could achieve this too, she knew, if she applied herself, sat still, laughed at the right times and didn't say anything dumb about *Star Trek*.

The next morning Esther swam with her cousins at a more distant beach with waves, though she knew the salty water would not help her hair situation. She joined them building a new fort soon smashed and flattened by the surf.

"You're way more fun today," she was told. She snorted and splashed;

somehow she had the idea that while she bobbed, Tennis Boy might be gazing at them, wondering who these people were, these people who acted so carefree.

Through the window of the cab home, she noticed a Walgreens. A hair iron waited in those aisles; the girls at school, if in her predicament, would buy it. Surely Esther's mom would never approve the idea: "What a waste," she'd say. "We're in a beautiful place and you want to go to a drugstore?" Yet the iron floated before Esther's eyes, a sacred object.

Later, Esther's brother and cousins embarked on a video game tournament. Esther sat alone, picturing Tennis Boy coming to visit her on her block at home, a red rose in his hands, and Lin's jaw dropping at the idea that a boy *like that* would go for *Esther*. In the vision, her hair was straight. Ironed straight.

She opened her eyes to the sunlight and there stood the real thing, with his racket, talking to her cousins at the entrance to the arcade. His shirt was off; his shorts slung below his waist revealed a trapezoid of fine-cut muscles. Esther draped a towel around herself, covering his indecency by proxy, and sauntered toward them, hearing phrases like "high score" and "next level."

"Hey Estie," the youngest cousin called.

"Hey, Chia Pet! Ch-ch-chia!" the cousin added as Esther struggled to formulate a socially acceptable way of saying hi back.

"Chia?" Tennis Boy said. He looked right at her and laughed like it was the best joke he'd ever heard. He quaked with it as her brother had, each peal a knife entering between her ribs and perforating her heart.

They began to talk about a tennis tournament but Esther couldn't pretend to care: she fled into the bathroom to weep pitifully into her resort-issue towel. What a loser she saw in the mirror there, too preoccupied with the rooms of her mind to tackle the halo of frizz that crowned them. She craved a friend, a girl to hand her tissues or coo. Instead, the shrieks of children on the waterslide battered her ears.

A thumping drumbeat began in her chest and spread down to her stomach. She had to act. Esther dashed upstairs to the room she shared with her brother, shivering from the hotel's air conditioning. Ignoring the wet stains spreading over her T-shirt from her thick hair, she pulled on the handle of the adjoining room and saw her mother asleep, her head framed by a pure white pillow.

Esther had never lied or stolen a thing. And her mother was so peaceful, so tired, as if the family's teasing, the tugging, had caused her to retreat just as it forced Esther to venture out.

Esther pushed back her pity: the moment demanded something harder. She grimaced, reached into her mom's purse and pulled out a wad of cash. Before she could reconsider her descent into petty thievery, she exited: out through the lobby with the slot machines blinking and bleeping and the sad old people throwing their money away, as her family described it.

She stood still on the sultry street. On their tour of the fort the first day here, they had learned about how horribly the Europeans, then the Americans, had treated the island. Oppression, poverty, just like the creepy Borg on *Star Trek*, traveling to different planets, assimilating people into slavery. Her family was like the Borg too sometimes: her father had gripped her shoulder on the way back and said, "Stay close to the Hilton, Estie." She had said, "I ride the bus into Boston all the time."

"Hey you. Hey Chia!" She looked up and saw Tennis Boy, lounging in front of the hotel with a drink in his hand. "Tennis later? Your cousins are coming. Ask them for deets. What's your name again?"

"Esther," she squeaked out.

"Okay cutie," he said. "Bring your racket."

She nodded and watched him glide away, "cutie" reverberating in the air. A window had opened with that word; a real one, not imaginary. She might puke with excitement. She had to see this mission through.

She walked toward Condado. Her thighs rubbed together and her shorts rode up inside them, about a centimeter. Her aunt said she wasn't growing taller. True, a small puddle of belly now spilled out over her bikini shorts. She should do sit-ups. Yes: she had to iron herself out from top to bottom. Sweat gathered behind her neck and beneath her breasts.

She stopped halfway across the causeway for a breath. The tide flowed beneath her feet from the wild Atlantic into the lagoon. Her hotel looked like a dollhouse. She felt dizzy but kept on down an avenue lined with shops whose windows held the little frogs, dolls and seashells that her family called *tchotchkes*, always in a singsong voice—chach-kees!

She passed two homeless men asleep on the sidewalk, one cop with a machine gun, dozens of tourists and six elderly people awaiting the bus. Where did the bus take them, and wouldn't it be nice to just sit on it until the end of the line? Esther imagined the ride, the bumpy road, the sea views, the small houses growing smaller and smaller as they left San Juan's center behind. Perhaps there was a perfect pink house for her and Tennis Boy, with laundry in the yard and some chickens.

Next to the bus stop she saw a group of teenagers, American boys. They reminded her of her cousins, but older. Like Tennis Boy, too. Their laughter was harsh; they barely saw her pass.

Esther hurried toward Walgreens and shoved the door open, standing still in an oasis of air conditioning and discount beauty products.

"You get them!" "No, you do!" a pair of teenagers giggled in the condom aisle.

Esther hid her face, sidestepped them on the way to the hair section. She had enough cash to buy the iron and for added kicks the cheapest eyeshadow, mascara and lipstick she could find.

At the register the woman gave her everything in a plastic bag.

"*Gracias*," Esther blurted out.

"That iron works good on curls," the cashier said in approval—or was it disapproval?

Tremors traveled through Esther's limbs: what if her mom woke up and missed her? But she was bursting with the need of it, to use her new purchases, to rip open the plastic and erase her face, tame her tangles. She slipped into the lobby of the Condado Plaza hotel and followed the signs to the ladies' lounge.

Once there, she savagely attacked the box with the iron in it, unsheathed it and plugged it in. While it began to heat up, she fell upon the makeup, hurling the pieces of packaging in the trash. She stood at the mirror: shadow, stroke, fill. She didn't know what she was doing but she was doing *something*: dab, line, stroke. Her eyes became encircled by big dark patches.

The iron radiated heat. Esther inhaled, then ran it down each curl, pressing it against the strands, stopping when she felt the singe, the crackle on the ends of her hair.

Oh, the sick smell of it. She had a friend who cut herself. Another friend who had stopped eating anything but balled up pieces of white bread. Esther kept going: lock by lock, kink by kink, she conquered the flyaways until a woman who reminded her of her mother barged in.

"Ugh! It smells like burning! Why are you doing this down here, honey?"

"My mom's sleeping." No lie. Still, she ought to return. Tonight they were going to Old San Juan for dinner.

"Giving yourself a makeover?" the lady asked

"Sort of."

"You're gorgeous. Don't change—you're too young." The woman went into a stall.

Shut up old woman, Esther wanted to say. Usually, she never even *thought* things like that. The woman began to pee. Esther looked at herself in the mirror and she couldn't help it; she grinned. She had done it; she was beautiful.

Esther held her head up high on the way home and let her hips sway, slightly, like Lin's did. She smiled to herself. *She had done it.* She noticed the American boys in college sweatshirts and backwards caps on the sidewalk, milling, and stared at them: frank, natural, bold.

This time they noticed her too.

"Yo. What're you looking at?" one asked. She froze.

They swarmed, like the bench spilling over after a school basketball game. They were fourteen or older; it couldn't be *her* they were lurching toward. She instinctively crossed her arms across her chest, looked down, walked on.

"Why is she not answering?" she heard. "Raccoon eyes."

"You were checking us OUT, girl. J, she likes you."

"Her tits are big!"

"Where's she going? So rude!"

"Hey chica!" They were tourists like her. Maybe they even went to her school, and she'd have to see them in January. Esther walked faster, engulfed by blasts of hot shame. Why had she looked their way? Why had she been excited when they looked back? Her face perspired; her eye makeup was running down the sides of her nose.

"Why won't you talk to us?"

"Ugh, fuck her!"

"Would you, though?"

"I'd hit it."

She lost them on the causeway, hearing over the din her raggedy breath. "Leave me alone!" she told the air.

Evening was arriving on the lagoon; she watched the white scrim of the waves hit the breakers. Salt settled on her tongue; air moved across her damp neck.

Esther lifted up her hand, weakly, and spent her last five dollars on a cab that took her 800 feet.

She looked at her selves, all six of them, in the mirrors of her hotel lobby. Gone was the frizzy hair, yes, but she saw now that the effect looked off, as if her head were straining against a leash. The tendrils near her face remained fuzzy: sweat.

Yes, her eyes looked like a raccoon's, her lips lurid, a cheap imitation of Lin or the girls at school. A *tchotchke*.

Tennis Boy, dressed in black shiny fabric, blocked her way to the elevator. "I kicked your cousin's ass in tennis," he said cheerfully. "Your mascara's running," he added, as if it were obvious that she would wear mascara. She put a hand to her face. "Well see ya, Chia! Hey, that rhymes," he said, finding her mute.

Esther slid down the side of the elevator and sat on the floor as it climbed. She was Chia Pet, yes, but he wasn't Tennis Boy. He was Andrew, Josh, Evan or Jake. Of course he had a girlfriend; boys like that just did. She saw Tennis Boy raising his racket and sending an ace over the net, leaving her relatives speechless.

Her mother paced the hallway, growing frantic. She pulled Esther by her arm and then wrapped her in a smothering hug—an act that led Esther to spill the details of her subterfuge and a few more tears.

In the taxi to dinner Esther learned *there would be consequences for her actions*. She heard the words "chores" and "grounded." But her mom wished it were easier, she did. She believed she had raised Esther to be herself, not underhanded. Esther, wretched, wished her mom would hug her again or go back to sleep.

The trees in the old city's plazas were festooned with lights that slid up and down like drops of illuminated water. Kids set off firecrackers and pigeons swooped, then hobbled around eating the clusters of crumbs.

"Whoa, you look different," said Esther's brother. "I miss your Jewfro."

"She looks good," said the older cousin.

"I see you're putting more into your appearance," her aunt whispered. "It's about time. Easier on the eye makeup, easier on the dessert."

"Your aunt has a problem," said her mother. "Don't listen, Estie."

Tunes engulfed the plaza, but Esther heard only the replay of the day: the rough talk of the boys, laughter from her would-be lover, her aunt's fretting.

Esther sought refuge in her mind, but imagined only the high balcony of her room and herself climbing the railing. She felt herself overtaken by a wave. She dodged a car swerving toward her on the causeway.

She sensed in a thousand ways her visibility, her invisibility. Maybe she even sensed a future of being overlooked, leered at, always wanting: objects packaged as salvation that never were, promised approval that never came.

The trees rained light. Somewhere close by, waves swept in against the rocks, the soft sand. Her cousins tossed a tennis ball in a circle. The moist breeze with its fingers began lifting each tendril of her hair and lacing it in a spiral, undoing her work.

Her journey to Walgreens felt filthy: a betrayal, a waste. But she felt she'd have to make it again, to flatten and press things down until they burned at the edges. How endless, how exhausting this would be, like the tide coming in each morning for years, wearing down the sandcastles the children built.

Esther squeezed her eyelids shut, then opened them. But wait—what if there was still a chance? She craned her neck, strained to get a glimpse of Tennis Boy walking the street toward her, hoping still for a rescuer, for a story that wasn't hers.

BETH KANELL

What Was Cut

W hen you are a girl who cuts herself, for years, with the clean antiseptic edge of a razor blade that once belonged to—well, no. Deborah never told anyone that. The first owner of the blade, that was her secret. But it never belonged to her father, or even her younger brother. She knew the therapist believed the slice of metal had family significance. But even a good therapist can carry a bad idea, a wrong idea.

Anyway, she never told, and years afterward, when the cutting had (mostly) ended and she only wore long sleeves to hide the scars, not to cover any new weeping wound, there came a day when she put the blade into a place she planned to forget. She didn't write the location, or even photograph it with her smartphone. Goodbye, little comforting knife. Goodbye, farewell, try not to rust.

Yet somehow she remembered the exact place. She didn't go back to check, but in her dreams she counted along the stone wall on the college campus, seventeen stones from the pillar, and found the single-edge razor blade gleaming, reflecting starlight. Not in her daily life, you see? Just in her dreams. Still, even a dream is a kind of memory, isn't it?

She found her soulmate, her *beshert*, the year after her daughter left home for college in another country. Text messages and occasional e-mails arrived several times each day, even now that her daughter's citizenship in the new place had become official. "I sent a seed into the world and it became a forest," Deborah hummed to herself, using a tune from the Friday evening prayer service that Louis attended every week, rain or shine, summer or New Haven winter with its icy winds and slick sidewalks. She liked being there with him—not in adjacent seats, of course, since he sat with the men and she davened with the women. But the gentle fluttering of the curtain between them comforted her, and the electric pulse from heart to heart never ceased. In fact, sometimes she felt the voltage of that pulse rise up, with certain prayers, like the *Shema*. How strange to wait until your silver hairs emerge to find the one meant for you. But it was true, and it was true love.

Even their bodies showed they were meant for each other. Each questing scar on Deborah's right arm matched a leaf-adorned branch inked onto Louis's left arm. And her left arm, to his right. Oh, she knew Jews weren't supposed to get tattoos. That echo of the cattle-car blue-ink numerals on the prisoners' inner arms, that painful assertion of labor demanded and death by starvation most likely to follow—Deborah knew about those memories. Her grandmother, her *bubbe*, used to point silently to the marks that Mrs. Worob down the block usually hid under her sweaters, displayed once each year, bared, at the swimming beach. Deborah understood silence, understood hiding, and the moment of revealing. Many times, she tried to shape those numbers from the fine red lines she cut into her skin, but the curves of the two and the five defeated her. You could still see the seven if you knew how to look.

The first night that she lay with Louis and traced the lines and leaves on his skin, she marveled. The Tree of Life, living and warm, stirring and vibrating against her own chest. On Louis, the twigs, branches, and finally trunk, accompanied by colorful birds that resembled exotic pigeons, came together in a rooted unity. He told her how he'd marked time with each added detail, and for him, the week that the last trembling leaf appeared on the back of his left hand, he saw her cross the road to the old cemetery, and he knew. A day after that, when he called out across the street to her, the thundering sky itself echoed the new connection. Something old, something new, something remembered that went deeper than a blade—or a needle—could reach. And it was Good. They married a month later, at the old synagogue, on a quiet November morning. Not much fuss, but still, they smashed the glass for luck and blessing. Meant to be.

One spring morning—New Haven spring: rain and hail interrupted by tender blue-sky hours, circling back to soft warm breezes, then a hint of frost, despite April—Deborah woke to Louis's absence from their bed. She tugged a velour robe around herself and padded on bare feet to the kitchen, where she found him, as expected. But he was not sitting at the round table with an early cup of coffee, not even fixing the coffee yet. Instead, he stood at the window, gazing across from their third floor to the little old cemetery at the end of the block.

Louis reached behind to hold her hand, without turning from the view. "Look," he said. "Someone is planting something. At the cemetery. Should we do something? What should we do?" Deborah paused to think before replying, and rubbed the warmth of Louis's hand, then stepped closer to curl under his arm, comforted against the side of his chest. Perhaps this comfort led her to the wrong words. She wondered afterward.

"Why should we do anything? It's a nice thing, to plant something there. With all the traffic and such dry soil, maybe it won't grow anyway. Let it be—and let the person feel good about it."

Person: She meant to say man, digging in the soil along the fence line of the dry, sorrowful place, but the more she looked, the more she thought, "Woman. Heavyset. Veil." Maybe what looked like a black veil from here could really be one of those insect-protection nets. She'd seen explorers wear them in nature programs, and even some advertised on TV. But grief is grief, and the darkness around the gardener's head spoke of mourning. "Veil," she said aloud.

"Might be." Louis glanced at her, unconvinced but not arguing. Morning and beloved, not mourning and sorrow. Louis started the coffee.

More people noticed as the season warmed and the plants grew. The person planting them tended them at dawn or in the last hour of twilight. As May turned to June, twilight came very late, and dawn very early, but still. "She must not sleep a lot," Deborah mused, thinking of how her mother became so restless among the dozens of deaths that old age witnesses. Buds formed on the new hedge of plants. Roses.

The cemetery association held a meeting. Louis attended. He told Deborah afterward, "Nobody knows who it is. But the roses—they have already taken over along the entire eastward wall. People are worried they will catch in the lawnmower when Harry mows that side. Harry's going to take them out."

Tuesday afternoon they saw Harry arrive with his mower, his truck of tools. Together, holding hands, Louis's leaves entwined with Deborah's thin net of scars, they walked down the block to sit by the west wall and watch Harry across from them, digging and tugging. Deborah felt bad that she couldn't help. Arthritis in her hands already, and the therapist said to choose tasks wisely. She waited as long as she could, then told Louis she'd be right back—at least she could fetch a bottle of ice water and some fruit to share with Harry. Maybe a slice of pound cake, too. Everybody liked pound cake.

By the time she returned, carrying it all (with paper cups, little plastic plates she could wash afterward, napkins) in a shopping bag, Louis had left the west wall. He stood across the cemetery with Harry. Deborah joined them to contemplate the roots in the pale, dry soil. She looked at their solemn faces.

"So, there's a problem, maybe? Some trouble with the shovel, a rock?" She didn't see anything like a rock in the long slice of open soil along the fence line, but who knew?

"It's not going to work, just taking them out like this," Louis explained, while Harry poked his shovel at the roots again. "They're already outside the wall, making a hedge along the outside. They could spread back inside any time."

"So you take them out from the other side too," Deborah commented. "If you really don't want them here, you have to do it all, right?"

Harry grunted a negative. "Can't do the other side. The cemetery stops here. That's someone else's land, that is."

Deborah watched the two men shake their heads. She turned aside to lay out her water, her food, on a nearby bench. Harry took a short break with them, then loaded his uprooted bushes from the near side of the wall and shoveled the soil back into place. In the back of the truck the displaced roses looked sad and crowded, but strong anyway. Some pink blossoms showed among the branches and sandy roots.

Along the other side of the wall, roses already had opened. From more heat on that side, sunshine soaked up by the wall, Deborah speculated. She tiptoed around to the other side, knowing she was trespassing, just to inhale the fragrance. She remembered her mother's rosewater scent, the least expensive and with a clean, gentle aroma that blended well. With his penknife, Louis cut a few blooms for her to take home.

After that, Harry often stopped at the cemetery for a few minutes on his way home from wherever else he mowed lawns, and pulled out any young rose stems that erupted on the cemetery side. Deborah noticed how quick he was, but also she could see how he frowned. It's just roses, she wanted to say—let them grow, let them bloom, no matter what the cemetery association says. But of course she didn't say it.

There was an argument with the city at the end of the summer, something about taxes. Louis sat on the committee doing the arguing. Deborah baked a little more often, with the cooler weather and with the need she saw in him, that need for comfort, for remembering what his mother used to serve. Rugelach, kichel, apple cake rich with cinnamon. The roses bloomed a second time, wild pink absurdity that lured passers-by to pause. It felt like a blessing.

One day Deborah saw in the paper a name she hated, a name she'd hoped to never see again. But it was in the Deaths column, which felt like removing a dark veil. Still, it stirred up something. She walked to the college campus and counted the stones along the wall. She didn't lift the seventeenth stone that day. She waited. Each day the bitterness, the shame, the old ache smoldered. Louis asked what was wrong, but she couldn't tell him. She began to grieve for this closed-off place between them.

So she went back to her wall, her stone wall, on a Saturday morning, and took the blade out of its darkness. Rust coated it, although the edge seemed sharp, not pitted. She rested it against her wrist, wondering. She ached to make a cut, a simple thin line where the red blood could ooze in relief. But—and this was a big important but—if she did this, her body and Louis's would lose their perfect match, their symmetry.

Instead, on the way home, she stopped at the old cemetery. She used the blade to cut the last roses, letting them tumble into the top of her shopping bag. Back in the apartment, with Louis still at his after-services meeting at the shul, she pulled out the old newspapers and found the obituary and tore it to carry with her. To carry, along with the roses.

It took almost an hour to walk across the city to the goyishe burying ground. She needed her freedom, after all these years. She paced herself, sipping now and then from a small bottle of water.

Statues of saints and rich men decorated the grounds. The last autumn flowers, mostly chrysanthemums, decorated many of the graves. She found the one she sought, easily enough, its green plastic blanket of fake grass and the white cross adorned with multiple wreaths calling out to her, the way he once called her to stay after school: too colorful, too charming, too dangerous.

Why were there no other living people visiting the dead in this place? Deborah puzzled over the absence. It was good. She stepped toward the raw grave and turned her shopping bag upside down, letting the autumn roses cascade down. She saw the glitter of the blade falling, and did not try to find it among the petals and thorns. No blessing or curse came to her to speak, just the roses, and a hope for freedom.

Beyond some trees, she thought for a moment she saw the rose gardener from the old cemetery, that hunched stocky form with the black veil. Just as she might have walked over to check, a new sound and scent and a flare of light by her feet stopped her.

Flames flickered on the ground. A thin column of gray-black smoke lifted and curled. It smelled like flesh burning, heavy with ash and bitterness. An ember landed in her shopping bag, and Deborah hastily dropped the burning bag onto what was, a few minutes earlier, a mound of cut roses.

"Remember."

Still, she let the blade vanish among the ashes. When she looked up, the figure in the veil had vanished also.

And a little New Haven snow began, the flakes hissing as they rested on the hot ashes, then melted, too soon for winter, after all.

HILA AMIT
translated from the Hebrew by Ilana Kurshan

Flash Flood

I.

Yoram stops the car just after the Arava Junction. The skies are spread out before and behind them, the horizon is blue and yellow. The girls, Naama and Yael, are strapped into their car seats in the back. Lily opens the car door, looks around.

Yoram raises the volume for the sake of the girls. "One Hundred Songs for Children, Volume 1," the blue cassette. Tzippy Shavit sings the song about the little bunny who forgets to close the door and catches a cold. The two front doors of the car are open. Yoram walks Lily around to the back so the girls won't see. It all happens silently—she vomits white fluid, with no traces of food. It's been two days since she's eaten a thing.

Hot. It's hot outside, and even hotter in the red Mini Minor—the air conditioning was broken even back when the car belonged to Yoram's mother. Lily leans against the back bumper. Her straw hat, white with purple plastic flowers and a wide brim, rests on the back of the trunk. There is no wind. The strap of her white dress has fallen off her right shoulder. Her pale skin is nearly camouflaged with the color of the fabric. Her bones protrude.

Yoram doesn't peer in at the back seat. He prefers to believe that the girls can't see a thing. Shula Chen sings "Hudie Cutie." There are no other cars on the road.

It is the end of September, and they're on their way to Eilat. It's their last vacation together. Yoram and Lily know this. They own an apartment in Eilat, on Hashmonaim Street. A long street, unvarying, with several roundabouts, overlooking the mountains. They travel there once a year, and the rest of the year they rent out their place. After this vacation Yoram will return only once, to fix up the place and remove the furniture. He will sell the apartment to pay for all the medical bills their health insurance won't cover. The girls will have no memory of it.

What Naama will remember most of all from that trip is the silence. On the Arava road, just past the Kushi Rimon rest stop, the cassette playing Sukkot songs got stuck. The tape unspooled, making a screeching noise that filled the car. Yoram kept driving along at the same speed. Naama will remember it as if in a dream: the noise, her father's forehead in the mirror, her mother's pale hand resting on her knee. Naama stopped singing. No one cried. The sound continued for several long minutes, invading their ear canals, blending with the whir of the engine, with the roar of the wind. Her father's foot pressed on the gas—he wasn't paying attention to the speedometer or to the empty noise. Finally her mother shook herself out of her daze and said, "Stop all that noise, Yoram, stop it already." Not loudly. Bitterly.

He managed to eject the tape without taking his eyes off the road. Then they kept driving a few more kilometers. The girls fell asleep, the radio reception was restored, and there were Hebrew songs playing. Lily's eyes gleamed and her entire face was flushed, and only her earlobes and the tip of her nose were still pale. "Do you remember the last time I threw up while we were driving?"

Yoram nods, but he is having trouble retrieving the memory.

"It was on those steep descents before the Arava road," Lily says. "I was pregnant with Naama, still at the very beginning. You didn't know yet. You thought I was just carsick. I hadn't told you yet," she continues, almost in a whisper, as if it's still a secret. "I wanted to get used to the feeling. I wanted to experience it myself first, alone."

That summer they bought the apartment in Eilat, and they even considered moving there. In the end they abandoned the idea: Naama was born, and they wanted to raise her close to their parents. They had no trouble finding tenants, and during vacations, between one rental period and another, they would drive down.

He casts a smile in her direction, wishing with all his might that he could hold her hand. His whole body is yearning for her touch, but he hesitates, knowing how sensitive she is, how weak her limbs are. Her thin pale fingers, too, stay where they are, interlaced with one another atop her sunken belly, the loose fabric of her dress bunched up beneath them.

In the apartment, on the first day, Yoram makes dinner for everyone. His plate is piled high with chicken wings, pasta with tomato sauce, and salad. Naama eats everything, just a bit less of each dish. He makes Yael a kid's plate: peeled cucumbers cut into circles, plain pasta, cut-up pieces of chicken. Lily's plate is similar: peeled cucumbers and white rice without seasoning. Even that makes her nauseous. The tensing of her bowels, the vomiting in the kitchen sink right on schedule—Lily is already used to it all. These days they can't insist that the girls finish all the food on their plates.

For dessert—four flavors of ice cream, fruit punch-chocolate-banana-vanilla, sold by the kilo. Lily slides a spoonful of pink along her tongue. She has already vomited everything, and whatever else she eats will remain in her stomach until morning.

In the evening Yoram fixes up the outside antenna, knocks on the back of the television, tries to improve the reception. Yael is already asleep in her crib. They are sitting on the old couch, Yoram's arm is around Lily's shoulders, and despite the pain, she is holding Naama on her lap, explaining to her what's happening on the screen. This was how they'd imagined their evenings when they didn't yet know if Lily was having a boy or a girl.

On Tuesday Yoram took the girls on a hike in Park Timna—it was only a twenty-minute drive. Lily didn't join them. At the entrance to the park, right after the ticket booths, he stopped to call her. He left the girls strapped in the back seat with the windows open and got out of the car. The guard refused: Visitors were not allowed to use the office phone. Yoram stood with his back to the car and explained the situation briefly, his head lowered. "Their mother is not well, you understand, just to make sure she's all right." The guard looked over at the two girls.

Lily answered after four rings. She said she was on the porch, resting, reading a book. Had she not answered, he would have turned around, speeding back in the Mini Minor like a police car with its sirens wailing.

He didn't know that afterwards, while the three of them were in the park, Lily was no longer resting on the porch. She was standing there, barefoot on the fifth floor, trying to make a decision. One of her legs was already swung over the railing.

On their second day in Eilat they sat on the Dekalim beach, caressed by the rays of the afternoon sun in autumn. One moment stood out from all the others: a silence in a world that was blindly dazzling, gold sparkling around them, and they are under a yellowish-orange beach umbrella. Lily and Yoram are lying on a straw mat, their heads touching one another on their folded-up towels. Lily's straw hat is next to them, moving slightly in the wind. The shadow of the beach umbrella extends almost to their knees, and Lily's thighs—pale and smooth compared to Yoram's dark and hairy ones—are baking in the sun. Naama is building a sandcastle, and Yael is feeling around in the wet sand next to her sister, alternately helping her and wrecking her handiwork. When the wind gets stronger it tousles Yael's curls, and sand flies into her eyes and she starts to cry. Yoram and Lily do not get up. Nothing can disturb the cocoon they have spun for themselves under the beach umbrella. Their eyes are closed, and as if in an unspoken agreement, they will not open them. Most of all Yoram remembers the smell of Lily's hair and the way it brushed against his shoulder, the image of their daughters playing in the sand, the sun disappearing behind the mountains.

In the years when they almost never spoke about Lily except on the anniversary of her death, which they always commemorated on a Friday so that everyone would be able to make it—during those years, Naama found herself drawn again and again to the beaches of the Red Sea, along with her husband and children. While the others were in the water, she would lie on the beach, covered in sunscreen, her skin fair like her mother's. She had a scattering of freckles, which had popped up as if overnight. But she is healthy and her kids are healthy. And there is no fear, just an elusive memory of her mother with all those tubes, before the very end—that was how she looked in the hospital, even though she didn't want anyone to visit her.

II.

Yoram silenced the engine, got out of the car, and removed Yael's stroller from the trunk. Lily, who seemed to have regained some of her strength, also got out and looked beyond the long line of cars, whose roofs grew smaller and smaller toward the horizon. All they could see from their vantage point were the cars and the mountains, and all they could hear was the raging of the water. Many people had gotten out of their cars. A public bus spewed out a group of boisterous teenagers, and behind them was a religious couple with their five children. There were cars whose doors were flung wide open, the passengers napping in the cool air, the car stereos blasting the latest hits.

When they had walked halfway there Lily's strength suddenly failed her, and Yoram reached out to support her while continuing to push the stroller with his left hand. When they arrived at the gushing water, he regretted that he hadn't taken his camera. You see a flash flood like this only once in a lifetime. The crowd that had gathered looked out in amazement.

Naama kept pushing the crowds aside. She held on to her mother's hand and pulled her forward in order to see better, dragging her farther from her father. The water was very high and the desert was yellow and calm; the storm had already turned into rainfall over the Red Sea. And then their grasp was broken when, worn out, Lily leaned against the very first car in the procession, and Naama cleared a path forward in order to see the water from up close. A young woman patted her on the head and said to her quietly, "Be careful, sweetie, it's dangerous." Naama looked up, expecting to see her mother, but the woman wore a different hat, greenish and without any flowers, and she wore a tight black shirt that her mother would never wear.

That moment the members of the family stood apart from one another: Lily leaning against the first car, Naama at the front of the crowd of curious onlookers snapping photos, and Yoram in the back, following them both with his eyes. The wadi swept away branches and uprooted shrubs, and the rising waters were a turbid brown. Naama looked on in awe, as if at an image from a movie. Yael slept in her stroller, until she woke and began crying. Yoram picked her up and hugged her.

Lily had already broken away from the car and she looked at the water in awe, astonished by its force. If her body were to fall into those waters, she would be swept far, far away, she thought, unmoving. The girls and Yoram were not paying any attention to her. The world was just patches of color blended together, and all the lines had blurred. Bright yellow coats floated before her, red Caution signs sharpened into focus, and she felt dizzy and weak, but she took two steps forward, or perhaps she only imagined it, that she was slowly approaching the flood water. The mountains were a blur and she pushed herself forward, or she just imagined it, getting swallowed up by the flow of the water, but then Naama emerged from the crowds and leaned against her legs like a stubborn little elf.

The two of them stood there, hand in hand. The horizon had become clear again, the lines came back into focus. The dizziness passed and Lily's throat was dry. The flooding gradually subsided and people began returning to their cars, waiting for the traffic to start moving, but the road was still impassable. A blue jeep splattered with mud emerged from the long line of cars and began crossing the water on a diagonal. Naama watched the spinning wheels. Then she saw her father in the crowd, and she pulled her mother by the hand to pass through everyone else, until their loose grasp came free. He drew her close and tousled her ponytail, and her mother, who saw them, began making her way toward them. When she reached them her hands were thrust as if by their own accord toward the handle of the empty stroller, and the four of them began walking back to the car. It was now afternoon. The sky cleared and the sun once again warmed the air. Lily pushed the stroller in front of them. She looked confused, her eyes unfocused and dreamy.

If Yoram had to identify the moment he lost her, before illness completely took over her body, this is the image that would come to mind: Lily making her way along the road, the line of stationary cars to her left, the white straw hat with purple flowers on her head, her yellow dress like the color of the desert sand. The stroller moved along the road in the direction of Eilat, as if they were just beginning their vacation—as if they'd come on foot, in a sort of desert pilgrimage, and Lily was advancing without looking back, growing increasingly distant, slipping away beyond reach.

Yoram continued holding Yael, her eyes still red from crying. He didn't pay attention to how distant Lily had become until they reached the Mini Minor. Only then did he yell to her: "Lily! Over here!" He had to yell just once. She stopped, turned around, focused her gaze, and her face brightened. A moment passed before she slowly turned the stroller around. In front of them impatient drivers prepared for the traffic ahead. Yoram folded up the stroller and put it back in the trunk. He strapped Naama and Yael into their car seats, opened the door for Lily and helped her sit down. He placed a new tape into the cassette player.

"You'll get married again," Lily suddenly said. The Arava road stretched out behind and ahead of them, the desert was silent, and the girls had sunk into that childish slumber that the whir of the engine induces. And even so, he cast a glance at the overhead mirror to make sure their eyes were closed. "You'll get married," she declared. It wasn't a question. Yoram wondered how to respond. He wanted her to know that he could not imagine ever loving someone else. He looked up at the mirror and debated whether to press on the brakes and wake one of the girls, but he kept driving and didn't say a word.

Lily wondered if she had said enough. She wanted to tell him, too, that he should have more children—maybe a son. But she remained silent. She saw the tremble in his hands, the sweat from his fingers on the burning hot steering wheel, small beads of sweat above his upper lip and between his eyebrows. Then, seemingly out of nowhere, she reached out her hand and caressed his cheek. It was the feel of her touch that he had been yearning for all that time. He'd already forgotten how his whole body woke to her touch. He was addicted to that feeling, and almost let himself close his eyes. Then she turned, took a long look at the girls, and declared, "They are looking more and more like you," as if she were trying to erase all traces of herself in the years ahead.

In the long silence that followed he was able to distract himself by switching lanes, concentrating on passing a long truck: the shift at just the right second to the opposite lane, the near-crazy acceleration of the engine, the appearance of a car in the distance, the rush to make it in time, and the hot wave that rushed over him, repressing their last conversation. And amidst all that, during that fraught and almost threatening silence, Yael suddenly stirred in the back seat. She opened her eyes and Yoram said, "Good morning, sweetie." With the girls awake, there was no place for Lily's prophecies. And it was true—Lily turned to look out the window and said, "We're coming up to Kushi Rimon. Stop here so they can pee."

All That Remains of Etta

T he saving grace about her mother's house, when Joan had dismantled it last spring with all the birds returning to the greenway, was finding her mother's hand in everything. Little notes, like the one on the newspaper clipping, found in the top drawer of her desk, *Simon Wiesenthal was a good man*. Or the slip of paper, yellowed and torn at the edge, an address for somewhere in Poland, *where your grandfather was born*. Joan had found all the notes—*to Joan, for Lisa, give to Philip*. On the bottom of the silver tea service, which Joan keeps in her living room, the yellow sticky read: *For Joan. You should know Aunt Edith sewed these into the lining of her coat and walked across Europe to escape. Keep, please*, to which Joan had added her own note: *For Lisa when I'm gone*. But there is nothing from Etta. No notes. No last words. No directions of who should get what. Just a cracked teacup she was holding when her heart gave out, a closet of tracksuits and housecoats and boxes of things stored in her basement. Even Etta's old cameras and her black-and-white photos, wrapped three times in bubble wrap, were left to Joan's discretion.

Joan tried. She tried to disburse what she could among Edward's sons and their wives but outside of the new television and a two-year-old computer, they wanted nothing. Even the boots in the white-and-blue Zappos box, never worn and in Merle's size, had been refused.

"They're good winter boots. You should take them," Joan said when Merle stopped by in between dropping her children off at preschool and picking up her mother for brunch.

"Oh, I couldn't take them," Merle had said. "I could never wear a dead person's shoes."

Joan shoves the last of Etta's velour tracksuits into the box for Salvation Army. Left to pack: a few things from the kitchen, some of the older linens and towels, a pillow needlepointed decades ago, the oil painting no one wanted. Joan has been at this so long that the discard pile is beginning to look fresh and she catches herself eyeing that needlepoint pillow for her living room. Enough! What she really needs is a good manicure; another two nails broken and the synthetic feel of velour caught in her cuticles. And coffee. She wants coffee. She would dig out the percolator if only she hadn't thrown out that can of Folgers.

But she is almost finished. She should beat the predicted snowfall home and meet Edward in time for dinner. Tomorrow at this time, the condo will be painted, the carpet washer is scheduled, and the For Sale sign readied. The last remaining remnants of Etta will be whisked away, bits and pieces of her life redistributed to strangers on the shelves of secondhand stores or in eBay auctions.

As she makes a final survey of her sister-in-law's condo, she feels the chill in the air. The windows have turned to smoked mirror from the darkness outside flecked with bits of frost along the edges. It is cold without the insulation of *things.*

Joan pulls the tissue from her sleeve and wipes at her nose before switching on the electric space heater. A burning smell closes in around her, mixes with a leftover stench of ginger and brine. Joan can still smell the dog. A mix of wet fur and urine.

It had been Edward's suggestion to put the dog down. "She's blind and pees on everything," he said at breakfast on the day of the funeral.

And so two days after Etta was buried, Joan had carted the dog, the little white Shih Tzu, to the vet. She sat with the dog in her car for almost an hour. When she finally went into the vet's office, she signed the forms to have the office dispose of the carcass and then returned to the task of packing up Etta's things.

"Did I get it right?" Joan says to the empty condo as she reaches for the last roll of packing tape and the scissors with the blue handle. She is startled by a knock at the door and drops the scissors to the floor, just missing her foot.

At the door is an elderly woman. Her face is slightly tanned, and she is wearing a black fur hat with wisps of gray hair curling out from underneath the rolled edge. Her coat is made of thick black wool that is familiar to Joan. *My mother's coat,* she thinks. Like a talisman for survivors, Joan remembers that her mother, her aunt, her grandmother, and a neighbor—she actually remembers a neighbor's coat from when she was small—all wore black wool coats to temple on Saturdays. The woman standing at Etta's door has petite hands that are gloved in black leather. Dangling from her right hand is a red leather leash.

"I've come for Leyke," she says.

At first Joan thinks this woman is talking about the old camera equipment. *Was there a Leica in the box? Did I drop it off for resale? Did someone take the cameras?*

But before Joan can answer, the woman says, "I am Mrs. Rutzel. I am here for the dog, Leyke."

And in that instant, Joan remembers the dog.

The elderly woman standing in front of her has a slight Polish accent, and her voice grazes at Joan's heart, and with a slight hesitation, Joan cannot help but think she has seen this face in one of Etta's photographs.

"Please come in," she asks Mrs. Rutzel.

"No," Mrs. Rutzel says. "I just need the dog."

"It's so cold out here, maybe you should come in."

"Thank you, no. I should have been to the funeral. I was in Boca and saw the paper, the *Jewish News*? Even in Florida you can get the Detroit issue! Ach! I am so sorry for Etta, may she rest in peace. She wanted for me Leyke. I tried calling, to make the arrangements, but the phone. It is out of order? So I come. The dog, please." Her Ws sound like Vs so that everything she says has a hard edge to it, and yes, Joan remembers how quickly everything was turned off, Etta's phone, her cable, the Internet service. She will wonder later why she knew nothing of this Mrs. Rutzel, never heard her name, never knew Etta had a friend, a visitor! Joan will remember later having seen unaccounted-for and unexplained waxed bags of cookies from a bakery in Oak Park, and she will think about all of the things overlooked and not known.

"We put the dog to sleep," she tells Mrs. Rutzel.

"To sleep?" says Mrs. Rutzel. "To sleep?"

"No one wanted to care for the dog; she was old. So we put her down. The vet, we had her put down?"

"She's dead? The dog? *Nebekh*, the dog, she is killed? You killed little Leyke?"

"We put her down."

"Down? Killed? She is gone?" Mrs. Rutzel's bewilderment is contagious, and Joan finds herself disbelieving the dog is actually gone: Perhaps the vet hadn't gotten around to it yet; perhaps it didn't take.

"They do that with gas?" Mrs. Rutzel asks.

The wind has begun to stir around the two women, one standing on the inside of an open door, the other on the outside. *Vit gas?* she asked. Joan is mesmerized by the start of a light snow, so early, and thinks about the killing. The dog.

"No. No. They do it by injection. Not gassed, the dog wasn't gassed. She was put down. Humanely," says Joan, thinking of the blue streak of numbers that ran across her mother's arm, visible only in summer when she slept in a white linen slip, and thinking that a similar row of numbers must exist on Mrs. Rutzel's arm as well.

"I am so sorry. I didn't know. No one said anything to me about you." Joan picks at her cuticles, drawing a drop of bright blood just at the edge of her middle finger.

"*Gvalt!* To kill a dog? Why?" Mrs. Rutzel's gloved hand, the one that does not hold the red leather leash, rises to her face. She holds her reddening cheek in her hand.

"If I had known . . . please come in, it's so cold," Joan says, opening the door wide, gesturing to Mrs. Rutzel to step over the threshold. *Coffee,* Joan suddenly thinks again. *If there were coffee, something to eat, she would come inside, they'd straighten this out—what's to straighten? The dog is gone.*

Mrs. Rutzel shakes her head, and the leash dangles in the quiet of snow falling, bells for the dead.

"Mrs. Rutzel, please," says Joan. "It was a mistake." It was all a mistake. Standing in the white cold, a leash dangling, Joan struggles to remember some conversation, any conversation, she had with Etta in which she asked more than *Do you need paper towels?*

"*Oy!* What a mistake!"

Joan whispers again, "It was a mistake."

Mrs. Rutzel, her hand still on her cheek, her head turning slightly from side to side, says only, "That Leyke, you know, she loved the cookies from the Polish bakery. Ach! *Nebekh.* Poor *hintele.*"

Swirling skies of white snow grow heavier around the two women, and Joan's vision is blurred by the thick downfall. Cookies for a dog, and Joan remembers her mother handing her a cookie meant for a dog but eaten instead by five-year-old Joan. She thinks about the pudding, the warmed pudding freshly made from milk—*use half jar sugar, Joan dear, and some whole milk always*—that her mother stirred up to take the bitter taste of the dog's cookie away.

In Mrs. Rutzel's gaze, her blue shining eyes, Joan feels her own disbelief at the hours spent relegating things, damn things, clothes and books and tchotchkes, and all the while it was the dog. The snowflakes have accumulated now on Mrs. Rutzel's black hat, her black-covered shoulders, each flake so different than the next, yet with the heat of Mrs. Rutzel's body, the flakes attach to each other and become a scarf knit in white just before they turn to droplets of water and time becomes fleeting liquid embers that burn through a mass of congested heartbreak. "I didn't know." *I didn't know!* But she understands there is nothing more to do, as Mrs. Rutzel walks back to her car, saying into the falling snow, "No dog. No Leyke. Poor *hintele.*"

"Wait. Wait," Joan yells as Mrs. Rutzel opens her car door. Joan holds her hands up to the air as if her open palms to the sky and to God as her witness can stop time. Joan runs back into the house; she yells one last "Wait, please" to Mrs. Rutzel.

In the house, Joan grabs the needlepointed pillow. Out to the car, slipping once on the wet walkway, she is breathless and crying when she reaches Mrs. Rutzel.

"For you," she says, gasping bits of cold air, "please, for you."

Joan hands Mrs. Rutzel the pillow and hopes she doesn't notice the small yellow stain on its backside.

"What is this?" Mrs. Rutzel says, although to Joan it sounds like Vos is dis? And the sound of the hard V stings.

Please, Joan is thinking. *Take this pillow. Forgive me the dog.*

Joan bends into the car and embraces Mrs. Rutzel. She holds onto the wool of her black coat, and she whispers into her ear.

"My mother was from Zloczow."

Inside the condo, Joan puts on her coat, her scarf, and tries to shake off the chill before she goes back outside. She turns off all of the lights. She unplugs the small floor heater. From her purse she finds a black Sharpie pen and writes in thick letters on the side of the box, *Take it all.* When she leaves, she makes sure the door is unlocked for the Salvation Army and then she is gone without ever looking back.

CAROLIVIA HERRON

The Comet Neowise Listens In

I remember you from before. Weren't you here the last time I came? It was before Gilgamesh, before Anansi, before Apollo. I saw you there. It was six thousand years ago, or seven.

Black Lives Matter, of course it's true. But the fact that something is true is NEVER the reason for saying it. So why say it? If you've got to ask why, then you don't get it, you don't understand. I know you want time to understand the saying of it. Is it a group? Is it an idea? Why do we need to say it if we already know that it's true?

I am a returning departing comet. The last time I was here Gilgamesh hadn't been born yet, but you were here. You're Black. You're Jewish. I saw you in tents, in huts, in booths, under canopies—corridors, hallways, chambers. You crossed the sand and came to the saltwater, you saw islands.

Black lives matter. Black lives started it. You all came from Africa. All of you. All of us. That's what I overheard returning and departing. All lives are Black lives that matter. But sometimes you forget. Say it so you don't forget. Black Lives Matter.

I overheard someone speaking, "I was not the one who did it." They were words coming up from Sixteenth Street in front of the synagogue, her congregation, Tifereth Israel, every Friday.

They were standing along Sixteenth Street, in support of Black Lives. I heard someone explaining, "I did not arrange it for everyone to stand along Sixteenth Street, six feet apart, social distancing." She was holding a sign. She said, "I do it because I want a change, I held a sign but so did the others. Did you see my sign? I got worried. What is my country doing? Why does my country hurt Black people so much? That's why I was there." That's what she said, that's what she does.

Do you want to know what I do? I make returns and curves and circles and ellipses around and around and around. I come back and back and back I was here six thousand years ago and when I came by this time I heard her say, "I want it to change."

Most of the words that were spoken the last time I came are lost now, but not all of them.

> I am black and beautiful,
> As the tents of Kedar,
> as the curtains of Solomon
> Black. Beautiful. Then. Now.

Hebrew words spoken all the way back. I was already there. Why are you saying it now? One said, "Y'all hear that, Chile? She went down to the Capitol Building, yes she did, She went all the way down to the Capitol Building to see the casket of John Lewis. That's what she did. She kept saying, Black Lives Matter. She went before to see the casket of Rosa Parks. She went this time to see the casket of John Lewis. The moments were different."

> Rosa was in the sunlight. John was by night,
> And there were floodlights on the Capitol Building.

When I was still approaching, back in 1987, I overheard when one said, "Black Power." She was there with Stokely Carmichael in the basement of Douglass Hall at Howard University. One said, "We've got to call ourselves something. We have lots of words to choose from. Let's call it something. Let's call it Black Power. We didn't know it would end up being a thing. We didn't know where it was going."

Black Power. It didn't say, nobody else has power. It didn't say anything about anybody else's anything. It just said, Black Power. And if you don't know that it's replacing black nonpower, that means you're clueless. You don't know what's going on. And if you think Black Lives Matter is trying to say Black Lives Matter instead of White Lives, instead of other kinds of lives, then you don't know what we've been going through.

But one said, "What about the word 'forbearance'? One day I hope somebody's going to have forbearance for some stupid thing I'm probably doing right now, and I don't even realize what it is. Forbearance. Give somebody a chance to learn something."

I overheard. One told a story. "The first day I showed up at Howard University, first-year student, first day of college, I started in the summertime. I arrived, and there were policemen there holding us all back as we were about to make the turn into the campus. One, two, three, four, fifteen, twenty buses came driving out onto Georgia Avenue and turn south, going to sit in somewhere. They were going to risk their lives somewhere. And I was a little first-year student, scared to death. I said, 'I'm glad they're going because I ain't going nowhere. I'm glad someone's willing to go there for me.'"

When those buses were gone, another one came up to that one and asked, "What are you going to do? Your country is a mess." And that one answered, "I don't believe my country would ever do anything to hurt me." Yes, that one said, "I don't believe my country would ever do anything to hurt me." That one is a descendant of Jews who were kicked out of Spain in the Inquisition, in 1492. That one is a descendant of slaves in America. That one is a descendant of slave-owning rapists and murderers. One of that one's ancestors signed a parchment with the words, "All men are created equal." That one said, "I don't believe my country would do anything to hurt me."

But there was forbearance. That one had time to learn something and figure things out. That one believes in teaching and forbearance. Someone taught her and had forbearance for her.

That one thinks about her friends. "One of the hardest things for me," she says about Black Lives Matter, "is not affirming that Black Lives Matter, but that all of my white friends are all feeling bad and searching their lives and hearts and dealing with all their pain about racism as if their lives are not connected to mine. Who am I supposed to have a cup of coffee with and a good laugh while they are out there in the midnight of their souls digging out their racism? Who am I supposed to have a giggle with while they're off attending antiracism seminars? And we're so close that it hurts my heart too. It's not like it's only hurting on one side of the friendship, and the others are home free.

"So, I keep thinking, maybe I'm the wrong person to listen to . . . Black Lives Matter . . . but too late now, I'm here, and I'm already talking, so you can't uninvite me.

"I feel so weird sometimes when I see the lack of forbearance. It's a new word that has never been heard before. Hold back a little bit, give somebody a chance to learn something, to teach something, to understand something."

This is what I overheard six thousand years on my way back, or maybe seven. Mostly I just lie down and wait for time to pass, lying down in space. And I remember you, all of you, from before. You were here the last time I came. Before Gilgamesh. Before Anansi. Before Apollo.

But there you were, Black, and Hebrew, and Jewish.

Black and beautiful
as the tents of Kedar
as the curtains of Solomon.

One said, "There were more barriers when I went to see John Lewis. I don't remember barrier for Rosa. John's dark was so beautiful, he changed the night. Rosa was joy, John was solemn."

One said, "You want to tell it as if I did it all myself. I looked at it, I, because I am a part of it, standing along Sixteenth Street holding a sign. Is that just performance? Is that nothing?"

Another one spoke to that one. "What do you think holding a sign on Sixteenth Street is going to do to help Black Lives?" White people were up there yelling at other white people, "All y'all are doing is performance. You're doing nothing, nothing. All you're doing is standing there holding a sign. That's just performance."

And yet I overheard young men, Black men speaking one to the other, "I've never seen this before. Usually when the trouble comes, white people disappear. Every other time they disappeared. This time they didn't run away." Performance. A way to get started.

Surely you were here the last time I came ellipsing around your sun, hearing your earth.

One remembers a song she sang as a child.

We're marching to Zion,
Beautiful, beautiful Zion
We're marching onward to Zion
the beautiful city of God.

But another one said to that one, "Zion isn't yours." . . . Yet the other said, "If you're a Zionist then something is wrong with you. If you want to be a Zionist you better be it secretly in your heart. You'd better not tell anybody. Send secret money to Israel while marching on the plaza with Black Lives Matter downtown."

"Do you think the land was given to Jews only forever for all time?" "Not exactly that, but I figure if G_d gave us that land, then let G_d set it up," that one said. "As for me, my joy is to have peace with the people around me. If G_d wants to make a change, then G_d you come in here and do it. I want peace. I want the people in Israel to know they don't have to worry about food. They don't have to worry about having a place to live and stay. My hope is that given the freedom of enough food and enough support, there will be time to know how can we live in Israel in peace."

I overheard as I ellipse around her sun. I remember that one. I saw her before, when I came by before, this is what I saw,

I saw Moses standing before Pharaoh. There was a little Egyptian girl behind a curtain listening. Hail was about to fall. Moses said to Pharaoh, "so tell your people to stay inside and get the cows in, or the hail will fall on them and they'll die."

And the little Egyptian girl behind the curtain said, "That's the first time any G_d has ever cared about what happens to the enemy, and tells the enemy to protect themselves. I've heard of many a god, but I've never heard of a G_d who cares about the enemy. So I'm going to follow this Moses. And I'm going to be there." And the little Egyptian girl left Egypt just behind the children of Israel, and spent forty years catching up with them, crossing the desert, and came to the land. To Israel. Black Lives Matter. We're Marching to Zion, beautiful, beautiful Zion.

> I remember you from before
> You are Black and beautiful
> As the tents of Kedar
> As the curtains of Solomon.

TO BELONG

Belonging is an elusive concept, perhaps especially for Jews. Involuntary displacement appears as a vivid thread in every Jewish history. The Bible is full of stories of people instructed—by God, by parent figures, by angels—to go, to move on. "Go to the land which I will show you." "Wherever you go I will go." Jews face exile after the Temple in Jerusalem is destroyed, twice. And displacement's burdens fall disproportionately on women, likely in biblical times as now. Who was rushing out of Egypt with the unrisen bread dough? And later, who packs the few possessions—those iconic Shabbat candlesticks—that a family fleeing Zhytomyr, or Alexandria, or Mashhad will take with them? Who carries the babies and figures out how they'll get fed?

It's hard to imagine any displacement as unalloyed sweetness, even if the move is to greater safety, better land, or useful adventures. Older women fear ending up in a nursing home in isolation away from what has become familiar, a shift they're told is for their own good. Feeling alien, and yearning to belong, is part of many processes of change. And innumerable Jewish women have felt they don't belong even in the comforts of a secure Jewish community, because their voices and their desires are stifled. In time, immigrants can blend into the societies around them. But the struggle for women to belong fully as Jews has taken much longer.

However uncomfortable the stance may be, there is some power in standing on the periphery, looking in, observing from the perspective of a reluctant outsider.

Flight

anina lives in Philadelphia now. Ever since her son decided she couldn't take care of herself anymore and imported her like a jug of olive oil.

"Like a fine old wine," he tells her the one time she complains.

He works for a French drug company that sells homeopathic medicines. Just like the drops and ointments her mother once bought in the Arab quarter all those years ago in Algeria—back when Arabs and Jews believed each other were friends, and before the French created a greater wedge than any differences about Mohamed and Moses.

Hanina counts her eightieth birthday in her son's Philadelphia row house. No one speaks to her all day. Her son is working and his children are abandoned in France, along with his ex-wife, who would never add Hanina to her daily obligations, now that the marriage is over. Hanina understands.

Every day she dusts his furniture and folds away his newspaper. Red circles dance across the pages to mark the words he wants to look up.

"I've started a new life here, *Maman*," he says.

Hanina feels too old to start anything new. But here she is, living in a foreign country for the second time in her life, wondering how she got from Constantine to Toulon to Philadelphia all in the space of eighty years when not one of the decisions was hers to make.

Once, she was in charge of the small daily decisions—like what to make for dinner for her husband and son. Or what fruit to buy at the market. Or what route to take home with the day's shopping in a basket looped over her arm. Like a passport to the city around her, that basket opened time so she could disappear for hours. Allowed her to wander to Toulon's port or to the cinema where she'd tuck the basket, filled with onions and apples, under her seat and take in the latest Bridget Bardot film that her husband would never permit. *Indecent*, he'd cry, *not for the eyes of a virtuous woman.*

She remembers all this as she prepares her son's dinner. He makes her life easy, he says, by ordering the groceries delivered to the house each week. Her son won't admit that he still welcomes the Sephardic cooking she's imported with her. He brags about the French food and wine he impresses his clients with over the long lunches that have added pounds to his lean frame. But Hanina knows not to think out loud. There's always the danger he'll send her back to France to some *maison de retraite* where she'll languish, forgotten. So she remains silent.

The mailman rings the door each day with some package for her son.

"How are you?" she tries, dragging the words from her mouth that could slide easily over French and once even recited poetry in Arabic.

"Good day, Missus," the man replies. Then he adds something about the weather—too hot, too cold.

"Bad today," Hanina says and points to the sky where the cold rain has formed ice crystals on the man's hat.

She wants to offer him tea like her own mother would have brewed in Constantine—sweet and fragranced with fresh mint. But she's afraid of what her son would say, or more, of what she could say to this man with her bad English.

"Watch television, *Maman*," her son instructs each day. "You'll learn English that way." Before he leaves, he hugs her like the Americans—with a broad clap to her back.

Some nights he takes her out so she doesn't have to cook. From her meticulously organized closet, she pulls a fine silk dress, polka-dotted with lime and tangerine. Her eyes are rimmed lightly with kohl and her lips are glossed peach. Once, even in winter, her skin would have been polished bronze by the Mediterranean sun, but now she rubs rouge onto her pale cheeks. She will not join the other American women in baggy pants and loose shirts.

She sits across from her son in the Italian restaurant. From the kitchen, she can make out some of the Spanish words the dishwashers mix with the empty plates.

"How was your day, *Maman*?" her son asks.

"I watch the stories on television," she answers.

"How many words did you learn today? Remember when you were a little girl, and you learned some English from the Americans who were in Constantine during the war?" He smiles at her as if he's discovered a secret and wants to share it.

"How-do-you-do?" Hanina repeats in English, remembering the Americans who were pleased to still be alive.

She watches the other people eat the Italian food that comes from the Spanish-speaking kitchen. They eat carefully, balancing their forks in one hand with the other hand quiet in their laps. Like dead birds. Not like Europeans, who use both hands to eat, knife and fork in constant motion, so that each morsel is tasted and enjoyed.

She looks down at her hands resting near the Veal Parmesan the waiter has raved about. Oil pockets against the fried meat. She saws away, not even hungry.

In the moment she pauses, she sees the old hands that belong to her now. The veins jump and wobble under the fragile skin. Then she allows herself to examine her wrists. She doesn't think about those two deep lines often, or how they came to be. She can't even see the stitches that once bound them together, even though the black thread had shocked her more than the lines themselves. They are camouflaged by time and age. By all the other cuts on her hands from chopping onions or grating oranges for a cake. From braiding bread and scrubbing floors. Those two deep lines have almost disappeared.

Her son is watching with a familiar narrowing of his dark eyes.

"*Maman*," he pleads, "there's a cake here, made by a French baker. Let me order it for you—for your pleasure!"

She crosses her wrists in her lap as he calls the waiter to their table.

Hanina is thirty-seven and lives in Toulon now. Her husband is a policeman in this South-of-France port. Her son goes to school with all the French children. Her mother-in-law stays home with her all day while Hanina tries to make a new home in France along with the other refugees from Algeria. There are only two tiny bedrooms in the apartment that is half-buried in the hills above Toulon. Her husband is proud that he can see the Mediterranean from their apartment—even if only a blue sliver when he thrusts himself from the balcony.

Her mother-in-law is unhappy with everything—even with the larger of the two bedrooms her husband insists they abandon for his mother's comfort. Hanina's son sleeps in the smaller bedroom, which she fills with books and toy cars and French flags. He would prefer tanks like the French recently used against the Algerians, who stubbornly insisted on their own independence. It is 1962, and she and her husband sleep on the pullout couch in the salon. He still wants to make love each night although she is tired, and his mother will surely hear his grunting. She covers his mouth with her hand, but he bites her and then sucks her nipples so hard, she is the one who cries out.

She tries to call the other woman mother, as her husband has requested. But the word seems reserved only for her own mother, who died just before Hanina boarded the plane for France and was buried next to Hanina's older brother. *He was simply walking home*, the family sages would recount as if telling a story from the Torah. Killed in an Arab riot because the French *pied noir* favored Jews over them.

"Weren't we all friends once?" Hanina asked.

No one would ever say, but Hanina knew that her brother had bled to death. His throat slit against the walls of their synagogue, like some lamb in a ritual slaughter, killed on an altar of hatred. Incomprehensible, that her brother should die so, the one who danced like a Bedouin to Oriental music, who shook his shoulders with pleasure, who played the flute like a street performer, who studied late each night to learn science, who brought her honeyed sweets from the market. Unforgivable, that her mother wailed as she washed his body for burial, not trusting the others to perform this last gift.

Unforgivable.

Hanina escapes from the apartment in Toulon with her basket over her arm. She knows her mother-in-law counts the hours until she returns and reports the missing time to her husband. *What does she do in the street all morning?* her mother-in-law whispers over and over. Each night, her husband climbs onto her to reclaim those lost hours.

He watches her with uneasy eyes. He's a policeman here, just as in Algeria, just like his father before him, and can understand peoples' secrets, he insists one morning before he follows her to the market. Slouching behind a post, he waits as she chooses vegetables and bread that some stranger bakes now. He calculates the minutes she spends watching the sea recoil with the same blue force that once gave her such pleasure on Algeria's coast. He watches until she boards the bus that will take her back to the apartment buried in the hill.

Hanina knows her husband has decided.

"You will no longer leave the house without me," he announces one day, as his mother peers from the kitchen. "It isn't safe on the streets. Young women are targets now—the French hate us for coming here."

"But our food?" Hanina manages to ask.

"Mother will go. She is more clever than you and older. The French will leave her alone."

It takes one week for Hanina to form her escape. She will kiss her son goodbye and tuck a special treat into his pocket for his snack. In the corner of his small room, she hides a note to try to explain. It will make no sense to him now—he's only nine; but later, she believes, he'll come to understand. She will wait until her mother-in-law places the basket over her arm. Hanina will only have a few hours before her son is back for lunch, and her mother-in-law returns from the market. Only a few hours.

She dresses carefully as if she might travel back to Constantine to see her old friends and her lost brother. She smooths her stockings and pins her hat carefully across her brow. She pulls the veil down across her face as she's seen Ingrid Bergman do in the movies. She passes through the bathroom on her way to her mother-in-law's bed.

Hanina doesn't think much before she drags the razor blade across her wrists. The burning of separated skin doesn't surprise her. She remembers how she burned when her son escaped her body. She carefully cuts through her veins, first one wrist and then the other. The pumping blood doesn't surprise her, either. Hadn't her own brother bled like this on that long-ago night?

She lies against the pillow and places her wrists downward on her mother-in-law's bed. Until she sleeps, Hanina thinks about the sea and Constantine. About her mother who baked each Friday. About her own fingers in that dough, learning to braid it in the ritual way for the Shabbat table. The dough is warm and rises against her hands, just as the blue tide rises against the shore. Hanina floats on a loaf of challah, and cradled against the deep braids, she safely rides the sea. Far away.

She is so far from shore that she can no longer see the hills of Algeria in the distance. Her brother calls: "Come, come." First from a distance and then in her ear. "Come back," the voice demands. Hanina turns her head.

"*Maman*, please come back." She hears someone crying. Then fierce hands hold her wrists in the air as someone binds kitchen towels around them. A body falls across her chest, but it is not her husband on his nightly errands. Her son's chest rises and falls with her own reluctant intake of air. She can hear men cursing because the stairs are too narrow for a litter, and they must carry her down the three flights of stairs that circle the building. She tries not to bleed on them.

After a year in the hospital, the doctors say she can go home. She has told the doctors about her brother and the challah. About the basket and her mother-in-law. She has finally cried out loud, and, at night, they let her watch old movies. Ingrid Bergman remains beautiful as she boards the plane from Casablanca. To do her duty, Hanina knows.

When she returns home, her mother-in-law has been moved to a daughter's apartment in the next village. Hanina has her own bed in the large bedroom now where her husband holds her in his arms and cries into her nightgown each night.

When she leaves with the basket on her arm, her son begs to come. He grasps her hand as they walk, even though he is ten, and the other boys his age run from their mothers.

Hanina is thirteen now and still lives with her parents in Constantine. Her older brother goes to the university each day and brings her a treat from the market when he returns at night. Sometimes it is a book from the antique stalls; one time it was a yellow bird that sang each morning when the swallows began their acrobatics in the sky outside their terrace. She has been bleeding for a year and her mother presented her with a box of chocolates to celebrate the occasion. She and her mother mysteriously cycle together.

"It is God's way," her mother laughs.

So she bathes away the stains of womanhood each month at the same time as her mother. Most of the women are naked in the *hammam*. They are still comfortable with each other, the Jews and the Arabs. Each month her mother chats with the same Arab woman. They talk about their children and laugh behind hands pressed closely to their mouths when they mention their husbands' names. Hanina knows they are sharing women's secrets. Sometimes, she prays the secrets will be hers, too.

Every afternoon she and her friends run through the streets of their quarter. They laugh when they see a group of boys who stand smoking on the corner and choose their sweethearts. The same boy watches Hanina each day with blue eyes that turn away whenever she notices. She knows all about his family because there are few secrets in her quarter. His father is a policeman and his mother was known as a great beauty, and the quarter tingles with the idea that this woman should have made a better match. Some kind of love, the women laugh again.

Some afternoons, Hanina slips away from the knot of friends and wanders the narrow streets until she reaches the Arab market. She is pulled by the scent of flowers and spices. The cinnamon and cumin reach out from their open sacks where they rest like the pollen of exotic flowers.

I'll travel the world, Hanina thinks. *I'll follow the route of spices and silks until I reach their origin—like a great explorer. Maybe I'll go to America.*

She has just read about Sir Richard Burton, who obsessively searched for the Nile's source. Beyond the mountains of Constantine, a desert unravels for thousands of miles. She will marry that young man on the corner and have two boys and two girls. But first, she will earn her education. Many Jewish women in Constantine live like the Arab women, inhabiting the world only of their homes—a place bordered by high walls. No matter how sweet the fountain in the courtyard, Hanina will not be captured.

Every Friday, her mother, who doesn't know Hanina's desires for the world, teaches her daughter the skills of maintaining a Jewish home. They prepare the Shabbat meal, the couscous and chicken stewed with prunes and honey. Most importantly, they bake bread together as Hanina's mother teaches her the mysteries of yeast and dough. It is to Hanina's smooth hands that her mother entrusts the braiding of the bread. Hanina is transported by the dough's heat and the smell of fermenting yeast. She carefully sections the three parts and begins to plait the dough as if she were dressing her own black hair for a festival.

As the bread bakes, Hanina stands on the terrace watching the swallows move across the sky. They soar and dive, filling the sky as they cry out to each other. The terrace is so high that the swallows fly directly in front of her. She can watch their spiked tail feathers spread while they catch the currents under those angular wings. Hanina knows they have begun to build their nests again. As they have for centuries.

Her mother places the dishes and silver on the table for her to arrange. Before Hanina leaves the terrace, she takes the cotton from her pockets and tosses the pieces, one by one, into the sky, so the birds can bury the soft material in their nests.

The cotton floats in the air for an instant before a swallow swoops down to catch it in its beak. One by one, the squealing swallows dive toward Hanina as she throws the last of the cotton into the air. One last time, the swallows pass in front of her, the cotton trailing behind them like gossamer flags.

Hanina watches with joy as those birds disappear into a flock that soars freely in the direction of the sea.

TAMAR BEN-OZER

The Miscreants

I played Bach's Prelude in C Major on Mrs. Z.'s piano this afternoon. Mrs. Z. is our downstairs neighbor, and she's old, maybe seventy. Since we don't have a piano at home, she lets me come over on weekdays to practice on her crumbling baby grand. Her husband died two years ago, in 1945, and their children all left for Palestine with their spouses and kids. She rarely leaves the house anymore because of her Parkinson's, so I'm pretty much the only person she talks to most days. I sang while I played, Gounod's "Ave Maria," just like Miss Weil showed me during yesterday's lesson. *Hear how Bach's Germanic harmonies sit perfectly underneath Gounod's French melody. Baroque and Romanticism perfectly entwined, reckless emotion and meticulous structure in flawless symbiosis.* I sat still for a long time, quietly contemplating the two partitures in front of me.

Mrs. Z. used to be more religious, back when her family was still around, but now she says offhandedly observance is a tribal practice and is not easily maintained on one's own. At first Papa would invite her to have the three Shabbes meals with us right after her youngest son left, but she'd always decline, and eventually he stopped asking.

In addition to being a pious Jew, Papa is also a Zionist. So are Mrs. Z.'s children. They left their mother alone in the withering Jewish quarter of our Transylvanian town so they could go live an ideological ideal in the Promised Land. Her youngest son and his newlywed wife packed up their belongings last summer: blouses and a white tie; a sterling silver, handmade candlestick set that had been in the family for generations; a rusted shovel he thought would prove useful in working the land. I snuck into their kitchen and asked him to stay, please, I'd said, *your mother is sick, your wife is pregnant, and you don't even believe in God, so why go there?* He ignored me and they left. His mother was rendered a sort of adult orphan, but as they were her children it was hard for them to see.

I swung my bag over my shoulder and stepped into the kitchen to say goodbye. "Ah gutten Shabbes." I spoke the familiar parting words, leaned over and kissed the age spots on her soft and wrinkled cheek. Her skin was thin as wrapping paper.

"*Ah gutten Shabbes*, my dear." She cupped my face in her trembling palms and pressed it close to hers.

Later that evening, after we'd finished eating and reciting the food blessing, I excused myself from the table, saying I'd forgotten something at Mrs. Z.'s house. I'd been doing this every day for the past month and a half, finding some excuse to get away and slip into her home once the sun had set. This practice demanded a certain degree of stealth on Fridays, to ensure my parents didn't ask any prying questions.

Once I made it to her apartment, I made sure all the curtains were shut. I walked through her three-room home and ended up in the bedroom, where Mrs. Z. lay waiting for me in her large antique bed. I walked over to her nightstand in the dark. On it lay a Yiddish translation of *Gulliver's Travels*. A small medicine jar. A tall glass of water with a straw. I lifted the box of matches that lay by a dark-blue candle, its color barely visible by the slivers of moonlight that shone through an obstinate crack in the drapes. It was a simple task, but one she could no longer manage herself, lacking sufficient control over the muscles and joints in her fingers. As I removed a match from the box a familiar chill raised the hair on my forearms. I sensed with a formidable surety that somehow Papa could see me, about to severely defy the Jewish code of law. I struck it quickly. The flame grew before my eyes as I brought it toward the wick and lit the candle.

A warm glow appeared by her bedside. It overpowered the moonlight and illuminated our faces in flickering light and dancing shadows. She smiled at me and placed the book in her lap, opened it to where the bookmark lay in one of the first chapters. She scanned the lines with her finger until she found her place. I made a half-turn away from her and waved the burning match around until it extinguished itself in a cusp of smoke, closed the matchbox and returned it to the nightstand. With a wave and good night I exited toward the living room.

I paused to look around before leaving. There were shelves upon shelves upon shelves of books, their titles, all of which I knew by heart, obscured in the darkness. Leather-bound editions of the Babylonian Talmud and Maimonides's commentaries; Bibles and Siddurs, prayer books; two shelves devoted entirely to Kabbalah teachings. Silent, dust-covered mementos of her deceased husband. He had always kept the faith alive in their house, defying his heretic wife. She stopped attending synagogue long ago, preferred to spend that time taking walks through the city or playing music at home.

Once, years ago, she went to Paris. She told no one but her husband and reappeared, weeks later, smelling of foreign perfumes, a vibrant green scarf wrapped around her hair and tall, gold-studded leather boots on her feet. No one she knew had traveled farther than neighboring Hungary, where they would often go visit family before the War. When she returned, she became the talk of the town, her name spoken askance in whispers at synagogue and overheard in the women's conversations at the market.

She told me stories of her adventures, over tea when I took breaks from practicing. The concerts she'd attended at the Opéra Bastille, how she had met Debussy and Satie; had approached them audaciously and shaken their hands, introduced herself in what I imagined to be impeccable French but in reality was just miscellaneous bits and pieces of the language. She used the proper accent when pronouncing their names, puckering her lips on the vowels. She spoke animatedly and raised her hands as they trembled, carried them up and sideways to illustrate the tale. It was as though she was shaking them on purpose: jazz hands invoking the zeitgeist of the '20s.

In bed that night I looked out the window at the stars. I saw Orion's Belt and the Great Bear. I recognized Betelgeuse, the star closest to Earth, except for the Sun. My younger sister was asleep on the other side of the room, her breathing soft and regular, pacing my own inhalations and exhalations. The starlight would suffice, I thought. I reached under my bed, took out papers and a pencil, and started to draw with a feverish imperativeness.

I drew dense forests and woodland creatures from the basin of my subconscious. Awake, I dreamt in outlines and sketches of trees. A hare was caught in the air mid-jump. It spread its paws forward and they merged with the bark and the leaves. Swirling upwards, you couldn't tell where fur ended and flora began. Grey pencil marks invoked shades of green and brown, a dawning purple sky. In lieu of a sun, a flickering flaxseed candle dripped tears of wax into the lake.

I woke up the next morning, graphite on my fingertips and the pencil clutched in my hand. Mama stood in the doorway. As per usual, she'd come to wake me up to eat. Our eyes met across the room and I saw that she'd already noticed the pencil in my hand, already registered my heresy and connected it to my time spent with Mrs. Z.

Two days later, I came home from school to find a black Steinway piano perched up against a wall in our dining hall. I walked over and gently fingered the keys. I stood upright at its far left; I didn't want to sit down and validate its existence just yet.

"Now you can practice at home." Mama smiled a smile that ended at her cheekbones, pursed her lips and clasped her hands to her chest.

"Yes. Finally. Yes, thank you so much," I said flatly.

Home

You think once you've crossed the desert you will find freedom; your belly will be full; your body will forget hunger and fear. After many months you reach the spot where the airplane will take you to the land and you think it will be like the words spoken by the kahenat on the Sabbath, full of milk and honey. You will touch trees and honey will drip into your cup. You will sit by the river and milk will gush toward the banks and you think your body will find its home and that you can finally rest. You want so much to rest, but there are others waiting to come here and you do not forget them, not once in your prayers, not even when you sit with your child on the terrace and smell the sea. You smile, but you do not forget.

When the plane lands, you nearly fall out in your hurry to kiss the ground your ancestors kissed. And the scented air is what you dreamed of when you crossed the Sudan—full of sweet promise. You meet the Israelis who tell you they only speak the holy tongue and that you must learn. They send you to school, like you are a child. But you are old. You point to your gray head to make them understand. The Israelis, who are smarter than you because they went to school and brought you here in their airplanes, believe you know nothing of the world and prod your shoulder to get you to move from one place to another, so that you wonder if crossing the desert has turned you into a goat. They find someone who speaks your language and he takes you to a place where buses shuttle people all over the countryside. You are glad there is a market nearby, but only men sell vegetables there. You do not understand why they would do women's work. And for the first time you wonder what you will do with your days now that you no longer need to walk across the sand.

The man who speaks Amharic brings you to this place. This is your home, he says. You must show him you can open the door with the key. At night you sleep on a mattress that fights your body, not like the sand in the desert that held you, not like the straw mat you shared with your husband that rustled with each movement. You find you miss the dirt beneath your feet that was home. You try hard not to think of the husband you left behind, but at night when the city dies to a whisper, you remember the feel of his hands drawing you to him.

You ask the man who speaks Amharic if there are spirits here, and should you bring a priest to cleanse the rooms? He tells you there are no spirits in the land, only God. But when you look out the window and see buses spitting clouds of black smoke, vendors shouting and people running, you see spirits everywhere and wonder can this place where nothing ever stops to rest be home?

MARKETPLACE

When she asks, you tell your child you are happy. But inside your body there is a rock pulling you to the ground. So you go to the market. You see a few black faces like your own and you greet each other politely and move on. Everything is rush-rush here and always buying-buying to make up for what you did not have at home.

Because no one speaks your language, you point to what you want: the eggplant, potatoes, tomatoes, peppers. You will make a stew for supper and hope your daughter will be home to eat it. Always cooking too much, as if your husband and sons were with you. And as the thought of food and family enter your head, you see the face of your boy before your eyes. You see Mengistu's men in their gray camouflage fatigues, their rifles cocked as they steal your son. Your husband tries to stop them, but he is sick and old. When he rises up against them, they laugh and slap him down. But you hold on to the boy who is crying your name. A soldier presses his rifle to your head. You think because it is metal it should be cold, but it is a brand against your skin. You remember that your youngest son is hidden in the root cellar, between the baskets of onions and yams, and let go of your first born. And you remember smoke stinging your eyes as huts are burned to the ground, the sound crackling like the keening of old women. In Gondar Province you are no more than straw. The thought of your son in Mengistu's army turns your feet to lead. The thought of your boy with a gun in his hands squeezes your heart. You ask God to keep him alive. You ask for half a kilo of red lentils and white beans for soup.

Your mind plays tricks because even while you walk through the market that swells with music and shouting and engines running, you are sitting with your husband and children on the carpet upstairs in the room the authorities gave you, a feast before you and all of you eating with your fingers. It is how you prefer to eat, but you have no strength to fight your daughter who tells you the Israeli way is to sit at the table and eat with utensils. Your hands, which embroider stories onto the bodice of a dress, feel like bricks when they hold a knife and fork. Only Arabs sit on the floor, your daughter says. Maybe I am Arab, you tell her. She laughs, then we could have stayed in Wallaka.

The vegetable vendor charges too much money and you shake your head and begin to walk away. He calls you back. You know this game. You have played it since you were a girl carrying a basket of fruit on your head—your body a slim reed swaying down the dirt path. The man who would one day be your husband stares until you feel there are ants crawling over your skin. The vendor calls you *Falasha*. But the word has no sting. He is right. You are a stranger here just as you were in Gondar Province. He calls you *kushi*. You nod, yes you are black, blacker than he. But soon he gives you the price you want. You take your basket and place it on your head. People stare. You keep your eyes down so as not to attract the evil eye. You miss the way you could step outside your hut and greet your neighbors and they would ask if you slept well and how were your husband and children and what a pretty robe you have on today.

Certainly, you are happy, you tell your daughter. After all it took to come here, you are finally home.

SAND BLIND

There are days when you forget where you are. Not even the sounds and smells of the market remind you. All you remember is sand—a river of it beneath your feet and waves of people, hundreds, maybe more marching in one direction. The journey begins with crying children. Mothers sob. Fathers shout. You tell your son and daughter to keep their heads covered. After the first twenty kilometers, everyone is too tired and too hungry to protest what they cannot change. They simply walk. There are two stops before nightfall, to eat, drink, and relieve yourself. The quiet surprises you. At first, you find it peaceful. But then you recognize it for what it is—the sound of your fear. Everyone carries their precious bits on their backs, some even bring their goats, believing they will be a boon on the journey. But soon the goats lie in the sand, and before they die, their masters slaughter them and dry their meat and eat well for a month. You used to think it was merciful to kill a suffering animal. Now you wonder if what it really wanted was to be saved. You still have your precious bits. There is the picture of your husband, your sons, and daughter. Next to them you place the gold bracelet your husband gave you as a wedding gift, a goatskin your father added to your dowry, and a small book of prayer that belonged to your aunt. You tied these bits in a cloth and dragged them across the desert. You wish now you could have brought something else here. When you crossed the desert you made sure to hold your son's hand. You love this boy. You knew he could be strong in this land; you made the journey. Mengistu took your older boy, so you thought, now I will thwart that man and take my son from this place. He is mine, you said, forgetting he belonged to God. Even at night you see sand. You feel it shift under your feet and are drawn back into the desert with your son and daughter. You lift your son onto your back. Your knees buckle at his weight. He is a big boy. Your daughter looks at you with pity. She knows what you refuse to see and walks ahead, her back straight, then bowing into the wind. When you stop to rest, you do not meet the hunger in her eyes, and take care not to look at your son's gray face. You are a master at not seeing. Your eyes travel the familiar past. They gaze into the future, and are shut to the present. You wonder if you have always been this way—sand blind. You make your way to the refrigerator in the dark and want to weep at the sight of all the food. You take out the butter and bread, the cheese and tomatoes, the milk and hot peppers, and sit on the floor in front of the open refrigerator, the light sharp in your eyes and you eat, though you are not hungry. You eat for the boy you saved from Mengistu's gun.

THE RIVER

You watch your daughter cross the room and think she wears the clothes of Israel real good—the blue jeans, the tricot shirt. She is a Western miss now. And though you smile at her happy face, you miss the girl you brought here—the skinny, angry child who thought you loved her brothers more, who helped you make *injera*, who poured the dough thin, and watched the pan while it cooked, who smiled when you weren't looking and cast dark looks when you were.

She is a beauty and you worry about the business of marriage. With no man around, who will take care of the dowry? Here we are scattered from Tel Aviv to Beersheva. How will she find a husband? You tell her you won't live in Beersheva—a city built on sand. No more deserts, the voice inside you shouts. She tells you, don't worry Ma. I'm Israeli now. No need to marry quick.

These matters were simpler in Wallaka. Her father would have found her a boy to marry and the families would have built them a hut. Sometimes you miss the village so much your bones ache. You miss the cluster of huts, the sound of the loom, the thump of a mallet on tin. You miss the women of your village. You miss the walks to the river, the way you sat braiding each other's hair and rubbing nut oil into each other's feet, and the talk, how you joked about young brides and about aging husbands. In your heart you wished for a younger man, but this one made you happy—sometimes.

At sunset you sit with your daughter on the veranda. "It's beautiful," she points to Tel Aviv. You nod your head. Yes it is beautiful, the white box buildings, the rooftop antennas like black arms stretching into the sky, but your mind is far away. It is with the river that winds around the village. It is on the path to the bathing spot. You know each tree and bush on this path. Your feet curl into the mud. You take off your robe and feel the morning air crisp on your skin. You belong there, hidden by those trees, walking into that river. Your body sinks under the water. On this day you will be washed clean. You open your eyes and see the wavering sky above you. The prayer rises from your lips like threads to the green surface. You rise all at once and stand pure before God and your village.

The children greet you with fierce hugs and chirp like birds. It was a long week, they say. For me too, you say. Your husband nods his head and tells you he will be back by sundown. You know he is going to the river. At night when he comes to you he smells of the grasses that grow near the banks.

You watch your daughter cross the room and wonder what she will do without the river to cleanse her, without the women of the village to ease her. Who will rub nut oil into her skin? Who will braid her hair when you are gone?

SHOES

Today they give your daughter a new name. You watch her step up to the podium in the auditorium at the agricultural school where she has learned to be a bookkeeper. Her head is full of numbers now and ideas about money, how much she will need to buy a car, an apartment, a dress she has seen in the mall that will make her look *eser*—a "10." Another number. You tell her, your future husband will buy these things for you, and she rolls her eyes. Lately, you feel foolish talking to this child.

She sits with her friends. All the girls and boys are glowing in their best clothes, their short skirts, and tall shoes, their black slacks and white shirts. They are happy to shed their Ethiopian names for Israeli ones. A teacher announces that from this day forth these children of Israel will be known by their new Hebrew names. The teacher calls your daughter Tali. She tells you the meaning of this name is morning dew. Your heart shouts for her to stop, but you are a stone in that seat, you and the other parents whose children are being reborn. And of course, you cannot help thinking of the day she was born, how she struggled to be free of you even then. Your mother said to you, this one is lively, call her Nikahywot, source of life. She will rejuvenate you in your old age.

Nikahywot, you whisper to the walls of your empty apartment. When she comes home for dinner you call her by her birth name. At first she doesn't answer and then she sighs.

Do you know what this street is called, she asks.

There is a sign on the corner, you tell her.

Not the name the municipality gave it, she says, but the one it's known by.

You shake your head.

They call it the street of shoes.

But there are no shoes here.

Not anymore, she says, but there used to be. Everything changes fast here, Ma, but underneath it is still the same.

Late at night you peer out the window and imagine yourself as a young woman on this street. You smell the leather and glue in the air. It is the smell of prosperity. You see shoe stores and shoe factories. The street is busy with shoppers. Everyone here wears shoes. You look down at your bare feet and remember them sinking into mud and sand, and small rocks cutting your soles. You put on your daughter's shoes. The heels are high. You sway like a leaf falling off a bough. You straighten your back and look at your long legs and then you sit on the window ledge. For the first time, you are really here, in this place, in your daughter's shoes. Tali, you whisper, trying on the name. She is asleep, your newborn child. The street of shoes murmurs its goodnight and, like your village that held onto its ghosts, you hear the ghosts of this place calling.

PAPER

Because you are new to this land, they take you to Jerusalem. The authorities hire a driver and a guide who speaks Amharic. You sit on a bus with the other women. Some are from your village and though you might not have liked them in Wallaka, you love them here. Today they come from as far as Dimona and Beersheva. You have not seen them for so long that you fall into each other's arms. Your voices reach the treetops when you greet one another and you realize with a start that you are happy.

When you are together you remember home and the people you left behind. You talk of your children and when the words are too painful, you whisper their fate. The guide points out the sights. "These are our monuments—here since 1948." You see a rusted tank, an upended jeep, a pine forest. "Today," the guide says, "you can pray for your family and God will listen." He gives out scraps of paper for you to write the names of your ancestors on, your husband, your children. "Roll them until they are no bigger than a pebble and press them between the stones of the Wall. God will read them."

You write the name of your husband and ask God to heal him and bring him here soon. You write the name of your daughter and wish for her a good man and many children. Then you write the names of your sons, the boy you carried in the desert, the boy you gave up to war, and you wonder again for the hundredth time if you could have saved them. You stare out the window, the rolled bits of paper crushed in your hand.

There are days now when you forget Wallaka. You forget the cluster of huts, the river, your children's laughter, your mother braiding your hair, the mat where you slept beside your husband, the heat of his body, the smell of burning straw, the blacksmith's ring, the clack clack of the loom. You forget the way night descended all at once, as if the day were swallowed whole. You forget everything when you see Jerusalem.

Your friends sing the song, "*BaShana HaBa'ah*, Next year you will see how good it will be." You clap with them and wave to the pedestrians on the street as you ascend to the holy city. Your eyes well at the sight. This is King David's city, the guide tells you. When you stand before the Wall squeezing your life between its stones, you weep. It has taken all your days to get here. Now I am happy, you say. But inside, where your thoughts are dark, you think if my boys were here then this would truly be a holy place.

The guide takes you to the Machane Yehuda market where you buy fresh bread and sweet dates rolled in coconut. He takes you to a restaurant where the menu is in Hebrew and Amharic. You eat *injera* and stew. You talk with your women friends about your daughters and how different they are from you. "These are not our daughters," someone calls out. "These are Israeli girls." The woman parades down the aisle, twitching her hips. All of you laugh. It is a good day.

The apartment is empty when you get home. You don't bother turning on the light until you reach the main room. You know these walls by now; they guide you. "Tali," you call, knowing she isn't there. She has left a note on the table. "Ma, be home at 10," it says.

What freedom these daughters have. This is what comes of having no man. Your thoughts stray to the hours you spent with your women friends. You are free too, you tell yourself. No cooking, no cleaning, no man.

You rip the scrap of paper in two. On one piece you write the name of the son you lost in the desert. On the other, the name of the son in Mengistu's army. You write their names in Hebrew, so God will recognize them. You roll the bits of paper into a tight scroll. These are your chosen ones, you tell Him. You chisel a small hole in the wall, big enough for your pinky to slip into, and push the scroll inside it. You pray for the soul of your boy in heaven. You pray God is watching your son—your soldier. Don't let him die, you beg, don't let him kill, don't let him hurt, or be hurt. You pray these words until every bit of your flesh feels stretched like a drumskin.

Night falls slowly. You step out onto the veranda, stare at the quiet street below and feel the presence of all those who came and went. The lights of Tel Aviv shine like eyes in the dark. You sit in your chair and wait for your daughter to come home.

NESSA RAPOPORT

The Woman Who Lost Her Names

She was named after her grandmother, Sarah, a name no one else had then because it was considered old-fashioned. Eight days after the naming, her father's brother died, and they gave her a middle name. The brother was Yosef—Joseph—so her mother went down to City Hall, Bureau of Births and Deaths, and Josephine was typed in the space after Sarah. "A name with class," her Aunt Rosie said. Sarah hated it.

When she got to school, the kindergarten teacher sent home a note. The family read it together, sitting around the kitchen table. "Dear Mrs. Levi, we have decided to call the child Sally for the purpose of school as it will help her to integrate and make the adjustment easier."

"What's to adjust?" the brother next to her asked.

"*Shah*," her father said.

Her father was a gentle man, remote, inaccessible. The books that covered the tables and chairs in their small apartment were the most constant factor in his daily life, and the incongruity of raising seven Orthodox children in the enlightened secularism of the Upper West Side never penetrated his absorption in Torah. Sarah grew up beside the families of Columbia intellectuals who were already far enough from Europe to want to teach their children civilization. The girls in her class had radios, then TVs, then nose jobs and contact lenses. They grew more graceful in their affluence, and she grew a foot taller than all of them, early. There were many blonde girls each year, and she'd stare at their fair, delicate arms whose hair was almost invisible. "Sally, how does your garden grow?" the boys would tease her in the hall, staring at her breasts, the dark hair covering her arms to her wrists, the wild hair that sprang from her head independent of her. She'd look down at her bigness, ungainly, and think, "Peasant, you peasant" to herself and the grandmother who'd bequeathed her these oversized limbs. No one would fall in love with her.

Her mother was intense, passionately arguing, worrying about people, disdainful. "She married for money," "he could have been a scholar," indicting these neighbors who were changing their names, selling their birthright. "Sarale," she'd suddenly gather her in her arms late at night when her brothers were sleeping, "remember who you are, and you'll have yourself. No matter what else you lose—" She never finished the sentence. Sarah would look into her mother's face, full of shadows, ghosts, and touch the cheek that was softer than anything. "You're a big girl, Sarah." Her mother shook herself free, always. "Go to bed." Her mother would sit at the kitchen table, alone, head in her hands, thinking. Once, long past midnight, Sarah saw her that way, shaking her head between her clenched fingers, and tiptoed in to say, "Mama, I understand." Her mother looked up, uncomprehending.

When she was seventeen and had given up hope, she suddenly bloomed. Her hair calmed down, and a kind of beauty emerged from within her. The boys in her youth movement started to talk to her after meetings, inviting her places. First, she said no, then she believed them and went gladly to rallies, campfires, lectures to raise money for the new state of Israel. She dreamed of Israel often, folk dancing in the orange groves of her imagination, fighting malaria, drowning in jasmine. None of the boys touched her heart.

At school, boys were thinking of college, and girls were thinking of boys. Graduation came on a hot day in June, and her parents watched her get a special award for poems she had written that no one but the teacher would ever read. "Poetry, Sarale." Her father was pleased. "My dreamer," her mother whispered. "We have a surprise for you. From Israel." The word was still strange on her mother's tongue.

Yakov Halevi was her cousin, a first cousin from Jerusalem she'd never met. He got up to greet her from the couch in her parents' living room, the room reserved for company, and she watched his thin, energized frame spring forward. He was meant to be dressed in black like the rest of her cousins whose pictures she'd seen, side curls swaying in an overseas wind. But his hair was short, startling, red, and the hair of his chest showed in his open-necked shirt. He spoke seriously, with a heavy accent, and she loved to watch the words form in his mouth before he released them. Yakov was a poet, only twenty and known already for his fervent lines. Great things were expected of him, and he carried their weight on his narrow Hebrew shoulders. Her Bible knowledge wasn't enough, and she struggled with the new language to read his book, tracing the letters of the title page, alarmed. *Jerusalem Fruit*, by Yakov Peniel.

"Who's Peniel?" she asked him. "Why did you change your name?"

"I didn't change it, I lost it." He laughed. "When the editor wrote to me accepting my poems, he had to ask my name, for I hadn't sent it. *'Hagidah na shmekha,'* he wrote, what Yakov our forefather asked when he wrestled the angel. 'Why is it that you ask my name?' I wrote back, as the angel answered, and he published me under the name Yakov gave that place, Peniel."

"But your letters come to you in that name. How did it happen?"

He shrugged. "People wanted to meet the bright young poet, Peniel. Then I was asked to talk, introduced that way. On the street, they would say 'That's Peniel,' and so it came to be."

"But you're the tenth generation of Jerusalem Halevis. You can't give it up, it's your name."

"Just a name." He smiled. "The soul underneath is the same, in better and worse."

She loved that humility, and the heart of Eretz Yisrael she heard in his chest when he held her. He loved her and loved her America. "It's not mine," she'd insist. "I don't belong here." But he stood in the middle of New York, looking up. "So big," he would cry in his foreign tongue. "So big."

He wanted to cross the country sea to sea, to marvel at mountains and chasms. She had waited so long to go home, to Israel, she could wait a little longer. Then he was her home, she became him, she loved every bone of his self, every line. The words of his mouth were her thoughts, what he touched she found worthy. It thrilled her, their sameness, and she'd wake in the mornings eager for the coming confirmation. They would say the same things at one time, and reach for each other, marveling. She wasn't alone anymore, she had found a companion. When she tried to explain about the Upper West Side and the girls in her class, he would say, "Everyone is alone. Man is alone before God, that's our state." Hearing him say it bound her to him even more. She wanted to breathe his breath, use his language, and searched through his poems, word after word, for her hidden presence.

"My muse." He sorted her hair. "Sarale," saying it the old Jewish way, as he'd heard his mother, also a Sarah, being called.

They knew they would marry, she floated for months on that knowledge, walking down Broadway to the rhythm of Solomon's Songs. "Sarale"—Yakov drew her to him one night—"we must talk of the name."

"It's all right. I don't mind Peniel. It's better in a way than Halevi, which is almost my name. No one would know I was married."

"It's the other name—Sarah. My mother's name. A man cannot marry a woman with his mother's name."

She turned white. "A man cannot marry?"

He noticed her face. "Oh, no, no, he can marry, but she, she must change the name."

She said in relief, "But what name? Sarah was my name."

"Do you have a middle name?"

She scowled. "Josephine."

"A *goyische* name, Josephine. So what do we do?"

She thought for a while. "I don't know. Josephine is Josie, but that's no good."

"Jozzi." It was clumsy. "There isn't a Jozzi in Hebrew."

She had no suggestion.

"Wait," he told her. "Jozzi is Joseph, Yosef, is that right?"

She nodded.

"Well, then, it's Yosefah." The Hebrew sound spun in the air. "Yosefah." He turned her around and around until the trees flew in front of her, dizzy.

They married in spring, and all summer they travelled as he fell in love with America. He loved New York City, the place where they'd started, he fingered the wheat of Midwestern fields, and stood on a rock high over the ocean as if he'd discovered the water. In the evenings and as she woke up, he was scribbling. Poems, letters, stories poured from his hand. She sat, amazed, as the papers grew and multiplied in hotel rooms, in the trunk of the car. The strange Hebrew letters leaped from the pages, keeping their secrets against her straining will. "Are you writing of me?" she wanted to know. He smiled. "They are all of you." He told her he sometimes took phrases she said and transplanted them into his work. She was grateful and mystified, peering through the foreign marks, not finding resemblance.

Yearning for Israel, they moved to New York. He studied small Talmudic matters on which great things depended. She had a son, then another. The boys laughed and cried with her all day in the house, surrounded by papers and books of ancient, cracked binding. When he finished his doctorate, they would live in Israel, and she counted the days as they lengthened to months, alone with her children and her longing. She was America to him, aspiring to be free, and he envied her readiness to leave such abundance behind. "It's your home," he tried to soften her, frightened by her single burning.

"It has nothing to do with me," she'd reply. He trembled in the face of seduction—the grandness of America's gestures, hundreds of plains crossed by rivers whose opposite shores were too far to see.

"We must leave," he said. "We must go."

She stopped her daydream of years and started to pack. The boat left in winter, and the grey piers of New York, city of her birth but not her death, she was sure, were left behind, unmourned. He stood watching the gap of water widen, then turned to her and was thankful.

There were cypress and palm trees as they traveled in, and a perfume heavier than air. Jerusalem approached them at twilight, her gold roofs and domes aching for heaven. She recognized the city as a lover, missing past time, a shock of remembrance. The boys were crying, tired, afraid, and she sheltered them under the sleeves of her coat. "We are home."

Jerusalem was designed for the world to come more than for this one. She washed, cleaned, shopped, scrubbed over and over again, as the dust blew in the summer and the winter wind seeped through the cracks. The boys got sick and well, and she was sick in the morning, pregnant with the next child. Yakov laughed as he smoothed her hair. "A girl, a *maidele* next."

From America letters came. A brother was hired, her mother was sick, Aunt Rosie was worried, family troubles, her mother was sick, Papa retired, a nephew converted, her mother was dying, gone. There was no money for planes, and the pregnancy was hard, so half a world away she guarded her pain, talking to her mother about the coming daughter. Her mother, sitting now at a kitchen table that was not of the earth, holding her head in her hands. Night after night, she lay on her back, her stomach a dome in her arms.

When the child was born, she could hardly know, groaning in a voice unfamiliar to her in this not-American hospital. Outside, the war in Sinai was sending soldiers into her ward, and sending her into the hall and then home, almost before she could stand. She bore the child alone, Yakov at the front, and when she looked down at her daughter, resting on her breast, she was full and at peace with this breathing body of her secret prayers, in love with the child, flesh of her flesh, bone of her bone, not a stranger. Yakov came home, exhausted, off for three days to see her and rejoice in his daughter. When he finally was there, she stared from her bed unbelieving, two ones loved so dearly, both whole in limb, wondrous. She ran her fingers up and down those tiny arms and legs hundreds of times. And Yakov, unmutilated, only tired, spoke to her, saying, "We must give the child a name."

"But I know the name," and she did, waiting for him to come home from the war, reading the Book of Psalms. "She is Ayelet Hashachar, the dawn star."

Yakov smiled over her, indulgent, "This is not a name."

"This is the name," she said firmly. "Ayelet, Ayelet Hashachar, it's beautiful."

"Yes," he said gravely. "It is beautiful. But it's not the child's name. Yosefele"—the smile—"your mother."

"My mother would love the name. She would love it," remembering her mother alone at the table dreaming her dreams long past midnight.

"Your mother was Dinsche," he told her, "and the child must be Dina. It is the Jewish way."

She looked at him, trying to find in herself some agreement, even a small accord and she'd bend to his will. But there was nothing.

"Yakov," she pleaded, "my mother won't care. I represent her, I know." Her mother holding her head in her hands. "It cannot be Dina. It can't be." Her voice was rising, new sounds that surprised her. "There's blood on that name."

She rose from the bed. "Look," and held out the Bible, shaking, to him. "Read." She tore through the page in her haste. "And when Shechem the son of Hamor the Hivite, the prince of the land, saw her, he seized her and lay with her and humbled her."

He stood before her in silence. "Rape," she said. "You want a daughter named for a rape."

"It is out of respect," he said. "For your mother. I don't understand what you want. A *goyische* name like Diana?" he asked.

"Ayelet Hashachar," she whispered in mourning, swaying like a rebbe in prayer.

"So what is it?" he asked.

"I don't care what you do," came the words in that voice, the one she had heard from herself giving birth. "Do what you want," turning her face to the wall. He stroked her hair straight back from her forehead until finally she was asleep.

When the day of the naming arrived, she was numb, jabbing the pins of her headcovering into her hair. She walked with her sons and her husband to the synagogue, and left them to climb the steps to the balcony for women. Below her, the men were lifting the Torah, opening and closing it, dressing, undressing it, reading the day's portion. The people in the synagogue were singing quite loud, and some of the women sang, too. The women around her moved their lips to the words. She stood still. She stood in her place, the place where the mothers always sat for their children. She closed her mouth, her lips pressed together, one on top of the other, and waited to hear her daughter's name.

NAOMI SEIDMAN

Raised by Jews

A long with the cart of groceries, my mother wheels in the jangle and cold breath of the world. This kitchen is her stage, small but crowded with incident, with ingredient: flanken in butcher paper, barley, big brown potatoes, three kinds of beans.

Loose-skinned onions spill from their net, a hairy turnip tips its tail over the edge of the counter. And then, like a gun in the first act, out comes a cellophane bag of candy corn, brash seasonal cousin of licorice whips, sugar-coated peanuts. My mother sighs as she clears a space for the candy on the counter. This is one of those kitchens where you could *eat off the floor*. It could be a television commercial, except for the speckles on the beans, except for the thick lenses my mother peers through, except that no one in this picture is going to eat that candy corn. Look at the little girl sitting there, staring at the Technicolor sunset candy, her mouth hanging open (adenoids). Look at the long braid down my back, blouse buttoned up to my skinny neck. This is 1966, before Paskesz dreamed up kosher cotton candy. You know I've never tasted a candy corn, never eaten anything that particular shade of orange or with quite so many ingredients. So what's this woman doing, dangling the forbidden artificial colors of the New World before her cholent-fed daughter?

My mother, having raised her captive audience, doesn't have to say a word. Impresario of the chopping block, she dices the onions with a virtuosity that in a better world would meet with drum rolls and applause. In this world I sit, swinging my legs to the rhythm of the knife and the bass line of the Frigidaire. The onions finally sizzling, my mother answers the kettle on the first ring and fills the glasses. For her baby she reserves the heel of the honey cake and a perfect white domino of sugar to go with her story. She breaks off a gooey piece and begins.

"You know what it is today, right?" she asks.

But I don't. What is it today?

"It's October, you know that it's October, no? Almost exactly fifteen years since I came here."

Having traveled over sea and land to this kitchen, my mother takes the long sip of sweet tea she knows she deserves.

"It wasn't easy for me, you can imagine, a new bride all alone in this country. Deddy was working hard, not just in the radio, he was traveling, giving speeches, Denver, Cincinnati, who knows where. A man like Deddy people wanted to hear, he had what to say about Israel, about the terrible things what happened in Europe. But it wasn't easy to get up and go to these places from one day to the next. Of course, he wasn't a well man then either."

Notice how we say his name, with two hard "d's," the word "dead" lurking in the silliness. Why? Who knows? But make no mistake—there's nothing silly about the man himself. His absence from this kitchen and the story is *important*. Everything my mother says about him has its own particular tang, served in every dish she cooks up like the recipes companies put out for their own products. She feeds her family pride in their father, slipping in a pinch of worry, peppered with a bite of resentment to which she's fully entitled.

"Only a short time I was here, maybe a month, two months. Let me see, I came right before Rosh Hashana and this was the end October, like today. I was by myself in this house where we lived in, in Queens. You remember. So I hear a knock. I don't know who could it be. In the whole Queens I don't know even one person. So I go to answer and I open a little the door and I see children, dressed up like Purim, but not really because they're not Esther and Mordechai, they're all in scary clothes. One is a ghost with a sheet, and one a cowboy, and one is . . . with the bones on his clothes."

"A skeleton?" I ask all those years ago, my voice hushed.

"Yes, a skeleton. You can imagine, I don't know what to think, and they say something I don't understand, ach, who knows what? It could be Chinese even. I didn't speak too much English then. I was scared what to think they want, these little goyim."

I gobble the honey cake to show my mother how to talk faster, so she gets past the scary part. This one I'll get to hear the end, because the end is America. But my mother goes on almost killing me with the way she's talking so slow, stopping every couple of words for a sip of tea while mine is still too hot.

"Then I see that they're holding out big bags full of candy like I should take and now I understand—it's Purim for the goyim. We have it in spring and they have it after Sukkes. I think I shouldn't hurt their feelings, even though I know it isn't kosher candy, so I put my hand in the bag and take a little and I put my hand in the other bag and take a little until I took from all the children, not to offend. And then I say a nice 'Thank you very much' and I close the door and first thing, I throw out all that *hazerei*."

My mother rides her heavy Transylvanian accent on the "Thank you very much," rolling the "r" like a slow train up a Carpathian slope, hamming up the part for her American daughter. And then she laughs, from the Olympian heights of her fifteen years of experience with the natives.

"So when I was in Waldbaum's," my mother continues, wiping tears from the corners of her eyes, "I saw this junk and I thought maybe I should give back some of that candy I took that time. If they knock, we'll have what to give."

My mother turns back to the cholent, but that isn't the end of the matter for me, since I have all the autumn afternoon to circle the candy, ruminating on its relation to food in general and corn in particular. No trick-or-treaters came that evening. Where would they come from, in that neighborhood? You could walk for a mile in any direction before you saw a pumpkin. The next day the candy is in the junk drawer, secure against assault in its protective cellophane armor. And there it sat, out of sight but not of mind, until April, when it was finally swept away in my mother's pre-Passover assault. They say that we are what we eat, but maybe it's also true that we are what we don't eat.

Okay, no trick-or-treaters. But we *knew* about them. We *participated* in this great country, we heard of its customs, thrilled to its purple mountains' majesty. How? Mostly, I think, the *Reader's Digest*, which lived in the bathroom. "I am Joe's Spleen." Survivors of airplane disasters. Adopters of orphans from ravaged countries. We knew. But did they know us? They should, they should. And so it happened that I sent my mother's story to the editor of "Life in These United States," which paid the unimaginable sum of $300. Working on the piece, I stumbled. How to explain? By the third draft, my mother was a nondenominational immigrant from "the

Old Country," grateful for the generosity of the New World. No Purim, no kosher. My mother, in this version, ate that candy and liked it. Looking up from my pad at the dining room table, I saw it unfold: She sat alone in that apartment, eating one candy corn at a time, licking her fingers between each bite.

I tried, reader. To have the story end the way I wanted it to end. To find some way to tell it. To cash in, if you want to look at it that way. One of those tries involved an MA thesis, called not "Life in These United States" or even "Death in That Europe" but rather "Varieties of Meaninglessness in Paul Celan and Nellie Sachs," presented to the Department of Literature at the University of Indiana, Bloomington. This history of mine isn't nondenominational anymore. Now it's academic.

Like other university students, I sometimes get on a plane and go home for Christmas vacation. But where I'm going isn't Christmas, and who could possibly think of Brooklyn in terms of vacation? Who else in this grand mid-December exodus has to do what I'm doing, changing from skinny black jeans to rumpled skirt in the redolent bathroom of the Eighteenth Avenue station? It doesn't really feel like going home either, since my parents are living in a second-floor apartment I've seen only once before, the address buried somewhere in the suitcase I drag down the street, gloveless fingers frozen around the handle and the wind feeling me up under the skirt. The brick row houses look on, uninvolved, unrecognizing.

I don't recognize them either. This block was Italian last time I was here, but now it's drowning in the Jewish overflow from Boro Park, the plaster Madonnas packed up and big wheels and strollers rolled in. Everywhere you look there's another windblown sukkah jammed into a driveway or perched on a porch. Then I see the last Italian holdout, staunch in the effort to combat cultural isolation, the last Christians in a world of Jews. The birth of the baby Jesus would not go unheralded. Every window shouts its joy, the pine tree lifts its twinkling branches in Yuletide wonder, radioactive-blue deer rhythmically genuflect toward the pavement, along the roof shining choir boys lift pious open-mouthed faces to the purple Brooklyn heavens. Santa Claus commands a view from the porch, waving a plastic hand up and down the street to the black hatters and pregnant housewives, to me. He could be a rabbi, a nice, fat Rabbi, I think, as I always do, and cheer up. What if Jews kept Christmas (kept! I think, observed! Not, for instance, "celebrated")? There would be laws about how tall the tree should be, where the angels and the pine cones should hang, the sharpness of the tree cutter's knife, the acceptability of burned-out bulbs. My father, at the ritual meal, would give an ingenious talk on the relationship between the red heifer, poinsettia, and the founding of the State of Israel. Reb Santa would stroke his beard thoughtfully, with feeling. The next two-family house is where I'm headed—I recognize the rusting deck chair on the upstairs porch from bungalow-colony summers.

My mother's face is confused when she opens the front door. Last time she saw me I had some hair. In the second before she recognizes me I see the face others see, the one not changed by love and watching. But then she beams and hugs me and my stiff arms go around her. Having broken her heart six or sixty times, having let my own shrivel to the size and density of an M&M, it's the least I can do. Up the steep flight of stairs, the apartment wears garish shades of sea green, remnants of the Mediterranean culture we've displaced to New Jersey. My mother grumbles to my father: "I thought she was the delivery boy from Landau." My father laughs. My mother shakes her head to her Greek chorus: "Why does he encourage her?"

When I get out of the bath the glasses are on the dining room table, special treatment for the guest. This is where my father spends his time, now that he's home from wherever it is men disappear to, scribbling furiously on notepads at one end of the table. A black yarmulke, the kind candidates wear in synagogues, sits pointed and shiny on his bald head. He pays no attention to us, otherwise my mother wouldn't say the things she's saying. She keeps her eyes on the spoon clinking the inside of her glass.

"You know, I was thinking about those girls in the camp, the DP camp I told you about, where I met Deddy. He was already a busy man then, collecting the names of who was alive, who wasn't. He made a newspaper every day, one short list on one side, on the other side very long ones. You should see how they waited for that paper every morning. Like hot latkes it went."

My mother clinks.

"The girls?" I prompt.

"The girls, the men, everyone wanted that paper. But I was saying about those girls, how they would look at me with big eyes. I was the only one with long hair. All the other girls were coming out of the camps and they looked at me like I don't know what. I wasn't a skeleton like them, even though I was plenty skinny. In Bucharest we weren't exactly living like a king. They would come over to touch my hair. Some of them asked why they didn't cut my hair. You know what they thought. I don't have to tell you."

She doesn't have to tell me. I rub my bristly scalp. My mother sighs and gets up, and then tries to remember where she was off to. "Come on. Just a short Scrabble and then we all go to sleep." But there's something I've been wanting to clear up.

"Ma, why do we call Deddy Deddy?"

My father raises his head and then goes back to his page.

My mother looks confused, "What *should* you call him?"

"I don't know," I shift uncomfortably. "*Tatty*?" Tatty was what most of the kids in the neighborhood called their fathers.

"No," my mother shakes her head in disgust.

"Papa?"

"*Papa*?"

"Daddy?" I venture, feeling foolish. What a strange word, Daddy.

"But that is what we call him—Deddy."

"Oh," I say for as long as it takes me to comprehend.

"What?" asks my mother, staring at her puzzling daughter.

I shake my head. "Nothing," and my heart gets a little runny at the edges. No, I conclude, I wasn't adopted. Look at us. Could there ever have been any doubt? Under my mother's kerchief (her wig perched now on its sightless Styrofoam head in the bedroom) and my jeans, we're punched from the same mold: square jaw, round nose, squat peasant calves. What is it that separates us? Nothing as substantial as flesh. Nothing but a truncated vowel, the thud of a consonant. Who says that it's the word, and not the way it's pronounced, that's the basic unit of meaning?

"Come on," my mother says, giving up on me once and for all. "Scrabble."

My mother, queen of the *New York Times* crossword puzzle, master of two-letter printers' measurements and Vietnamese currency, turns the letters over to hide their secrets. We get to work. Halfway through her third turn the silence breaks. It takes a second to hear:

"'Tis the season to be jolly,
Tra-la-la-la-la, tra-la-la-la."

I walk out onto the porch to investigate, and then, suddenly, I'm angry. To hell with Reb Santa. I'm already talking as I lock the door behind me. "I can't believe it—they have some kind of megaphone or trumpet pointed straight at us. And it's after ten. Does this go on *every* night? I'm calling the police."

My mother peers at the board, counting aloud. "I have fifty-four. It's your next." She puts her hand in the bag.

The wry look in my father's eye travels straight to my gut. I see myself as he sees me, and it isn't pretty. The crew cut, the Anti-Defamation League attitude, my American birth—but isn't that his fault as much as mine? I want to whine. My mother finally catches what's passing across the table and looks up, "Oh them, they don't bother us."

I snort. "What are you waiting for? A *pogrom*?" We fall into three separate silences. My mother is hurt silent, my father is shrewd silent, I'm defiant silent, but with a squeezed heart. Outside, the Christians hit a scratch and tell us to deck the, deck the, deck the. I turn, stumble into the back room, close the door and with the long practice of adolescence, fling myself on the bed and try to get miserable. But I can't do it—something's wrong. Am I too old? Is the room too neat? That's it. My mother's gotten into my things, books on the windowsill, clothes on the cabinet. I don't like this, and then I remember why I don't. I get up and pull the suitcase from under the bed, searching for a particular balled-up sock. I find it alongside its sibling in the top drawer of the dresser, as flat and emptied as my own heart. My goodie bag, my self-medication, having survived the drug-sniffing dogs and X-ray vision of Indianapolis International, had fallen prey to my keen-eyed, sharp-nosed mother. I shut the light and lie down, waiting for the neighbors to pull the plug, my galumphing heart to settle down, my parents to give themselves over to sleep.

Finally, I tiptoe into the quiet kitchen. By the glow of the night-light I open the junk drawer, the mother lode, where all good things come to rest. Purple-gold buds of Humboldt's finest glint through the Ziploc baggie, nestled among rusty hardware and out-of-date Jewish Home for the

Aged calendars. The refrigerator shifts gears, a radiator hisses. Outside the F train hurtles toward Coney Island, a garbage can rattling after it down the empty street. I close the drawer and sit down, uncannily alert, thinking about what it would feel like to expand my lungs with enough smoke to fill the space in this kitchen, until the walls come close as a warm blanket, until the house fits like a glove, like a shell, like a home.

Acknowledgments

The editors of this collection are deeply indebted to *Lilith*'s wonderful early fiction editors, first Julia Wolf Mazow and then Faye Moskowitz, who selected the short stories that appeared in the magazine prior to 2001.

What *Lilith* magazine puts forth in the world is cheered on by our indefatigable board of directors, which has included, over the many months of creating this book, Frances Brandt, Eve Coulson, Barbara B. Dobkin, Charlotte Friedman, Heidi Gralla, Yvette Gralla, Michal Hart Hillman, Natalie Pelavin, Moji Pourmoradi, Marci Rosenberg, and Mildred Weissman. Without them the magazine's many manifestations—print, digital, and more—would not exist as robustly as they do.

We are deeply grateful to Elaine Reuben, a longtime supporter of *Lilith* magazine and of this book. She has been the midwife to this project. Elaine's vision made possible our careful readings of hundreds of *Lilith*'s stories, and her wide-ranging intelligence and thoughtful suggestions once the compilation took shape have been invaluable.

Current *Lilith* staffer Arielle Silver-Willner provided patient, careful, and clear-eyed administrative support that moved this collection toward completion. We also acknowledge with great appreciation our editors at Brandeis University Press and our partners at the Hadassah Brandeis Institute and the Brandeis Library Special Collections, home to *Lilith*'s archives and to those of other writers and organizations that together document the powerful roles Jewish women play in contemporary feminist movements.

Contributors

PHYLLIS CAROL AGINS (b. 1947) has long found inspiration in Philadelphia, where she lives. Two novels, a children's book, and an architectural study of synagogues and churches were all published during her years there. Recently, more than fifty of her short stories have appeared in literary magazines. www.phylliscarolagins.com. The story here was published in *Lilith* in Spring 2006.

HILA AMIT (b. 1985) grew up in Kfar Saba and divides her time between Tel Aviv and Berlin. Her short story collection *Moving On from Bliss* was published by Am Oved in 2016. She was awarded the Israeli Ministry of Culture prize for debut authors in 2017. The story here was published in *Lilith* in Summer 2017.

TAMAR BEN-OZER (b. 1995) has a bachelor's degree in classical music, a background in journalism, and a law degree in the making. Currently based in Tel Aviv, she writes, sings, and engages in various forms of social activism in her free time. The story here was published in *Lilith* in Spring 2018.

AMY BITTERMAN (b. 1962) has fiction published in the *Cream City Review*, the *Chicago Quarterly Review*, *Kerem*, Jewishfiction.net, and *Poetica*, among other publications. In 2015, she was awarded a Special Mention for the Pushcart Prize. She teaches at Rutgers University School of Law-Newark. The story here was published in *Lilith* in Fall 2014.

ZEEVA BUKAI (b. 1958) was born in Israel and raised in New York. Her work has appeared in outlets including *The Master's Review* (Fall 2019 Fiction winner), *McSweeney's Quarterly Concern*, *December Magazine* (Curt Johnson Prose award), Jewishfiction.net, and in the anthology *Out of Many: Multiplicity and Division in America Today*. Honors include an Emerging Writers Fellowship at the The Center for Fiction in New York City and artist residencies at Hedgebrook and Byrdcliff. She is an academic support specialist at SUNY Empire State College. www.zeevabukai.com. The story here was published in *Lilith* in Fall 2009.

CHANA BLANKSHTEYN (1860?–1939) is almost entirely forgotten now, reports translator Anita Norich, but she was a well-known figure in Vilna between the two world wars. She was an activist, committed to women's causes and vocational training for women. As a publisher, editor, and journalist, Blankshteyn defended women's rights to social, sexual, and political equality. She belonged to the Folkspartey, which argued that Jews were an ethnic minority with a distinct secular linguistic and cultural identity that should be acknowledged and cultivated. Her collection of nine Yiddish short stories, with an introduction by noted Yiddishist Max Weinreich, was published in July 1939. That such a book appeared in Vilna just before the Second World War is remarkable. Even more remarkable are the modern stories in that book. This story is one of them. The story here was published in *Lilith* in Summer 2020.

MICHELLE BRAFMAN (b. 1964) is the author of the novel *Washing the Dead* and a linked short story collection, *Bertrand Court*. Her work has appeared in *Tablet*, *The Forward*, *Slate*, the *Los Angeles Review of Books*, and elsewhere. She teaches at the Johns Hopkins MA in Writing Program and lives in Glen Echo, Maryland. The story here was published in *Lilith* in Winter 2006–2007.

ELIZABETH EDELGLASS (b. 1950) is a fiction writer and book reviewer living in Connecticut. During the Covid pandemic, at the age of seventy, she turned to writing poetry in response to the world—personal, national, and global. The story here was published in *Lilith* in Spring 2015.

AUDREY FERBER (b. 1949) moved from Brooklyn to San Francisco, where she remained after college. She teaches writing and literature at the Osher Lifelong Learning Institute and the Writer's Grotto, and is currently working on a collection of essays. The story here was published in *Lilith* in Spring 2017.

RUCHAMA FEUERMAN (b. 1960) was born in Nashville, lived in Israel, and now resides in New Jersey. She is the author of *Seven Blessings* and *In the Courtyard of the Kabbalist*. Her short stories have appeared in *Narrative Magazine*, *Michigan Quarterly Review*, *Tablet*, *Moment*, and elsewhere. She helps people create their own novels, memoirs, stories, and books of nonfiction. The story here was published in *Lilith* in Summer 2015.

EMILY FRANKLIN (b. 1973) has published in the *New York Times*, *Guernica*, *New Ohio Review*, *Cincinnati Review*, *The Rumpus*, and *Cimarron Review* among other places. She has been featured on NPR, long-listed for the London Sunday Times Short Story Award, and named notable by the Association of Jewish Libraries. Her debut poetry collection *Tell Me How You Got Here* was published in 2021. She lives in Boston. The story here was published in *Lilith* in Winter 2018–2019.

MYLA GOLDBERG (b. 1971) is the bestselling author of *Bee Season*, *Wickett's Remedy*, *The False Friend*, and *Feast Your Eyes*, which was named a finalist for the National Book Critics Circle prize and the Carnegie medal. She lives and teaches in Brooklyn, New York. www.mylagoldberg.com. The story here was published in *Lilith* in Spring 2001.

HARRIET GOLDMAN (b. 1950) lives in Great Neck, New York. Her work has appeared in numerous journals, including *Confrontation* and *Kalliope*. "The Curiosa Section" is an excerpt from a novel in progress set in the 1940s about forbidden love and women who face impossible choices. The story here was published in *Lilith* in Winter 2017–2018.

AMY GOTTLIEB (b. 1958) is a novelist and poet. Her debut novel, *The Beautiful Possible*, was a finalist for the Edward Lewis Wallant Award, Ribalow Prize, and a National Jewish Book Award. Recent work has been published in *On Being*, *Ilanot Review*, *Paper Brigade*, and elsewhere. She lives in New York City. The story here was published in *Lilith* in Spring 2005.

RACHEL HALL (b. 1964) is the author of *Heirlooms*, selected by Marge Piercy for the G. S. Sharat Chandra Prize. This book was also runner-up for the Edward Lewis Wallant Award and winner of the Phillip H. McMath Post-Publication Book Award. She has lived in Rochester, New York, for almost thirty years. The story here was published in *Lilith* in Winter 2015–2016.

BARBARA HARSHAV (b. 1940) has published several translations of Hebrew and Yiddish works. She received the Ralph Mannheim Prize for life work in translation in 2018. She lived for several years in Israel and currently lives in North Haven, Connecticut. The story here was published in *Lilith* in Spring 1991.

CAROLIVIA HERRON, PhD (b. 1947), teaches classics at Howard University. Her books include *Peacesong DC: A Jewish Africana Academia Epic Tale of Washington City*; *Always an Olivia: A Remarkable Family History*; and *Asenath and the Origin of Nappy Hair: Being a Collection of Tales Gathered and Extracted from the Epic Stanzas of Asenath and Our Song of Songs*. The story here was published in *Lilith* in Fall 2020.

PENNY JACKSON (b. 1961) is an award-winning novelist, playwright, and screenwriter. Her novel *Becoming the Butlers* was chosen by the New York Public Library as one of the best books for young adults. Awards for her writing include a MacDowell Colony Fellowship, the Elizabeth Janeway Prize in Writing (Barnard College), the Pushcart Prize, and the Gideon Poetry Review prize. www.pennybrandtjackson.com. The story here was published in *Lilith* in Spring 2021.

ERICA W. JAMIESON (b. 1963) came of age in the Jewish suburbs of Detroit. She currently lives in Los Angeles where she writes and teaches fiction and memoir. The story here was published in *Lilith* in Spring 2013.

BETH KANELL (b. 1952), a poet, historian, and novelist, lives in northeastern Vermont with a mountain at her back and a river at her feet. She grew up in the strongly Jewish town of Montclair, New Jersey, and rediscovered her passion for Jewish life in a place where there may be only three Jews per town—each with a fierce and remarkable story, and great appreciation for miracles. The story here was published in *Lilith* in Summer 2018.

BETH KANTER (b. 1969) is a Washington, DC-based writer whose fiction, creative nonfiction, and essays have appeared in a range of publications. She was awarded a James Kirkwood Literary Prize for her novel in progress and is the author of six books about Washington, including *No Access DC*. She earned her MSJ from Northwestern's Medill School of Journalism and, when not writing she leads narrative writing workshops. www.bethkanter.com. The story here was published in *Lilith* in Spring 2020.

Short fiction by EMILY ALICE KATZ (b. 1975) has appeared in *Meridian, Confrontation, Jewish Fiction, South Carolina Review*, and other publications. Her short story collection, *The Book of Nut and Other Stories*, was designated a finalist for the 2019 Eludia Award. She lives in Durham, North Carolina. The story here was published in *Lilith* in Summer 2019.

ESTHER SINGER KREITMAN (1891–1954) was a Yiddish-language fiction author, born in Vistula Land. She and her family fled World War I and moved to London, where she married and eventually began to publish her writing. She was the author of two novels and a short story collection. The story here was published in *Lilith* in Spring 1991.

ILANA KURSHAN (b. 1978) is the author of the memoir *If All the Seas Were Ink*, published by St. Martin's Press; it won the 2018 Sami Rohr Prize for Jewish Literature. She lives with her family in Jerusalem. The story here was published in *Lilith* in Summer 2017.

JANE LAZARRE (b. 1943) is a writer of fiction, memoir, and essays. Her most recent books are *The Communist and The Communist's Daughter*, and *Beyond the Whiteness of Whiteness: Memoir of a White Mother of Black Sons*. Her first collection of poems is *Breaking Light*. Lazarre lives in New York City. The story here is a chapter in her novel *Inheritance* and was published in *Lilith* in Summer 2009.

After Abel and Other Stories, the debut collection from MICHAL LEMBERGER (b. 1971), where this story appeared in a slightly different version, was named a finalist for the National Jewish Book Award, Honorable Mention for the American Library Association's Sophie Brody Medal, and a National Jewish Book Club pick. Her fiction has appeared in *The Nervous Breakdown*, *LitroNY*, and elsewhere. Her poetry, essays, and journalism have been published widely, including in the *Bellevue Literary Review*, *The Rattling Wall*, *Real Simple*, and *Slate*. Born in New York, she now lives in Los Angeles. The story here was published in *Lilith* in Summer 2014.

GINA BARKHORDAR NAHAI (b. 1960) was born in Tehran. She is the author of five novels as well as numerous short stories, articles, and book reviews. She is Emeritus Professor of Creative Writing at the University of Southern California, and lives in Los Angeles. The story here was published in *Lilith* in Summer 1991.

ANITA NORICH (b. 1952) is Collegiate Professor Emerita of English and Judaic Studies at the University of Michigan. Her translations include *Fear and Other Stories* by Chana Blankshteyn (2022) and *A Jewish Refugee in New York* (2019) by Kadya Molodovsky. She is also the author of *Writing in Tongues: Yiddish Translation in the 20th Century*; *Discovering Exile: Yiddish and Jewish American Literature in America During the Holocaust*; and *The Homeless Imagination in the Fiction of Israel Joshua Singer*. The story here is from *Fear and Other Stories* and was published in *Lilith* in Summer 2020.

NESSA RAPOPORT was born in Toronto, Canada, in 1953. She is the author of two novels, *Evening* and *Preparing for Sabbath*; a collection of prose poems, *A Woman's Book of Grieving*; and a memoir, *House on the River: A Summer Journey*. Her essays and stories have been widely published and anthologized. She lives in New York City. The story here was published in *Lilith* in Issue 6, in 1979.

REBECCA GIVENS ROLLAND (b. 1980) is the author of *The Wreck of Birds* and the forthcoming nonfiction book *The Art of Talking with Children*. She won the Dana Award in Short Fiction and has published fiction in the *Michigan Quarterly Review*, *Slice*, and *The Literary Review*. The story here was published in *Lilith* in Summer 2021.

RACELLE ROSETT (b. 1960) is the author of *Moving Waters*, a short story collection described by *Lilith* as a "stunning debut." Rosett is the winner of the Moment Magazine-Karma Foundation Prize for Jewish short fiction, and "Unveiling" won the 2011 *Lilith* Fiction Prize. As a television writer, Rosett won the Writers Guild Award for "Thirtysomething." After three decades in Los Angeles, she has moved to the Pacific Northwest, where she is working to create a retreat for writers and artists. The story here was published in *Lilith* in Summer 2011.

MICHELE RUBY (b. 1950) is from Louisville, Kentucky, and has been an enthusiastic Louisvillian for most of her life. Her fiction has appeared in *Arts & Letters* (winner of 2015 fiction prize), the *Adirondack Review* (Fulton Prize finalist), *Literal Latte* (Winner, 2017 Short Shorts contest), *Ellery Queen Mystery Magazine*, and other journals. She has taught fiction writing at Bellarmine University, and was a fiction editor for Best New Writing. The story here was published in *Lilith* in Spring 2007.

ILENE RAYMOND RUSH (b. 1954) has had her fiction published widely, including in *The Threepenny Review*, *Philadelphia Stories*, and the O. Henry Prize collection. She lives in Philadelphia where she works as a freelance health and science writer. The story here was published in *Lilith* in Winter 2016–2017.

KATE SCHMIER (b. 1985) received the Virginia Voss Memorial Scholarship for Excellence in Writing from the University of Michigan. Her writing has appeared in *Tin House*, *Apogee Journal*, *Alma*, and elsewhere, and has aired nationally on NPR. Her work has received support from the Freya Project, the Virginia Center for the Creative Arts, and the Elizabeth George Foundation. She lives in New York City. The story here was published in *Lilith* in Spring 2020.

NAOMI SEIDMAN (b. 1960) is the Chancellor Jackman Professor of the Arts at the University of Toronto. Her fourth and most recent book, *Sarah Schenirer and the Bais Yaakov Movement: A Revolution in the Name of Tradition*, won the Barbara Dobkin National Jewish Book Award in Women's Studies. She divides her time between Toronto and Berkeley. The story here was published in *Lilith* in Summer 2010.

SARAH SELTZER (b.1983) was named a winner of the 2013 *Lilith* fiction contest, and eventually took a job at the magazine, where she now serves as executive editor. A self-described "old millennial," she is working on a novel about a family of folk singers. The story here was published in *Lilith* in Summer 2013.

ADRIENNE SHARP (b. 1957) lives in Los Angeles. She is the author of the story collection *White Swan, Black Swan*, a Barnes and Noble Discover Book and a national bestseller; the novel *The Sleeping Beauty*, one of Booklist's ten best first novels of 2005; and the novel *The True Memoirs of Little K*, a finalist for the California Book Award and translated into six languages. Her latest novel, *The Magnificent Esme Wells*, which includes this episode, was published by Harper in 2018. The story here was published won *Lilith*'s fiction prize when it was published in Summer 2016.

ELENA SIGMAN (b. 1965) is a writer in New York City. Her fiction has been published in *Little Star* and *Orim: A Jewish Journal at Yale*. Her essays have appeared in *Salon* and elsewhere, including the anthology *Dog Is My Co-Pilot: Great Writers on the World's Oldest Friendship*. The story here won *Lilith*'s fiction prize when it was published in Summer 2012.

KATIE SINGER (b. 1960) has said that the appearance of "News to Turn the World" in *Lilith* led to the publication of her novel *The Wholeness of a Broken Heart*. Her other books include *The Garden of Fertility* and *An Electronic Silent Spring*. She writes about nature and technology (www.KatieSinger.com and www.OurWeb.tech). The story here was published in *Lilith* in Spring 1995.

MIRYAM SIVAN (b. 1959) lives in Tel Aviv and teaches literature and writing at the University of Haifa. She has published scholarly work on American and Israeli writers, including Cynthia Ozick and Jane Bowles, and translated *On the Blossoming*, a book of poems by the Israeli poet Leah Goldberg. Her short fiction has appeared in *Arts and Letters, Wasafiri, Jewish Quarterly*, and other publications. Her collection of short stories, *SNAFU and Other Stories*, came out in 2015, and her novel *Make It Concrete* in 2019. The story here was published in *Lilith* in Spring 2003.

DIANA SPECHLER (b. 1979) is the author of the novels *Who by Fire* and *Skinny*. Her work appears in the *New York Times, GQ*, the *Guardian, Esquire*, the *Washington Post, Harper's, Playboy*, and many other publications. She lives in Austin, Texas. The story here was published in *Lilith* in Summer 2004.

ILANA STANGER-ROSS (b. 1975), a former *Lilith* intern, currently lives in Victoria, British Columbia, where she works as a registered midwife. She is the author of *A is for Advice (The Reassuring Kind): Wisdom for Pregnancy* and the novel *Sima's Undergarments for Women*. The story here was published in *Lilith* in Summer 1991.

ANCA L. SZILÁGYI (b. 1982) is the author of the novel *Daughters of the Air*, which Shelf Awareness called "a striking debut from a writer to watch." Originally from Brooklyn, she has lived in Montreal and Seattle and currently lives in Chicago. Her second novel, *Dream Under Glass*, will be published by Lanternfish Press in 2022. The story here was published in *Lilith* in Winter 2017–2018.

ELLEN S. UMANSKY (b. 1969) is the author of *The Fortunate Ones*, which Booklist named one of the best debut novels of 2017. Her fiction and nonfiction have appeared in numerous publications, including the *New York Times*, the *New York Sun, Slate*, and *The Forward*. She grew up in Los Angeles, and now lives in Brooklyn. The story here was published in *Lilith* in Summer 2011.

The debut novel from CHERISE WOLAS (b. 1961), *The Resurrection of Joan Ashby*, was a 2019 International Dublin Literary Award nominee, a 2018 PEN Debut Fiction Prize semifinalist, among other honors, and was named a Top 10 Novel of the Year by *Kirkus Reviews*. Her second novel, *The Family Tabor*, was a *New York Times Book Review* Editors' Choice, among its other accolades, and was optioned for television. She lives in New York City. The story here was published in *Lilith* in Fall 2010.

JUDITH ZIMMER (b. 1956) has published short fiction in *Five on the Fifth*, an online literary magazine. The author of several nonfiction books, she has written for the *New York Times*, *Psychology Today*, and other outlets. She lives in New York City and Connecticut, and is working on a novel. The story here was published in *Lilith* in Summer 2016.

QUESTIONS FOR DISCUSSION

What makes a collection Jewish and feminist?

Consider that each person holds multiple identities, and often we bring more than one identity—and emotion—to an encounter: scholar, laborer, child, artist, parent, warrior, lover, antagonist, elder. How do you see this assertion being played out in the collection? And what happens when a character's identities or desires are in conflict?

Photographs have a role in several of the stories here, including in "The Wedding Photographer's Assistant" and "Street of the Deported." In what ways do visual cues trigger memory, with its attendant emotions of joy, nostalgia, sadness over time passing, and also, as Holocaust documents do, bear witness to the past?

Why do you think traditions—familiar rituals or prayers, a baby naming, marriage rites, an unveiling—also can be occasions for transgressions, or for reshaping norms? Is it precisely because they are so telescoped, compressing close relationships or religious fealties, and come freighted with expectation? In which stories do female characters' relationships to tradition shift through time?

Have you ever participated in a ritual that left you feeling erased or demeaned? Which traditions or rituals in this collection feel authentic to you? Or . . . deeply inauthentic? Why? Referring to the stories here, how would you want to shape (or reshape) a ritual or celebration so that it has meaning for you?

There is considerable range in what passes for intimacy in "Boundaries," "Unveiling," "Glass," and "A Wedding in Persia." Are there particular expectations Jewish women and Jewish men have of one another as romantic partners? The stories set in Israel—"Flash Flood," "Road Kill"—offer a different angle on intimate connections between Jewish protagonists. What could explain this difference?

Women in almost every culture bear responsibility for caring for the young, the elderly, people with disabilities, and those who can't fend for themselves, so the depredations of war and its aftermath take a special toll. How does this play out in the stories in the section "War?"

"News to Turn the World" deals with an illegal abortion and its aftermath. What does this narrative signal to readers about the mother-daughter connection?

We believe that one of fiction's reasons for being is the opportunity it presents to enter empathically into the experiences of another. Yet there has been considerable discussion about whether an author is permitted to write fiction that steps into a life dramatically different from her own. What do you think? Does telling a story this way violate a precept enunciated by some marginalized groups: "Nothing about us without us"?

Short stories let readers take a sidelong glance at narratives we think we know. Like . . . what goes on in the mind of a widow? How should one sort through the belongings of someone who has died? Is there a microaggression in not knowing or remembering the name of an employee? Which stories here revealed something surprising about a situation familiar to you?

About the Editors

YONA ZELDIS MCDONOUGH has been *Lilith*'s fiction editor for over twenty years. She is also an award-winning author of nine novels, most recently *The Dressmakers of Prospect Heights*, which was published under the pen name Kitty Zeldis. She has written over thirty-five books for children, and her middle-grade chapter book won the Once Upon a World Award presented by the Simon Wiesenthal Center. Her short fiction, essays, and articles have been published in many national and literary magazines. She was born in Chadera, Israel, holds degrees from Vassar College and Columbia University, and lives in Brooklyn. Her story in this collection was published in *Lilith* in Spring 2002.

SUSAN WEIDMAN SCHNEIDER is *Lilith*'s editor-in-chief and CEO of the non-profit Lilith Publications, and was one of the magazine's founding mothers. She is the author of three acclaimed books, among them the groundbreaking *Jewish and Female: Choices and Changes in Our Lives Today* (1984). Her writing in *Lilith* includes innovative reports on women's philanthropy, the Jewish stake in reproductive rights, and the persistent stereotyping of Jewish women. Among her recognitions: a Polakoff Lifetime Achievement Award in journalism, inclusion in Women's eNews "Leaders for the 21st Century," journalism prizes for individual articles in *Lilith*, and being named a National Council of Jewish Women "Woman Who Dared." She was born in Winnipeg, Canada, and lives in New York City.